DALENGOUR

Nethergar Book I

CLARE L. HOLLAND

Nethergar Publishing

This book is dedicated to my Mum.
You were the strongest person I ever knew. You taught me to believe
that I could do anything with some hard work and imagination. Now,
I am putting that to the test.
I miss you every day.

PROLOGUE

February 1922 - Nethergar

NERISSA LARIMORE TORE THROUGH THE DENSE, shadowy trees, their deep green cascading branches contrasting starkly with the whiteness of last night's snow. Her breath danced in clouds of mist as she forcibly exhaled the winter air, the smell of fresh pine needles filling her nostrils as she ran. Her limbs ached with the effort of her haste, but she could not slow. She had to reach the gateway. She had to stop her.

Forging further into the forest, she stumbled clumsily across the uneven ground. The black trails were barely illuminated, the full moon struggling to infiltrate the sombre canopy, darkness obscuring the path as she headed towards the kirk. Her long woollen coat caught on a fallen branch, tearing as she wrenched it free. Her heart hammered in her chest, but still she ran, desperate to save Elspeth the pain of losing a child.

The web of thickly tangled branches began to thin, allowing the silvery moon to peek through vagrant clouds. In the distance, she could see the foreboding silhouette of Castle Dalengour, home only to malignant weeds ransacking the now derelict walls. For centuries, it had stood empty, no-one willing to overwrite its treacherous past. Looming like a sinister memorial to all those lost, the passing of time could not dim the memories of torture and persecution. An age-old battle for power waged against her family.

Frost glittered on the pale stone walls of the kirk nestled in the clearing, the bright red wooden steeple coated in a pearlescent layer of cold. Long forgotten as a place of worship, the rectangular church seemed out of place amongst the austere buildings of Dalengour, a burst of colour in an otherwise dour landscape.

Nerissa quickened her pace as the trees fell away, the mossy blanket slumbering beneath the thin layer of snow deadening her footsteps as she approached the heavy wooden door. She had not been here for an age. There had been no need. The gateway was closed. Tentatively, she pushed the door ajar, unsure of what she would find inside. Squinting against the darkness, she could see a few feet into the gloom. All was still.

The hinges protested as she entered, candles springing into life as she crossed the threshold, the dormant building sensing the presence of Larimore blood. The flickering flames bathed the pulpit in light, giving an appearance of warmth that belied the ambient temperature. Nerissa walked between the pews flanking each side of the aisle, her footsteps echoing around the desolate chamber. The air was stale, decades of dust awakened by the movement of her coat as it flared behind her. She coughed as the airborne particles caught in her throat. Hastily, she ran towards the colourful saints immortalised in a stained-glass window behind the altar. The frame stretched from floor to ceiling, the intricate detail scarcely visible in the lambent flames.

Her attention was drawn to the only woman in the scene, her long blue gown falling from one shoulder. A book was clutched in her left hand, a magpie perched on the other. Her eyes stared out from her beautiful face, opaque and lifeless. Saint Oda, a blind princess whose sight was restored by faith. Nerissa too felt blind. She needed to see. See into another world.

Tentatively, she reached out and touched the cold glass image, the warmth of her skin leaving a cloudy trail as her fingers crossed Oda's hand. She traced the leaded outline, ripples appearing in the wake of her caress, the surface becoming liquid under her touch. She felt the ground trembling beneath her feet, yet nothing around her was affected by the tremors. The surface of the window was now a molten silver lake, the saintly images obliterated by waves crashing from side to side, affected by an internal tide. The gateway.

Nerissa drew back, unsure of what would happen. She had always known the gateway was here, but it had been closed for so long. She watched as the undulations calmed and the waves rolled back to the edges of the stone window frame, leaving a clear shimmering pool where the ornate glass had once been. She stepped forward to get a better view. It was as if she were looking through a mirror that reflected the kirk behind her. Yet her own image was not there.

A woman came into view, carrying a child as she moved soundlessly down the aisle. Nerissa spun around. There was nothing behind her. She turned back to look through the window. The woman continued to approach the altar, the baby cradled at her bosom. Nerissa ducked back behind the frame afraid the woman would see her. Yet she went about her business, laying the child on the plinth, paying no heed to the window that was to her, a mosaic of glass and lead depicting long dead saints.

With no indication she could be seen, Nerissa stepped out to stand in the centre of the window, peering voyeuristically into another world – a world that seemed oblivious to being watched. The woman facing her was only a few feet away as she stood resting her hands on the altar stone where the infant squirmed in his blankets. She seemed to be waiting for something, glancing periodically at a gold pocket watch laid beside the child. As Nerissa stared at her, she had no doubt this was Morwenna Darroch, the emerald feline eyes alive with excitement in her exquisite elfin face. Her dark hair was pulled back, secured with pins at the nape of her neck, the severity of the style taking nothing from her overt sexuality. Nerissa felt a fleeting stab of jealousy as she looked at Morwenna before remembering the callousness her beauty concealed.

Morwenna began to pace around the altar, hands on hips, the beads on her knee-length black dress catching in the candlelight with every change in direction. She seemed agitated. The baby must be crying as she mouthed angrily at him. Nerissa watched Morwenna unwrap the child, making no attempt to offer comfort, leaving his tender skin exposed to the chill evening air. She saw her withdraw a knife from the folds of the infant's blankets, the silver blade glinting as she ran the tip across the child's face, the metal reflecting in her eyes fixated on the baby's wriggling form. An excited, satisfied smile curled her full lips as beads of blood formed on the child's cheek. Pain made the infant scream louder, his small face contorted and perfused with colour by the power of his yells.

Morwenna seemed undisturbed by the cries as she deliberately drew the blade slowly across the palm of her hand, allowing her own blood to drip onto the child's naked chest. Nerissa knew she must act. She must act now.

She reached out to touch the surface of the molten glass. It felt cold, watery. One step and she would leave this world with no assurance she could return. It didn't matter. She couldn't let Morwenna succeed. With a deep breath, Nerissa stepped through the window. The liquid engulfed her, the viscous fluid gliding over her skin, leaving no trace as she emerged in the kirk face to face with Morwenna Darroch. The sounds of this world forced their way into her mind, displacing the silence from whence she came. The cries of a child in pain, the scream of anger let go by Morwenna as she suddenly appeared.

'You! You can't be here! You're dead! He assured me you were dead!'

'It seems he was mistaken.'

Her sense of calm stood in contrast to the panic now overwhelming Morwenna who was muttering chaotically under her breath, shaking her elegant head in disbelief.

'You can't be here. You can't. He killed you!' Morwenna screeched, her voice cracking as she began to lose control.

'As you can see, he did not. If it makes you feel better, he did try. When he left, I was almost dead. Almost...'

Morwenna showed no signs of calming, pacing frantically in front of the child, leaving a trail of blood dripping along the tip of the knife as she clutched it tightly in her injured hand. Nerissa was on edge. She needed to get her away from the boy. Morwenna's instability could cause her to act rashly.

Now she knew Nerissa lived, killing the baby would not bring about what she wanted. But she could not be sure Morwenna would turn away now. Her hatred for the Larimores was complete, and revenge could be reason enough to kill the child.

'Morwenna, the boy is innocent. He may be a Larimore, but Darroch blood runs through his veins as well. Doesn't that mean anything to you? Are you so corrupted by a need for power you would spill your own grandson's blood?'

The laugh that escaped Morwenna's lips extinguished any hope she had of reaching the woman's emotions. There was nothing behind the beautiful façade except loathing, madness and cruelty.

'Do you think I care about this mongrel? He should never have been born! If my son had not been such an arrogant idiot, he wouldn't have been!'

Nerissa took a step towards Morwenna as she jabbed the knife in the boy's direction.

'Not so fast. One step nearer and the brat will die.'

Morwenna hovered the knife over the infant's heart, the trembling blade alluding to the turbulence within. Nerissa stopped, bringing her feet together, her spine straight and her hands clasped tightly. She could feel energy building between her palms, the tingling giving her the confidence she needed. She didn't speak, her eyes fixed on the blade, her senses on high alert as she witnessed the unravelling of the woman before her.

Morwenna's eyes flicked back and forth, her troubled mind trying to see a way out of the situation, sweat collecting on her forehead as she realised her plan had failed. Nerissa stood silently, waiting. Her stillness seemed to unnerve Morwenna and she shifted her grip to grasp the weapon with two hands, the tip still poised over the child who had fallen eerily silent.

Certain Morwenna intended to drive the blade through the fragile skin of the baby boy, Nerissa inhaled deeply, closing her eyes as the world around her slowed. With each deliberate breath, seconds became minutes. As she opened her eyes, the scene before her progressed in slow motion, as if the players were wading through deep water.

Nerissa's vibrant blue irises glowed with energy. She was in control now. She had time. She watched as Morwenna plunged the knife downwards, her face twisted in insanity, intent on spilling Larimore blood. Nerissa raised her hand and the blade came to rest barely an inch above the child, halted by some unseen force. The infant's wide eyes stared up at his attacker as Morwenna let out an anguished scream, the sound muffled by the denseness of the surrounding atmosphere. The weapon was snatched suddenly from her hand, flying across the altar to clatter on the stone floor with a dulled thud.

Morwenna's eyes glittered with tears of frustration as she found herself unable to move. Although nothing seemed to be holding her, she was rooted to the spot, her limbs immobilised by the weight of the air. Nerissa stepped forward and gathered up the child, tucking his blankets around him, the cut on his face healing as she ran her finger across the wound. The security of her hold settled him as he nestled against her, content to feel warm and coddled.

The sound of footsteps echoing on the stone floor announced the appearance of a dishevelled man, his rasping breath suggesting recent haste. Coming to a stop, his eyes darted from Nerissa, calm and serene as she clutched the child, to Morwenna screaming and struggling against invisible bindings. He cast around, noting the ripples undulating around the stained-glass window, the discarded silver knife stained with blood laying at his feet. Unfazed, his eyes settled back on Morwenna who let out a raucous laugh as she registered his identity.

'Get the knife!'

He didn't move.

'Get the knife you imbecile!' Morwenna shouted again, her voice shrill and grating now as it penetrated through the heavy air.

Still, he did not move, shifting his gaze to Nerissa who stood silently watching.

'I swear, if you don't do as I say, you won't live to see another day!'

This caught his attention, a tick visible in his cheek as he tensed. He knew what Morwenna was capable of. Nerissa took a step towards him.

'Pay her no heed. She's in no position to make threats. Take the boy back to his mother. I'll deal with Morwenna.'

Tentatively, he took the child from her arms, Morwenna's ranting momentarily quietened as she realised he was ignoring her commands. He turned slowly and began to retrace his steps out of the kirk, Elspeth's son cradled protectively to his chest, Morwenna's threats resonating off the barren walls.

The sound of silence stopped him, the irate screeching of Morwenna gone, only his own breath and the gentle gurgling of the infant now audible. Slowly, he turned around. The cold glass eyes of Saint Oda glared back at him from the solidified window-pane. The space occupied by Morwenna now vacant, emptiness remaining where Nerissa had stood. Both were gone and he was alone. He furrowed his brow in confusion. Only the glint of the silver blade laying on the stone floor evidenced what happened here. But there was no time to worry about this now.

The man looked down at the child in his arms whose innocent cornflower blue eyes were heavy with sleep.

'Everything's going to be alright,' he said soothingly. 'I'm going to take you home.'

CHAPTER 1

Kirkholm Cottage

May 1920– Cairndarroch

THE RHYTHMIC TICKING WAS INTERRUPTED BY A mechanical grinding sound as the cogs in the mantel clock made ready to announce the hour. Raising her eyes from the book she was pretending to read, Elspeth checked the time. Seven o' clock. The sun was low in the sky, casting a golden glow over the wild Highland landscape, the occasional splash of pink erupting from the heath as heather flowers opened to the warmth of the season.

The longer days always filled her with hope as the chilly, Scottish spring gave way to summer. Elspeth had watched the seasons change in the village of Cairndarroch her whole life. She had lived all her twenty-six years in this small cottage on the edge of the Dalengour estate, cosseted by the love of her family. She had taken for granted the happiness that lived within these walls, never considering things could change.

With no interest in returning to her reading, she glanced around at her family gathered in the rear living room of Kirkholm Cottage. Although much smaller and not as nicely decorated as the front room in the house, this was where they spent most evenings. Unlike the rich blues that bedecked the front drawing room, this room continued the pastel yellow and green florals of the kitchen that Elspeth much preferred. It also had the best views, the large sash windows looking out over the garden towards the hills and forests beyond. The front drawing room was only ever used for special occasions and there had been very few of those this past year.

Her mother sat in her usual place by the fireside. Despite the warmth of the day, flames danced in the grate, protecting against the coldness that permeated the thick stone walls of the cottage in all but the height of summer. The needle and thread in her hands moved expertly as she kept her attention focused on her work. Anything to avoid staring at the empty chair.

Elspeth let herself remember her father sitting there, his nose buried in a book or composing a sermon. She remembered his deep blue eyes, the crow's feet at their edges crinkling in ready laughter, his strawberry blond hair so like her own. Consumption had cruelly taken Connor Larimore twelve months ago. The loss of her father was still overwhelming.

The sound of her mother's heavy breathing caught her attention. Exhausted from the toils of the day, she was beginning to nod, the tapestry threatening to fall as her grip loosened. Charlotte Larimore was the strongest woman

Elspeth knew, and this had never been more tested than when she lost the love of her life. She had watched her mother struggle to keep the family together, trying to keep the lives of her four children as normal as possible and fill the void left by the death of their father.

There were times when she would catch her mother weeping, usually at the sight of some memento or possession that was dear to her father, or because of an unexpected kindness from a friend or stranger. In these moments, Charlotte would tell her they were lucky. Lucky her father had not suffered long. Lucky they had been allowed to stay in Kirkholm Cottage after Connor's passing. Elspeth did not feel lucky. Her father had been a good man. A man of God. Yet God had seen fit to take him anyway.

Not wanting to disturb her mother's rest, she tiptoed across the polished wooden floor that peeked out between threadbare rugs, to rescue her needlework. She noted her mother's reddened, chapped hands, responsible for their comfortable and clean home now the servants were long gone.

Returning to her seat, Elspeth stared out of the window, watching as the fading light cast shadows across the gardens that had grown wild since her father's death. He had always kept them neat as a pin. Her mother didn't have time or energy to care for the garden and although Elspeth had tried to tidy it herself, her knowledge and expertise of flowers and plants were wanting. Raised voices drew her from her thoughts. The twins were arguing. Nothing new.

At almost seventeen years of age, Kaliope and Agatha were as different as any twins could be. Like all the Larimore's, both had cornflower blue eyes that contrasted with their pale skin blemished with a smattering of freckles in the summer months. They were shorter than Elspeth who had inherited her father's tall, angular frame. But where Kaliope was slender with womanly curves in all the right places, Agatha was rounded and homely.

'What's the matter now?'

Disturbed from her nap, her mother's voice hinted at the exasperation of continued intervention in the twins' squabbles.

'Agatha won't let me do her hair. I know I could make it…pretty.'

Kaliope attempted to smooth the unruly mop of auburn curls on Agatha's head. People said she inherited her Grandmother Larimore's hair that had apparently been just as wiry and wild. Kaliope in contrast had her mother's dark brown curls that hung obediently down her back in manicured waves at all times.

Unlike her twin, Agatha had no interest in dressing up in pretty things. It was as if she knew she would never attract male interest and rather than spend her life trying, she decided to do the things she enjoyed with no heed to finding herself a husband. Kaliope was opposite in every way. Her head was filled with dreams of love and romance, and nothing brought her more pleasure than a new dress.

The twins hated and adored each other in equal measure. Elspeth smiled as she listened to her mother trying to settle their spat. This was her life, her family, and she would miss them so much if she accepted him.

Kaliope started to sulk as her mother came down in Agatha's favour, trying to explain for the thousandth time that she couldn't make people do something they didn't want to. Elspeth knew it was falling on deaf ears. As soon as the twins were alone, Kaliope would start on Agatha again and she would give in, emerging with some elaborate hairstyle that did nothing except make her uncomfortable. That was

Agatha's way. Eager to please, always bending to keep the peace.

'Now look what you've done!'

Her mother moved to the basket wedged between cushions on the best sofa, her lips fixed in a thin line as she feigned annoyance with the twins for waking their brother. Soothing the griping child with her voice, Elspeth noted the sting of tears welling in her mother's eyes as she tried to lull her son back to sleep. Calder Larimore had been a surprise, born four months after the death of his father. Charlotte had been so consumed in nursing her ailing husband, and then grieving his loss, she had not recognised the signs she was with child. It hadn't even occurred to her that another pregnancy was possible with her age and history. She had lost two infants at birth between Elspeth and the twins.

Calder's safe arrival was heralded as a miracle, dragging Charlotte from mourning with his constant needs and wants. She wouldn't let him out of her sight, afraid he might be whisked away if she wasn't watching him. This was the reason he was sleeping on the sofa rather than being bedded down in the nursery upstairs.

With her son settled, Charlotte returned to her seat by the fire, beckoning Elspeth to join her as she resumed her sewing. Uneasy about sitting in her father's chair, she perched on the footstool that served as an additional chair or table as required.

'I see Riordan Darroch was here again today,' her mother said softly, not looking at her. 'He's become quite a frequent visitor.'

Elspeth shifted uncomfortably.

'Yes, he called in this afternoon.'

'Was there a special reason for his visit?'

Her mother tried to keep her tone casual, but Elspeth knew she was prying.

'No special reason,' she said dropping her eyes to the floor to conceal her lie.

Riordan had come for a reason. To ask her to marry him – again.

'I don't know why you keep his company Elspeth. There's something really odd about him,' Kaliope chimed in from across the room, her nose wrinkling as she spoke of Riordan.

'Kaliope! That's not a very nice thing to say. Riordan is a good man from a good family and Elspeth should be honoured by his attentions.'

Kaliope looked falsely contrite at her mother's reprimand, pulling a face at Agatha when she turned away, making her sister giggle.

'He seems quite nice,' Agatha interjected, trying, as usual, to smooth over her sister's slight.

Elspeth didn't know what to say. She didn't want to talk about Riordan until she decided how she felt about him and his offer. He was a good match for her in many ways. He was wealthy, titled and had always been courteous and kind. But she couldn't understand why he wanted to marry her, a clergyman's daughter with nothing to bring to the marriage except herself. In her view, that wasn't much. She wasn't rich or beautiful, or even all that interesting. He should marry someone more equal to his position. Yet he seemed intent on wooing her and was doing everything possible to get her to agree to become his wife.

Elspeth sighed, absently tracing the outline of a hole worn in the upholstered fabric of the footstool with her finger. She didn't love him, but maybe that wasn't the point. Marrying Riordan would secure her future and that of her family. It would make her mother's life easier, maybe allow her to get some help with the house, with Calder. The problem was, she wasn't even sure she liked him. Kaliope was right. There was something strange about him. She couldn't voice this to her mother. Charlotte wanted her to marry and Riordan would, in her eyes, be quite a catch.

Elspeth became aware that all eyes were on her, waiting for some explanation for why Riordan was around so much.

'We're friends, that's all. I think he's lonely at Dalengour with just his mother for company.'

It felt unconvincing and the looks on her family's faces suggested it was. She searched around for something else to say.

'Besides, I don't think his mother would even allow him to seriously pursue me.'

'Nonsense,' her mother snapped. 'I'm sure Morwenna, I mean Lady Darroch,' she corrected, 'would only want her son to be happy.'

Charlotte and Morwenna Darroch had been friends at one time, before their life choices led them in opposite directions. Her mother, to a simple life as a clergyman's wife, Morwenna to become Lady of the Manor when her father, Lord Darroch had succumbed to an early and unexpected death.

Elspeth had been in Morwenna's company only once since Riordan began to court her. She had been invited for afternoon tea at Dalengour and unable to find a plausible excuse not to accept the invitation, she had gone. She instantly hated the place. Castle Dalengour was an imposing fortified house on the outskirts of the village, surrounded by a dense pine forest that gave it an endlessly gloomy appearance in every season. The salmon pink harling did little to improve the austere outside, the small windows reminiscent of a beady-eyed stone monster watching over its lair.

The interior was little better. Opulence filled every room but to Elspeth it seemed coarse and ostentatious. Displays of wealth adorned every inch, yet the atmosphere was empty, lifeless. Even the sound of it was desolate, everywhere echoing, the lives of the inhabitants making no impression on the house. Dalengour did not feel like a home. If she married Riordan, Dalengour would become the place she lived, but it would never be her home. Her heart would always be here, in the slightly shabby cottage she shared with the people she loved.

For two hours, Elspeth had endured Morwenna's scrutiny. Riordan's mother made it blatantly obvious she didn't approve her son's choice of company. Afterwards, she was sure Riordan would end their friendship, but somehow his mother's disapproval made him even more determined to have her.

Elspeth shook off thoughts of Dalengour and Morwenna Darroch. She needed to make this decision about Riordan, not his mother or where he lived. If she married him, she would be spending the rest of her life with this man. She needed to be sure she could abandon her childish dreams of marrying for love and be a good wife to Riordan Darroch.

The last of the spring sunshine began to fade and the drawing room took on a comforting glow from the corner lamp. Its flouncy shade tainted the light, bathing the room in a rosy hue. The colour warmed the peeling sage green paint that could be seen above the rows of dark wooden shelves lined with books and porcelain trinkets collected by Charlotte and Connor throughout their marriage. The last of the logs carried in by her mother earlier that day burned in the grate, the smoky smell mingling with a faint trace of lye and the scent of blooming lavender emanating from the white vase on the table.

A sound outside the window drew Elspeth's attention. A rider on horseback came out of the shadows, heading towards the cottage, his black coat flaring out behind as he cantered down the hillside. Elspeth recognised the large black gelding belonging to Riordan Darroch, and her heart sank. He promised to give her time to think, yet here he was, at an inappropriately late hour.

'Who's that?' Kaliope asked craning her neck as she peered out of the window. 'Oh no, it's Riordan Darroch again,' she said drawling out the last word, her shoulders slumping.

'I...I'm sorry. I didn't invite him,' Elspeth stammered staring at her mother and feeling the need to be apologetic.

'It's rather late for a social call but I suppose someone should go and let him in,' Charlotte said wearily, starting to rise from the chair.

'You stay here Mother. I'll go,' Aggie said, reluctantly leaving the room to admit the uninvited guest.

Moments later, Riordan appeared in the doorway of the drawing room, removing his hat and making excuses for his evening intrusion. He was a tall, angular man, with a thin nose too long for his face and slitty green eyes lacking in noticeable eyelashes. His skin appeared pock-marked from childhood measles, the indentations grey against his pale complexion. His lank hair looked almost black as it fell limply to his collar accentuating his hard features and giving him a solemn and unforgiving appearance. He doffed his hat and attended to Elspeth's mother.

'Please accept my apologies for disturbing you at this late hour Mrs Larimore,' he said staring around the simply furnished living room, his nostrils flaring slightly as his toneless voice broke the silence. 'My mother asked me to come and invite Elspeth to dine with us tomorrow at Dalengour.'

Elspeth was caught off guard. She hadn't expected an invitation and certainly not in the name of Morwenna Darroch. She stared blankly at Riordan whose eyes were now fixed on her. When her lack of response became embarrassing, her mother intervened.

'And how is your mother Lord Darroch? I don't know if she told you, but we used to be friends. In our younger years anyway.'

Riordan looked unimpressed and for a moment, Elspeth was sure she saw a fleeting look of contempt before his thin, bloodless lips curled upwards in a forced smile.

'She's well thank you,' he said tightly with a slight dip of his head.

He turned his attention back to Elspeth.

'So, dinner, tomorrow evening, around seven o' clock? I can tell my mother you'll be there Elspeth?'

She could think of nothing to get out of it.

'Yes, that would be lovely Lord Darroch.'

'Elspeth, we've discussed this. You must call me Riordan. After all, I hope we will all be family soon enough.'

Elspeth was mortified. She wasn't ready for her family to know about the proposal. She looked at the faces of her loved ones who were all staring at Riordan. Unsure his words had resonated, she looked for signs of surprise or questions, but there were none. Elspeth turned back to Riordan, expecting him to take his leave now she had agreed to the invitation. But he showed no signs of moving. He was staring at Kaliope, his eyes alight with something disturbing. Something that made Elspeth wish for him to leave.

'It's late Lord...Riordan. Was there something else you wanted to talk to me about?'

'No, no. That was all. I look forward to seeing you tomorrow evening Elspeth. Now, please don't trouble yourselves. I'll show myself out.'

Placing his hat back on his head, he backed out of the room, his eyes lingering covetously on Kaliope who fidgeted uncomfortably as his gaze raked over her for an inappropriately long time. He turned without a glance at anyone else and they all listened as his riding boots clacked across the wooden floor of the kitchen towards the back door.

They all remained silent until the sound of hooves moved away from the cottage. Elspeth let go her breath, her shoulders relaxing for the first time since his arrival.

'I'm sorry Elspeth, but that man's odd. He makes me so uncomfortable. The way he stares at me!'

'Kaliope, contain yourself. Riordan is Elspeth's...friend,' Charlotte chastised.

However, Elspeth tended to agree with her sister. There was something about the way he always leered at Kaliope that bothered her too.

'It's fine Mother. I know Riordan can be... intense, but I think he's a good man underneath.'

Elspeth's voice trailed off as conviction failed her. This was part of the problem. She wasn't sure he was a 'good man'. He was a good potential husband for someone like her. But was his character good? She had no reason to doubt him. All their interactions had been courteous and polite. He was a little pushy - turning up here tonight when she specifically asked him to give her time to think. Maybe that was just an indication of how much he wanted her to accept his proposal?

The thought of tomorrow evening's dinner weighed heavy. Even though she was unsure of her feelings for

Riordan, she was sure she didn't like Morwenna Darroch. She didn't want to spend the evening at Dalengour. She would be on trial, being assessed by her potential mother-in-law who would pass judgement on whether she was good enough to join the Darroch clan. A glimmer of hope in being found unworthy lightened her spirit before it was quickly extinguished by the weight of responsibility. She would be a fool to refuse Riordan if he wanted her.

'I think I'll turn in,' Charlotte said, laying a protective hand on her eldest daughter's shoulder, leaning to whisper in her ear.

'If you love Riordan, I will be happy for you my dear. But please don't marry him for any other reason Elspeth.'

Her mother had understood Riordan's unspoken intentions. Elspeth sat motionless, lost for anything to say. She felt her mother's wispy touch on her cheek before she turned and left the room. Kaliope followed their mother, calling goodnight as she left. Agatha hung back, her eyes following her sister from the room, listening as she ascended the narrow, wooden staircase to the bedroom they shared.

'Are you alright Elspeth?' she asked once sure they couldn't be overheard.

Her concern caused a tightening in Elspeth's throat. She had always been closest to Agatha, her sister usually knowing how she was feeling even when she tried to conceal it.

'No Aggie, I'm not.'

She tried to swallow the emotion as she spoke, bringing Agatha immediately to her side. Her sister wrapped comforting arms around her, and Elspeth began to weep. She wasn't even sure why she was crying. The loss of her father? For her mother's pain? For the decision she had to make?

Elspeth clung to Agatha until her tears were spent. Pulling away to wipe her eyes on the crumpled handkerchief retrieved from the sleeve of her dress, she looked down into her sister's face, now full of concern. Agatha didn't speak. She just waited patiently for Elspeth to regain composure and explain what was worrying her.

'Riordan wants to marry me Aggie.'

If her sister was surprised, she didn't let it show. Elspeth slumped down on her mother's well-worn chair feeling a sense of relief in finally speaking the words out loud.

'And that's making you cry?' Agatha asked, her arched auburn brows raised questioningly.

Elspeth couldn't help but laugh. Aggie could always say the right thing to lighten her mood.

'Seriously Elspeth, is this what you want? To marry Riordan Darroch?'

'I don't know. I always knew I would marry, even welcomed the idea. Before father died, I thought my husband would be someone I fell in love with. Nothing but that would have pulled me from Kirkholm Cottage. But now, I have responsibility – responsibility to marry well so that I can provide for you all.'

'Pish! No, no you don't Elspeth!' Agatha said sternly. 'We'll be fine no matter who you decide to marry!'

Elspeth smiled at Aggie, hoping her naivety would never be challenged by the real world.

'Riordan is a good match for me,' she said simply. 'I'd be a fool to turn him down if he wants to make me his wife. Marrying into the Darrochs would secure all our futures.'

'But you don't love him?'

'I… I'm not sure,' she lied, dropping her gaze to fixate on her crossed ankles.

'Maybe love can grow between two people. Marriage isn't always about love Aggie.'

'Well, it should be,' Agatha said resolutely, 'and especially for you Ellie. I would hate to see you trapped with a man you didn't love, and I know Mother would feel the same.'

'I'm just not sure how I feel. I find it hard to understand why Riordan would want me. He could take a wife from any one of the wealthy families. Why would he want me?'

'Oh Elspeth!'

Agatha came to perch on the arm of her chair.

'If only you could see what the rest of us do. Then the question would be why wouldn't he want to marry you? You're kind and caring and you look after the rest of us without ever complaining. You're such a beautiful person Elspeth, outside and in.'

'You're biased Aggie,' she said, smoothing a curl escaping the garish red ribbon tying back her sister's hair. 'If I do marry Riordan and move to Dalengour, I'll miss you so much.'

'You won't get rid of me that easily,' Agatha replied, her bright eyes crinkling in a ready smile as she looked warmly into Elspeth's face. 'I'll be by to visit so much you'll soon bar me from the place! Now come on. You're going to need your beauty sleep if you're to impress Morwenna Darroch tomorrow.'

Smiling reassuringly, Agatha stood and pulled at Elspeth hand. Sighing, she rose reluctantly to her feet, her sister sliding her arm through hers as they headed up to bed.

CHAPTER 2

Dalengour

RIORDAN SENT A CARRIAGE TO COLLECT ELSPETH from Kirkholm Cottage the following evening. She sat stiffly on the burgundy velvet padding, taking deep breaths to settle the swirling of her stomach as the wheels rattled along the driveway to Dalengour. The horses began to pick up speed, the draw of a good feed and warm stable spurring them on. The carriage swayed more violently, aggravating her nausea, making her feel faint.

Bracing herself against the door, she closed her eyes in an attempt to stop her head spinning. It made things worse and the carriage became suffocating. She tried to lower the window but her fingers, clad in the only silk gloves she owned, slid ineffectually over the glass. Ripping them off, she managed to force the window open, relishing the breeze that now cooled the sweat gathering on her brow.

Her panic subsided with the fresh air.

'For goodness sake Elspeth! It's only a dinner invitation!'

Her internal monologue didn't help. It didn't feel like 'just a dinner invitation'. It felt like a trial.

Opening her eyes, she looked towards the castle looming ahead. Its tall, angular walls were broken by the occasional turret topped with battlements, the placement of the front windows and large heavy door making it look like a face ready to devour her. Windows across the rest of the façade were few and far between and Elspeth thought every room must be shrouded in perpetual darkness. Her one previous visit had taken place in a windowless parlour that was so sombre the light assaulted her eyes when she returned to the brightness of the day.

The carriage drew up to Dalengour and with one last deep breath to steady her nerves, Elspeth stepped out into the warm summer evening. She was pleased with her appearance tonight. She was wearing her best grey taffeta dress, fitted at the bust to make the most of her underwhelming curves. The high waist, although not fashionable now, accentuated her slenderness before the skirt fell away from her body. It made a satisfying swishing noise as she moved, the beads added by her mother catching the light as the fabric rippled.

The colour suited her, bringing out the blueness of her eyes that were pale by comparison to the rest of the Larimores. Kaliope had done her hair, drawing it up on top of her head in a mass of pale red curls, making her look even taller than usual despite the flat grey pumps on her feet. Elspeth had never felt so elegant.

Stealing herself one last time, she raised her hand to the doorbell. Before she had a chance to press, a young man dressed in a butler's uniform and a huge grin threw open the door. His bright hazel eyes and warm smile offered a ray of light in an otherwise dark and shadowy hall.

'Jenson!'

'Hello Elspeth – sorry, Miss Larimore.'

She laughed as he made a decorous bow, sweeping his hand to guide her inside.

'I didn't know you worked here,' she said passing into the gargantuan entrance hall.

She was so happy to see her childhood friend, the foreboding feelings about the pending dinner were momentarily forgotten.

'I've been here about a year. I'm training to be a butler. I'm not really supposed to admit guests, but when I heard you were coming tonight, I convinced Gadsen, the Head Butler, to let me open the door to you. I thought you might appreciate a friendly face,' he said, cocking his head towards the inner rooms and raising his eyebrows.

He wasn't wrong. Jenson Tanner had been Elspeth's best friend growing up. His family lived a mile north of Cairndarroch and they had been inseparable as children. As they aged, the feelings she had for Jenson had matured, but always self-doubting, she had been unsure whether he felt the same. On occasion, she had thought there was something different in the way he looked at her, but they never got the chance to explore their changing relationship.

Elspeth hadn't seen Jenson for over ten years, losing touch when his family moved into the city. Elspeth remembered Jenson as a lanky youth, all arms and legs. He was always the clown and from memory, exceptionally clumsy. The thought of him being a butler made her smile.

Yet the man who greeted her bore little resemblance to the boy she knew. He was even taller than she remembered, towering a head above her. He had filled out in all the right places and looked exceptionally handsome in his uniform. His sandy-coloured hair rested foppishly on his collar, the light catching tawny flecks in his otherwise green eyes. Elspeth felt her heart flutter as he looked at her, heat rising in her face.

'May I say, you look beautiful tonight Elspeth.'

Her cheeks flushed fiercely at his compliment, her coyness amusing him as his full, rose-coloured lips parted in a grin revealing slightly crooked teeth.

'Thank you. I'm not used to being done up like this. It feels a little weird,' she said shrugging her shoulders but avoiding his gaze.

'Well, you look wonderful.'

Her heart started to beat a little harder as she raised her eyes to meet his. He was staring admiringly at her and the old sensation that there was more than friendship between them, stirred.

'Sorry,' he said, suddenly remembering his position. 'Please follow me Miss Larimore.'

Seeing Jenson had made her forget why she was here. The nervousness she felt in the carriage was now replaced with disappointment. She would much rather stay here and catch up with Jenson.

'Lord Darroch is waiting for you in the drawing room with his mother.'

Jenson's formal tone surprised her after the warmness of their greeting. His outstretched arm indicated an open doorway across the hall.

'Th…Thank you,' she fumbled, taken aback by the sudden change in his manner.

In step, they started towards the door, footsteps ringing out on the stone floor as they walked. Elspeth's anxiety returned and stopping suddenly, she turned to face Jenson.

'I don't think I can go in there!'

'Elspeth, you'll be fine. You look every inch the lady and Riordan is a lucky man.'

Elspeth thought she detected sadness in Jenson's tone as he said this, but as she raised her eyes to look at him, his face was passive, unreadable.

'But I don't belong here.'

'Of course you do, and don't let them, or anyone else ever tell you differently.'

Jenson glanced quickly around the hall and seeing they were away from prying eyes, took both her hands in his own. The feel of his warm skin through her gloves both calmed and excited her.

'Now deep breaths and remember, they're just people like you and me. It's only money that separates us. Nothing else. You are just as worthy as they, even more so to me.'

She stared into his kind eyes, glad he was here to help her through this ordeal. She took the deep breaths he instructed and felt better.

'Ready?'

'I think so.'

As Jenson stepped away, this time she was sure a look of sadness momentarily clouded his eyes as he once again assumed his formal role. Elspeth lingered, wanting to stay here with him, wanting to walk out of this imposing house and rekindle the friendship they had shared years before. But Jenson started to move forward, readying to make introductions to her hosts.

Grudgingly, she dropped in behind him as he escorted her into the drawing room of Dalengour Castle. Elspeth felt she was in some kind of theatre production, playing a role she had no right to, the guest of Riordan Darroch. The prospective wife of Riordan Darroch.

'Miss Elspeth Larimore.'

The sound of her name resurrected the feeling of dread as she walked past him. Jenson left without looking at her, closing the door and trapping her in this alien world. She shivered slightly as cold sweat settled on her skin and her legs were like jelly as she moved further into the room. Riordan came to her, his bony hands outstretched. He pulled her towards him and kissed her lightly on the cheek. His lips felt cold and hard as they brushed her skin. They offered no reassurance or welcome.

'Elspeth, so glad you could join us.'

He led her by the hand to stand in front of his mother. She felt like a prize cow being presented for inspection. To her surprise, Morwenna rose from her seat and embraced her, bumping cheeks with her in a mock kiss.

'Elspeth, I was so pleased when you accepted my invitation.'

She held Elspeth at arms' length, casting her emerald eyes over her, an unreadable expression on her face.

'You do look lovely my dear.'

The endearment seemed to stick in her throat, and Elspeth couldn't help but feel she was going through the motions of a sincere warm welcome. But still, even this act contrasted sharply with her open hostility in their last encounter.

'Eh…thank you Lady Darroch.'

'Oh please. We're going to be family. You should call me Morwenna. Now please, won't you take a seat. Riordan, pour Elspeth a sherry.'

Elspeth did as she was told, feeling she would never dare do anything other than follow Morwenna's commands. Riordan handed her a small crystal glass filled with an amber liquid that had an unfamiliar pungent smell. Sherry was not found in the frugal larder at Kirkholm Cottage. At a loss for what else to do or say, she took a sip, trying not to cough as the sweet sickly liquid caught in her throat. The drink did nothing for the nausea that had now returned with a vengeance.

Feeling observed, Elspeth looked up to find Morwenna's gaze boring into her. The heavily lashed eyes seemed to be appraising every inch of her, a forced smile cemented on her full sensuous lips. The scene sat well with her analogy of a theatre, Morwenna playing the part of someone who wanted to be in her company yet deep down, resented her very presence in the house. Riordan stood watching the two women, assessing the hidden machinations of his mother's mind. But the results of her inspection were well concealed.

'Dinner is served Lady Darroch.'

Elspeth jumped as a grey-haired elderly man announced the readiness of the dining room. She guessed this was the Head Butler Jenson was studying under.

'Thank you Gadsen. Shall we go through?'

Riordan offered his mother an arm to escort her through to dinner. Elspeth followed behind, grateful for a moment of relief from Morwenna's visual invasion of her person.

An imposing mahogany table dominated the room, laid for three people but easily seating twenty guests, the silverware and crystal in such abundance Elspeth had no idea where to start. Morwenna seated herself at the head of the table and Riordan guided Elspeth to the seat on her left before taking the chair opposite. Silently, Gadsen came to her side, filling her glass from an elaborate gilded decanter. Instinctively she thanked him although no one else around the table offered him that courtesy.

As the butler withdrew, Elspeth again felt Morwenna's eyes on her. She began fiddling with the beads on her skirt

for something to do to avoid meeting the older woman's
stare.

'How is your mother Elspeth?

The question broke the uncomfortable silence.

'She's well Lady Darroch. Thank you for asking.'

'I told you, Elspeth, please call me Morwenna.'

With this, she reached over and patted Elspeth's arm in a
gesture that seemed contrived, something people did when
trying to show they cared for someone. There was no genuine
candour or comfort in her behaviour.

'I was so sorry to hear about your father Elspeth. He was
a good man. It must be difficult for your mother to manage
without him. We used to be close you know, your mother and
I. But our lives took us on different paths.'

Morwenna   smiled   condescendingly,   and   Elspeth's
countenance hardened towards her hostess. How dare she
comment on her father's character, a man she hardly knew?
She took a deep breath, suppressing the unreasonable anger
rearing within her. She knew she was being unfair.
Morwenna was just trying to be nice to her. Yet somehow,
something in the way she spoke did not feel well-meaning.

She was saved from making a response by the arrival of
soup, carried less than expertly by Jenson who gave her a
surreptitious wink as he entered. Elspeth's heart lurched as
he entered the room and she lowered her head to conceal her
blushes.

The crockery rattled, Jenson's hands shaking as he
crossed the large space between the door and sideboard, his
polished black shoes echoing on the barren wooden floor.
Placing the tureen down, he proceeded to fill three small
porcelain bowls, decorated with a garish pattern of brightly
coloured fruits and finished with gilt edges. Under the careful
scrutiny of Gadsen, Jenson placed one in front of each person

seated at the table, then withdrew quietly, receiving an approving nod from the venerable butler as he left.

Elspeth suppressed the intense desire to leave with him. She stared around the opulence of the table setting – at least she knew which piece of cutlery to use for this course. Selecting the silver soup spoon, she filled it with the thick, grey-coloured liquid. The smell was repulsive. Keeping her face passive as she pushed the glutenous mass into her mouth was difficult. Reluctantly, she swallowed, the desire to gag immense as the overpowering taste of slightly rancid fish permeated her taste buds. The glue-like substance gripped her throat on the way down and she was grateful to note Jenson had poured very little into her bowl.

Stealing herself for a second mouthful, she looked around the room, trying to distract her brain from processing the unpleasant odour rising from the soup. The décor was hideous. The walls were covered in a flocked wallpaper with swirls of burnt orange rising from a tangerine background. Garish, gilded frames surrounded pictures of long-dead Darroch ancestors, shared history embedded in their sallow complexions and almost black hair. The furniture was heavy and dark, every available surface covered with animals preserved forever, teeth bared, their glassy eyes joining the portraits to gawk at the inhabitants of the room. Directly in front of her, a pine martin stared, immortalised by a less than skilled taxidermist. Its body contorted unnaturally, a dead wood mouse hung from its open jaw, red welts painted on its tiny side to tell the story of a violent death.

Elspeth shivered, pulling her eyes away from the sickening creature. The contents of her bowl were congealing into a dense grey mass languishing beneath a watery layer of grease. She pushed another spoonful into her mouth and fixed her eyes on the stag's head pinned to the wall above the gruesome pine martin as she tried to swallow. Being surrounded by a mortuary was not helping her nausea, the fishy soup adding to her already delicate constitution.

They ate without speaking, only the sounds of silverware scraping on china and the ticking of the grandfather clock in the hall penetrated the deafening silence. Elspeth was relieved when Morwenna returned her spoon to the bowl, signalling the butler lurking a short distance away, always ready to do his mistresses' bidding. It seemed when Morwenna was finished, everyone was. Although Elspeth had not managed to force in the rest of the bowl's contents, she was more than happy to see it lifted from the table and passed to a maid loitering outside the door.

'Please tell Mrs Pegg the soup was excellent,' Morwenna said as the butler removed the tureen from the sideboard and left the room.

Elspeth took a few deep breaths, trying to calm the churning in her stomach and the panic over what might turn up next. No one spoke. She could feel perspiration gathering on her top lip as she covered her mouth with her hand, desperate not to vomit. Morwenna returned to scrutinising her, adding to her discomfort.

It seemed like an age before the butler returned to fill their glasses with a red wine. The last thing Elspeth wanted was to add an acidic drink on top of the fish soup. Out of politeness, she raised the glass to her lips and feigned a sip.

Jenson appeared with a silver platter, serving Lady Darroch with two slices of meat perched precariously in a pair of silver tongs. Elspeth was relieved to see it looked like chicken. He moved around the table to serve Riordan before coming to her side, followed by a footman delivering potatoes and beans. Thankfully, she was left to add her own gravy, Jenson presenting the jug on a tray so she could add a little of the unappetising pale brown sludge to her plate.

A discrete nod from Morwenna dismissed the servants, leaving only the butler who resumed his position by the door. They continued to eat in silence, Elspeth sure the ticking of the clock ebbed, time doing its best to extend her purgatory. At least the food was edible, the meat and vegetables taking away the foul fishy taste that seemed intent on lingering.

Gravy avoided, Elspeth's stomach started to feel better, perhaps settled by the food she managed to eat, or her relief the meal was almost over. Plates were cleared and the main course replaced by a mass of crowdie cheese and fruit doused in honey and whisky. The cranachan dessert was overly sweet and sticky, but Elspeth managed to make a reasonable attempt before it was whisked away on Morwenna's command.

The meal finished, Morwenna rose from the table, announcing they should retire to the library. Riordan took his mother's arm again and led her out, leaving Elspeth to follow in their wake. Jenson smiled broadly as she caught his eye, earning him Gadsen's scowl as she scurried after her hostess.

The library was in almost total darkness. A small desk lamp cast a limpid pool of light on the worn bottle-green leather inlay, and two candles on either side of the hearth flickered as they grappled with the oppressive shadows. Morwenna seated herself in a high, wing-backed chair by the fireplace, the empty grate adding to the bleakness of the room. Riordan guided Elspeth to a dark brown leather sofa opposite his mother, the low seat ensuring her head was well below that of Morwenna.

Goosebumps formed on her arms as the chill air grazed her bare skin, the cold of the leather seeping through her thin, taffeta skirt. Elspeth took the brandy Riordan offered, relishing the warmth spreading through her chest as she swallowed, the pervasive cold of this dank, lifeless room temporarily diminished. Riordan came to sit beside her, too close, making her shift along to put more distance between them as he threw his arm along the back of the sofa behind her. His hand glanced across her back, his possessive gesture making her stiffen and shuffle forwards, out of his reach. He seemed to take her discomfort as modesty, his thin lips twitching in amusement.

Again, silence stretched ahead with only the infernal ticking of another clock marking out the slowest seconds Elspeth had ever experienced. She stared down at ripples forming in the brandy as she clutched the glass with a shaking hand. It felt so alien to her to sit, no-one with anything to say. At times, she wanted to quiet the endless chatter of Kirkholm Cottage, but she would give anything to hear her sisters bickering now.

As if seeing what was in her mind, Morwenna returned to the topic of her family.

'Are your sisters still living at Kirkholm Cottage?'

Elspeth's voice croaked as she responded, her vocal cords seeming to have forgotten their job.

'Yes, yes they're both still at home.'

'They must be a great help to your mother.'

'Well, Agatha is a help. Kaliope is more of a free spirit.'

Elspeth noticed Riordan fidget as she spoke Kaliope's name, his reaction also seen by his mother who glared at him.

'You have a brother too I understand?'

'Erm, yes, Calder was born shortly after my father passed away. He was a surprise. Mother didn't think there would be any more children but, well...'

Elspeth tailed off. She was rambling and had no idea why

she was offering this information. Morwenna's weak smile failed to reach her eyes.

'It will be good for her to have company in the house when you marry.'

Elspeth met the intenseness of Morwenna's gaze, trying to read between the lines, trying to guess what she knew.

'Yes, I suppose so, if and when I eventually marry.'

Morwenna sighed, then widened her smile as she leaned closer to Elspeth.

'I know my son has made you an offer of marriage my dear, and I want you to know I would welcome you into our family.'

She did know then. Despite the words, Elspeth doubted her genuineness. What was meant to be reassuring, even welcoming, seemed contrived. She had not expected so bold a statement of acceptance, whether meant, or not. She hadn't expected any acceptance at all. She had even been hoping Morwenna would flatly refuse to accept her, giving her the perfect excuse to turn Riordan down. Yet here she was, approving of her as a daughter-in-law.

What she couldn't understand was why?

'Thank you La... Morwenna.'

Silence again. Elspeth groped around for another topic to avoid having to discuss her joining the house of Darroch and to break the uneasy quiet that had again descended on the library. However, Riordan prevented her having to find anything else to say. It seemed the purpose of the evening had been fulfilled. Morwenna had said she was an acceptable daughter-in-law and now she was being dismissed.

'Well, I think I should escort Elspeth home. It's getting late.'

Rising, he extended his hand to her, his bony hand feeling coarse and dry to her touch. Elspeth had no idea what time it was or how long she had been here. Every second had felt like an hour and in this windowless room, it was impossible to age the day by the fading light. She was sure it couldn't have been much more than an hour though. It was hardly possible this was enough for Morwenna to get to know her prospective daughter-in-law. She had barely spoken more than a few words all evening. Yet, desperate to get out of there, she wasn't going to prolong the ordeal if they were allowing her to escape. Elspeth let Riordan help her from the low seat and relieved her of the empty brandy glass still clutched in her hand.

'Thank you for a lovely evening L … Morwenna. It was nice to see you.'

Morwenna rose and took Elspeth's hands, pulling her in to sham kiss both cheeks.

'Thank you for coming. You're most welcome anytime.'

Elspeth felt she was in another scripted scene, the finale of a play about a dinner party.

'Come again and visit soon Elspeth.'

Morwenna released her hands, and Elspeth, stammering her thanks again, followed Riordan into the hall. Jenson stood stiffly waiting to open the door, to set her free.

'The carriage is waiting outside Elspeth. I won't be a moment.'

Riordan turned to Jenson, the gentle tone he used when speaking to her now commanding.

'You, help Miss Larimore into the carriage while I fetch my hat.'

As Riordan disappeared through a doorway off the hall, Elspeth closed her eyes and exhaled. Feeling Jenson's eyes on her, she turned to look at her friend. She opened her mouth to speak, but he gestured for her to stay quiet as he opened the front door. Elspeth was surprised by the onslaught of light that confirmed the shortness of her visit. Squinting to allow her eyes to become accustomed after the bleakness of Dalengour, she stepped outside feeling like a fly that had managed to escape the spider's web.

'What time is it?' she asked as Jenson closed the heavy door behind them.

'Half past eight.'

'You mean I've only been here for just over an hour! It felt like years.'

Elspeth noted how Jenson's skin crinkled around his eyes when he smiled. He had a beautiful smile. She felt the heat rising in her face again and quickly looked away.

'We should get you settled in the carriage before he comes back.'

Elspeth was reluctant. She wanted to stay and breath the fresh air, needing to evict the staleness of Dalengour from her lungs. She wanted to stay here with Jenson.

Knowing Riordan would be back momentarily, she moved towards the open carriage door. Jenson caught her elbow, turning her to face him, his eyes searching her expression for... something.

'Elspeth, are you going to marry him?'

Sadness – there was definitely sadness in the question, the emotion dulling his eyes as he waited for her answer. Taken off guard, the nearness of him making her head swim, she couldn't get her thoughts straight. Her head was full of Jenson leaving no room for rational thought or sense.

'I... I don't know.'

Her answer seemed to kill a spark within him. He held her gaze, opened his mouth as if to say something, then closed it as his shoulders dropped. Suddenly, he stood aside, making space for her to step into the carriage, his head erect, his gaze fixed above her head, the familiarity between them once again replaced by cold formality.

'Jenson I... I'm confused. I don't know what to do. Please look at me. Let me explain!'

He continued to stand rigidly by the carriage door, somehow closed down, all evidence of their friendship evaporating.

'There's really no need Miss Larimore. You don't owe me any explanation. I'm just a servant here at Dalengour and you will soon be Lady of the house.'

Jenson kept his eyes anchored on the wall ahead, refusing to look at her, his voice passive.

'I haven't accepted him yet!' Elspeth blurted, wanting him to know that she was still free. It didn't have any effect as Jenson stood wordlessly waiting for her to step into the carriage. His stoicism suggested this wasn't the point. Elspeth had disappointed him somehow by even considering marriage to Riordan Darroch. She just wasn't sure why. Jenson was no fool. He must understand the need for her to make a good marriage. Especially now her father was gone.

Further conversation was impossible as Riordan appeared in the doorway. Tears began to sting the back of her eyes as she climbed into the carriage, afraid now to look back at Jenson and see his indifference. Riordan clambered alongside her taking the seat opposite and closing the door behind them.

'You don't have to take me home Riordan. I'm sure the driver will make sure I get back to Kirkholm safely,' she said curtly, trying to regain control of her emotions.

'Nonsense, it's my pleasure. Besides, I thought you might appreciate some more relaxed company after the strain of my mother. I know she can be quite intimidating.'

Elspeth forced a weak smile and Riordan took this as

confirmation of her need for his company. She wanted nothing more than to be away from Morwenna Darroch - that was true. But she wanted to make the journey home alone. Riordan's company was not welcome. She wanted time to think.

Riordan banged on the roof and the carriage swayed into motion. They made their way down the long drive of Dalengour, Elspeth staring out into the fading light to avoid looking across at her suitor. Riordan's vapid voice demanded her attention.

'I think the evening went very well. My mother likes you a great deal Elspeth.'

Elspeth blinked, trying to hide her amazement at this summary of the evening.

'I must admit I was quite surprised. I didn't think she would be so welcoming. I remember she didn't seem keen on having me at Dalengour last time we met.'

'I think it just took her by surprise. She knows how I feel about you now and is eager to get to know you better before the wedding.'

'I haven't consented to be your wife yet Riordan.'

Elspeth smiled feebly to soften her waspish response, then returned to staring out of the window. Suddenly, Riordan was beside her, clasping her hand in his. She stared into the pallid face that was now too close as he gazed at her. She could feel his breath on her skin, smell the remains of the repulsive fish soup and brandy as he exhaled through wine-stained teeth. She tried to pull back, trapped by the side of the carriage.

'Elspeth, you know how I feel about you don't you? I want to marry you.'

She noted the absence of a declaration of love. But then she didn't love him either.

'I'm honoured that you want to make me your wife Riordan. Really I am,' she said, trying to bow her head to avoid the assault of his bad breath on her nostrils.

She attempted to free her hand from his grip, but he just held on tighter as she struggled.

'Then why are you holding back? Say you'll marry me Elspeth?'

'I – I need a little more time.'

'What is there to think about Elspeth? We belong together. I just know it. I'll make you a good husband. I can give you, and your family a good life.'

Elspeth looked into his eyes, looking for something. Some indication that his words stemmed from a depth of feeling for her. Yet she could see nothing. She felt confined by his nearness, pressured by his insistence she except his proposal. He was an excellent match for her, titled, wealthy. She should accept him. Yet there was a certain sense of defeat in agreeing to marry him. She would be giving up on dreams of marrying for love, being cherished by a man she adored. Giving up the dream of Jenson.

The carriage pulled up at Kirkholm Cottage, the sudden halt throwing her into Riordan's arms. She arched her back to keep her face as far away from him as possible while trapped in his grip, afraid he was going to kiss her.

Thankfully, he relaxed his hold, allowing her to draw back, the tension easing.

'Goodnight Riordan. Thank you for bringing me home.'

He reached across and opened the carriage door, his arm barring her escape. He leaned towards her and brushed his thin, passionless lips across her cheek.

'I'm not a patient man Elspeth. I won't wait forever. Give me your answer soon and put me out of my misery,' he whispered close to her ear.

There was something almost threatening in his plea as she sat trapped between him and the side of the carriage. Not knowing what else to say, she bade him goodnight and pushed his arm out of her way to step into the night air. Riordan kept his eyes on her as he pulled the door closed, then banged on the roof to signal the driver to move off.

Elspeth stood sombrely by the door of Kirkholm Cottage and watched the carriage turn around. She didn't move until the sound of the horses faded away. She rubbed the goosebumps starting to form on her bare arms, partly due to the chill in the night air and partly due to the memory of Riordan's touch. How could she marry a man whose affection left her so cold? But then, how could she turn down such a man as Riordan Darroch? Elspeth sighed as she made ready to deal with the tirade of questions that would begin as soon as she opened the door. She fixed a happy smile on her face and prepared to lie about the pleasantness of her evening.

CHAPTER 3

Morwenna's Fairytale

CLOSING THE DOOR TO HER BED CHAMBER, Morwenna leaned back on the cold, wooden slab. She was exhausted. The evening with the Larimore girl had been excruciating. The idea of her marrying into the Darrochs was abominable, but necessary. One step in the chain of events that must happen for her to get what she wanted. She just hoped Riordan could convince her to accept him.

Morwenna moved through the darkness to light candles on her dressing table, the extravagance of electricity averted. The flames cast a becoming glow across her face as she seated herself on the tatty, upholstered stool, staring at her reflection in the mirror. Not yet forty-five years of age, she was still a beautiful woman, her pale skin youthful and bereft of tell-tale lines of age, her body curvaceous and taut, unaffected by the ravages of bearing her child.

She ran a carefully manicured hand across the non-existent wrinkles under her eyes and sighed. She would not remain beautiful for long. Time was at this very moment doing its best to steal her looks. She needed her plan to work and soon. Then her beauty would be eternal.

This thought cheered her as she carefully removed the emerald earrings and placed them back in the velvet box standing open on the dresser. She admired them as their facets reflected the orange glow of the flickering flames. Tenderly, she laid them on the black fabric next to a matching necklace and ring, also shining with precious green stones and diamonds. These were the last of the Darroch jewels, all that remained, the rest long gone.

Closing the lid on their richness, Morwenna sighed and began to remove the pins holding her dark hair in its neat chignon. Normally, the maid would undress her, but tonight, she had allowed her to help Mrs Pegg in the kitchen to maintain the charade of a full complement of staff at Dalengour. Thanks to the extravagances of her father, the money was gone. She managed to keep six servants to run the house. Selling paintings, jewellery and renting some estate farmland paid their wages and put food on the table, but if things didn't change soon, she would have to let more staff go. But things were going to change. Elspeth Larimore was going to change the fortunes of the Darrochs.

Morwenna began to drag the silver brush through her hair, the natural waves accentuated having been tightly wound in the nape of her neck all day. Leaving the mirror, she strode towards the bed where her nightgown lay, the grey tinge of the white cotton attesting to its age. She braided her curls into a loose plait as she walked, then changed quickly before the chill of the room cooled her skin. She slipped the threadbare garment over her head, shivering as the cold fabric enveloped her body. Drawing a shawl around her shoulders, she pulled the comforter from the bed, taking it to the chair by the window where she settled to wait for Riordan's return.

Morwenna's eyelids begin to droop as the warmth of the blanket relaxed her. Suddenly, she was surrounded by her past, a husky voice in the distance, telling her the story. She was seven years old, staring up at the wizened face and pale green eyes of her grandmother, always dressed head to toe in black, rose water fighting to disguise the fusty smells of old age. She was sitting at her feet, listening, eyes wide as she became immersed in the tale she had heard so many times before.

'*You know the Darrochs are not from here?*'

The younger Morwenna nodded, her wide eyes expectant as they fixed on the aged woman.

'*We belong in another world called Nethergar.*'

Her grandmother's voice took on a lilting quality, the cadence of her words bringing the tale to life. Morwenna rested her head on the storyteller's bony knees. The feel of her skirts rough under her cheek, the weight of the gnarly fingers on her head as her grandmother stroked her hair, vivid in her dream.

'*Nethergar is a mystical place – a place where wonderful things can happen. It is a place of magic and the Darrochs were once very powerful in Nethergar.*'

Her grandmother seemed to drift off, her thoughts absorbed by the past. Morwenna waited patiently, listening to the old woman's raspy breath.

'*We lived in a beautiful castle, very much like this one and we were happy, contented. But one day, some of our Darroch ancestors became lost. They found their way to another world, to this world and they became trapped here, in Cairndarroch. We have been looking for a way home ever since.*'

'How did they get lost?' Morwenna said, turning her face eagerly to look at her grandmother.

The old woman smiled, her papery skin crinkling even more, accentuating the furrows already deeply etched in the worn face.

'Nethergar was a peaceful place until the Larimore family moved into the village.'

'Are they like the Larimores that live here?' Morwenna interrupted, earning her a stern stare from the watery green eyes.

Morwenna shrank back and turned away to lay her head on the old woman's protuberant knees.

'The people of Nethergar welcomed the newcomers at first. But soon, strange and dreadful things started to happen. Fields that were previously fertile became barren, illness and death plagued the village, houses burned to the ground and floods swept through the streets.'

Her grandmother paused for dramatic effect, settling against the scrolled back of the velvet clad armchair with a sigh.

'Why did bad things happen?' Morwenna asked innocently without looking up.

'It was the Larimores,' she said conspiratorially. 'They were the reason bad things happened in the village. They were very powerful witches you see, who were using their gifts to torment the people of Nethergar.'

'But why? Why did they want to hurt them?' Morwenna asked, sitting upright and turning to face the venerable old woman.

Morwenna's eyes shone brightly, the flames from the drawing room fire reflected in their brilliance. Her grandmother raised her eyebrows, pursing her lips as she blinked slowly.

'Because they enjoyed it,' she spat. 'They enjoyed hurting people.'

Her stare was hard now, full of hate. Morwenna's young brow furrowed, confused by the depth of her grandmother's anger towards the mythical Larimores in her story. The aged woman was lost in emotion, her granddaughter's presence momentarily forgotten. Coming back to the present, her grandmother reached out a wizened hand, tracing the outline of Morwenna's face with a spindly finger, a wistful look in her once-striking eyes.

'Their gifts made them very wealthy,' she went on. 'Every time something terrible happened in the village, the Larimores would offer their help. No-one suspected they were the cause of whatever tragedy had befallen Nethergar and in their ignorance, the villagers gratefully accepted their offer to use their gifts to fix things. Over and over again, they wreaked havoc on the people of Nethergar, then stepped forward and used their powers to restore the village. Doing this, earned them the gratitude of the people who willingly paid for their services in money or goods. Only the Darrochs saw them for what they really were. Ruthless witches willing to hurt and maim people for their own ends.'

Her grandmother reached for the sherry at her side and took a slow sip. Morwenna fidgeted at her feet, eager to hear more.

'The Darrochs began to hunt the Larimores down and as each one was removed from the village, things began to improve for the people of Nethergar. Eventually, the villagers saw that the Darrochs were right and joined them in eradicating the witches from their home.'

'Where did the Larimores go?' Morwenna asked, prompting her grandmother to get on to her favourite part of the story.

'Most were slain as they tried to flee,' the old woman said with a resigned sigh. 'But the most powerful witch was able to open a gateway to another world and escaped Nethergar, coming here to Cairndarroch. But before she had time to close the gateway, one of our ancestors followed her through, determined not to let her escape. Unfortunately, when the gateway closed, they also became trapped here, in Cairndarroch, with the Larimore witch.'

'Why didn't they just open the gateway and go home?'

Morwenna knew the answer. Her grandmother leaned forwards, bringing her leathery face close and lowering her voice to a croaky whisper.

'Because once away from Nethergar and with the gateway closed, *the power to reopen it was gone. Magic is not strong here in Cairndarroch and when she passed through, the Larimore witch was no longer able to find a way back.'*

Her grandmother bowed her head, staring at Morwenna from under hooded eyes as she spoke in a hushed tone.

'But legend has it that the gateway will be opened again - when the blood of a Larimore with the gift of magic is spilled in the place where the gateway lies, hidden from the eyes of this world. Then, the Darrochs will return home. The gateway will restore everything that is our right. We will be powerful again. So powerful nothing, not even time, will be able to stall us.'

Morwenna's innocent eyes burned with wonder. Her imagination fired by dreams of a world of magic hidden beyond a mythical gateway.

'I wish you wouldn't fill her head with such nonsense.'

Her mother's meek voice broke the thrall of the story. Her mother, kind, loving, pathetic. If only she had been stronger, protected her, Morwenna's life could have been different. If only her mother had born a son, but she couldn't even manage that.

'It's not nonsense!' her grandmother snapped, contempt for her daughter-in-law evident in her tone. *'These stories contain our truth and I have a feeling my little Morwenna will be the one to find that gateway home.'*

Her grandmother ran a knurled hand down Morwenna's cheek, a smile deepening the furrows in her drapey skin as she looked down on the naïve face. Her mother looked on, anger momentarily tainting her usually placid expression as she noted the possessive way the old lady talked about Morwenna. It was as if she herself had no claim on her daughter, no role to play in her own daughter's life.

From the shadows of her dream, a tall man entered the scene, his angular face and prominent nose framed by almost black hair hanging limply to his jawline. The darkness of his attire accentuated the sallow skin. Only his vibrant green eyes seemed alive as he looked around the room. Her father. The little girl in the dream ran to wrap her arms *around the legs of the father she adored. The sleeping adult Morwenna became agitated, eyes flickering under closed lids, moans of fear escaping her torpid lips.*

She awoke with a start, her breathing raspy and fast, perspiration gathered on her top lip. The blanket was stifling in her panic. Throwing it off, she leaned forward, breathing in the cool air. Tears prickled her eyes, her anger rising. Anger for what he took. Anger that the thought of him could still bring back the fears of a helpless child.

Morwenna went to the washstand and tipped cold water into the bowl. Splashing her face, the fear washed away as the icy droplets ran down her skin. Now only the resident hate remained. She dried her face on the towel and returned to sit before the mirror. The hair around her forehead was damp, the moisture causing it to wrap into tight curls.

She reached up to tame the unruly strands, a smile threatening her lips as she let the image of her father, his face contorted, enter her mind. She remembered his wrinkled, deathly white pallor, bile oozing from the corners of his mouth as he clutched at his throat, the poison invading his tissues. She remembered the young woman she was then, standing serenely over him, holding a glass identical to the one shattered on the floor except, in hers, the wine was untouched.

As her father lay writhing in agony, the seventeen-year-old Morwenna had watched, waiting for his struggle with life to end. When the rattle of death had come, she placed her glass on the table and calmly stepped over the corpse. She had wanted to feel something at that moment– some sadness at his loss, even happiness that he got what he deserved. But there had been nothing.

It was the day her father died that Morwenna Darroch realised her grandmother's story might be true. Leaving her father's body in the library at Dalengour, she had retreated to her rooms and waited. The scream of the housekeeper had brought hurried footsteps clacking on the stone floor as Gadsen came to investigate the commotion. Her mother's voice was heard asking what was going on before an unassailable wail of shock and grief escaped her lips at the sight of her dead husband.

The young Morwenna had hid in her rooms, her eyes closed as she visualised what was going on below stairs. She could see the servants, one running from the house to bring the doctor from the village, another returning to the room with a sheet to cover the distorted body. Gadsen, the butler, was trying to disentangle her mother from the shell of her father.

In her mind, the scene had become so vivid, like she was standing in the middle of the commotion, a passive observer unseen by the actors. She could see tears running down her mother's reddened nose, the pale welts on the housekeeper's bottom lip as she bit down her teeth to keep her emotion in check, the ripple of the white cotton bedlinen as it hovered above the body before settling to cover the contorted grimace of death. The smell of vomit had filled Morwenna's nostrils as the sheet settled, wafting the aromas of her father's last moments into the room, the housekeeper gulping, her nose wrinkling in disgust. Detail – the detail had been too clear, the sights, sounds and smells palpable. Morwenna was in the room. Somehow, she was there.

With realisation, the connection to downstairs was lost. She had opened her eyes, the images in her mind replaced by what was immediately in front of her. The heavy framed bed, the small leaded window admitting the burgeoning light of dawn, the ashy remains of last night's fire piled in the grate.

The days that followed the end of her father's life were

overtaken by the façade of grief and it wasn't until after the funeral that she was able to visit her grandmother. The once forbidding dowager languished in her bed, irascible at her growing infirmity. But only her grandmother would believe her. Morwenna explained the feelings of witnessing something happening elsewhere, avoiding the detail of what she had seen and when. It didn't matter. Suspicion in her grandmother's eyes told her she knew of Morwenna's role in her son's death. There was no sign of judgement or recrimination reflected in her crumpled face. Just resignation, as if she had expected it.

Her grandmother's voice was hoarse, age drying her out from the inside, making everything about her arid and flaky.

'You have the gift now Morwenna. It did belong to your father, but now he's gone, it's passed to you.'

'What gift?'

'I told you that in Nethergar, things exist that seem impossible to those who live in this world. Gifts are common amongst the people of Nethergar. The Darrochs have the ability to observe – we can see things, witness things happening in other places without being there. The gift passes from one Darroch to another on death. Your father had it, now it's yours.'

'My father? But he never told me?'

'The gift isn't strong here in Cairndarroch. Your father didn't recognise it for what it was. He didn't believe and so never recognised his gift.'

'But I could? I could choose to see things?'

'With practice, you might be able to train your mind to see into other people's lives. But it would take access to Nethergar for your gift to truly develop.'

That was the last conversation Morwenna had with her grandmother who was found dead in her bed the following morning. Standing at her graveside in the Darroch cemetery, Morwenna grieved for the child she had been. The child who loved the old woman unconditionally. The child who listened to her stories of the Darrochs of Nethergar with wonder and awe. On that day, her young son clasped her hand, bewildered by his second visit to this consecrated place in his short life. Once to bury his grandfather and now, to bid farewell to the old woman he never really knew. Looking into his innocent face, the sadness Morwenna felt at her grandmother's death was quickly replaced by hatred for what the old woman had done.

Even now, thirty years later, memories of hushed conversations between her father and grandmother, the sound of her mother's pitiful sobs as she begged them not to do it, haunted her dreams. She could still feel the fear and shame of the thirteen-year-old Morwenna as her father took her innocence in the name of producing an heir. Every week, she was subjected to the writhing of her father as he raped her, justifying his act by the need to pass the Darroch title to a son – something her mother had been unable to provide.

The week before her sixteenth birthday, her physical ordeal had ended. Her grandmother came to her rooms as she was undressing, scrutinising her naked body as had become routine. On this day, she declared her with child. Morwenna was grateful for the baby in her belly. It kept her father from her bed.

Plans were made, lies were told to make the world believe she was travelling in the Americas. Both Morwenna and her mother were confined to their chambers, away from prying eyes so when the child came, it could be passed off as the son of Lord and Lady Darroch. Morwenna never considered what would become of her child if it was a girl. She never considered the swell of her belly as containing a child at all.

With the due date approaching, Morwenna's mind turned to what she would do after the baby was born. She couldn't stay here, especially if she didn't produce a son. She would never let her father touch her again.

Morwenna hadn't seen her mother since her confinement but heard rumours about her descent into insanity. The morning her father came to her rooms with news of her mother's death, she was glad. She revelled in the imagery of her mother hanging by the neck from her bedsheets, taking her own life to escape the shame of letting her daughter be used as a breeding sow. One less person to hate.

The demise of her mother spoiled her father's plans. It was impossible to keep his wife's death a secret until after the baby was born and so a tale was concocted that Morwenna had met and married an American man on her travels. Her young husband had been tragically killed shortly after their wedding, leaving Morwenna pregnant and alone in an unfamiliar country. She had therefore decided to travel back to Dalengour to have her baby. As improbable as this seemed to Morwenna, it did allow her some freedom in the last weeks of her maternity. She attended her mother's funeral and played the grieving daughter, accepted condolences as a grieving widow and plotted the murder of her father.

Late in October, six weeks after she buried her mother, her son was born. She wanted to hate the child for everything he represented, yet she found herself loving him from the moment he was placed in her arms. She swore she would protect him from the treachery of her family. He would never know the truth of his paternity. The story of her hasty marriage and subsequent widowhood shielded him. If anyone doubted its veracity, the power and influence of the Darrochs prevented them voicing their opinions.

The sound of the carriage drawing up to the front of the house dragged her mind back to the present. Riordan was returning from taking the Larimore girl home. Morwenna wiped away the tears of the past and waited for her son. She was so close now. The world of her grandmother's stories had been her sanctuary every time her father forced himself on her. As she felt his nails digging into her skin, felt him push into her most intimate places, her mind had hidden in Nethergar.

Finding a way back to the home of their ancestors had become an obsession. Morwenna spent years poring over Darroch history, listening to myths and legends retold about the Larimores, and now she was sure Elspeth was the key to finding the gateway. Nethergar would again be her sanctuary but this time, not only in her mind. With access to Nethergar, the wealth and status of the Darrochs would be restored. With the power of the Larimores, no one could ever hurt her again.

CHAPTER 4

The First Night

AUGUST 1920 - CAIRNDARROCH

ELSPETH STOOD IN FRONT OF THE MIRROR, HER eyes too blurry to see the reflection staring back at her. Her chest heaved as she forced air into her lungs, her heart feeling as if someone's hands were gripping it tightly, trying to prevent it doing its job. She could feel her legs trembling beneath her, threatening to give way, leaving her in a crumpled heap of white lace and wilted flowers. She'd done it. She was now Mrs Riordan Darroch.

Laying the bouquet on the dressing table, she tried to focus her eyes on the pale peach freesias and ivory gardenias already turning brown. She ran her fingers across the curling petals, feeling an affinity with their fading expectancy of being left to grow in the sun. Wiping her eyes, she rallied her composure. She must ready herself for the first night with her husband.

With shaking fingers, she fumbled with the veil, pulling painfully at her hair as she tried to disentangle the clips holding it in place. She laid the white tulle carefully next to the flowers, straightening the fabric to make sure the beads did not tear the delicate net. Her wedding outfit was beautiful, a gift from Morwenna with no expense spared. The carefully designed bodice, cut to disguise her broad shoulders and accentuate her slim waist, was adorned with pearls and glass beads matching those on the now discarded veil. The full-length satin skirt skimmed her ankles, layers of lace decorated with more beads visible on the petticoat beneath when she moved. Her mother's pearls dangled from her ears – the only piece of jewellery Charlotte Larimore had ever possessed. They had been a gift from her father when Elspeth was born.

She looked around the rooms that would be her chambers from now on. Her eyes were drawn to the dominating four-poster bed she would share with Riordan, the quilt sewn by her mother and sisters looking forlorn on its huge mattress. Her possessions had been brought here from Kirkholm Cottage. Elspeth welcomed their familiarity, yet their brightness did little to offset the cold, funereal atmosphere of the room.

The bed caught her attention again. He would soon be here, expecting her to succumb to him, expecting her to be his wife. The thought of his nakedness made her reel as she fumbled for the stool at the dresser. Her chest tightened again, the room starting to spin, the blood draining from her face. Sitting down heavily, Elspeth held her head in her hands, elbows resting on her knees, breathing deeply.

A gentle knock at the door startled her.

'Elspeth, may I come in?'

Her mother come to help her out of her dress. Morwenna had offered her the maid, but she had declined, not wanting to spend this time with a stranger.

'Yes, come in.'

Charlotte Larimore entered looking radiant in the mauve-coloured dress gifted to her by Morwenna for the wedding. Her blue eyes sparkled, her skin glowing, the usual tiredness banished now Riordan had engaged a housekeeper and maid for Kirkholm Cottage. Looking at her mother, Elspeth remembered why she had agreed to the wedding. Her mother and sisters' futures were secure now, their lives easier.

Forcing a smile, she stretched her hands towards her mother, too weak to stand and greet her. Charlotte came and kneeled at her feet, her eyes examining her daughters face, her brows drawn together in worry.

'What's the matter Elspeth?'

'Nothing… I'm fine. Just a little tired and nervous I think.'

Charlotte caressed her cheek, her palm feeling cool against Elspeth's flushed skin.

'Of course you are! It's to be expected on your wedding night.'

Elspeth nodded, not trusting herself to speak. Her mother must never suspect. It would break her heart if she thought Elspeth had felt responsible for providing her with a better life, had married from a sense of duty to better their situation. Charlotte Larimore would willingly have worked herself to the bone if it meant her children would be happy.

'Elspeth, you do know what will happen tonight?'

Her mother blushed as she asked the question. They had never spoken about what happened between men and women in the bedroom.

'I think so. I know what will happen, just not how it will feel,' Elspeth said, her watery eyes fixed on her mother, her bottom lip trembling. 'I'm scared Mother.'

Charlotte wrapped her arms around her, smoothing her hair as she spoke.

'There's nothing to be afraid of Elspeth. There's nothing more wonderful than laying with a man you love.'

Elspeth gritted her teeth, trying to keep her tears in check, not wanting to give way to the tide of emotion swelling in her chest.

'Come now, dry your tears. We must get you ready for your husband.'

Charlotte ran her thumbs tenderly under her daughter's eyes, attempting to brush away her sorrow. Elspeth saw concern in her mother's expression and knew she had to pull herself together or there would be questions about the depth of her sadness.

'I'm fine Mother, really I am. It's just unnerving to realise I won't be going back to Kirkholm Cottage tonight, that I'm now a married woman. I suppose I'm all grown up,' she said, shrugging her broad shoulders as she smiled weakly.

Elspeth turned to face the mirror, wiping her nose on the handkerchief her mother passed her, taking a deep breath to steady herself.

'I'm all red and blotchy! I'm not even sure Riordan will want me now!'

She feigned a laugh as she looked at her mother in the mirror. Charlotte began to unpin her hair, allowing the long, rose gold ringlets to fall down her back. Once free of the clips, Elspeth's hair returned to its poker-straight natural state, all signs of Kaliope's efforts to arrange it in curls and waves in vain. Her mother picked up the brush and began to smooth the non-existent tangles. Elspeth was transported back to a memory of her heavily pregnant mother trying to control a wriggling nine-year old child as she tied ribbons in her hair, her father shouting at her to stand still. It was the day the twins were born, her mother already in labour, still trying to make sure Elspeth looked pretty.

Charlotte worked in silence, helping Elspeth out of her dress and petticoats and into the new, crisp white nightgown and lace shawl. Once her undressing was complete, her mother led her to stand in front of the full-length mirror. Placing her hands on Elspeth's shoulders, a wistful look on her face, Charlotte's eyes were brimming with tears.

'You look beautiful.'

Elspeth turned away from her reflection to look into her mother's face.

'I wish your father was here. He would be so proud to see the woman you've become.'

Charlotte looked down, wiping her eyes on the sleeve of her dress having given her handkerchief to her daughter.

Elspeth wrapped her arms around her mother.

'I miss him so much.'

Charlotte pulled back and held Elspeth at arm's length, looking intently into her face.

'So do I. But he will always be here with us, watching over us.'

Elspeth wasn't sure she believed that. She wanted to believe her father was by her side, looking down on her from… somewhere. But she couldn't feel it. To her, he was just gone.

Her mother embraced her again, clinging tightly, not wanting to let her go. Elspeth was content to stay in the protection of her arms, hide there for a while, forget what was to come. Charlotte released her reluctantly and standing straight, stared at her as if it was the last time she would ever see her daughter. It was the last time her mother would look at her as a child. After tonight, she would be a woman, a wife.

'I should go. Riordan will come up soon and you should have a few moments by yourself.'

'Don't go!'

Elspeth grabbed her mother's hands, desperately trying to delay her departure.

'Elspeth, I must. You'll be fine. There's really nothing to be afraid of,' Charlotte's voice trying to soothe her anxiety.

It didn't work and Elspeth was afraid. Afraid of her husband.

Pulling free of her daughter's grip, Charlotte patted her arm consolingly and left Elspeth alone. Determined not to let the panic overwhelm her, she turned back to stare at her reflection in the mirror. She didn't recognise the woman who stared back. Something had changed without her even noticing. Becoming Riordan's wife made her seem matte, the shine of possibility dulled. Now her future was written, known, the lustre of dreams had vanished from her face.

Elspeth felt numb. This day had mapped out a future she now realised she did not want. The image of Jenson Tanner forced its way into her mind. She had slavishly pushed all thoughts of Jenson away since she agreed to become Mrs Riordan Darroch, but now, on her wedding night, thoughts of him refused to be abjured.

The night of the dinner at Dalengour was the last time they had spoken with the familiarity of friends. Since that day, Jenson had treated her with the same reverence and formality he afforded Riordan and Morwenna. She had been hurt by his refusal to look at her, to talk freely to her. She had wanted to explain why she was considering marrying into the Darrochs. Wanted him to give her a reason not to. It was after yet another failed attempt to talk to Jenson, his desire to be out of the conversation and as far away from her as possible obvious, that she had finally decided to accept Riordan's proposal. Now she was Riordan's wife, thoughts of Jenson Tanner had no place in her mind.

The door opened and her heart began to beat uncontrollably in her chest. Slowly, she turned to see Riordan, standing in the weak pool of light cast into the room by one of the few illuminated lamps in the hallway. He was still in his wedding suit, the expression on his face strange, unreadable. Elspeth's mouth felt dry, like the bottom of a birdcage, the air gritty in her throat as she tried to swallow.

Riordan stood, unmoving, silent. He stared at her, his eyes emotionless, concealing any thoughts behind them. His black hair, usually slicked back, fell across his forehead in greasy strands, giving him an uncharacteristically unkempt air. She shifted uncomfortably, not knowing what to do or say. The quiet felt expectant, ominous. Goosebumps stood to attention on her arms, her legs ready to collapse under the weight of silence. Undoing his jacket, he pushed the door closed and came to stand in front of her.

'Mrs Elspeth Darroch, my wife.'

There was no sentimentality in his voice. Elspeth thought it sounded like mocking disbelief, as if he couldn't believe it was true. He reached out to touch her hair, letting the silky strands run through his fingers until his hand was level with her breast. Thrusting his hand beneath the delicate fabric of her nightdress, he groped at her chest, his eyes never leaving her face, watching for her reaction.

Elspeth gasped, having never felt the hands of a man on her before, fighting every desire to push him away. He pinched her flesh between his fingers, making her cry out in pain as she pulled away from his caress.

'You're hurting me!'

Riordan's face contorted into a licentious grin. He lurched forwards and wrapped his arms around her waist, pulling her against his wiry body.

'I can do what I want now that we are husband and wife my dear Elspeth.'

Fear gripped her and she struggled against him. He held her for a few moments, laughing while she tried unsuccessfully to get free. Beaten, she quietened in his grip, breathing heavily. As she stilled, Riordan released her and she staggered backwards until she met the edge of the bed, trying to put as much distance as possible between them. She wanted to run, to get far away from this man – the man she had just married.

Riordan looked at her now as she cowered against the bedpost, her face drained of blood, every muscle in her body trembling in fear, and his face softened as much as the hard features allowed.

'Elspeth my dear, why so scared? I was just having some fun. I would never hurt you. You're my wife. Now come, sit with me and have a drink. It'll relax you.'

Riordan removed the black tailcoat and threw it across the bed. He went to pour two shots of brandy from the decanter in the adjoining room that was to be Elspeth's private sitting room, holding one out to her when he returned. Taking the drink, she eyed him suspiciously. His sudden change in character unnerved her. He gestured to the chair facing the waning fire, lit hours before to warm the room but dying now with no additional logs to restore its life.

Elspeth took the seat, never taking her eyes from her new

husband, everything about her tense. Riordan remained standing, gulping down his brandy and unbuttoning his collar.

'Are you feeling better now?' he asked.

She wasn't. She nodded feebly, her palms sweating despite the chill permeating the room, winning against the weary flames.

'If you're afraid Elspeth, we don't have to consummate our marriage tonight. We have our whole lives ahead of us. There is time to take things slowly.'

He spoke kindly now, more like the Riordan who had paid her such attention during their courtship. Yet she couldn't forget the malevolence that had been present moments before.

'I – I am nervous Riordan and the way you just behaved, it scared me.'

He put down his empty glass and came to her now, crouching at her feet, his cold hands resting on her knees. Elspeth clamped her thighs together as he touched her, protecting her intimate bare skin from his nearness.

'I'm so sorry my dear. I didn't mean to make you uncomfortable. Would you like me to go? I can leave you alone and we can try this again tomorrow, when you're more used to the idea.'

Inside, she was screaming for him to get out, to never come back. She saw herself packing her bags, running back to Kirkholm Cottage, forgetting this day ever happened. Elspeth knew she didn't love Riordan, but she had never expected it to be so hard to be with him as a wife should. Yet there was no point regretting her decision to marry him now. No point putting off the inevitable. It was too late for regrets.

'No, there's no need for you to go. Can we just take things a little more slowly, more gently?'

The muscle in Riordan's cheek began to twitch as he clenched his teeth. Elspeth saw something flash in his eyes. The emotion disappeared as quickly as it had appeared and Riordan plastered a condescending smile on his sour lips.

'Of course. We can take things slow.'

Standing, he relieved Elspeth of the remains of her drink, then drew her to her feet, letting the shawl around her shoulders fall to the floor. Taking her hand, he led her to the four-poster bed.

'Why don't you settle yourself while I undress?'

Elspeth did as she was told, sliding her legs between the cold sheets, watching as Riordan disappeared into the dressing room leading off their shared bedchamber. She pulled the covers high up to her chin, straightening the hand-stitched quilt over the bed. The bright squares of fabric, decorated by her mother's hand felt comforting under her touch, a small injection of colour in an otherwise bleak room. Her thoughts turned back to what was about to happen and she threw the quilt across the room. She didn't want something so beautiful to be sullied, to bear witness to an act devoid of love and feeling.

Riordan returned, wrapped in a burgundy dressing gown, his bare legs pale and grey protruding beneath the hem, the black hairs stark against the paleness of his shins. Elspeth fixed her eyes on his feet, the gnarly toes with yellowing deformed nails and callouses doing little to warm her arousal. All she could think was how scratchy they would feel if they touched her. She did not dare look up, afraid to see his nakedness as the dressing gown crumpled around the ugly feet.

She kept her eyes averted, feeling Riordan climb into bed beside her.

'Lay down,' his said, his hand resting lightly on her hip. She shuffled down and stared up into his face.

She was still clutching at the bedclothes, her heart beating wildly.

'Relax Elspeth or this will hurt more than it needs to.'

She tried to release the tension from her muscles as he gently caressed her face. His lips came down on hers and she felt his tongue, slimy and insistent, push into her mouth. She resisted the urge to gag at the pungent smell of his breath, saliva building in her mouth, his kiss becoming harder.

She was glad when he moved his lips down to her neck, but now his hands began to roam over her body, his breathing intensifying. He crushed her small breasts, squeezing the delicate flesh in his bony fingers, the too-long fingernails biting into her tender skin. She heard the fabric rip, his hands pulling viciously at the top of her nightgown, exposing her nipples to his eager mouth. She cried out as he bit and sucked, begging him to stop.

Her pleas seemed to arouse him more, his hands now searching between her legs. Panic gripped her and she started to scream at him, trying to push him away. Riordan clamped one hand over her mouth, muffling her cries, the other continuing to explore her most intimate area. She couldn't breathe, her chest crushed by his full weight as he pushed two fingers inside her. Tears sprung to her eyes – tears of pain, fear.

Riordan took his hand from her mouth, allowing her to gulp air into her lungs. He shifted his weight to push her legs apart. On his knees, he threw back the blankets and pulled her legs up towards her head. With every part of her on show, the humiliation was overwhelming as her husband inspected her.

'You're as dry as an old hag Elspeth. Not that I expected there to be any passion under that sexless exterior.'

She tried to struggle against him, to close her legs, restore some dignity. But he held her firmly behind each knee, pinning her ungraciously. He laughed as she fought, tightening his grip, spreading her legs even further. Realising it was futile to try and escape him, Elspeth begged.

'Please Riordan, please, let me go!'

The tears were streaming down her face, but he was untouched by her distress.

'No my dear. We're going to see this through.'

He spat on his hand and ran the silky spit between her thighs, using a finger to work the saliva inside her. Elspeth lay silent now, resolved to what was going to happen. She turned her face away, distancing herself from Riordan's actions. She closed her eyes as she felt him push inside her, biting her lip against the pain, not wanting to give him the satisfaction of hearing her cry again. He began to pound his hips against her, every thrust tearing into her flesh.

Elspeth lay as still as the dead, willing it to be over. Riordan began to grunt, his movements becoming faster, harder. Opening her eyes, she fixed her gaze over his shoulder, staring vacantly at the bedframe. She was outside her body, her mind retreating to a place where this horrible man was not writhing around on top of her. She tried not to feel the sticky warmth as blood flowed down her thighs, the searing pain as he brutalised her femininity. Her disembodiment freed her from the degradation. She was not here. This woman, being raped by Riordan Darroch was not her.

Elspeth watched the scene, a passive observer in her own violation. Every detail was so clear, the vacancy in her eyes, the sweat forming on his pock-marked back, so white it glowed in the dim light as he bucked. His knuckles, bloodless with the power of his grip on her thighs. She saw it all but felt nothing.

Riordan lifted up further on his knees, pulling her towards him, forcing her legs higher, his thrusts penetrating deeper into her broken skin. Turning her head away, Elspeth blinked away the tears. She wouldn't cry again.

Something stirred in the room, catching her blurry eyes. She tried to focus but could see nothing. Yet something… she sensed something, someone. Someone witnessing her humiliation. She tried to move to see. Nothing. There was nothing. No-one was in the room except her and her writhing husband. But she couldn't shake it. She couldn't shake the sensation that someone was watching them.

Riordan's breathing was becoming faster. She looked up to see his face contort, his nails digging into her thighs, his muscles trembling in his release. He collapsed forward, the weight of him trapping her legs above her head, the air in her lungs being forced out. It was over – for now.

Riordan rolled away panting, evidence of her innocence and his pleasure smeared across his crotch as he laid, exposed, flaccid. Elspeth righted herself, pulling down her nightgown, torn and stained with blood. Half-moon welts from his fingers suffused with colour, the bite marks on her breasts bruising even now. She clutched the torn garment to her chest, curling up like a small child, shuffling as far away from him as the bed would allow, turning her back on his nakedness.

His breathing steadied, and she felt him get up from the bed. She didn't move, afraid he might touch her again. She listened to his shuffling, willing him to leave.

'Well, my wife, you're as frigid as I expected you to be. You offer no pleasure for a man.'

Elspeth spun around to look at him, thankful to see his body now wrapped in his dressing gown again. He sat on the edge of the bed as Elspeth flinched, instinctively shuffling a few inches away. A condescending smirk escaped Riordan's lips.

'Don't panic Elspeth. I can promise you that I will share your bed as infrequently as possible. You see, I want a son and heir and you're going to produce one. Until you do, I will have to endure visits to your bed to plant seed in your belly. If we're lucky, it may have already happened.'

Riordan grinned, eyes fixed on her stomach. Elspeth drew her legs up tighter, even his gaze assaulting her.

'I must be going now to get a good night's sleep. Today has been very draining. All that smiling and feigned happiness.'

He got up to leave, speaking to her like some acquaintance, as if they had taken tea together.

'Goodnight Elspeth. Sleep well and I'll see you at breakfast.'

She waited for him to close the door behind him before she dared breath. His footsteps became fainter as he walked down the hall and sure he wasn't coming back, at least not tonight, she clambered tentatively off the bed. Everything hurt.

She shuffled over to the washstand and removed her tattered nightgown. She dared not look at the damage he had done, focussing instead on cleaning herself up. The water was freezing but the cold felt soothing on her burning skin. As she rinsed the cloth, the water turned pink. She wanted to scrub away all traces of Riordan Darroch, but the pain was too intense and all she could manage was a gentle wash of her most sensitive areas.

Her administrations complete, she found a clean

nightgown and sliding it over her head, returned to the bed. The sheets were stained where she had lay. She threw the covers over the marks and went around to the other side. Retrieving the comforter from Kirkholm Cottage, she climbed on top of the bed, wrapping herself tightly in the familiarity of home. Alone, Elspeth Darroch cried herself to sleep.

CHAPTER 5

A Breath of Fresh Air

October 1921– Cairndarroch

She wanted to hate this room. The room that had witnessed her greatest humiliations at the hands of Riordan Darroch – her supposedly loving husband. For the first two months of their marriage, Elspeth had endured Riordan's visits to her bed. At first, his lovemaking was tortuous, the bruises on her skin attesting to his revelry in causing her fear and pain. But later, it became almost perfunctory, Elspeth's determination to lie like a soundless dead fish no matter what he did, cooling his pleasure. His visits had ended abruptly when her pregnancy was confirmed. Since then, she had seen her husband only briefly at meals, their interactions courteous and cold... perfunctory.

Her son, Robert Connor Darroch was born two months

after her twenty-seventh birthday. Born here, in this room –
the room that had witnessed her greatest humiliations, but
now, her greatest joy as well. The moment her son was
placed in her arms, the abasement she had suffered to bring
him into this world faded. That was five months ago, and she
had rarely seen her son since.

Elspeth laid looking up at the heavy burgundy canopy of
the bed, her eyes needing no time to adjust to the gloom as
she roused from sleep. All she did was sleep. Since the birth,
she had rarely left this room. It was an easy pregnancy.
Robert arrived on schedule. His eagerness to make an
appearance meant a short labour of just a few hours before
the arrival of a healthy boy, robustly screaming to announce
his presence. But since then, her health had been failing.

She had been allowed to hold her son for less than an
hour before he was whisked away so she could get some rest.
She had been grateful then, the tiredness of birthing
weighing heavy on her eyelids. The maid had deftly changed
the sheets and helped her into a clean nightgown. After
eating a little food, she had drifted into a contented sleep,
images of the screwed-up face of her new-born son
swimming through her dreams.

Elspeth didn't know how long she slept, but when she
awoke, the doctor was standing over her, talking to someone
in the room. She strained her ears, trying to make out what
they were saying, but only the occasional word penetrated
the haze of her mind. Morwenna was at her side.

'I think she's waking up. Elspeth? Elspeth, can you
hear me?'

'My son… where's my son?'

Her voice scratched as she spoke, as if there was no
moisture left in her throat. She tried to focus on her
surroundings but couldn't see anything further than the

imposing bedposts, the damask patterned drapes tied back to expose her.

'Robert's fine Elspeth. Nanny's taking care of him and he's doing fine,' Morwenna said dismissively.

'I want to see him.'

'Soon, when you're stronger. I'll get nanny to bring him in for a visit when you're stronger.'

The doctor was back at her side now, shining a light into her eyes, blinding her momentarily.

'It's good to have you back with us Elspeth,' he said before turning to Morwenna. 'See that she stays in bed and rests. I'll be back in a few days to check on her.'

Elspeth felt the bed move as he stood and heard the rattle of instruments being put back into his medical bag.

'How long have I been asleep?' Elspeth asked groggily.

'You've been drifting in and out for five days,' Morewenna said matter-of-factly.

'Five days! But Robert, he needs me.'

'Don't you go worrying about a thing except getting well. Robert's fine.'

With that, Morwenna patted her arm, muttered something about her getting some sleep, and left with the doctor.

Elspeth had wanted to scream out after them, to ask what was wrong with her. But she didn't have the strength. They wouldn't have been able to tell her anyway. That had been five months ago and still, she didn't know the cause of her ill health. Every bone in her body ached, the pounding in her head never let up and the constant nausea and dizziness had kept her almost bed-bound since the day she had birthed her son.

Visits from the doctor had become rare and unhelpful as he administered some routine tests every time, only to prescribe more rest. She had seen no-one other than the doctor, Morwenna and the maid who scurried silently around the room, refusing to look at her let alone speak. Riordan had been conspicuous by his absence, as had the rest of her family.

Steeling herself to sit up, Elspeth turned towards the narrow windows, trying to gauge the hour of the day by the level of light infiltrating the room. She knew the summer had passed, but the days confined to bed had blurred the passing of time. She had no idea what month or day it was. The sun streaked through the restricted opening, a golden hue illuminating the floor where it fell, but bringing no warmth. The sun in the windows meant it must be morning, the afternoons in this place being devoid of any natural light. The yellowish tint suggested it was early, the glare still low in the sky.

Elspeth wearily pulled herself up to a sitting position, the muscles in her arms trembling with the strain of supporting her weight. Her chest heaved from the exertion of this small act and she flopped back against the pillow, angry and frustrated at her frailty. As her heartbeat slowed, she swung her legs out of bed, and using the support of the bedpost, pulled herself to a standing position. The room began to spin. She closed her eyes against the wave of nausea, gripping the drapes to steady herself as her stomach lurched.

Taking deep breaths, she walked slowly towards the window. Air, she needed air. Her fingers fumbled with the catch, her muscles resisting instructions from her brain. Finally, she managed to push the window open, the fresh breeze rippling the stale air of illness in the room. The sun kissed her pale skin and she raised her chin upwards to expose as much of her face to the light as possible. The brightness fortified her, and she wanted to stay bathed in its glow forever. The need to leave this room overwhelmed her. She had to get outside.

Dressed, she needed to get dressed. The thought of escaping the sourness of Dalengour, even for a moment, strengthened her. Elspeth pulled a plain lavender dress from the closet. The long sleeves and high neck would protect against the morning chill and with a shawl, she would be warm enough. Shoes were more of a problem as the only ones she could reach were the grey ballet pumps she wore with her best gown. All the others were pushed too far back in the wardrobe for her limited mobility, so they would have to do.

She took the clothes over to the bed, retrieving some underwear on the way. Getting dressed was laboriously slow. She had to rest between each garment, but her resolve to feel the sun on her face kept her going. Elspeth folded her nightgown neatly onto her pillow, and fully dressed, went to the washstand. She splashed some cold water on her face and looked at her reflection in the full-length mirror for the first time in months.

It was hard to recognise the girl who moved to Dalengour as the woman who stared back with a gaunt pale face, grey circles surrounding deep set eyes. Elspeth's cheekbones rose prominently from her haggard face, the skin papery as it stretched across their boniness. Her head looked too big for her scrawny body, the dress hanging in empty pleats, her athletic frame ravaged by months of sickness. The only flesh that didn't cling directly to bone was her belly, her pregnancy still evident from the rotund appearance of her stomach.

Her strawberry blond hair was matted and dry. Reaching for the brush, Elspeth started to detangle the ends. It felt alien to her, like the mane of a horse, textured and coarse. Her hair had always been strong, wilfully silky and straight, resisting any attempts to make it curl or wave. Now, it hung limply in dull, straw-like strands around her angular face. Using a few pins, she twisted it into the nape of her neck, not wanting to see it as a reminder of how ill she looked.

Ready now, she pulled a grey woollen shawl across her shoulders and stepped out of her rooms for the first time since Robert was born. Standing in the dimly lit hall where no natural light was permitted entry through the heavy stone walls, she desperately wanted to see her son. She had no idea where the nursery was, or even if he would be there if she found it. She didn't have the strength to go looking. Elspeth resigned herself to her plan of getting outside. The fresh air would make her feel better and then she could look for Robert.

Tentatively, using the walls for support, she made it to the staircase that descended into the main hall. Clutching the bannister, she put her foot on the top step, fixing her eyes on the door leading to freedom – leading into the sun. Her legs felt like jelly, every sinew protesting as she forced her muscles to carry her down the steps. Stopping every few to rest, finally she made it to the bottom.

Elspeth leaned against the newel post, her heart hammering in her chest. The ticking of the grandfather clock that stood sentry in the hall echoed in her woolly head, the shuffling of servants in the surrounding rooms indistinct. The sounds blurred into white noise as her addled mind tried to make sense of her surroundings. She felt her body wanting to slip back into unconsciousness, to give up and collapse where she stood. She wouldn't let it. She needed to get out of the house.

Bracing herself with both hands on the bannister, Elspeth lowered her head, letting her eyes close, focusing on her breathing. The dizziness began to subside.

'Elspeth, Elspeth! Are you alright?'

She felt an arm rest on her shoulder. Turning, she saw Jenson Tanner, his hazel eyes full of concern. Standing so she could face him, she summoned all her strength to meet his gaze.

'I'm fine thank you Jenson.'

The formality of her tone made him drop his hand and step back. With his feet together and spine stiff, he fixed his gaze above her head.

'Can I get you something Mrs Darroch?'

It was the first time Elspeth had seen Jenson since the birth of her son and the first time she had the chance to talk to him alone in almost a year. She didn't know what to say. Since her marriage, he had avoided her as much as possible. Whenever they spoke, it had been as mistress and servant, Jenson rarely meeting her gaze and never allowing the conversation to stray off essentials.

'I don't need anything thank you Jenson. I just feel like going out for some air.'

Jenson's brow furrowed as he continued to fixate on a point above her head. Clearly, her appearance made him think she shouldn't be on her feet.

'Would you like me to fetch Lord Darroch to accompany you?'

'No, no,' she said rather too enthusiastically, causing Jenson to glance briefly at her, eyebrows raised. 'No, I don't want to bother him. I probably won't be long anyway,' she clarified quickly.

Elspeth smiled weakly and turned towards her escape. She had only made it a few steps when Jenson called after her.

'It's good to see you up and about Elspeth. I've been so worried.'

He caught her off guard with his sincerity. She spun around and their eyes met. For the longest moment, they stood, silent, their gaze conveying more than words ever could. Elspeth wanted to tell him everything, spill out every emotion she had been trying to hide since moving to Dalengour. She had longed to see him look at her this way and wanted to throw herself in his arms and tell him so. But she couldn't. She was another man's wife and now, a mother.

Quickly she lowered her eyes. Having him look at her, his face reflecting his depth of feeling was wonderful, and dangerous.

'I… I'm feeling better,' she lied. 'I think I just need to get out more, build up some strength.'

'I won't keep you,' he said, standing aside, formality restored.

She walked across the hall as quickly as her weakened legs allowed. She could feel his eyes watching her and fought the desire to turn around and look at him again. Pulling open the door, the brightness assaulted her, and she raised a hand to shield her eyes from the sun. Elspeth stepped outside for the first time in months. She let the door fall closed behind her and took a few faltering steps away from the shadow of Dalengour.

The sunlight felt wonderful. The morning was cool, a chill breeze caressing her pallid cheeks. For a few moments she stood, revelling in the fresh air, feeling the layers of dust from months cooped up in the prison of her rooms being blown away. She began to walk slowly towards the forest, wanting to be hidden from the prying eyes of the house. The tall pines stretched skywards, standing guard along the path, protecting her for a while from her life as Elspeth Darroch.

Within the safety of the trees, she indulged her thoughts of Jenson as she wandered aimlessly, revelling in her freedom. She couldn't suppress the whirl of excitement in her stomach when she remembered the way he had looked at her. She was sure his concern had been more than worries of a servant for their mistress, more even than the worries of one friend for another. But what difference did it make? They could never be together. Not now. It was too late for them. She sighed, meandering further along the shady paths away from Dalengour.

Elspeth wasn't sure how far she had walked, but now, she was beginning to tire, the light-headedness and sick feeling returning. The forest felt oppressive now. The heavily leafed branches formed an interwoven net above, blocking out all but dappled specks of light. The musty smell of the decaying pine needles turning brown underfoot became suddenly cloying and her breath laboured as her feeble chest fought for sufficient air. Eager for brightness, to feel the sun on her skin again, she headed towards an area where the gnarled trunks of the ancient trees seemed to thin.

The clearing opened out before her, basking in a golden glow as the dense canopy let in the rising sun. Exhaustion now threatened to overwhelm her, with only anger at being laid waste by such a short stroll keeping her putting one foot in front of the other. The small kirk surprised her. Never in all her walks around Dalengour had she come across this rundown church nestled in a ring of trees.

The shattered windows, glinted, sunlight bouncing off shards of glass still wedged in their frames. Red paint on the wooden steeple, faded now, would once have stood bright and cheery against the dark green backdrop. Ranging weeds suggested the heavy wooden door had remained closed for many years. Brambles invaded the crumbling brickwork, the kirk ensnared by a botanic predator trying to wipe its presence from the earth.

Elspeth felt drawn to the building. Despite its dilapidated state, she wanted to go inside. She would rest there. Regain her strength. Birdsong suddenly startled her. The sound was somehow unexpected as it penetrated the eerie quietness settled on the clearing. It was as if this place existed out of time with everywhere else, the normal rustles of the forest stilled.

Turning suddenly to stare back into the trees, Elspeth had the familiar feeling that seemed to haunt her these days – the feeling of being watched. She squinted back into the darkness but could see nothing. All was still, silent except for the sound of her laboured breathing. Her legs were like lead now and every step was like wading through mud. The kirk looked fuzzy as her head began to spin and she could feel sweat beading on her brow. She was trembling all over, waves of nausea washing over her weakened body. She had no more fight. She would lay down, right here, not caring if she lived or died.

Her son. The vision of Robert sleeping in her arms, the thought of never seeing him again, leaving him at the mercy of Morwenna Darroch, drove her forward. She must live for her son. With every ounce of remaining strength, she dragged her feet towards the kirk. Progress was painfully laboured, but at least she was still moving. She stretched her arms out in front, relief flooding her body as she felt the grainy wood of the door beneath her fingers. Tears sprang to her eyes. She had made it and now, with no rhyme or reason, she felt safe.

The heavy door pushed open more easily than expected, the hinges protesting noisily but offering no resistance. Air rushed past, blown out as if a breath had been trapped inside, waiting to escape. Elspeth coughed as dust carried on the air caught in her throat, then stepped across the threshold.

Inside the church was bathed in light that streamed in through a stained-glass window, the beams coloured by the decorated images. A woman stared out from the centre of the frame, her vibrant blue gown casting silvery ripples across the stone floor. Elspeth walked towards her, steadying herself on the pews lining the aisle. There was something familiar about the window, as if she had seen it before. Yet she was sure she had never been in this place.

Compelled towards the leaded glass woman, she moved further into the kirk. Her feet scraped along the floor, her muscles too weak to lift them. The step leading to the altar looked like a mountain to her weary body, but somehow, she had to get to the window. Gathering what was left of her strength, she hauled herself up the step and staggered the last few yards to lay her hands on the cool glass.

At her touch, the surface ruckled. She could feel the glass, cold and solid. Yet she could see ripples emanating from each depression made by her fingers. Her brow furrowed, her brain struggling to make sense of the conflict between sight and touch. The ripples moved outwards to the edge of the frame as more formed around her hands. She stood watching the swirls of glass, her heavy breath misting the surface in front of her face. Surely her foggy brain was playing tricks?

There it was again – the sense that someone was watching. Elspeth purled around, scouring the kirk for signs that someone was here. Nothing. She was alone. Fearing now for her sanity, she looked back at the window, glowing brightly in the sun's illumination. It was solid – as glass should be. What she had seen must be due to the delirium creeping over her tired body.

She stepped back against the altar stone, her legs crumpling as she slid to the floor. Everything in the church was swimming now, fading further from view. She was looking at everything through the wrong end of a telescope, reality retreating, surrounding her in blackness. Then, even the emptiness was gone.

Elspeth could hear someone in the distance calling her name. She couldn't see or feel anything. Only the sound of panic in someone's voice as they called her over and over again permeated the haze of her mind. She needed to open her eyes. She needed to see what the matter was. She should try and help them. But she didn't want to wake up. She was so tired. She could just go back to sleep if only they would stop calling her name.

The someone was shaking her now, their attempts to rouse her more insistent. Elspeth could feel two hands on her shoulders, the voice now sounding afraid, the calls of her name louder, more determined.

'Elspeth! Wake up! Please Elspeth, come back. Please don't leave me!'

Her eyes flickered open. Kneeling by her side, framed against the stained-glass scene, tears streaming down his cheeks, was Jenson Tanner.

'Thank God!' he shouted as he gathered her into his arms, holding her tightly, smoothing her hair, his lips against her forehead.

Elspeth could feel the warmth of his skin through his shirt. She wanted to stay wrapped in his arms and drift back into sleep. But why was he here? Where was here? She couldn't remember. Everything seemed so confused, dreams weaved with reality in a nonsensical dance. She remembered a kirk, feeling like she was being watched, falling, a woman dragging her across the floor towards the window, the window moving. Blood, there had been blood.

Jenson still held her, his body shaking, tears flowing.

'Jenson, what's going on?'

Her voice was thready, hoarse. Wiping his eyes, he released her from his embrace. Awareness began to seep back in. She could feel the cold stone of the floor against her back and the vaulted ceiling above her told her she was still in the kirk. She felt stiff and shivery now Jenson had relaxed his hold.

'I...I'm not sure. I found you here, passed out on the floor. I thought you were...dead.'

His voice was shaky, his eyes red, a mixture of panic and relief on his face.

'Can you help me up?'

He got to his feet and came to her side as she tried to put weight on her palms to sit up. A searing pain shot through her right hand when she put pressure on the floor. Jenson supported her into a sitting position, and with his help, she managed to stand. Dizziness overwhelmed her, falling again, a real possibility. Jenson steadied her and she gripped his arms waiting for the world to stop spinning.

When the light-headedness passed, she noticed blood seeping from under her right hand, staining his white shirt. She turned it over to see a deep laceration spanning the width of her palm. She didn't remember hurting herself and the wound looked clean, fresh, almost as if it had been done by a sharp blade. Seeing her confusion, Jenson nodded over to the altar. A silver blade mounted in an ornate bone handle glinted as a stream of sunlight came through the stained-glass window. Beside it stood a small pewter bowl filled with red, viscous liquid – blood, her blood?

She looked back at Jenson, her eyes full of questions.

'How did you know I was here?' she croaked.

'I didn't. I was worried when I saw you in the hall. You looked so frail.'

He brushed a hand over her cheek, his eyes still swimming with unshed tears.

'I watched you head into the forest and as soon as I could get away, I followed, just to make sure you were alright.'

'It looks like it was a good job you did. What happened here?'

'I don't know. When I found you, you were unconscious, and the knife was where you see it now.'

'There was no-one else here?'

'Not that I saw. Can you remember anything?'

Elspeth took a step away from him, feeling able to support her weight now.

'I came in here because I wasn't feeling well. I thought I could rest a while. But something felt familiar, like I'd been here before... the window, I think I've seen it somewhere, but I don't know where. I touched it and it...'

She didn't want to tell him what she had seen. Jenson was looking at her intently, his eyebrows drawn together over his heavily lashed hazel eyes.

'You're not making much sense Elspeth. Have you walked this way before?'

'No... maybe. I really don't know. Everything's so fuzzy, confused.'

'But you don't remember anyone being here with you, someone who hurt you?'

He picked up her injured hand and turned her palm upwards. The blood was still flowing, reluctant to clot. Jenson pulled a cotton handkerchief from his trouser pocket and wound it tightly around her hand to try and stem the bleeding.

'No, I don't remember anyone being here...I dreamt there was a woman, but it was just a dream.'

Elspeth swooned, the blood loss accentuating her already

woozy state.

'We should get you back to the house, get your hand looked at properly.'

She nodded. Never had her gloomy rooms at Dalengour sounded so appealing. She would try and sort out all the confused thoughts another time. Now, she just wanted to be back in her bed – to sleep. Jenson came to her side and placed a supportive arm around her to help her walk.

'Wait... I just need...'

Elspeth left Jenson and shuffled back towards the stained-glass window. She needed to touch it again, to reassure herself she had just been seeing things. She reached out her wounded hand and laid her palm on the woman in the blue dress. The glass felt solid, cool under her touch. She dropped her hand, leaving behind a small patch of blood that had leached through the makeshift bandage. Unsure why, she felt disappointed. Turning away, she took a step back towards Jenson.

The kirk was suddenly flushed with a bright light that made her raise her arm to protect her eyes from the glare. A rumbling sound shook the ground, the stone trembling beneath her feet.

'Elspeth, what is it? What's wrong?'

Jenson's voice penetrated the growling of the earth, but Elspeth's eyes, still blurry from the sudden onslaught of harsh brightness, wouldn't focus. She staggered a few paces, losing her balance as the floor shook beneath her. She felt Jenson's arms pull her in, her body trembling against him with the force of the vibrations rising from the ground.

'Elspeth, Elspeth, look at me? What's happening to you?'

'The floor, the shaking, it's too bright, I can't see?'

'What shaking? Elspeth, what shaking?'

He sounded alarmed as she tried to get her eyes to focus

on his face. She was still squinting, her eyes struggling to adjust against the flare of light. She could make out his silhouette against the glare, the shadows on his face allowing her to see the worry furrowing his brow.

'Can't you feel it? The ground... it's trembling. And the light...'

'Nothing's happening Elspeth.'

'But I... I can feel the floor moving, hear it. You can't feel anything?'

'No. Everything's the same.'

She clung to him, afraid. What was happening to her? Her body was failing and now, her mind? No, this had to be real – it felt too real.

The brightness slowly began to fade, and Elspeth could again see the inside of the kirk. Spots were floating in front of her eyes, but she could see where she was. The tremors also began to subside, the stillness accompanied by a return to quiet. She let go of Jenson, confused but certain it had really happened.

Elspeth turned back to look at the stained-glass window. The colours seemed more vibrant, the surface shining like someone had recently polished it. Drawn back to the image of the woman in the blue dress, she reached out to where her bloodstain smeared the glass. Her fingers touched the mark and the surface rippled, as if she was dipping her hand into a pool of molten lava. She was mesmerised as ripples traced her movement across the surface, a calmness resting over her

.

Jenson appeared beside her.

'What the ..? What is going on?'

'You can see that?' she asked, wanting to confirm this wasn't just another trick of her addled mind.

'It's moving!'

'Yes. It happened when I first came in here, but I thought I was seeing things because when I checked again, the glass was normal. But now... it feels like water, like I could just step inside.'

With this, she pushed her hand though the liquid glass and it disappeared below the surface, just as if she had plunged it into a vat of water.

'Elspeth,' Jenson cried, trying to pull her hand back.

'It feels warm,' she said simply, her eyes still fixed on the shimmering window.

'Elspeth, stop. You should come away. This isn't right.'

'But it feels right' she said resolutely. 'I can't explain it, but it feels like I should be here, like I should... step through.'

'Don't be crazy Elspeth. This is... well it can't be true. There must be something in here that's making us see things. Something in the air. Please, let me take you out of here, take you home.'

He was pleading now, the weirdness making him uneasy, her calm certainty that this was normal adding to his discomfort.

'I can't Jenson. I just know I have to trust what I'm seeing.'

With this, she took a step closer to the viscous surface undulating around the window frame. Jenson grabbed her arm, pulling her round to face him. He stared at her, opened his mouth to protest again, but something in her expression made him close it. He sighed, casting a furtive look into the shadows. He seemed to be considering something, his mind working behind a glazed expression directed towards the darkness beyond the pews.

With his decision finally made, he returned his gaze to Elspeth who was watching him intently.

'Fine,' he said, 'but can you please explain exactly what it is we are seeing?'

'No, I'm afraid I can't. But somehow, I just know I have to step through this window Jenson.'

He searched her face then shook his head resolutely. He wound his fingers tightly around hers.

'Well, if you think you need to try this, you aren't doing it alone.'

Elspeth smiled with as much sincerity as she could manage. His decision to go with her buoyed her spirits. With a deep breath and Jenson's hand clutched tightly in her own, Elspeth turned towards the window frame and together, they stepped through.

In the darkness, Morwenna Darroch watched as Elspeth and Jenson disappeared behind the shimmering sea of silver. Once they vanished out of sight, she rushed forwards, her arms outstretched as she reached the glass. It did not give. The liquid surface had hardened back to its solid state. It was just a window again, the serene expression on Saint Oda's face seeming to mock her. Morwenna's maniacal scream echoed around the empty chamber.

She slammed her palms against the cold glass, but still, nothing happened. Quickly, she retreated, pressing her body against the wall beside the window. She didn't want to be seen should Elspeth look back though from the other side. Resting her forehead on the edge of the stone frame, her throat tightened as she struggled to regain her composure. She had been right. The gateway *was* here, and Elspeth Larimore had reopened it. She should take comfort from this. But right now, she was just angry. Angry she had been denied. Angry she was not in control. Well not yet…

CHAPTER 6

A Different Kirk

October 1921 - Nethergar

STILL CLINGING TO JENSON'S HAND, ELSPETH stepped out of the frame and into a kirk. She looked around what were familiar surroundings. Going through the window hadn't done anything. They were in the same place. But she felt different. She felt strong for the first time in months. The weakness in her limbs, the dizziness that plagued her mind, were gone. Standing here, she was restored – her old self again.

Elspeth looked down at her bandaged hand. She untied the handkerchief to see the wound completely healed. No sign of injury, no scar, no remnants of blood. She turned her hand over and over in front of her face.

'Jenson, look.'

He took her hand and ran his fingers across her palm, now soft and whole. He continued to move up her wrist, to her arms, a caress that made her skin come alive. He pulled her nearer and peered into her blue-grey eyes.

'You seem... better,' he said tentatively, his head cocked to one side, his eyebrow raised in contemplation.

'I feel better. Better than I have in a long time. I feel... strong.'

They held on to each other, both reluctant to spoil the intimacy that had sprung up between them. Jenson eventually broke the silence, casting his eyes around the kirk.

'What's happened here Elspeth? What happened when we stepped through the window?'

'I'm not really sure. We seem to be in the kirk but...'

Elspeth whirled around to look at the glass, now a tranquil lagoon, only a slight cresting at the edges speaking to its fluidity. The reflection of the kirk shimmered on the surface, but there was no image of herself or Jenson there. She reached out, the molten glass still rippling at her touch. She could see the knife sitting on the altar, the argentine bowl stained with her congealed blood at its side. She looked back over her shoulder – no knife, no bowl.

'I don't think we're in the same kirk. This isn't a reflection of where we are. See?' she said pointing towards the altar mirrored in the window. 'We aren't visible and there's no knife in this room, yet we can see one in the window. I think we're looking back into the kirk where you found me. But this is a different kirk, a different place.'

She saw something flicker across Jenson's golden eyes, too quickly for her to read. Her brow furrowed as she looked at him, trying to see what was on his mind. There was a moment where she thought he looked nervous, afraid. Quickly, he looked away, not wanting to meet her gaze. His sudden distance confused her, at odds with their earlier familiarity.

'Jenson, wh...'

She didn't get chance to ask her question. Jenson moved away from her quickly, hands on his hips as he stared around in feigned distraction. He was blatantly pretending not to have heard her begin to speak. He took a step closer to the window inspecting the reflection, then looked back at Elspeth ignoring her concerned facial expression.

'I don't understand. Where are we?'

'I'm not sure,' she replied guardedly, unsettled by his behaviour.

'Hmm...' Jenson said sauntering away from her again.

He seemed dissatisfied with her answer, like he expected her to know where they were. She watched him for a few moments, baffled by the change in his demeanour. Something had quelled the affection between them in an instant, something he didn't want her to question.

Elspeth left him wandering in front of the window and began to walk away. Her strength restored, she moved quickly between the pews.

'Where are you going?' Jenson called after her.

'To look outside,' she said absently, her voice echoing as she shouted back over her shoulder.

Jenson followed, catching her up at the door. She reached for the handle, and he cupped his hand over hers. At his touch, her unease instantly dissipated. He was here with her, and she needed the security of him.

'Are you sure about this Elspeth?'

'I know it's strange, but I've never felt surer of anything.'

Jenson nodded and released her hand. The door creaked open, and she peered out into a forest clearing almost identical to the one they had left in Dalengour. The trees rose majestically in a circle around the kirk. Sunlight bathed the mossy floor, the dappled light disappearing and reappearing as the brown-tinged leaves of ferns were ruffled by a gentle breeze. There didn't seem to be anything to fear. It looked like the same forest she knew, just her awareness of it seemed heightened. The colours, noises and smells were more vivid, like she was noticing them for the first time.

The sounds of the forest assaulted her ears as the door opened. Sounds she usually barely noticed. She could hear rustling of wings as birds moved in the branches of trees, the trunks creaking as they swayed, their great height making them vulnerable to the slightest wind. In the distance, the burbling of a stream, the lowing of cattle in a field beyond the forest.

Stepping out, Elspeth looked around – looking for anything that would tell her where they were. She looked back at the kirk. It was the same, except now, all signs of disrepair and neglect were gone. The windows shone as sunlight bounced off the panes of glass, now intact, new-looking. The brickwork showed no signs of wear and the red painted steeple glowed as if the painter had just set down his brush.

Elspeth took a few more steps into the clearing, swivelling around, taking in everything surrounding her. The pine trees looked lush and full, pinecones weighing down their branches and threatening to fall at any moment. If they did, they would land amongst the mushrooms, their smooth-brown caps visible in rings clustering under the shade. The air smelled damp, and she could see silvery raindrops perched on the leaves of downy thistles guarding the walls of the kirk.

It was as if someone had turned up the brightness. The clarity of every detail in the landscape was wondrous. Her eyes drank in the beauty of the place. Why had she never looked at the forests of Cairndarroch this way? Jenson was still standing in the doorway, unnerved by what was happening. She couldn't explain it, but for her, it didn't seem all that strange. She knew she wasn't in Cairndarroch anymore, but it didn't concern her. It excited her.

Reaching the edge of the clearing, Elspeth ran her fingers across the gnarled trunk of an ancient tree standing sentry at the entrance to the path winding into the forest. As she trailed her hand over the bark, a golden glow followed her movements. She watched it fade when she dropped her hand, only to luminesce when she touched the tree again. She placed both palms flat on the roughened trunk, heat gathering under her hands, the brightness beneath them intensifying. The light seeped into her skin, her hands becoming translucent as it travelled up her fingers, reaching her wrists before continuing up into her arms. Her skin rose in goose pimples, her muscles tightening in excitement.

She stood transfixed, unable to pull her hands away from the tree. There was no fear. She could feel a tingling warmth where the light touched, her skin bristling with energy as it moved towards her chest. Slowly, it engulfed her in a shroud of gold. She could feel life coursing through her body. It was as if she were one with the tree, connected to the web of life that linked it to the forest, to the earth.

Elspeth could hear Jenson calling her. Reluctantly, she dropped her hands from the bark, but the light did not dim. It surrounded her, moving with her as she stepped back. She felt more alive than ever before, powerful, protected. Slowly, the brightness began to wane, disappearing as Jenson pulled her around to study her face.

'Elspeth, what happened? Are you alright?'

His voice sounded panicked, his fingers digging into her arms as he held her still.

'Yes, yes, I'm fine. It was strange, beautiful. It felt like I was drawing energy from the tree, like I was connected to the forest for a moment. It was amazing.'

She looked up into Jenson's eyes, her expression alight with excitement.

'Your eyes...they're...'

'What? What about my eyes?'

'They're kind of glowing... they look golden.'

Elspeth blinked instinctively, trying to sense the change he described. She looked around the clearing. Everything looked even more vivacious, more vibrant, more alive.

'I feel different.'

'Different how?'

'I'm not sure how to explain it. It's like I'm on the edge of something... something powerful. I feel stronger that I have ever felt before, full of energy, of life.'

'You look different.'

He ran the back of his hand down her face. His touch felt more intense now, like everything around her, augmented by this place. She closed her eyes and pushed against his caress, enjoying his nearness. His arm slipped around her waist and he drew her closer. She could feel his breath on her face, just inches away from her own. Looking up into his eyes full of things he shouldn't say, she smiled. She had longed to see this look on his face, but now it was too late. She wasn't free.

Elspeth pulled away, her heart tearing, sadness displacing the love in his eyes. Before she could say anything, movement in the tree line caught her attention.

'Someone's there.'

Elspeth began to walk quickly towards the edge of the clearing, squinting into the darkness. Someone was hiding unsuccessfully, their shoulders broader than the trunk they had chosen. As she approached, a hand with dirty fingernails appeared from behind the tree, followed by the face of a small boy, no more than ten years old. Elspeth crouched down so her head was level with his.

'Don't be afraid. Come out here and let me introduce myself.'

The child stepped out into the open, his heavily lashed, amber eyes wide as he stared at her. He was dishevelled, dirt smeared across the white cotton shirt that had come untucked from his grey trousers, his feet bare, spattered with mud. The clothes were good quality, and Elspeth thought his grubby appearance more likely attested to fun in the forest rather than poverty.

'My name is Elspeth, and this is my friend Jenson,' she said cocking her head over her shoulder.

Jenson walked over to where they stood, smiling warmly at the boy.

'What's your name young man?' he asked.

The boy blinked his large eyes, their golden flecks catching in the sunlight. His long dark hair curled around his forehead, damp with sweat. He was a handsome child.

'I'm Darian.'

'Nice to meet you Darian.'

Jenson extended a hand to him in a formal gesture. The boy took it, and they shook a manly greeting that made Elspeth smile at the absurdity of the action in one so young. Darian fixed his gaze back on her.

'You came through the gateway,' he said simply.

Elspeth and Jenson exchanged looks.

'I suppose we did. Yes. Do people often come through the gateway then?' Elspeth asked encouragingly.

'No. No-one's ever come through. At least, I don't think they have.'

Elspeth thought for a moment.

'Darian, can you tell us exactly where we are?'

The child furrowed his brow, the answer obvious to him.

'You don't know where you are?'

'Well, it looks like the forests around Dalengour, but I think we may have got a bit lost and so I just want to make sure.'

'It is Dalengour,' the boy said matter-of-factly, looking at Elspeth as if she was stupid.

She felt stupid, confused. How could she be somewhere else but still be in the same place? Maybe they hadn't left Cairndarroch at all and she was imagining all this. But Jenson was here. He had seen the same things.

'Do you live at Dalengour?' Elspeth asked him.

Darian screwed up his face.

'Noooo! No-one lives there. They haven't in years! It's horrible, haunted. I live at Cunygar,' he said proudly, puffing out his chest.

Relief flooded over her. This was a different place. She wasn't going insane. The Dalengour she knew was lived in, and she had never heard of a house called Cunygar in Cairndarroch.

'Where is Cunygar?'

Darian pointed somewhat randomly to the right.

'It's over there, on the edge of the village.'

'The village?'

'Nethergar,' he said, his brows knitted together again at the stupidity of her question.

Jenson had been standing quietly behind her, listening. Now he crouched down beside her and spoke to Darian.

'This gateway you say we came through, do you know where it leads to?'

'My dad said it takes you to another world. He said there are people there, just like us. I've never seen it open – I don't think anyone has, but I come here a lot just to check,' he said importantly. 'No one has ever come through though... until you.'

The young boy's eyes were wide with excitement. He seemed thrilled to have come across visitors from 'through the gateway'. Jenson looked at Elspeth and she knew he was wondering if they would be able to get back home. Images of Robert swam though her mind. She must get back to him. Darian's voice interrupted her thoughts.

'You look like her.'

'Like who?' Elspeth asked, focussing on the boy again.

'The woman who lives at the cottage.'

'Is the cottage near here?'

Darian pointed again in the same direction he had indicated his home.

'Will it take long to get to the cottage?' Elspeth asked.

Darian shook his head.

'I can take you there if you like?'

'Yes, I think I would like that.'

'Elspeth, wait!' Jenson grabbed her arm as she stood up preparing to follow Darian.

'We should go back.'

'I can't Jenson. I need to know where we are and maybe this woman can tell us.'

'But what if the gateway closes? What if we get stuck here?'

'We won't.'

'How can you be so sure.'

'I don't know, I just am. Please Jenson, I need to do this. You go back if you want, but I'm going with Darian.'

Conflicted, Jenson sighed. Elspeth turned towards the boy, willing Jenson to come with her but not daring to ask. He had to make up his own mind. Relief flooded over her as he came to her side.

'I just hope you're right about getting back,' he said, shaking his head in disbelief at his own actions and taking her hand.

Comforted by his touch, Elspeth smiled and Jenson despite his concern, couldn't help smiling back.

'Are you ready now?' Darian asked impatiently.

'Lead the way,' said Elspeth standing aside, letting him pass in front of them as he headed across the clearing and into the forest.

They walked for about twenty minutes, the dimly lit trails occasionally illuminated by a break in the dense canopy overhead. Elspeth tried to take in the route, needing to be sure they could find their way back to the kirk, find their way back home. Jenson seemed to be doing the same, his head pivoting around, looking for landmarks in their journey.

In time, the trees began to thin, and they emerged from the forest blinking into the brightness of clear, open skies. They were looking down from a hilltop at a pathway leading towards a small cottage nestled in the base of a valley. It was unmistakably Kirkholm Cottage, Elspeth's family home.

'She lives there,' Darian said, pointing towards the cottage.

They followed him as he descended the path. There was no gate or fence marking out the back garden as in Cairndarroch, and the doors and curtainless window frames were dark wood, not the colourful green Elspeth knew. This house was trying to blend into the landscape, avoiding anything that would make it stand out or be noticed.

Darian marched purposefully on, turning towards Elspeth and Jenson a few feet from the door.

'Are you going inside?' he asked, his eyes wide.

'Well, I'd like to talk to her if she's in,' replied Elspeth and she took a few steps towards the cottage.

'I'm not coming in.'

The boy backed away as Elspeth knocked on the plain weathered door. No sound came from inside.

'I don't think anyone's home,' Jenson said, almost hopefully. 'We should go.'

A crack appeared in the door and Elspeth could see a keen, blue eye peeping out in the gap. An eye that was cornflower blue, like Agatha's.

'Who are you? What do you want?'

Taken aback by the obvious hostility in the voice behind the door, Elspeth stammered.

'I..I... Sorry to bother you but I wanted to ask you some questions. My name is Elspeth and Darian here thought you might be able to help me.'

She gestured back to where the young boy stood, out of sight of the eye in the door. Whoever was living at Kirkholm Cottage stood silently scrutinising her, the eye looking her up and down. Suddenly the door slammed shut. Elspeth jumped as the sound echoed through the valley.

'Please, please,' she begged, placing her palms flat on the door and banging on the wood. 'Please, I really need to talk to you. I don't know where we are or what's happening to me!'

The owner of the eye did not return. Elspeth leaned her forehead on the door, the sting of tears prickling her eyes. She felt Jenson's hand on her shoulder as he drew her away.

'Come on Elspeth. Let's get back to the kirk and try to get home.'

'But...But I want to know. I need to know what's happening here.'

Her voice sounded pleading, even panicky at the thought of leaving. The sound of hinges creaking jerked her head back towards the doorway. A middle-aged woman, vibrant red hair cascading wildly around her shoulders, her bright blue eyes fixed warily on the visitors, stepped out into the light.

'Is that you Darian McGillvaray? Bringing strangers to my door?'

The woman placed her hands on her hips, irritation in her voice as she spoke to the boy. Darian ducked behind Jenson, who instinctively placed an arm protectively around him.

'You better run back to that grand house of yours Master McGillvaray. You know you aren't supposed to be in these forests.'

Darian freed himself from Jenson, turned and ran back up the hill as fast as his legs could carry him. Elspeth watched him go, then turned to face the red-haired woman who was staring at her, eyes boring into her, trying to see her insides.

'You're a Larimore.'

It was more of a statement than a question.

'Yes. Yes I am. My name's Elspeth.'

'How did you get here?'

The woman was eyeing her suspiciously and Elspeth shifted uncomfortably under her scrutiny.

'Darian brought us from the kirk at Dalengour.'

'That's not what I meant,' she snapped. 'You aren't from Nethergar. How did you get *here*?'

She emphasized the last word to make the question feel like a demand.

'I...I'm not actually sure. We were in the kirk in

Cairndarroch, then something happened and... Well, it sounds crazy now but the window sort of melted away and we stepped through. Then we were here – wherever here is? Nethergar the boy said.'

'Hmph,' she grunted. 'You opened the gateway.'

'I did what? I didn't do anything!'

'Obviously you did. What happened in the kirk before the window 'melted'?'

'I don't know for sure. I wasn't feeling well and went into the kirk to rest. I passed out and when I woke up, my hand was cut but I don't remember it happening.'

'Did you touch the window?

'What?'

Irritation flared in the woman's tone again as she marked out each word of her next question.

'Did you touch the window with your cut hand?' Get blood on the glass?'

'Maybe... I think so. But what does that have to do with anything?'

'Your blood opened the gateway,' she said matter-of-factly, as if such a thing was normal, to be expected.

'I don't understand,' Elspeth said.

'Of course you don't,' she said waspishly. 'Who's that?'

The woman nodded towards where Jenson stood.

'This is Jenson Tanner. He's my friend. He was with me when I fell ill in the kirk.'

She leaned around Elspeth and squinted mistrustfully at Jenson who pulled back his shoulders and met her eyes defiantly. A knowing smile appeared fleetingly on the woman's lips.

'Your friend you say?' she said, raising her eyebrows and looking back at Elspeth.

Colour unexpectedly flushed Elspeth's cheeks and she didn't meet the woman's penetrating glare.

'Well, I guess you should both come inside. It seems there is much I need to tell you Elspeth Larimore.'

The woman turned and beckoned them into the cottage. For some reason, Elspeth didn't mention she was now a Darroch, thinking it better to lean on her Larimore heritage for now.

'Can I ask who you are?' Elspeth said approaching the entrance to Kirkholm Cottage.

The woman straightened her spine proudly.

'My name is Nerissa Larimore, and I'm the last of your relatives here in Nethergar.'

CHAPTER 7

An Ancestor's Tale

THE KITCHEN AT KIRKHOLM COTTAGE WAS ODDLY familiar although this one lacked the brightness and colour of her family home. The painted grey walls surrounded a large brick fireplace containing the remains of the last fire to burn in the grate, the cupboards the same dark oak as the barren slab of a table and six heavy chairs. The whiteness of the gleaming butler sink was stark against the colour palette, but what struck Elspeth most, was the absence of mementos or trinkets gathered through life.

All the surfaces were bare, with only the essentials of a kitchen on display. The large, austere dresser held a single cup, bowl and plate evidencing the loneliness of Nerissa Larimore. The walls were pictureless, bereft of family portraits or scenes of the spectacular Highland landscapes. Despite the warmth of the day, there was a coldness to the room, almost an emptiness. Nerissa could walk out today and if someone happened upon the place, they would never know she lived here.

'Sit down,' Nerissa barked, indicating the chairs wedged tightly under the table.

The thick legs scraped across the wooden floor as Elspeth and Jenson pulled them free, the sound echoing around the spartan kitchen.

'Do you want tea?'

'Yes, that would be nice, thank you,' Elspeth said politely, looking over at Jenson who also murmured thanks.

Nerissa began to move around the kitchen, retrieving the solitary cup from the dresser and then disappearing into the pantry to return with two more that had been hidden away, unnecessary in her everyday life. Elspeth watched as she filled a copper kettle and set it on the stove, looking for the similarity in appearance the boy Darian had seen.

They shared the same colouring, although Nerissa's red hair was a shade darker, and wild and unruly - more like Agatha's. She was tall and statuesque, her long grey linen dress as plain as her surroundings, hanging loosely over her slender frame. It was her eyes that were unmistakably like Elspeth's. Brighter blue, but the same almond shape framed by dark blond lashes, and with an intenseness that seemed to absorb the detail in everything she looked at in an instant.

Nerissa set down the tea and took a seat at the table.

'Tell me more about what happened before the gateway opened,' she said, staring intently at Elspeth. 'You said you were ill?'

'I've been unwell for a while, or at least I was until I came here.'

Elspeth glanced around the kitchen, still not entirely sure where 'here' was. She felt Nerissa's glare on her face and shifted as she met the unwavering observance.

'It's been very strange really because I've never suffered ill health before,' Elspeth went on. 'But for the last five months, I haven't even been strong enough to leave my rooms. The doctor didn't know what was wrong with me and so I've just laid in bed, waiting for things to get better. Today, I was desperate. I needed some fresh air, so I got up and tried to go for a walk.'

'And you found your way to the kirk?' Nerissa interrupted, her eyes now alight with interest.

'Yes. Even though I've walked the forest many times, I hadn't seen it before. I guess I must have always taken a route that missed it.'

Nerissa's eyebrows raised but she didn't speak.

'Anyway, it was stupid of me to try to go outside by myself after such a long confinement. I hadn't gone far when I began to feel nauseous and faint. I went into the kirk to rest and think I must have passed out.'

Nerissa turned her shrewd eyes accusingly on Jenson.

'You found her?' she barked.

'She was unconscious in the kirk when I got there. Her hand was bleeding and there was a knife. It looked as if someone had been trying to collect Elspeth's blood in a bowl.'

'But there was no-one else there?'

'Not that I saw, just Elspeth.'

'And you? You don't remember anyone else being there?

Nerissa turned pointedly back towards Elspeth.

'Not really. There was a woman, but it must have been just in my dreams.'

'Maybe – maybe not,' she said reaching across the table and taking Elspeth's hand.

She turned her palm over, looking for any sign of the wound. Nothing remained. Nerissa didn't let go. Instead, she encased Elspeth's hand between her own. Heat, like she'd felt when she touched the tree began to build at her touch. Elspeth looked down as a thread of light began to weave around their hands. It entwined around and around, spinning a net of gold connecting her to Nerissa. She watched as light began to move up her arms, leaving a prickling sensation where it touched. It moved through her body as if it was searching, looking for something.

A smile passed across Nerissa's lips as she nodded, having found evidence for something she suspected. The light began to recede, retracing its journey back to Nerissa's hands.

'What's happening? Please tell me what you just did?' Elspeth asked, her brow creased in puzzlement.

'All in good time.'

Nerissa let go and settled back against the hard wooden chair, taking a large gulp of tea with her eyes still fixed on Elspeth. Jenson began to fidget, leaning forward, about to speak. Nerissa raised her hand, stopping him before he could form a word.

'You're impatient Jenson Tanner,' she said simply, glaring at him like a schoolteacher reprimanding an unruly student before turning her attention back to Elspeth.

'You were being poisoned,' Nerissa said simply, as if announcing the weather.

'What? I can't have been,' Elspeth stammered.

Nerissa didn't respond, her eyes unblinking, continuing to glare. Elspeth tried to process what she had said. Poisoned? Surely not.

'How do you know?' she ventured tentatively.

'I have... gifts. I can sense what's inside you.'

'That was you I felt moving through me?'

'In a way.'

Elspeth thought for a moment, her mind reeling with new information, new experiences. This place was another world, a world that challenged everything she had ever known. She had family here – this woman who could do strange things. Yet somehow, none of it seemed that strange. However incredible, it felt comforting and real to her. But the thought that someone was trying to do her harm...

'Who would do that? Who would want to poison me? And why?'

Her voice became tight, high pitched at the incredulity of the suggestion.

'You can answer the first question better than me,' Nerissa said, running her finger round the rim of her cup. 'But I might be able to help you understand why someone would want you dead.'

Elspeth's eyes widened.

'Dead? Someone was actually trying to kill me?'

'Eventually. I suspect the poison was just meant to incapacitate you. Whoever did this wanted your blood. Someone wanted to use it to open the gateway. But once they had access to Nethergar, they would probably have killed you.'

Nerissa turned to face Jenson. He shifted uncomfortably under her gaze, his cheeks colouring, his cup suddenly holding immense fascination. Nerissa's pause seemed to challenge him. She was waiting for him to speak, to admit something, but Jenson didn't meet her stare. Ripples formed on the surface of his tea as his hand trembled but still he kept silent, his hazel eyes downcast.

Elspeth's brow furrowed, unsure of what was passing between them. But her mind was too full of questions to wait.

'I'm sorry, but I don't understand,' Elspeth asked. 'What has my blood got to do with any of this?'

Nerissa sighed, her shoulders dropping along with the rancour that had been rattling her since Elspeth turned up at her door. This time she spoke softly, resigned to answering Elspeth's questions.

'There are things I need to tell you and then you will understand.'

Nerissa absently rubbed a dribble of tea from the side of her cup.

'Elspeth, you feel better here because you are home.'

'Home? I don't live here.'

'But you come from here. All the Larimores originate here, in Nethergar.'

Elspeth's eyes narrowed as she tried, and failed, to understand what she meant. Seeing her confusion, Nerissa leaned forward and placed a hand maternally on her arm.

'Centuries ago, the Larimores in Nethergar were persecuted. Some managed to flee through a gateway to another world. Once there, they closed the gateway so they would be safe – safe but trapped there. Until now.'

'You mean Cairndarroch? They went through the gateway to Cairndarroch?'

'Yes. You have come back here through that same gateway.'

Elspeth paused, trying to make sense of what Nerissa was saying. A gateway between worlds? It didn't seem possible. But then, she was sitting here in Nethergar.

'Why were the Larimores persecuted?' Elspeth asked, focusing on something that felt easier to tackle.

'Because we are powerful. The Larimores have always had special gifts. We are connected to nature and can use the energy that is part of all living organisms to change things, to manipulate things.'

'Are you talking about magic?' Jenson asked, scepticism colouring his tone.

Nerissa blinked thoughtfully and Elspeth expected her to snap at Jenson again. But surprisingly, she didn't.

'I suppose it might seem that way to you, but we don't think of it as magic,' she said in response, her tone more even and considered. 'We can harness the power of nature, use it make things happen, or even stop things from happening. Some of the Larimores have this ability. I have it, and it seems Elspeth here does too.'

Nerissa turned back to Elspeth.

'The power we each possess cannot be destroyed. On the death of a Larimore who has inherited the gifts, what they possess is passed on to another Larimore, provided one exists with the potential to harness it. Someone like you,' she said, jabbing a finger in Elspeth's direction.

For a moment, no-one spoke. Elspeth's head was spinning with new information, improbable information she wasn't sure she believed. Nerissa waited, drinking her tea, staring at Elspeth over the rim of her cup.

'And they were persecuted for this?' Elspeth asked, her forehead creased, her mind struggling to accept what she was hearing.

'There were some who coveted the power we had and tried to take it from us.'

'Is that possible?'

'Only when there are no more gifted Larimores left.'

Nerissa stood and cleared away the tea, leaving Elspeth to muse on what she had said.

'So, when the last Larimore with the potential to carry the gifts dies, what happens then?'

'That depends. If they die naturally, the power will be released, back to nature. But if their life is taken by another, the murderer could take their gifts.'

Elspeth pondered this.

'You said you're the last Larimore here in Nethergar?' Elspeth said to the back of Nerissa as she washed their cups and placed them on the side to drain.

'Yes. There were just a few of us left here after the gateway was first opened. All were killed except me. I managed to stay hidden until they were driven out of Dalengour.'

'Who were driven out?' Elspeth asked.

'At the time of the persecutions, the village was governed by the Darroch family who lived at Dalengour. They turned the people against us, telling them we were a threat because of our gifts, and the villagers believed them. What they really wanted was to take our power by eliminating us all.'

Jenson shot a look across at Elspeth who shook her head almost imperceptibly to keep him silent. Nerissa turned to face them now, leaning back against the sink, lost in her own thoughts for a moment.

'What happened to them?' Elspeth asked as a look of sadness swept across Nerissa's face.

'The Darroch's rallied the villagers, convincing them that anyone with Larimore blood should be killed to keep Nethergar safe. We tried to escape, but they hunted all of us who stayed here until only my sister and I were left. We were eventually captured and taken into the village square where the eldest Darroch son decapitated my pregnant sister and drove a sword through her unborn child in front of everyone in the village.'

Elspeth flinched. Tears were pooling in Nerissa's eyes, intensifying their blueness.

'Something about the relish on his face when he murdered an innocent life broke the hold the Darrochs had over the villagers. I remember the cheers that had echoed around the square were suddenly silenced as everyone stood staring in shock at the bloody corpse of my sister, her swollen belly sliced open.'

Sadness filled the room and Elspeth felt the loss with Nerissa. The two women stared at each other, joined by grief for lost family, and by anger for what had been done to them. Jenson broke the silence.

'And then what? What happened to the Darrochs?'

Nerissa came back into the moment, hastily wiping her hand under her eyes.

'The villagers saw their cruelty, saw the Darroch's revelry in the murder of the innocent. They freed me and chased them from Dalengour. They have never returned.'

'And you are the only remaining Larimore?' Jenson asked.

'I thought I was the only Larimore still alive in either world until Elspeth arrived on my doorstep. I assumed those that had escaped to Cairndarroch had long perished as they never managed to find a way back here.'

'There are still Larimores in Cairndarroch. I have two sisters and a brother. My father, Connor Larimore died a year ago. He was an only child, so I suppose that means there are four of us left on the other side of the gateway.'

'There are Darrochs too, living at Dalengour,' said Jenson. 'Elspeth is m... .'

Elspeth aimed a kick at him under the table. She didn't want to explain her involvement with the Darrochs yet.

Nerissa's face became grave as she looked at Elspeth.

'You know them? The Darrochs?'

'Well yes. They've always been in Cairndarroch as far as I know.'

'We suspected one of Lord Darroch's sons had followed the Larimores through the gateway. I guess we were right. The Darrochs in your world may well know.'

'Know what?'

Jenson's question sounded churlish. Nerissa's glare dripped with barely concealed irritation. Elspeth didn't understand why Jenson seemed to rile her. She waited patiently for Nerissa to continue, hoping she would answer Jenson's question despite her annoyance.

'After the Larimores crossed into Cairndarroch, the gateway was sealed. To protect both worlds, we ensured it could only be reopened from the Cairndarroch side by a Larimore with our gifts. I think that Larimore is you Elspeth. When your blood came into contact with the gateway at the kirk, it opened and allowed you through.'

'But I don't have any gifts!'

'Yes, you do. I sensed it as soon as I touched your hand. You have the potential to inherit the Larimore gifts, but you also have some power of your own, even now. It has just been sleeping because you and your ancestors have been away from Nethergar for so long. It re-awoke when you came back here.'

'Something did happen when I came through the gateway. Something strange when I touched the tree,' Elspeth mused. 'It was like I could feel it – I could feel the tree's energy.'

'Your gift was stimulated when you returned. I'll show you.'

Nerissa left the table and disappeared through a door that led deeper into the house, leaving Elspeth and Jenson alone.

'Are you alright?' Jenson whispered, leaning across to take her hand.

'Yes, I think so. It's all a bit overwhelming, but somehow, it doesn't feel as strange as it should.'

Jenson didn't get the chance to respond, pulling his hand away as Nerissa returned carrying a dead plant in a dull grey pot. She placed it on the table in front of Elspeth and took her seat again.

'I want you to try and revive the plant,' she said, pushing the shrivelled plant towards Elspeth.

'What? I don't know how to do that.'

'Yes, you do. Now try.'

Elspeth looked at the brown curled leaves with no idea what she should do. She reached out her hand and carefully touched the decaying stems, not wanting to crush their precarious form. As she traced her fingers over the arid husks, she became mesmerised by their shape, the kitchen at Kirkholm Cottage fading away. She thought about how the plant would have looked when it lived, wondered what the flowers would have looked like, what colour were they? How did they smell?

The plant began to shiver under her touch, a brightness appearing where her skin connected to the leaves. Where there had been dull, brown waterless crinkles, lush green leaves began unfurling towards the light. The stems thickened, strengthening to stand upright, buds forming on their tips. Nerissa's voice came to her as if from a distance.

'That's good. Keep going. Make it bloom.'

Never taking her eyes from the plant, Elspeth focused hard on the natal flowers. The buds swelled and burst, petals opening to reveal pinks and purples, their centres, a vibrant yellow and black. More buds began to form as the plant grew, striving upwards towards a non-existent sun.

Elspeth was so focused on what she was doing that she didn't notice Nerissa lean in. As her hands closed over Elspeth's, she felt a surge of power rush to her fingers, the glow extending around the plant becoming brighter, the rate of growth accelerating. More and more stems forced their way through the earth. Leaves unfurled and flowers appeared apace until the plant was a riot of colour barely contained by the pot.

Nerissa released her hands and sat back. The connection faded and Elspeth was left staring at the plant, full of life, the stems still reverberating with the energy she had pushed through its lifeless shell. Finally, she dragged her gaze away from the flowers and looked up at Nerissa who was smiling back at her, and then to Jenson whose mouth hung open.

'I... I did that?' she asked Nerissa.

'Yes, you did. You have the gifts Elspeth. You just need to learn how to access and control them.'

'I felt you helping me.'

'My powers are much stronger because I have remained in Nethergar and because, as the last Larimore here, I have inherited the gifts of my ancestors as they died. All the Larimore power from Nethergar resides in me now.'

'And me? What will happen to me now when I go back home, to Cairndarroch?'

'You will keep the gifts that have been awakened for now. But they will fade in time if you don't return here or will grow in strength if you do.'

'And will I remain healthy? As I am now?'

'You will. Passing through the gateway is restorative.'

Elspeth sighed in relief. She needed to be strong, for Robert.

'There's something else you should know,' Nerissa went on. 'Passing through the gateway fixes you as you are.'

'What do you mean?'

'Think of the gateway as a mirror. When you first look into it, the self you see reflected becomes fixed. No matter how much time passes, you will always see the same reflection every time you look in that mirror in the future. This is how the gateway works. Every time to step through, it will restore you to that reflection – the way you were when you first looked through the mirror.'

Elspeth's eyes clouded over as she tried to understand.

'Are you saying that every time I pass through the gateway, I will go back to the way I am now, no matter how old I have become?'

'Yes. You will always be returned to this version of yourself, at the age you are now. It won't be the same for you,' Nerissa said, pointing jarringly towards Jenson.

'Me?'

'If you stayed here, you would age much more slowly. The energy in this world prolongs all life. But the restorative effects of the gateway only work fully on those whose bloodline originated in Nethergar.'

Something clicked behind Jenson's eyes, like a switch had flicked, answering a long-pondered question. He leaned towards Nerissa, his earlier discomfort forgotten, his interest piqued.

'So, someone from Nethergar who could access the gateway could stay young forever, effectively become immortal?'

Nerissa surveyed him suspiciously, then turned back to Elspeth, a look of warning on her face.

'The gateway could prolong a person's life indefinitely if they originated from here, yes.'

Her voice was wary, as if she was imparting information against her better judgement.

'That would be a powerful reason for someone to want access to Nethergar,' Jenson said absently, his eyes glazed as his mind turned over.

Lost in thought, he was oblivious to Elspeth staring at him.

'Jenson, what do you mean?'

Elspeth's voice brought him back.

'Er... Just that if someone knew about this, someone whose bloodline originated here, it would be a good reason for them to want the gateway reopened ... a good reason for someone to hurt Elspeth.'

He directed the last part towards Nerissa whose hostility immediately returned.

'It would.'

Tension vibrated between Jenson and Nerissa, but Elspeth ignored it. She had too many questions.

'So now the gateway is open, anyone will be able to pass through to Nethergar?"

Nerissa turned to face her, still shooting Jenson icy daggers between words.

'No. The Larimores control access to Nethergar and so only those with Larimore blood can pass freely through the gateway. Others can, but only if accompanied by a Larimore. Even if their bloodline originated here.'

Nerissa glared at Jenson now with open animosity. But Jenson didn't challenge it. He dropped his gaze to the floor in submission and Nerissa looked back at Elspeth, her eyes softening.

'Or if provided with a guide from Nethergar.'

'A guide?' Elspeth asked.

'You can give someone without Larimore blood a guide that will allow them to pass through the gateway. No-one has done this in my lifetime, but the guides of the past usually took the form of animal spirits that appears corporeal when someone passes out of their home world.'

'And I can do that?'

'I could teach you. I could teach you many things if you stay here, in Nethergar.'

She couldn't stay. She had to get back.

'I can't stay. I have to go back.'

Panic swelled in her as she realised she had no idea if they could go back through the gateway to Cairndarroch.

'I can get back, can't I?'

Nerissa's jaw tightened as she fought to keep her face neutral. But her eyes gave away sadness at Elspeth's obvious eagerness to leave Nethergar.

'Now the gateway is open, you will be able to come and go as you please.'

Elspeth let out a sigh, her shoulders relaxing again.

'I do want to learn from you. I do. I just can't stay here. I have a life in Cairndarroch, a family.'

'Family?'

'Yes... my mother and siblings,' she stammered.

Nerissa's expression didn't falter, but Elspeth recognised that *all-knowing* glare common on her father's face when she tried to hide things from him.

'I see,' she said, lowering her eyes. 'Remember Elspeth, your gifts will fade if you don't return.'

'I will come back. I'll come back as soon as I can.'

She meant it. She was eager to come back, to learn. But now, she had a more pressing need - to see her son. Turning to Jenson, she began to push back her chair.

'I think we should be getting back before we're missed.'

Nodding his agreement, Jenson stood quickly, anxious to be out of there. He headed to the door and had stepped outside even before Nerissa got to her feet. Elspeth followed him outside into the bright sunlight, squinting after the dimness inside Kirkholm Cottage. Nerissa leaned against the open door, arms folded, her expression leery as she looked at Jenson.

'Thank you for telling me all this and helping me understand what was happening to me. I promise, I will come back.'

Elspeth leant forward and embraced Nerissa Larimore who seemed surprised by the show of affection, but she returned the gesture warmly. Elspeth stood back as Nerissa hung on to her hands.

'Elspeth, if there are Darrochs in your world, you must be careful. They will try to get back to Nethergar.'

Nerissa looked pained, her eyes trying to convey more than her words. Elspeth sensed her fear.

'How would they even know about it? Or know that I've been here?'

'You should know, gifts are common here. Not all of them are as strong as ours, but many families possess abilities that would be thought unusual in your world. The Darrochs are no exception. Their ancestors had the ability to project their conscious mind to other places. They could use this to observe people's lives in secret – to watch them without being physically present. I don't know if any of the Darrochs in your world inherited the family gift, or even if they would know how to use it if they did. But if they can, you need to be very careful.'

Nerissa kissed Elspeth's cheek in a maternal way and turned reluctantly to go back into the house closing the door behind her. Elspeth heard the lock turn as Nerissa shut out the world. It wasn't surprising that the past still tormented her, and Elspeth realised letting her in had been an enormous leap of faith for the solitary Nerissa Larimore. She didn't trust anyone, except perhaps the boy Darian.

Turning away from the secluded, barren cottage, her mind

pondered over everything she had learned. She lingered on what Nerissa had said as they parted - about the Darroch's gift. She didn't want to believe Riordan or Morwenna would try to hurt her. The idea they could have been secretly watching her was appalling. But those moments when she had felt someone's presence haunted her memory as she followed Jenson back into the forest.

CHAPTER 8

Secrets and Lies

JENSON HADN'T SAID A WORD SINCE THEY LEFT
Nerissa Larimore. Elspeth had been watching his back as he
walked quickly through the trees, determination to get away
from this place reverberating in every step. She was almost
running to keep pace.

'Jenson wait! Slow down will you!'

'I need to get you back,' he called over his shoulder,
without turning or easing his speed.

Elspeth hurried after him, her heart pounding from
exertion and annoyance. She broke into a run, determined to
catch up, intent on challenging him about what was going
on. Her foot caught on a twisted root. Pain seared through
her stubbed toe as she fell forward, crying out as her hands
grazed across the woodland floor. Jenson was quickly by her
side, helping her to her feet, a look of concern on his face.

'Are you alright?'

Elspeth righted herself, looking down at her hands, rubbing them together to clear away the dirt.

'I'm fine,' she said curtly, wiping her stinging hands down her skirt. She looked at her feet. Her delicate shoes were ruined, scuffed and torn by the gnarled bark. She felt irrationally annoyed.

'Can you walk?' he asked, concern now replaced by his eagerness to be on the move again.

'Yes, but..."

He had already turned about and resumed his course through the forest.

'Jenson! Wait a minute. Wait will you! I want to go to Dalengour.'

Her tone stopped him in his tracks. Slowly, he turned to face her, his body language retaliatory.

'That's where we're going. I'm taking you home.'

'Not my Dalengour. I want to see it here.'

Jenson sighed heavily. He folded his arms and raised his eyes up to the sky as if she were being testy.

'I want to see it and I'm going with or without you!'

Elspeth was even more rankled now, turning to march off in the direction of Dalengour. Jenson didn't move to follow but after a few moments, she heard his footsteps fall in behind her. He kept his distance and didn't speak, but at least he was coming. Despite her doggedness, she didn't really want to go alone, unsure of what she would find there.

The imposing pine trees came to a sudden end as she stepped out into the grounds of Dalengour. But this was not the Dalengour she knew. It had the same domineering presence, a complete lack of welcome or homeliness, but this castle was derelict, invaded by the surrounding forest. Parts of the roofs and walls were gone, scorch marks from flames that had licked the sides, still visible.

Elspeth walked over to the castle, something driving her to get a closer look. She reached the façade that was covered in the same salmon-coloured harling she recognised, cracked and faded to an insipid greyish pink. As she ran her hand across the crumbling brickwork, her mind was invaded by images of the villagers charging on Dalengour, their anger fuelled by the actions of the Darrochs. Flaming torches were held aloft, ready to set the house alight. She could hear yells of rebellion, feel their collective fury as they searched for the family. She sensed the fear of the Darrochs preparing to flee their family home.

She dropped her hand, the images fading, her thoughts bothered by conflicting emotions. It was difficult to feel empathy for the Darrochs after what they had done. But she couldn't reconcile the heinous acts Nerissa had described with the Darrochs that were, whether she liked it or not, now part of her family. Her son was a Darroch.

Elspeth began to wander around the castle, the hatred of those who had lived there and those who had destroyed it, echoing in its remains. Despite its dilapidated state, the house was still forbidding, an angry smear in an otherwise serenely magical place. Dalengour did not belong in the beauty of Nethergar.

Couch grass grew unchecked around the walls, the white funnel-shaped flowers of bindweed long since overpowering the cultivated plants that would have decorated the gardens. The sparse windows were glassless, brambles growing though the openings indicating that the inside had also been reclaimed by the forest. There was something wild and untamed about the infiltration of life into this place. Nethergar was doing its best to obliterate the evil that had lived here.

Jenson hung back, watching her intently as she explored

Dalengour, but showing no signs of wanting to be with her. Elspeth was confused, hurt. She felt the stab of tears behind her eyes, the emotion of the day lurking in the pit of her stomach, threatening to spin out uncontrollably. She headed back towards him, ready now to leave this place, to get back home to see her son.

'Ready?' Jenson asked as she approached, his eyebrows raised, irritation on his face.

It was anger that reared in her first.

'Yes, I just wanted…actually no! I'm not ready to go until you tell me what the hell is wrong?' she burst out. 'Something's been bothering you since we met Nerissa. And now you seem angry with me for a reason I can't fathom!'

Indignation flared in her eyes as she rounded on him. Jenson fidgeted from foot to foot, avoiding her stare. He opened his mouth to speak, but closed it again, dropping his head and becoming momentarily fixated on a small rock that he kicked absently with his toe. He reminded Elspeth of a small child caught in misbehaviour who was now trying to find something to say to rationalise their actions.

'I…I'm just worried about you! What if the Darrochs do know about this place and it was them who were trying to hurt you Elspeth?'

He looked up, but still, his eyes didn't seem to see her. He was unsettled, twitchy, looking through her to the forest beyond.

'How can they know? There's only Morwenna and Riordan left and if they had heard stories about this place, I'm sure they'd think they were just that – stories. I certainly wouldn't have believed it if someone had told me about Nethergar.'

'I wish I could be as sure as you,' he murmured.

Elspeth waited for him to say more, to elaborate, but he

wasn't inclined to. She sighed heavily, the sound of her breath making him finally look at her. The ghost of a smile caught on his lips.

'You chew your bottom lip when you're angry,' he said, the smile creeping into his eyes.

She stared at him, awareness of her teeth gripping her bottom lip releasing the tension. She laughed. Jenson moved towards her, reaching out to push a stray strand of hair behind her ear. Elspeth felt her heartbeat quicken as she took in the contours of his face, the first signs of shadow across his chin, his eyes sparkling.

'What is it Jenson? There's more going on in your head than you're telling me. I know the Darrochs can be arrogant, even unpleasant at times. But I find it hard to believe they would actually hurt me.'

Jenson backed away, needing to put some distance between them before he spoke. He leaned against a nearby tree, picking at the bark with his fingers.

'I know you want to believe that Elspeth. I can understand why you don't want to think them capable of hurting you. But I hear things.'

His eyes fixed on the pile of bark pickings growing at his feet.

'Hear from who? Hear what?' Elspeth probed.

'From the other servants. They talk. The Darrochs can be cruel, especially Morwenna. If she did know about this place…'

His eyes roved around the trees, coming to rest on Elspeth.

'If she knew what the gateway can do, I'm sure she'd go to any lengths to get through. She's cruel, not to mention vain and greedy. Nethergar offers her everything she values.'

Elspeth knew he was right about Morwenna's nature. She

had seen it for herself in the way she treated the staff at Dalengour. But she had always treated Elspeth reasonably. She wouldn't go as far as to say she was kind, but never directly unkind.

'She can't know – she can't know this place exists,' Elspeth replied, deciding to ignore the issue of whether Morwenna could hurt her for now.

'I hope not,' said Jenson, starting back along the path to the kirk.

Elspeth fell into step behind him. The pace was slower now, although they still walked in silence. Her mind mulled over the possibility that Morwenna could be behind her illness. She wanted to dismiss the idea as ridiculous, but somehow, it festered in her mind.

It was ten minutes before either spoke again. As the path widened, Jenson slowed down, allowing Elspeth to come to his side. They walked together for a few moments before he stopped and turned to face her.

'I'm sorry about how I behaved when we first left the Cottage. I was annoyed.'

'Annoyed about what?'

'Nerissa seemed suspicious of me, almost hostile. I think she thought I'd contrived to get you to bring me with you. That I had some kind of ulterior motive.'

'I don't think the hostility was just about you. She didn't seem all that keen on having either of us there at first,' Elspeth said, smiling at him.

He couldn't help smiling back.

'True, but I think she got over it with you. She seemed to doubt what I told her about finding you.'

'You can't really blame her after what her family, …my family, went through. I think Nerissa is very astute. If she doubted anything, it's that we're just friends.'

Elspeth felt patches of heat bloom on her cheeks and looked away. She waited for him to speak, the redness intensifying under his gaze. He swallowed audibly, taking the thread of what she had said and burying it deep in his stomach. He cleared his throat, pushing her insinuation of more than platonic feelings aside.

'I suppose so. She just seemed to think I had planned all this out.'

Elspeth's disappointment at his blatant avoidance removed the glow from her cheeks. She looked up, her eyes coming to rest on his unreadable face. In a poor imitation of composure, she pressed her lips together and raised her eyebrows. Inwardly, her heart clattered like a train hurtling down the tracks.

'I think that's in your imagination. How could she think you knew anything at all about Nethergar!' she said, her voice rising uncharacteristically at the end of the sentence.

Jenson quickly averted his eyes, shifting uncomfortably again. Elspeth watched him as his eyes scanned the ground, a tic visible in his cheek, his mouth forming a thin line.

'You didn't know anything did you?'

Elspeth put her hand under his chin, forcing him to look at her. His bottom lip trembled, and his eyes looked watery.

'Jenson – what is it? What did you know?'

'Nothing, nothing I promise,' he said too quickly. 'I didn't know anything about this place.'

'Then what is it?'

'It's just that I... I... well I'm so scared for you. If anything happened to you...'

He turned away and started to walk slowly on. She stared after him, eyebrows raised, her mind bothered. She wanted to believe it was just concern that was making him behave this way, but something niggled. She couldn't help thinking he was keeping something from her.

The kirk came into view, its bright red steeple vibrant under the bright skies. Elspeth took one last look around before following Jenson inside, the stale smell of a long-forgotten place assaulting her senses. She hadn't noticed that before. Sunlight flowed through the stained-glass window, throwing dapples of blue and orange onto the stone walls, dust disturbed by their presence dancing in the streams of light. Elspeth stepped in front of Jenson and raised her fingers to the hand of the immortalised Saint Oda, majestic in the centre of the frame. Immediately, the glass shimmered, ripples forming where she touched before clearing to reveal the kirk in Cairndarroch. The room was empty, the knife still glittering on the altar, the pewter bowl still at its side.

Elspeth went to step though the molten glass. Jenson grabbed her hand and pulled her back.

'What is it? What's wrong now?' she asked, exasperation in her question.

Jenson grabbed both hands and pulled her close.

'Elspeth, I need to tell you something.'

He was breathing heavily, struggling to find the right words to tell her whatever was on his mind.

'Tell me what? Jenson, we're friends. You can tell me anything.'

'But that's just it. I don't want to be just your friend Elspeth. I've been in love with you since we were children. I took the job at Dalengour to be near you. I wanted to better myself so I could support you as my wife.'

His intense gaze blocked out everything, his nearness making her insides swirl with excited anticipation. Elspeth's heart soared. He loved her. Her first instinct was to throw herself into his arms. The man she loved was telling her he loved her back. As they stared at each other, the connection between them wrenched her insides, a flutter of butterflies tickling the walls of her stomach. Then reality struck. She couldn't be with him. She was married! Married to Riordan Darroch. The butterflies came to rest, a numbing sadness placing them in a state of torpor. Tears stung her eyes as she continued to look at Jenson, his feelings openly displayed on his handsome face.

'I was so hurt when I found out you were thinking of marrying Riordan.'

'You should have told me how you felt!' Elspeth spluttered. 'You should have told me then, before I married him.'

'I didn't want to stand in the way of you being with the man I thought you loved.'

'But I don't love him!'

Anguish flooded her voice as the words burst out. A crease appeared in Jenson's brow.

'I don't understand. Why did you marry him if you don't love him?'

'Oh, don't be so naïve Jenson! I married him because as his wife, my future and my family's future would be secured. I had a responsibility after my father died to make sure they were provided for. I could do that as Elspeth Darroch. But I will never love him. Never!'

She paused, colour flushing her face again.

'It's you I love Jenson.'

Her voice was quiet, almost timid, wavering at the boldness of her own declaration. A broad grin spread wantonly across his face as he pulled her into his arms.

'You love me! Oh Elspeth, I've waited so long to hear that. I never thought you would ever say it.'

He stroked her hair as she lay her head on his chest. She

could hear the strong, steady beat of his heart, feel the warmth of him. She had never felt so safe, so protected. She could have stayed there forever. Elspeth felt him place a hand under her chin, tilting her face up so he could look at her. He was going to kiss her. She wanted it so much but was afraid that if she let him, she wouldn't have the strength to do what she must. She pulled back quickly, stepping away from him. He let her go, but his arms remained stretched towards her, inviting her to come back into his embrace.

'Jenson, we can't. It's too late. I'm married to Riordan now. And I have a son who needs me. I can't risk his future.'

Jenson dropped his arms. His eyes glazed over, and she watched a silvery trail glisten on his cheek as he looked away. Elspeth clasped her hands together, her spine straight, using every bit of resolve she possessed to hold her ground while he felt the pain of her words.

Sadness choked in her throat, tears spilling that she quickly wiped away, not wanting Jenson to see her weakness. It took him a moment to pull himself together, but when he finally raised his head, his eyes were dry.

'I understand,' he said simply, two words being all that he could manage. 'We should get back.'

He didn't look at her, fixing instead on the blank patch of wall above her head. Elspeth nodded and with a deep breath, turned away from the man who would always have her heart, to return to the man she despised. Jenson must never suspect what her life with Riordan was truly like. She couldn't bear the thought of him blaming himself for not speaking up and protecting her from marrying a man whose cruelty was so degrading.

Emerging from the kirk in Cairndarroch, they walked back to Dalengour, the air heavy with the weight of their declaration. They paused on the porch of the castle, Elspeth fighting the urge to grab Jenson by the hand and run back into the forest. He took a deep breath, then opened the door to let in Lady Elspeth Darroch. As she entered the sombre hall, Riordan came running from the drawing room. His black leather boots clacked noisily on the stone floor, stomping out her dreams of being with someone she loved.

'Elspeth, oh my god Elspeth, where have you been? I was so worried!'

Riordan crushed her to him, his bony arms leaving her cold, his concern, the emotion expected from a worried husband.

'I went out for a walk,' Elspeth said disentangling herself from his arms. 'I started to feel unwell while I was out but thankfully, Jenson found me and helped me back to the house.'

Elspeth indicated Jenson standing behind her, all formality of mistress and servant restored. Riordan completely ignored him, grabbing Elspeth by the arms and holding her at arms-length as he scrutinised her face.

'What were you thinking of, going out alone after being so poorly?'

It sounded like he was reprimanding a child. Elspeth fumed, raising her shoulders, her eyes filled with contempt. She wanted to lash out, shove him away. But she needed to be careful. She inhaled deeply before pushing the air out, trying to exhale both breath and tension. Blinking, she relaxed her lips enough to let them to twitch into a forced smile.

'I was feeling much better. I am feeling better. The walk did me good. I just tried to go too far.'

'You should have called me. I would've gone with you,' Riordan said, running his dry, cracked palms down her arms. She felt the rough skin catching on the sleeves of her dress.

Instinctively, she snatched her arms away, clamping them to her side in a 'don't touch me' way.

'I wanted to be alone.'

Despite the feigned pleasantness on her face, something about the look in Elspeth's eyes stalled him. He cocked his head, eyes narrowed as he scrutinised her.

'Well, you're back now, safe and sound.'

His voice patronised her, the inflection dripping with insincerity.

'Mother's been worried sick. We'd better go and show her you're alright and then it's straight back to bed for you.'

He stood aside, his outstretched arm encouraging her towards the drawing room.

'I don't want to go back to bed. I've spent far too much time in my rooms of late. I want to see Robert.'

Elspeth's voice was commanding and she felt a momentary flicker of satisfaction as uncertainty paid a fleeting visit to her husband's pallid features. Maybe he sensed the change in her, sensed her fear of him was gone. Sensed that she was more in control now.

Within seconds, the doubt evaporated, replaced by a condescending smile on his cadaverous lips.

'Well maybe a visit to Robert after you've looked in on Mother,' he said, the arrogant façade fully restored now as he placed his hand possessively in the small of her back, propelling her forwards.

Elspeth cast a glance in Jenson's direction. He was standing stiffly, his hands clasped behind his back, his eyes staring blankly at a portrait of some long-dead Darroch.

'Thank you, Jenson, for escorting me home'

'You're welcome my lady. Glad I could be of assistance.'

He didn't look at her and her heart tore. She turned back to Riordan in time to see him shoot an evil glare at

Jenson who didn't acknowledge it, his eyes still glued to the wall.

Reluctantly, she let Riordan lead her in to see her mother-in-law. Morwenna was holding court in the drawing room, a fitted dress in her traditional black accentuating her tiny frame. On seeing Elspeth, she rose from her chair, stretching out her hands, inviting her to take them.

'My dear! I was so worried when Riordan told me you were missing. Whatever possessed you to go outside? And on your own!'

Elspeth didn't take the outstretched hands. She stood looking at Morwenna, everything she had heard from Nerissa at the forefront of her mind. It was the first time since meeting Riordan's formidable mother that she didn't feel diminished in her presence. Standing at least a head taller, she looked down into Morwenna's feline eyes.

'I was feeling better and wanted some air. As you see, it has done me the world of good.'

Morwenna, ignoring Elspeth's reluctance to come nearer, took the initiative and stepped towards her. She analysed the younger woman's face, tilting her head from side to side as she inspected her. Elspeth kept her eyes fixed keenly on her mother-in-law, following her every movement with a defiant stare.

'Yes, you do look better. Much better,' she said, eyeing her with what Elspeth could only place as suspicion. After a moment, Morwenna seemed to remember the role she was playing, smiling forcibly as she continued.

'That's wonderful my dear! We've been so worried about you, haven't we Riordan?'

Morwenna looked over at her son, inviting him into the conversation.

'Yes, yes, very worried,' Riordan replied, surprised at being asked to participate.

'It's wonderful to see you feeling better. Wonderful!'

Elspeth couldn't help the smile loitering at the corners of her lips as she witnessed their pathetic attempts at feigning concern. How many more 'wonderfuls' would Morwenna vomit out in her stab at authenticity? Her mother-in-law suddenly lurched forward, grabbing Elspeth's hands.

'It's so wonderful to see you looking better Elspeth. But make sure you don't overdo it won't you?'

Elspeth was certain Morwenna ran her fingers across her palm as she spoke. Looking for the wound she expected there?

'I met someone while out walking today,' Elspeth said casually, deciding to test the waters.

'Oh yes, who?' asked Morwenna sweetly, letting go of Elspeth and returning to her seat.

'Someone who said they knew me. She said she was a relative of mine, a Larimore.'

A greyish tinge overtook Morwenna's usual healthy glow. All pretence of concern was replaced with unchecked hatred. The silence vibrated as the two women glared at each other. It was Morwenna who backed out first, dropping her eyes momentarily before returning her gaze to her daughter-in-law, this time, with a trite smile plastered on her face.

'A Larimore you say? I didn't think there were any others except you and your siblings?'

'Neither did I,' replied Elspeth, trying to sound nonchalant. 'But it seems we were wrong. She said her name was Nerissa Larimore.'

As she spoke the name, Elspeth stared intently at Morwenna, looking for signs of recognition, but there were none. Yet the thought of more Larimores had definitely rattled her.

'I can't say I've ever heard the name,' Morwenna said dismissively.

'Well, no matter. We didn't talk for long, so I didn't find out much about her. If I see her again, I'll ask how we're related.'

Elspeth smiled sweetly, her eyes still absorbing her mother-in-law's behaviour. But Morwenna gave nothing away.

Not wanting to prolong the conversation any longer, Elspeth was desperate to get away. She needed time to think about everything that had happened. But first, she wanted to see her son. Morwenna's leonine eyes were fixed on her, burning with dislike despite the grin fixed on her tight lips. Elspeth ignored her.

'I think I'll take your advice Riordan and go for a rest.,' Elspeth said, casting a glance at her husband who was watching the exchange between the two women intently. 'But first, I'm going to the nursery to see Robert.'

With this, Elspeth walked serenely out of the room, feeling two sets of eyes boring holes in her back as she left.

ONCE MORWENNA WAS CERTAIN ELSPETH WAS OUT of earshot, she rounded on Riordan, her face alight with excitement.

'It's true!' she burst out, pacing the room unable to contain the restlessness coiling around her stomach. 'My grandmother's stories were true! Elspeth has been through to Nethergar. The gateway has restored her! That's the only explanation for why she's so clearly well again.'

Morwenna was rambling and Riordan looked uneasy.

'Do you think the gateway has awakened her gifts?' he asked his mother, slowing his speech in the hope his drawling voice would calm her agitation.

'Maybe. It could have. But I'm more concerned about this woman she claims to have met and what she might have told her. If she's a Larimore, she'll need to be dealt with.'

'Could this Nerissa Larimore have their family's abilities? Their... gifts?'

'Its likely. And if she does, because she must have remained in Nethergar after the gateway first opened, she will be much more powerful than Elspeth.'

Morwenna's eyes glowed, greed intensifying their greenness.

'And Elspeth, will her powers develop now that she's been there?'

Morwenna stopped her pacing and smirked at her son.

'Riordan, are you afraid of your wife?'

'No, no, of course not! But it would be good to know what she's capable of, especially if I'm going to have to dispose of her!'

Morwenna nodded and began marching around the room again, tracked by Riordan's narrow eyes.

'Even if she knows about the Larimore gifts, she might not realise that she has them. And even if she does, she will still need to learn how to use them. So, you're safe for now,' she said, grinning condescendingly at her son.

'But we have to be careful. I couldn't get through the gateway. If we're going to get to this 'Nerissa', we'll need to gain Elspeth's trust.'

'How are we going to do that? My wife didn't trust us before and if this woman she met is filling her head with tales of the past then...'

'I'll think of something,' Morwenna interrupted. 'Now go

play the doting father and husband and keep an eye on Elspeth. I need to know if she makes any attempt to go back there. And send Jenson in here as you go.'

Dismissed, Riordan left the room to do as his mother ordered. Seconds later, Jenson knocked quietly on the door and entered.

'You asked to see me Lady Darroch?'

'Tell me what happened,' Morwenna barked without preamble.

'I did as you asked. I made sure she went through the gateway.'

'Why couldn't I follow you?'

Jenson's shoulders dropped a little as he lowered his head.

'Well?' Morwenna prompted, her voice irate.

Jenson looked up but still didn't meet her gaze. He fixed his shining, hazel eyes on the shelf filled with embalmed dead animals behind her.

'It seems that Elspeth, as the Larimore who opened the gateway and the one who now controls it, chooses which people she allows to pass through.'

'What do you mean, 'allows through'? How does she do that?'

Morwenna moved around the room as she questioned him, her words tripping over each other in her eagerness to get them out.

'She can take a person through, or she can assign a guide to them so that they can cross without her.'

Morwenna's pacing became frantic again, her black taffeta skirt making a swishing noise with each change in direction. Jenson was tracking her now, his watery eyes fixed on her, his guard raised.

'Who was the Larimore woman she met?

'Her name was Nerissa, but I don't know any more than that.'

'You're lying,' Morwenna said coming to stand close to Jenson.

Her breath warmed Jenson's face. He pulled his neck back, trying to distance himself without moving his feet.

'What did she tell Elspeth?' she asked, her poorly veiled threat causing Jenson to fidget uncomfortably.

'Only the story of how the Larimores fled Nethergar.'

Morwenna narrowed her eyes. Jenson did his best to hold his ground, keeping his eyes focused on a stuffed buzzard, beak open, talons piercing a dead vole.

'Did she have power, this Larimore witch?'

She looked at him from under hooded lids, surveying his features mistrustingly.

'Not that I saw.'

'And Elspeth? Does she know about her own gifts?'

'I don't think so.'

This time, Jenson flinched at his lie, but Morwenna lost in her own thoughts didn't notice. She had resumed her pacing, skirt rustling as she patrolled to and fro.

'You can go now,' she said, flicking her wrist to signify his dismissal.

Jenson turned his eyes on her and looked directly into her face for the first time since entering the room. The sound of the grandfather clock ticking matched the beating of his heart as he mustered the courage to speak again.

'I've done what you asked. Are you going to keep your end of the bargain now?'

Morwenna laughed.

'You think you've done enough do you? Well, I don't! I'll keep my end of the arrangement, but at a time when I decide it!'

To Jenson, she looked manic as she spat the words at him. He knew there was no point in pressing her further now.

'Very well,' he said. If that's all...'

With a curt nod of his head, Jenson backed out of the room.

CHAPTER 9

The Child in the Tower

November 1921– Cairndarroch

'Have you been back?' Agatha asked eagerly now they were alone.

'I haven't had the chance. Morwenna's watching me like a hawk,' Elspeth replied.

'Do you think she knows about Nethergar then?'

I'm not sure. Sometimes, the way she looks at me, I think she does. But it's still hard to imagine how she could know. Even if someone told her, it does seem rather farfetched doesn't it? Like a story someone made up or an old folk tale. Why would anyone believe it?'

The sound of her son giggling as Kaliope tickled him drew her attention. This was one of the rare visits Agatha's twin made to Dalengour. Agatha was a frequent visitor, but the leering and hovering of Riordan Darroch made Kaliope uncomfortable and so she made the journey to visit Elspeth only rarely. But today, she was here, sitting on the carpet of the drawing room playing with her nephew.

Elspeth and Agatha were sitting at a small occasional table, enjoying afternoon tea and each other's company. Elspeth lived for visits from her family. Life at Dalengour had improved in the month since she had returned from Nethergar. Riordan seemed almost wary of her and stayed out of her way as much as possible. Morwenna was being insipidly sweet and over-attentive. Today was unusual as Morwenna had left her alone to visit with her sisters. Normally, she held court while they talked, orchestrating the topics of conversation and the schedule of their visit.

Since she married Riordan, Elspeth had concealed much from her family. She never wanted them to know how unhappy she was, nor the cruelty she endured at the hands of her husband. But she had entrusted Agatha with the secrets of Nethergar and meeting Nerissa. She had told her everything except the niggling doubts she had about Morwenna being responsible for poisoning her to get through the gateway.

Robert was crawling unsteadily across the floor followed protectively by Kaliope, ready to catch him should he fall. Elspeth looked towards her husband, seated in a chair by the window pretending to read a newspaper while leering at Kaliope's behind as she crawled on all fours after his son. Elspeth felt the familiar unease seeing Riordan ogle her younger sister.

'And Jenson? Have you spoken to him since you came back?'

Agatha was staring pointedly at Elspeth as she brought her attention back to their conversation. Her skin flushed at the sound of Jenson's name. She quickly lowered her eyes, focusing on the delicate daisies embroidered on the lacy overlay of her dark blue skirt, suddenly mesmerised by the intricate detail of their white petals and silver-coloured stems. Agatha knew about Jenson's confession of love, but Elspeth still felt ashamed when her own feelings surfaced. She was a married woman, for better or for worse. She had her son to think of and he would always come first.

'We haven't really spoken since. It's probably for the best,' Elspeth murmured, avoiding her sister's knowing stare, concealing the sting of tears always ready to spill at the realisation she could never be with the man who owned her heart.

'Rubbish! He would be far better for you than Riordan! You aren't happy here Elspeth, I can see that. And you so deserve to be!'

Elspeth couldn't lie to Agatha. Her sister would see through any untruths in an instant.

'Things are much better these days. Riordan and I have fallen into a routine, we see relatively little of each other now. I'm getting to spend more time with Robert as well.'

'That's not enough Elspeth. You shouldn't have to settle for this. Not you. You deserve more. Your son deserves to be brought up surrounded by happiness. Come home with me. Leave this mausoleum. We can deal with whatever the Darrochs throw at us. Especially now you can access the gifts Nethergar has given you.'

Elspeth looked into the pleading face of her sister. Her heart swelled as she saw only sincerity reflected back. Agatha was her rock. The one person in all the world who knew her completely. Her need to protect Agatha from the harsh reality of the world was overwhelming. She would do anything to keep her innocence undamaged. She wanted her younger sister to see the world as full of possibilities and dreams, to remain certain in her belief that family and love could solve any problem.

'I love you for saying that Agatha, but it isn't possible for me to leave here. I'm Riordan's wife and we share a son. I have to do the right thing for them both.'

'You don't owe that man anything!' Agatha spat, glaring hatefully across at Riordan Darroch.

Elspeth was taken aback by the hostility in her sister's tone. Agatha usually saw only good in everyone, but for some reason, her dislike of Elspeth's husband had grown even though she kept most details of his behaviour from her. She followed Agatha's gaze. Riordan was now sitting awkwardly cross-legged on the rug close to Kaliope on the pretence of interacting with his son.

Elspeth recognised the real motive in her husband's action as in the seven months since her son was born, she could count on one hand how many times he had even looked at Robert. There was only one reason why he would come to sit so close beside him now. Elspeth was not stupid. Neither was Agatha. The obvious lust in Riordan's eyes when he was around Kaliope fuelled Agatha's dislike of him. It was the reason Elspeth didn't try to encourage Agatha's twin to accompany her to Dalengour more often.

Elspeth shifted in her seat and leaned forward to break Agatha's focus.

'Besides, I still have a lot to learn about how my gifts work and if I can't get back to Nethergar for Nerissa to teach me, they'll be useless.'

'You need to find a way Elspeth,' Agatha said vehemently, her eyes still fixed on Kaliope and Riordan.

Their conversation ended abruptly as Kaliope, eager to

remove herself from Riordan's nearness, appeared at their side, cradling a sleepy Robert in her arms.

'I think it's time we headed home Aggie,' Kaliope said, shooting a look back over her shoulder and raising her eyebrows. 'Besides, this little man is spent.'

She passed her much-loved bundle to Elspeth whose face softened into a gentle smile. She stroked the cheek of her first born son and his eyes flicked open, then closed again, too heavy now as he slipped into sleep.

'Must you go?' she whispered as Robert's breathing deepened.

'I think so. Mother will be expecting us back for dinner soon,' Kaliope said, eager to get away, her tolerance for Riordan's leering exhausted.

Elspeth pressed her lips together and nodded, swallowing back her disappointment. Agatha reached forward and placed a hand reassuringly on her arm.

'I promise I'll come back soon Elspeth.'

Her sisters stood up and Agatha placed a kiss on both hers and Robert's cheek.

'Remember what I said. You can come back to Kirkholm Cottage for good anytime.'

Elspeth nodded, not trusting herself to speak without her voice cracking. Kaliope bent to hug her, then brushed her lips lightly on Robert's forehead. He didn't stir.

'See you soon Elspeth.'

Agatha's eyes lingered on Elspeth and her son for a few moments before they turned and headed into the hall. There was no sign of Riordan now. He had probably disappeared the moment Kaliope had extracted herself from his company. He would have no desire to spend time with Robert now. That suited Elspeth fine.

Watching her son sleep on, she was content to stay in the drawing room and watch the sun drop down behind the trees through the window. As the shadows lengthened, she remained at the small table, listening to Robert's gentle breathing. She didn't know how long she sat there before the nanny appeared at her side, looking disapprovingly at the sleeping child.

'He should be in the nursery by now. He needs feeding.'

Robert stirred in Elspeth's arms as the shrill voice of Josephine Dennings, the austere nanny Morwenna had hired to look after Robert, broke the silence.

'I am quite capable of knowing when my son needs feeding Miss Dennings. I will bring him up shortly.'

The nanny did not respond to Elspeth's surly dismissal, remaining at her side, glaring at her.

'Is there something else?' Elspeth asked curtly.

'I have his bottle ready now and his bath is being drawn.'

Tension had grown between Josephine Dennings and Elspeth since she had come back from Nethergar, her health restored. During her illness, the nanny had enjoyed complete control over Robert's care. Now that she was well, they seemed to be locked in a constant battle over doing the simplest and most mundane tasks for the child. But Elspeth didn't have the energy to fight today. Reluctantly, she handed over her son, who was now starting to gripe. Miss Dennings clutched him to her ample bosom and marched towards the door, satisfaction etched on her dour face.

Elspeth shivered. The air felt chill as the fire waned. She placed the teacups and pot onto a tray and carried them out into the hall, intent on taking them down to the kitchen, hoping to catch sight of Jenson. Riordan was crossing the hall as she entered. He paused when he saw her.

'Have your sisters gone?' Riordan asked.

'Yes, they left a while ago.'

Elspeth was sure she saw a look of disappointment flit across her husband's face.

'I thought they might stay for dinner.'

'Why? They never have before and it's not as if you or your mother have ever invited them to,' she snapped.

Riordan glared at her. A year ago, she would never have dared talk to him like this. But recently, she had become emboldened, mostly because he seemed to have become more wary of her. He chose to ignore her quip.

'It's probably for the best that they aren't staying as dinner will be late tonight. We'll wait for Mother to get back.'

'She's not here?'

Elspeth's heart skipped a beat. If Morwenna wasn't here, maybe she could go back to the gateway.

'No. She's been out all afternoon. She's gone into the city to see some friends. I expect her back about eight.'

She had three hours. That was enough time to get there and back to see Nerissa. Riordan was looking at her suspiciously. Elspeth tried to fix a nonplussed expression on her face and stared defiantly back at him. He fidgeted uneasily, unsure of how to end the conversation. She was eager to escape and so she helped him out.

'If we're eating late, I think I'll go and rest in my room for a while.'

'Fine,' he said, relieved to be able to leave her.

Riordan disappeared into the library and Elspeth waited until the door closed behind him. Careful to stop her heels clacking on the stone floor, she tiptoed across the hall towards the front door. As she reached for the handle, she heard her name being called softly from behind her.

'Elspeth.'

Jenson was heading towards her, his eyes fixed on the door where Riordan had just disappeared. An involuntary smile spread across her face as she saw him, a tickling feeling dancing around her stomach.

'Jenson,' she said openly, taking a step towards him. 'What is it?'

'I…I just wanted to check you were alright. We haven't really had a chance to speak since… well since we came back, and I've been worried about you.'

'There's no need to worry. I'm fine. Riordan is avoiding me which suits me, and Morwenna is being surprisingly nice.'

'That's what worries me,' he said with a wry smile. Then more seriously, 'I've seen the way she is around you. It's not normal for her.'

Elspeth laughed.

'You're right about that!'

There was a pause where they continued to look at each other, each waiting for the other to say something.

'She isn't here,' Elspeth said noting Jenson's continued furtive glances towards the library door.

His shoulders dropped as he relaxed. With his eyes now fixed on her, he reached out tentatively and took her hand.

'Elspeth, I… I.' He struggled to find the words.

She desperately wanted to hear him say he missed her, wanted her, loved her. But she didn't want to hear it in equal measure. If he gave her reason, she didn't trust herself to do what was right. Didn't trust herself to continue playing the dutiful wife.

'Don't say anything,' she said dropping her eyes.

She could feel Jenson's disappointment as he released her hand and stepped back. Sadness threatened to crush her chest as she fought with the eager young girl buried inside that wanted to throw her arms around him and run from this place, never looking back. Then she heard Agatha's words ringing in her ears, telling her she deserved happiness, telling her she should leave Dalengour and be happy. She looked up to see tears pooling in the corners of the kind eyes she so loved, and her sense of duty crumbled.

'Jenson, Morwenna has gone out. I am going back to visit Nerissa. Come with me.'

His eyes lit up, his full lips curving into a broad smile.

'It's probably best if you go first in case anyone sees you crossing the lawn. I'll go around the back of the house and follow on in a few minutes. Wait for me at the kirk.'

Elspeth nodded, excitement flooding through her body at the thought of Nethergar and spending time alone with Jenson. She watched him as he almost skipped back to the kitchen stairs before turning to head out the door.

The eye peering through the crack in the library door watched Elspeth leave. Furious, Riordan Darroch reeled around to face his mother who was concealed in the shadows of the cavernous library.

'She's going to the gateway?' she asked her son who was pacing agitatedly around the room.

'Yes! And she's taking that devious butler with her!'

Morwenna tracked his pacing, her green eyes narrowing.

'Calm down Riordan,' she said eyeing her son suspiciously. 'It doesn't matter if he goes with her.'

'Of course it matters! Elspeth is my wife!'

'And? Why is that so important. It's not like you ever wanted her. Why are you bothered if the butler befriends her? As long as it doesn't interfere with our plans, it's of no consequence.'

Morwenna was scrutinising her son, who was still stalking angrily around the library, hands on hips, his thin lips pursed tightly so the little colour they normally possessed faded to white. He was jealous, possessive, and that could be a problem. She had wanted to keep Jenson around in case she needed him again. But looking at Riordan's reaction, his presence could be a risk to her plans.

'It matters because she's mine! He has no right to take what belongs to me!' he spat, glaring thunderously at his mother.

Never taking her eyes off Riordan, Morwenna reached for the black candlestick telephone on the sideboard, waiting for someone to answer from below stairs.

'Gadsen, bring the child down from the tower.'

Riordan looked confused as his mother replaced the receiver.

'Why are you asking for my son?'

'I'm not,' she replied simply. 'Jenson Tanner is an easy problem to solve.'

'What do you mean?'

'Wait for Gadsen and I'll explain.'

Riordan resumed his pacing while they waited in silence for the venerable butler to arrive. The sound of the library door creaking open announced him, the scrawny wrist of a child about twelve years old clasped in his gnarled hand. The young girl was gaunt-looking, dark circles standing out around her hazel eyes. Her skin was pale and stretched across her cheekbones, giving her face a look of poverty and starvation. Her grey dress was dirty and hung from her scrawny shoulders, like it belonged to someone much larger than she. The girl cowered behind Gadsen's legs when she saw Morwenna. The butler looked down at her, as if she were an unwelcome feral cat twisting around at his feet.

'The child Ma'am,' he said stepping sideways so the girl was on view again.

'Thank you Gadsen. You can leave her here.'

Gadsen looked down at the girl, his nose flared in obvious

disgust. He seemed reluctant to leave this dirty child unguarded in the presence of his mistress.

'Very well,' he said, nodding stiffly, leaving the child vulnerable and alone in the middle of the room.

Morwenna didn't speak again until the butler had closed the door behind him. The child was visibly shaking, her wide eyes filled with fright as they flicked between the two Darrochs. Riordan stared from the pitiful girl to his mother, waiting for her to explain.

'This is Gwen Tanner,' Morwenna began. 'She has been our guest here at Dalengour this past year.'

'What? You've been keeping this child here all this time?' Riordan said incredulously.

'Yes. She's been enjoying our hospitality in the east tower.'

The girl's eyes were now so dilated they were at risk of popping out of her skeletal face. Her hands were screwing up the front of her dress as she gripped tightly to the dismal fabric.

'But why?' Riordan asked.

'She has been my insurance plan.'

Riordan raised an eyebrow and looked at Morwenna from under furrowed brows.

'Insurance for what?'

'I didn't trust that your wife's commitment to you would keep her at Dalengour long enough to find the gateway.'

Anger flared in Riordan's mean eyes as he opened his mouth to protest. Morwenna raised a hand to silence him.

'I needed another reason for her to stay. I wanted someone who could help me nudge Elspeth in the right direction to find the gateway. Someone she trusted, like her old friend Jenson. Getting him here took some persuasion, but he came round to my way of thinking once Gwen became our guest.'

'But now the gateway is open, why is she still here?'

'I wasn't ready to let her go yet. I still haven't got into Nethergar myself, so I've kept her here in case I needed to make use of Elspeth's attachment to Jenson again. But now I think it would serve our purpose better if Jenson left. He may take some convincing to leave, but I think we have the upper hand.'

Morwenna looked at the child who was trying to shrink away from her glare.

'If you hurry, you may be able to catch Jenson before he goes after you wife.'

Riordan's face registered understanding and he grabbed the child roughly by the arm, dragging her out into the hall.

'Come on,' he growled, the girl whimpering as his nails dug into her flesh.

She had to run to keep up, stumbling occasionally, her weakened muscles unaccustomed to moving at such speed, failing her. She would have fallen to the ground had Riordan not been hauling her along.

They reached the kitchens to see Jenson pulling on his jacket. His face fell when Riordan entered, dragging the child behind. He stood staring at the little girl, not daring to move in case he was imagining it and she wasn't really there.

'Gwen?'

Jenson's voice was shaky as he uttered her name. The little girl tried to run towards him, but Riordan was still holding firmly on to her arm.

'Not so fast,' he said, pulling the child back.

Jenson stared at him, the hatred he normally tried to hide burning clearly in his pinched eyes. He was fighting every impulse to run and snatch the child. He stood rooted to the spot waiting for Riordan to make his move.

'This is a simple proposition that I think even you will be able to understand Tanner. You can take this child and leave Dalengour now. Or you can carry on with your plan to meet my wife and I will take the child back up to the tower. The choice is yours.'

Jenson's eyes flicked between Gwen whose sallow cheeks were now wet with tears, and Riordan who was standing with a smug expression on his face. He knew Jenson didn't have a choice and he was enjoying the sense of power.

Jenson could feel his teeth clench together, his fists balled by his sides as he fought to control his anger.

'You bastard,' Jenson snarled.

'Name-calling is not going to solve your problem Tanner. Now what will it be?'

Jenson closed his eyes, trying to steady himself.

'Let her come to me,' he said stretching his arms out towards the child.

Riordan held on to Gwen who was now struggling against his hold.

'I trust it won't take you more than an hour to collect your things and leave here? And I'm sure I don't need to say it, but just so we're clear, you are never to come back. Do you understand?'

Jenson nodded.

'Please, let her go.'

Riordan released the child who ran into Jenson's waiting arms. He clung to her, tears running freely down his face as he held her close.

Riordan watched the scene with distaste.

'One hour Tanner. Then you and the brat will be gone.'

He turned dramatically and headed back upstairs feeling

exhilarated. He was disappointed to find his mother gone from the library. Pouring a large slug of whisky from the decanter, he drained it in one and took up position in the window seat. His stomach lurched with anticipation of the hurt Jenson's departure would cause his wife and a smile twisted his insipid lips.

Relaxing into his vigil, he stared out towards the gloomy trees surrounding Dalengour. As darkness closed in, the tangled branches cast ominous shadows across the lawn, swallowing what little light permeated the dour rooms of the castle. Movement caught his eye on the edge of the forest as he saw his mother disappearing into the tree line. He stared at the place where she had vanished and smiled again.

At the kirk, Elspeth paced impatiently. Where was he? She couldn't wait much longer if she was going to get to Nerissa's cottage and back before dinner. She wrapped her arms around herself and rubbed the tops of her arms to ward off the chill permeating the kirk. In her eagerness to get out of the house, she hadn't had time to collect her warmer coat and her cardigan was proving ineffectual against the cold November evening. Why hadn't he come? Her throat felt dry and her eyes stung. He had obviously decided not to.

Pushing away her disappointment, she focused on the reason she was here. She walked purposefully towards the stained-glass window, fixing her eyes on the looming image of the woman in the blue dress, dimly lit as the failing light filtered weakly through the pane. A sound coming from the shadows halted her and for a moment her heart soared at the thought of Jenson.

'Jenson? Is that you?'

'No my dear. Your friend is indisposed.'

Morwenna Darroch took a step into the light, her green eyes burning, a scornful smile on her flushed face.

'Morwenna, I…I thought you were out. I decided to go for a walk before dinner,' she stammered, stumbling over the words, her heart racing.

'Really? And you just happened to find yourself here again?'

Her mother-in-law's tone dripped with sarcasm as she took another step forwards. Elspeth breathed deeply and quickly regaining her composure, pulled herself up to her full height to square up to Morwenna. This time, she would not be intimidated.

'What do you want?' Elspeth said calmly now, the surprise at Morwenna's presence waning.

'You're going to take me through the gateway.'

Morwenna's words released a tidal wave of realisation in Elspeth's mind. She did know. Nerissa was right. She knew about Nethergar. Morwenna was the one who had poisoned her, who planned to use her blood to open the gateway. Comprehension made her want to run from here, run from this woman who was capable of such cruelty. The woman who had been willing to sacrifice Elspeth's life for access to Nethergar.

But she wouldn't run. She was strong, powerful and had the advantage here. She had what Morwenna wanted. Holding her ground, she breathed slowly to stem the trembling in her legs.

'Why would I do that?'

The smile on Morwenna's face contorted as she glared at Elspeth.

'Because if you don't, I'll hurt him.'

Morwenna pulled the long silver blade from inside her cloak – the same blade Elspeth recalled seeing on her last visit to the kirk, and pointed it threateningly towards the shadows. Elspeth's eyes followed the direction of the knife and saw her son, sleeping peacefully in his basket.

'You wouldn't!' she gasped, staring incredulously at her mother-in-law. 'He's your grandson!'

Elspeth made a move towards where Robert lay, blissfully unaware of the scene unfolding around him.

'Not so fast,' Morwenna said, pointing the knife towards Elspeth who stopped in her tracks.

Morwenna moved to where the boy lay sleeping, keeping the blade pointed menacingly at Elspeth. She picked up the basket and carried it to the altar, laying it on the bare stone. Elspeth's heart was racing, sweat beading on her brow. She clenched her fists, her eyes flicking between the silver weapon and her son.

'He looks so angelic, doesn't he?' Morwenna said, running the knife blade across Robert's cheek. 'Seeing him laid here so peacefully, I could almost forget Larimore blood runs through his veins…almost.'

She raised the hilt of the knife and hovered it over Robert's chest that slowly rose and fell in the peace of his slumber.

'No! Please don't!'

Elspeth stretched out her arm in anguish, her fingers trembling uncontrollably as she tried ineffectually to reach out for her son.

'What will it be Elspeth? The blood of your son or are you willing to take me through the gateway?'

She didn't get a chance to answer. The door of the kirk burst open, and Riordan Darroch raced towards the altar. His eyes darted around the room, taking in Elspeth, white as a ghost, tears running down her cheeks, eyes wide in panic.

His mother, madness on her face as she held the knife over Robert's chest.

'Mother! What the hell are you doing?'

Riordan's voice was filled with rage as he stared disbelievingly at Morwenna Darroch. His appearance seemed to have rattled her, the knife beginning to tremble in her hands, her eyes darting from her son to her grandson.

'Stay out of it Riordan. This is between me and your wife.'

'What? What the hell's going on? Elspeth?'

'Your mother is threatening to hurt our son unless I take her through the gateway.'

'What gateway? What are you talking about?'

Was it possible he didn't know? Elspeth wasn't sure, but he was here, and he could help her.

'Riordan, please save our son.'

Elspeth looked at him pleadingly, hoping beyond hope he would get Robert away from his insane mother. Riordan looked at her, his face expressionless. For a moment, Elspeth panicked, believing he would turn away from her, side with his mother, let her drive the blade though their innocent son. It felt like an age while Riordan stood motionless, his eyes scrutinising his wife.

'Mother, you need to put down the knife.'

His words were clear, deliberate, ringing through the silence of the kirk. Relief flooded through Elspeth as Riordan fixed his attention on Morwenna, taking a few tentative steps towards where Robert lay.

'Don't come any closer,' Morwenna screeched.

There was fear in her voice as she lowered the blade until the tip grazed against the delicate flesh on Roberts exposed neck. Elspeth drew in a sharp breath and began to move forward, but Riordan raised his hand to halt her. Still, Robert slept on, oblivious to the impending danger.

Riordan took a few more steps towards his mother.

'Stay where you are!' Morwenna screamed again and Elspeth's heart skipped as the blade dimpled Robert's skin.

'You won't hurt him Mother. You're not a monster and nothing is worth taking the life of an innocent child. I'm sure you know that,' Riordan said calmly, still creeping towards his mother and son.

Morwenna didn't move, her hand clutching the knife that now trembled ferociously.

'This is worth it. Nethergar is worth it!'

Confusion creased Riordan's brow, but he maintained focused on his mother, taking a final step bringing him within reach of Robert's basket. Elspeth wasn't breathing. She wanted to rush over and rescue her baby but knew one move could cause Morwenna to plunge the knife into his neck.

'Give me the knife Mother.'

Riordan reached out his hand.

'You don't understand. I've waited all my life to get through the gateway. And now... now it's so close.'

Tears of frustration and anger sprang from Morwenna's eyes, and she shook her head in disbelief as everything she had ever wanted slipped away. Riordan held his ground, his hand still outstretched, his pale slitty eyes fixed on Morwenna.

'Give me the knife,' he repeated calmly.

Still, Morwenna didn't move. Riordan slowly reached across and cupped his fingers gently over Morwenna's trembling hand, steadying the weapon and drawing it slowly away from the sleeping child. Morwenna let him guide her, reluctantly surrendering the knife and dissolving into desperate sobs, encircled in Riordan's arms.

Elspeth flew forward and picked up her son who began to

stir as she cradled him close to her breast. Quickly, she examined him but there was no sign of a wound. She showered his face with kisses as her tears fell onto his cheeks. For a moment, nothing else mattered apart from the baby in her arms. Her love for him overshadowed everything, the wails of Morwenna fading into the background.

'Elspeth, I'm going to take Mother back to the house.'

Riordan's voice broke into her mind and a fury like she had never felt bubbled up from deep within her.

'She needs locking up! That woman tried to kill our son! How can you stand there comforting her. She's evil!'

Elspeth was screaming, the realisation of what Morwenna was capable of fuelling anger she could no longer control.

'Elspeth, I understand. We need to talk. There is a lot going on here that needs explaining. But right now, I need to deal with Mother. We have some… accommodations at Dalengour where she can be secured for now until I understand what's been happening. Meet me back at the house and we'll talk once Robert is settled back in the nursery.'

Elspeth nodded, anger rendering her unable to speak. She was trembling again, but now from rage. She watched Riordan shuffle out, Morwenna clutching him as he coaxed her towards the kirk door. Once they had left, she settled her son back into his basket and rocked him gently until his eyes closed, sleeping once again.

CHAPTER 10

The Worm Turns

RIORDAN RELAXED BACK ON THE SOFA IN THE library, sighing heavily as he took a swig from the tumbler of whisky in his hand. Elspeth watched his features as he tried to make sense of all she had told him.

'You're saying Mother believes there is another world that can be accessed through some gateway in our kirk?'

He was looking at her, one brow raised, his lip curled in disbelief. She had just finished telling him the tale of Nethergar and the history of the Larimores and Darrochs. She owed him some truths after his actions in the kirk. Elspeth could understand his scepticism. The story did sound incredible, even to her who had first-hand knowledge that it was true.

'Your mother desperately wanted to get to Nethergar. She was willing to poison me and kill our son to get there.'

Riordan leaned forward, his elbows resting on his knees, his fingers buried in his lank black hair.

'I just can't believe that. I know Morwenna can be a hard woman but to kill Robert...'

His voice trailed off as he looked up at Elspeth sitting across from him. She could see tears pooling in the corners of his pale green eyes. The uncharacteristic show of emotion surprised her. In their eighteen months of marriage, never once had she seen genuine feeling on his face. But here he was, signs of damage showing in his expression.

'You saw it Riordan. How can you deny it!'

'I know, but she's my Mother! How can she be capable of such an act? And for what? Access to some other fantasy world she believes exists?'

Elspeth looked down, deciding how much more she should tell him. As he sat there, trying to reconcile Morwenna's actions, she felt sorry for him. This was new. Her hatred had kept her from seeing him as a man, a son. But this Riordan was grieving for the mother he thought he knew. He was trying to come to terms with this new version of Morwenna Darroch, a woman who had the capacity to cause pain, even to murder.

'Riordan,' she said softly, 'Nethergar really does exist.'

'What? What are you saying?'

'What I told you about the Larimores and Darrochs coming to Cairndarroch through a gateway from Nethergar, it's true. Some Larimores do possess gifts, abilities that allow them to do improbable things.'

'I don't understand.'

Elspeth came to sit beside him. He shifted his knees around so he was facing her.

'I've been to Nethergar. Do you remember the day I went for a walk and came back recovered from my illness?'

Riordan nodded.

'Well, that was the day I opened the gateway to Nethergar. I went through and met one of my ancestors, Nerissa Larimore. It was she who told me about the feud between the Darrochs and the Larimores.'

'I...I still don't understand. What do you mean 'you opened the gateway'?'

'My blood. The gateway could only be reopened again from the Cairndarroch side, by the blood of a Larimore.'

She didn't add in the details of Morwenna's involvement in opening the gateway, or that Jenson had gone with her. Her husband was struggling enough. Riordan knitted his brows together and it was a few moments before he spoke again.

'What do you mean the Larimore's have gifts? What gifts? Do you think you have special gifts?'

His tone irked her.

'I don't suppose you would ever think me capable of anything special!'

'No, no! Honestly, that's not what I meant. I don't know what you mean by gifts. All this seems so impossible.'

He shook his head wearily and Elspeth sighed. He was right. It was impossible.

'I know. If it hadn't happened to me, I don't think I would have believed it either. But I did open that gateway. When I went through to Nethergar, something happened to me. It was as if something had awakened in me. While I was with Nerissa Larimore, I did feel a connection to something, some sort of power.'

'And that's what healed you?'

'No, Nethergar healed me.'

Riordan looked confused again.

'One of the reasons your mother wants to get to

Nethergar so badly is because of what it offers. There is an energy there, a restorative energy is the best way I can describe it.'

'Just being there made you well again?'

'Yes, but it's more than that. When you pass through the gateway, you're sort of fixed in time. You can stay for many years on either side of the gateway and live your life, age as any normal person would. But for those who are from Nethergar, the moment you step back through the gateway, you will be restored to how you were when you first went through it. You'll be put back to the age you were when you first passed from one world to another.'

Riordan's eyes burned more brightly now but he didn't speak.

'Can you see now why getting through the gateway was so important to Morwenna?'

'I think so. Mother panicked about getting old and I guess the idea of freezing the ravages of time would have been appealing. But Elspeth, this all seems... well insane. Like something from a fairy story.'

They sat in silence for a while, Elspeth sensing he needed some time to process everything she had said. He relaxed back on the sofa and stared out at nothing. Elspeth focused on the ticking of the clock in the hall, the only sound to penetrate the quiet. When she could bear the silence no more, she broached the subject of Morwenna.

'What are we going to do about your mother?' she asked, trying to keep her tone even, unemotional.

Riordan looked down at the golden liquid in his glass and absently swirled it around.

'I don't know.'

His voice shook slightly as the last word cracked. He

blinked a few times, the rawness of Morwenna's deceit etched in the lines around his eyes.

'I think she needs help,' he said, turning his face towards Elspeth.

She fought the desire to demand Morwenna be removed from the house, that she be arrested, incarcerated in some grim prison cell.

'Where is she now Riordan?'

'We have some secure rooms in the top of the castle. They are comfortable. Gadsen and one of the maids are attending her needs. She can stay there until we decide what to do.'

Elspeth noted the use of 'we' and was grateful that she was being included in the discussion of Morwenna's fate.

'She should be punished for what she tried to do to Robert.'

'I know, really I do. But she's my mother and I think she's sick. Otherwise, she would never have tried to...,' he couldn't say the words now. 'She would never have tried to kill my son.'

Another first. He had referred to Robert as his son. Elspeth's hostility towards him softened. He looked like a worried father. But she doubted whether Morwenna's actions were down to madness, as Riordan wanted to believe. Morwenna was dangerous.

'I'm worried Riordan, for the safety of our son.'

'I understand that. Elspeth, I know you have no reason to trust me. I have treated you dreadfully since our marriage. I am deeply ashamed of my actions. But I will keep you and Robert safe. I promise you that.'

Elspeth shifted back in her seat, taken aback by his words, unsure of how to respond. Riordan placed his glass on the floor and turned to take her hands. His skin felt coarse as his bony fingers with their long nails circled her palms, the whisky on his breath reaching her nostrils as he drew closer.

'I want us to try to be a proper family, you, me and Robert. I know I've been an awful husband, but I want to do better. I do care for you Elspeth. I know we can be happy if you can forgive me?'

'I..I don't know,' she stammered, off balance by his declaration. 'What about your mother?'

'I'll get her some help. She can stay in her rooms until she's better.'

'You're going to keep her locked up here? At Dalengour?'

'I can keep her confined if it will make you feel safer my love?'

The endearment gave her shiver. She wasn't ready for that. His sudden change in attitude was making her dizzy and she wasn't quite sure she trusted it.

'She must stay confined and away from Robert and I until I can be totally sure she no longer presents a threat. Can you promise me that?'

'I promise. Will you give me a second chance?'

Before she could answer, voices drifted into the room from the hallway. Jenson! She heard Jenson talking to someone, a child asking where they were going.

Elspeth rose from her seat, but Riordan caught hold of her arm.

'Elspeth, where are you going? Did you hear me?'

'Yes, I heard you, and I'll be back. But now, I need to speak to Jenson.'

She snatched her arm from her husband's grasp, noting a fleeting look of anger that he quickly subdued. She could feel his eyes on her back as she walked from the room. But she didn't care. She needed to ask Jenson why he hadn't met her in the kirk.

The heavy wooden front door was coming to rest, drowning out the excited chatter of the child as it closed. She almost ran across the hall, desperate to see him. Pulling open the door, she saw Jenson settling a young girl into the carriage, a single, battered suitcase at his feet.

'Jenson!'

He turned slowly around, but his eyes did not meet hers.

'Hello Lady Darroch.'

His tone was cold, unfeeling, surprising. She looked from him to the suitcase and into the carriage door where the girl sat huddled in the corner, clutching a dirty dress around her skinny body, the bones of her shoulders jutting pointedly through the worn fabric. She looked terrified, her wide eyes fixed on Jenson as she tried to cower lower into the leather seat, afraid to be seen by Elspeth.

'What's going on Jenson? Where are you going?'

Still, he didn't look at her, but bent down and hoisted the suitcase into the carriage.

'I'm leaving. I have another position in the city.'

'Leaving? But why?'

'I think it's for the best. There's nothing for me here.'

He put his foot on the step of the carriage, ready to haul himself inside.

'Wait! Jenson, has something happened? Have you been sacked? Is it because of me?'

Stepping back, he turned to face her again.

'Why would it be about you?'

'Well, we.. you…we were supposed to meet at the kirk, but you didn't turn up. I thought you…'

She couldn't get the worlds out under the coldness of his stare.

'That's precisely why I've made up my mind to leave. I realised that my infatuation with you is just that. While ever

I believed you to be unattainable, it made you more alluring. But, this afternoon, when I realised you were willing to risk your life at Dalengour to be with me, the shine went off the rose. I realised I didn't want that. I didn't want you.'

Elspeth couldn't believe what she was hearing. This wasn't the Jenson she had known all her life. He had never been cruel.

'I don't believe you.'

'Suit yourself. Now if you'll excuse me Lady Darroch, I need to be on my way.'

He swung himself into the carriage. Pulling the door behind him, Jenson settled beside the frightened child, cradling her in his arms as she nestled closer to him. He banged on the roof and the driver raised his whip.

'Wait!' Elspeth shouted, raising her hand to halt the driver.

Jenson leaned out of the window, looking agitated at being delayed.

'Jenson, please! I know you aren't telling me everything. Please don't go. I have so much to tell you.'

'Elspeth, understand this. I have no desire to stay here or to hear whatever you have to say. I just want to be away from Dalengour, away from you.'

As he spoke, his eyes still did not meet hers. He was looking anywhere except into her face, but his voice was softer now. She didn't understand, but something about the way he was behaving didn't feel real. She placed her hands on the carriage window, trying to stall his departure.

'Who's this?' she asked nodding in the direction of the girl who was trying to conceal herself behind Jenson.

'Her name is Gwen.'

He didn't elaborate and Elspeth began to feel irritated at his obvious desire to be away from her and his reluctance to tell her the truth. She tried to peer around him to see the girl, maybe to introduce herself, but he seemed determined to bar her view. She drew back from the carriage, feeling beaten and annoyed. If he wanted to leave, she couldn't stop him. Jenson disappeared from the window, and she thought he was going to leave without even saying goodbye. But suddenly, he reappeared and beckoned her closer.

'Elspeth, please be careful won't you?'

This was the Jenson she knew. The golden flecks in his hazel eyes caught in the fading light as he looked at her for the first time since she had come outside. His finger brushed over her hand, his touch barely noticeable. She looked at him, imploringly, trying to encourage him to say whatever was on his mind. Instead, he settled back into the carriage and this time, she did not try to stop the driver as he brought the whip down on the horses. Inside the carriage, Jenson clung onto Gwen, trying to conceal the tears running down his cheeks as he left the woman he loved.

Elspeth strutted back to the house, anger welling up from within. She wasn't sure who she was angrier with. Riordan because she suspected he had something to do with Jenson's leaving? Or Jenson? He seemed to have given up. He had left her. She obviously didn't mean that much to him after all. Or was she angry at herself? Had she tried hard enough to stop him, to find out what was going on?

As she reached the hall, her heart was pounding in her chest, the muscles in her face tense as she pressed her lips against her teeth to stem the tide of tears waiting to break free. She had other things to deal with now. Mourning Jenson's departure would wait. Riordan was the current priority. She must go back into the library now and talk to her husband.

Damn that infernal ticking! The sound of the clock

seemed to accompany every moment when her actions changed the course of her life. Here was another. What was she going to do about Riordan?

Elspeth looked into the hall mirror and ran her hands under her eyes to wipe away the signs of sorrow. She smoothed her hair and gazed at the reflection staring back. Taking a few deep breaths, she closed her eyes and pushed away the anger. When she opened them again, her mind was empty, blank. It matched how she felt inside. Empty. Blank.

She walked back into the library. Riordan stood up as she entered, his tall, angular body wrapped in his customary black made him look almost skeletal silhouetted against the dim lamps now burning on each side of the barren fireplace. He cast a shadow across the floor that stretched to her feet, shrouding her in darkness as he approached. The familiar sense of being trapped, like a fly in a spider's web threatened her. She wouldn't let it in. If she was going to stay here, stay with the man she had married, she wouldn't feel like the victim, resolved to her fate. She would only stay on her own terms.

The ticking of the clock penetrated the silence. Her decision was made.

'Riordan, I will stay here with you for now. I made a commitment to you when we married, and I am a woman of honour. However, if there is even the smallest sign of you returning to your old ways, I will leave and take Robert with me.'

Riordan crossed the space that remained between them and gathered Elspeth into his arms. His show of affection seemed almost rehearsed. She let her arms slip guardedly around Riordan's bony body, allowing him to hold her. His embrace tightened in response to her acquiescence, the pressure on her body becoming uncomfortable. She fidgeted and he released her. She immediately stepped away, not enjoying his nearness. Her memories of his physical attentions in the past, too raw.

'You've made me so happy Elspeth!'

The words did not resonate with happiness. But maybe she was being unfair. He had never been emotionally demonstrative. She searched his sallow face, looking for a flicker of genuine emotion. His eyes were brighter than usual as they peered out of their narrow slits, a smile playing at the corners of his bloodless lips.

'We can start again Elspeth. I'll be a good husband to you. I promise I'll do my very best to make you happy.

As he gushed, Elspeth couldn't help but feel she would never be truly happy with him. But maybe she could get to feeling content. If that was going to happen, she had to commit whole-heartedly to being Elspeth Darroch.

'I hope you abide by your words Riordan. Really I do.'

She smiled weakly and he seemed reinforced by her expression.

'I would like to understand more about Nethergar, if you'll tell me?'

Suspicion poked her in the back. She shook it off quickly. She needed to trust him if her marriage was going to work. After all, he had turned on the one woman Elspeth thought he truly loved to save their son.

'I will. But not tonight. It's been a long and tiring day. I want to go and say goodnight to Robert and then go to bed myself.'

'Of course. I completely understand.'

He leant forward and brushed his hard lips briefly against her cheek, then stepped back. She was relived he wasn't coming in for another embrace.

'Goodnight Riordan.'

'Goodnight Elspeth. Sleep well.'

She backed away, keeping her eyes on her husband, trying to reconcile the uneasiness still seeping into her consciousness. Tomorrow, she would try to put the past behind her. But for now, she was too tired for that.

RIORDAN WATCHED ELSPETH'S BACK AS SHE LEFT the room. He moved to the door to see her traverse the stone floor and mount the stairs to the nursery. A sardonic smile twisted his lips. He went back into the library and refilled his glass with whisky, knocking it back in one, before breaking into smug laughter. It had been too easy.

Replacing his empty glass on the table, he left the library and followed in Elspeth's wake up the stairs. He didn't stop on the first floor where the nursery was, instead heading to another staircase in the east tower hidden behind a locked door disguised by wooden panelling. He took an ancient wrought iron key from the dresser on the landing and opened the door revealing a dark passage climbing upwards. Dalengour was always a few degrees colder than the outside temperature, but here, the chill air also carried a staleness reminiscent of a lost space never inhabited by the living.

Closing the door behind him and plunging the passage into total darkness, he began to feel his way up the twisting staircase. He quickened his pace, his eyes becoming accustomed to the gloom. Light from a slitted window illuminated his way as he turned the next corner. The staircase continued twisting upwards, but he stepped out onto the first landing and crossed to a door, the only feature of this colourless space. Pausing to catch his breath, he listened for sounds coming from within. All was quiet. She was alone.

Riordan thrust open the door and came face to face with his mother. For a second, they stared at each other blankly. Then Riordan could contain himself no longer and a broad grin spread across his sour face, reaching his beady eyes.

'Well?' Morwenna asked sharply. 'Tell me?'

'Putty in my hands Mother. She fell for it hook, line and sinker!'

He laughed now, arrogance at his success spilling over.

'Are you sure?'

'I'm sure. But I think I have some way to go before I earn her trust completely. We have agreed to talk about Nethergar tomorrow.'

'Talk!' Morwenna shrieked. 'You mean she hasn't agreed to take you there?'

'Patience Mother. Elspeth is not so easily won over. I'll need to prove my loyalty first. But I'm confident she'll take me there soon.'

'Soon! Soon! And in the meantime, I suppose you expect me to stay locked up in here?'

Morwenna raised her arms to indicate the surroundings that were not exactly terrible. There were two adjoining rooms decorated in pale, summery colours that seemed out of character for Dalengour. The rooms were simply furnished with stocky, oak pieces and bright textiles. There were no dead animals here, or portraits of dour ancestors. The walls were adorned with landscapes in gilt-edged frames and tapestries of flowers and trees. Whoever had decorated these rooms had very different taste from Morwenna Darroch.

'You must stay here mother. Elspeth will never come around to me if I allow you to roam free so soon. It won't be for long I'm sure.'

'It'd better not be!' Morwenna said waspishly. 'I want to get to Nethergar and soon.'

'I promise, a few days at most.'

He smiled again and Morwenna's ire faded a little.

'You got rid of Jenson?'

'Yes. He left a while ago. I had to be careful though. Elspeth saw him leaving. But he played his part well.'

Riordan sat down on a dusky pink chair, throwing his arms across the back and crossing his legs.

'What are you doing?' Morwenna asked staring hard at her son.

'What do you mean? I'm sitting down.'

'Don't you think your time would be better spent trying to woo your wife rather than sitting up here with me?

Riordan sighed. He knew better than to answer her back. He rose and smoothed his shirt.

'Very well. I'll bid you goodnight then.'

He left the room, his movements tracked by the feline eyes of his mother. He descended the staircase, locking the door to the tower and replacing the key in the dresser draw on his way out. He didn't go to Elspeth. He knew if he turned up in her chambers tonight, it would undo all the good work he had done so far. And anyway, he had no wish to feign the desire to be in her company or her bed.

CHAPTER 11

Meeting of Enemies

RIORDAN STARED UP AT THE LARGE STAINED-GLASS window in the kirk.

'I haven't been in here since I was a boy,' he said to Elspeth, craning his neck to stare into the face of the woman in the centre of the frame.

'And this is the gateway?

He turned towards Elspeth who was trying desperately to convince herself taking him to Nethergar was the right thing to do. It had been two weeks since Riordan had turned on his mother and since then, he had been as good as his word. A model husband and father. Kind, caring and supportive. Elspeth had been surprised to find herself talking to him more and even enjoying his company.

'This is how I got through to Nethergar the last time, so yes, I think so.'

'How do you open it?'

'I'm not really sure. Last time, it just opened when I touched it.'

They stood staring at the leaded window, the midday winter sun adding vibrancy to the coloured panes and throwing dappled patches of light that shimmered with reds and blues as they danced on the stone floor.

Elspeth had agreed to take Riordan through the gateway after an enjoyable evening where he had sat attentively, listening as she talked eagerly about her family – about her father and the story Nerissa had told her about the Larimore's feud with the Darrochs. Never once had Riordan asked to go to Nethergar. He had never pushed and had even seemed reluctant to go when she mentioned it might help him to understand if he experienced it. In her mind, taking him to see Nethergar was a way of helping him believe what she knew must sound like a tall tale.

She hadn't seen anything of Morwenna Darroch since that day in the kirk. Riordan had hired a nurse to care for his mother, who remained confined to rooms in the east tower. Doctors were frequent visitors, employed to soothe Morwenna's ills. But as Elspeth deliberately avoided the east tower, she rarely encountered any of them.

Riordan never discussed his mother with Elspeth, her continued presence at Dalengour being a silent bone of contention. It seemed to Elspeth he didn't want anything to disturb the fragile peace that had developed between them. On the occasions when Morwenna's name came up in conversation, it was usually in relation to Nethergar. Riordan told Elspeth that his mother's insane monologues were always about the gateway and returning home. He seemed to be struggling with deciphering the truth in the ramblings of Morwenna's troubled mind.

Now they stood together, about to cross in to Nethergar. Although it had been Elspeth's idea, the feeling of closeness to her husband that had developed as they talked the previous evening had now waned, and she was less sure about taking him through the gateway.

Riordan sensed her hesitance.

'Elspeth, are you sure you want to do this? We can leave and go back to the house if you like?'

She looked at him blankly, her mind agonising over the right thing to do. She could walk away from here now. He wasn't pushing her. But she desperately wanted to go back and see Nerissa again. She wanted to know more about the powers she possessed. If she could learn to control her gifts, develop them more by visiting Nethergar, she would feel safer. Riordan was playing the dutiful husband at the moment and Morwenna was contained, getting help, but it might not always be that way. She didn't trust this new life. If she were more powerful, she could protect herself, protect Robert. Nerissa was the answer.

'No, we should go through,' she said with more certainty than she felt.

Elspeth stepped towards the window and reached out her hand to touch the glass. It felt warm under her fingers, the winter sun imbibing the usually cold surface with heat. As her hand traced the leaded outline of the woman's hand, the glass melted away to reveal a molten lake of silver that rippled under her touch. Riordan's eyes widened as he witnessed the change in the window, the reflection from the mirrored glass echoed in their greenness.

'I..I don't believe it. It's true. There is a gateway here!'

Elspeth laughed.

'I knew that you didn't really believe me!'

'Well, I wasn't sure. It seemed so...so unbelievable.'

He stepped towards the viscous surface lapping against the frame as the tide within appeared to ebb and flow.

'Can I touch it?' he asked uncertainly.

'Of course.'

Elspeth watched Riordan tentatively raise his bony hand to the glass. He dipped one long finger into the liquid.

'It feels strange. Like oil but it leaves no trace,' he said pulling his hand back to examine his hand.

'Are you ready to step through?' Elspeth asked.

'Yes, I think so.'

There was an uncharacteristic tremor in his voice as he reached for Elspeth's hand and laced his fingers through hers. She was still unaccustomed to his touch. Although they had developed a friendship over the last two weeks, there had been no intimacy between them. Elspeth had been in no rush to enter back into a full marriage with Riordan, his treatment of her in the bedroom still painful in her memory. But today, she did not baulk at his touch. She found it surprisingly comforting.

'Wait,' Riordan said sharply, turning to face her. 'What do I have to do?'

'Nothing, just walk through with me.'

'Right. Ready when you are then.'

Together, they stepped into the fluid surface, emerging a moment later in another kirk. Riordan dropped her hand and spun round to look back through the window. His eyes were sparkling with excitement as he gazed from Elspeth to the scene they had left behind.

'That's it? We're here? In Nethergar?'

His words tumbled out as he began staring around the kirk. He placed his nose close to the shimmering surface of the mirror and his pale eyes narrowed as he peered back through.

'That's Cairndarroch?' he asked pointing through and glaring wide-eyed at Elspeth.

'Yes, you can still see back into our world until the gateway closes.'

Riordan contemplated this for a moment, his lips pressed tightly together, hands on his hips.

'Can we go outside?'

He reminded Elspeth of a young boy, his eagerness to explore this new place rather endearing.

'Yes, of course we can look around,' she responded. 'I want to see if I can find Nerissa. There are so many things I want to ask her.'

They headed towards the door, Riordan's head still spinning as he tried to take in everything around him. The brightness as they stepped outside caused them both to squint until their eyes became accustomed to the light. Elspeth was again taken aback by the vividness of the forest clearing. The lush green pines mixed with the autumnal yellows and browns of fading plants. The dried husks of thistles adorned with fluffy clouds of white seed heads surrounded the kirk, regularly interspersed with the vibrant red of rose hips still glistening where they had been caressed by the damp night.

Riordan seemed mesmerised, casting his eyes from one side to the other as he walked across the mossy floor. She had never seen him like this, so interested, his whole body resonating with excitement.

'Its beautiful!' he exclaimed. Everything seems so much brighter, so much more alive.'

'That's because it is in a way. All living things are more vital in Nethergar, more alive I suppose. It's the energy you can sense that restored me to health when I last came here.'

Riordan shot her a sideways glance as she referred to her illness inflicted by his mother, then lowered his eyes quickly. He didn't speak for a moment, but curiosity got the better of him. He started to walk around the clearing again, touching the gnarled bark of trees, running his hands along the lush pine branches and kicking his way through the decaying ferns tanging around his feet.

'Come on,' Elspeth said. Nerissa's cottage is this way.'

He joined her and they began to head towards the tree line. The sound of rustling coming from a short distance away stopped them. They turned quickly to see a young boy emerge from behind the kirk.

'You're back!' he shouted, running across to Elspeth.

'Darian! How very nice to see you again.'

'I knew you'd come back. I told Nerissa I'd wait for you. I've been coming here every day. It's been ages!'

'I'm sorry it took so long,' Elspeth said, smiling at the babbling boy.

He was as dishevelled as the last time she saw him, his feet still bare and his good quality clothes splatted in mud and soil. Riordan cleared his throat behind her.

'I'm sorry,' she said, steeping aside to allow Riordan to join the conversation.

'Riordan, this is Darian McGillvaray. He lives in a house close by here. He was a great help to me last time I visited Nethergar.'

Riordan stepped forwards and bent low to the boy, his spindly arm outstretched.

'Hello. Nice to meet you Darian McGillvaray. I'm Riordan Darroch.'

Darian didn't take the offered hand. His eyes rounded like

saucers at the sound of the Darroch name and Elspeth realised he must know something about the events of the past.

'You aren't welcome here,' he said defiantly, and Elspeth was amused by the set of his jaw as he drew himself up to his full, if diminutive, height.

Darian peered around Riordan to get a clear view of Elspeth.

'Why haven't you brought the other man back? I liked him better.'

Riordan straightened up and turned to Elspeth.

'Other man?'

Elspeth flushed.

'Jenson Tanner was with me last time I visited,' she said without meeting Riordan's gaze.

'Jenson? You brought Jenson here?'

Now she looked up and glimpsed warning signs flashing in his eyes. Guilt flooded her momentarily, quickly displaced by anger. He had no right to feel aggrieved that Jenson had been here. She felt her back stiffen and she met his glower head on.

'Yes, he found me unconscious in the kirk,' she said, staring pointedly at Riordan. 'It was after he revived me that the gateway opened. I was sure it was the right thing to come through immediately, but I wasn't strong enough. So, Jenson helped me.'

Her eyes flashed with a determination not to be cowed by him. He sensed her resolve and backed down, returning a smile to his face if not to his eyes. Riordan turned back to address Darian.

'Perhaps you can give me a chance young man? I assure you, I'm not the monster you might think I am just because my surname is Darroch.'

Darian fixed his amber eyes on Riordan, the golden irises catching the sunlight filtering weakly through the trees. He raised one eyebrow quizzically, cocking his head as he considered Riordan's words. He didn't speak for a few seconds, but then seemed to accept the stranger's assurance of non-monsterness.

'I suppose I can,' he said pushing his balled-up fists into his waist. 'If you promise to be nice to Nerissa.'

'I promise,' said Riordan with a smile Elspeth could see was forced. The discovery that Jenson had been through the gateway still hung like a cloud between them, the superimposed joviality pretentious.

Darian spoke to Elspeth.

'Are you going to see Nerissa now?'

'I think so, If she's home.'

'She is,' he said simply. 'I have to go home for lunch or my mother will kill me for being late. Although I think she will kill me anyway,' he said looking guiltily at his grubby white shirt, untucked from the dark blue shorts, the hem torn with finger-shaped smears down the front where he had rubbed his dirty hands.

'Bye Elspeth,' he shouted turning to run back the way he had come. 'Come back soon!'

She watched as the boy disappeared, then turned her attention back to Riordan. He was gazing after Darian, his eyes filled with something like animosity as the child went out of sight. Sensing Elspeth's eyes upon him, Riordan came out of his reverie, plastering a grin back on his sallow face.

'Shall we go?'

He extended his hand for her to take. Now, the gesture felt far too familiar. The interaction with Darian had unnerved her, shaken her trust in him. She ignored Riordan's outstretched hand and walked ahead into the forest towards Kirkholm Cottage.

Nerissa Larimore was standing in the open doorway as they approached, as if she knew they were coming. Her blue eyes watched them intently as they walked down the path out of the forest towards the small cottage nestled between the rolling hills. Her wild red hair blew across her face, catching in the gentle breeze. She pushed it away, holding it down with one hand and extending the other in greeting. A warm smile curved her lips and she pulled Elspeth in to kiss her cheek.

'I'm so glad to see you. I'd almost given up on you coming back!'

'I know it's been a while. Things at home have been… difficult,' Elspeth said, returning her smile.

Nerissa peered over Elspeth's shoulder to look at Riordan who was loitering a few feet behind, waiting for an introduction.

'Who's this?'

Elspeth couldn't stop a fleeting expression of concern from clouding her face and it didn't go unnoticed by Nerissa. But there was nothing she could do about it now. She steeled herself, her heart pounding a little more quickly. She stepped aside to let Riordan approach.

'This is Riordan… Darroch.'

She kept her eyes fixed firmly on Nerissa's watching blue eyes. Riordan stepped forward, but before he could speak, Nerissa whirled around to glare angrily at Elspeth.

'Darroch? You brought a Darroch here?'

Nerissa's words dripped with incredulity, red patches burning on her cheeks as her easily stirred hostility gathered. Elspeth dropped her eyes, fixating on her boot laces, her hands clasped tightly in front of her.

'It's very nice to meet you Miss Larimore,' Riordan said ignoring Nerissa's truculence, his twisted smile not reaching his eyes.

Slowly, Nerissa turned her head away from Elspeth to look at him. Her face was completely unreadable, but Elspeth could sense fury prickling under her skin.

'You're not welcome here.'

Riordan looked stunned at the hostility in her tone, her body language aloof and unyielding. For a moment, they stood glaring at each other, Nerissa's face impassive, Riordan fighting to control his irritation at her belligerence. It was Riordan who broke the impasse.

'I've heard that a lot since I arrived here and I can understand why you feel that way, really I do. Elspeth told me what my family did to you, the pain they caused. But I assure you, I'm not like the Darroch's you remember. I have no desire to hurt you or anyone.'

Nerissa did not look convinced. She looked towards Elspeth for confirmation, but something was making it difficult for her to corroborate her husband's character. The nagging doubts left by his reaction to Darian McGillvaray when they first arrived lingered, making her question her judgement in bringing him here. Riordan was looking at her now, expecting her to offer some support for him. Elspeth met Nerissa's gaze.

'Riordan and I have been married for eighteen months Nerissa,' Elspeth said, realising this was not exactly the resounding confirmation of him being a good person and unlike the Darrochs of old. But it was the best she could muster.

Nerissa obviously didn't think this sufficient either as she continued to glare at Elspeth coldly. Riordan's pale green eyes were also boring into her, expecting her to say something more, to elaborate on the goodness of his character.

'We have a son together and he has been a good husband and father of late.'

This again seemed weak, but it was all she had. She couldn't stand there and lie to Nerissa. She couldn't espouse the genuineness of Riordan's claims because until two weeks ago, she had thought him a monster. Although he had been kind and attentive recently, she had seen the ghost of the old Riordan when Darian had crossed their path.

Riordan realised Elspeth was not going to offer him any more support and shot her a disappointed look.

'I really am sorry for everything my family put the Larimores through in the past,' Riordan said, taking the matter of his character into his own hands. 'But it is just that, all in the past. I am not one of the Darrochs who hurt you and I hope you will give me a chance to prove we are not all bad?'

'Are you the Darroch who hurt Elspeth?' Nerissa asked acerbically.

'No, but I'm ashamed to say my mother was.'

Riordan looked down in a sort of feigned shame. Nerissa shot Elspeth a questioning look.

'It's true. It was my mother-in-law who poisoned me and later tried to kill our son to get through the gateway to Nethergar. Riordan saved him from her.'

This part at least was true. She could vouch confidently for Riordan's role in rescuing Robert and dealing with Morwenna.

'My mother is ill. She's now confined at Dalengour and is receiving help. Elspeth and Robert are now safe from her.'

Riordan directed a sickly smile towards Elspeth.

'I care for my wife and son a great deal and will always protect them.'

Nerissa cocked her head to one side.

'Care? Not love?'

Elspeth caught her breath.

'Of course I love them,' Riordan said, challenging Nerissa's glare.

This was the first time Riordan had ever said he loved Elspeth or Robert. He had been a better husband over the last two weeks, but Elspeth would never label what had developed between them as love. Friendship was even a stretch for her. She still didn't trust him and no matter how hard she tried, she couldn't forget his cruelty towards her when they had first wed. That they had come to respect each other was as far as she would go.

Her surprise at Riordan's declaration of love must have been written on her face as Nerissa was now staring at her, a wry smile twitching the corners of her mouth.

'You'd better come inside then,' Nerissa said, retreating into the kitchen at Kirkholm Cottage.

Riordan gestured for Elspeth to go ahead of him, and they followed her into the house. Nerissa was filling the kettle and lighting the stove as they entered.

'Sit down,' Nerissa said, indicating the wooden chairs around the table.

Elspeth noted the plant she had revived on her last visit sitting on the windowsill, its colour and vibrancy stark against the rest of the greyscale kitchen. Nerissa placed tea in front of both Riordan and Elspeth, then came to join them, still eyeing Riordan warily.

'Tell me what's happened since you were last here then? What's happened to Jenson?'

Elspeth felt Riordan stiffen at her side at the mention of Jenson's name.

'Jenson has left Dalengour,' she said quickly. 'He was offered a position in the south and felt that was the best place for him.'

'I see,' Nerissa said nodding slowly.

Elspeth knew Nerissa didn't believe this as the whole truth, her pause loaded with knowing. She didn't press though, turning to the other matter.

'What's this about your mother-in-law being the one who poisoned you?'

'It seems you were right. Morwenna did know about Nethergar. She wanted to get here.'

'And she was willing to kill you and your son for it?'

Riordan leaned forward agitatedly.

'You must understand, she isn't in her right mind. My mother isn't a monster. She would never hurt anyone normally!'

Nerissa gave him only a cursory glance, then focussed back on Elspeth.

'Is that how you see it?'

Elspeth hadn't expected to find herself defending Morwenna.

'I…I don't know,' she stammered. 'I'm not sure I ever knew Morwenna when she wasn't…ill.'

Nerissa was reading between the lines and whatever she saw seemed to confirm her thoughts.

'Well, I'll give him the benefit of the doubt for now,' she said as if Riordan wasn't there. 'But I don't trust the Darrochs and neither should you.'

Nerissa shot Riordan a pointed stare and he fidgeted uncomfortably. Elspeth was eager to break the uneasy silence and move away from the discomfiting topic of Morwenna Darroch.

'I came back because I want to learn about the Larimore gifts. I want to explore what I can do. I was hoping you would teach me.'

Nerissa took a slow gulp of her tea, keeping her eyes fixed on Elspeth over the rim of the cup. For a long time, she didn't speak, replacing the tea on the table and looking into the brown liquid as if searching for answers there. Eventually, she raised her eyes and looked earnestly into Elspeth's face.

'I will teach you, if only to make sure you can protect yourself against them.'

She cocked her head again towards Riordan but didn't look at him. She seemed to have decided to ignore him now. Elspeth glanced at her husband who looked angry, the insinuation that he was not to be trusted irking him. She reached out a hand under the table and placed it briefly on his bony knee, wanting to keep him from speaking out and angering Nerissa rather than with the intention of offering reassurance to him.

'When can we start?' she asked.

'Now, if you want to?' Nerissa said, leaning forward, eyes fixed firmly on Elspeth.

'Yes, yes please,' Elspeth replied, a feeling of excitement rising in her stomach.

Nerissa pushed her tea away, her chair scraping on the wooden floor as she suddenly shoved it back to stand.

'Come, let's go into the garden then.'

CHAPTER 12

A Garden of Flowers

ELSPETH FOLLOWED AS NERISSA LEFT THE KITCHEN
and walked around to the back of the house, Riordan lagging
behind them. They approached a high stone wall with a
decrepit wooden gate, barely hanging on its hinges on one
side. Nerissa pushed it open and Elspeth caught her breath.

'Come on in then,' Nerissa said brusquely. Elspeth
stepped into the garden, wild and alive with colour, life
shouting its presence from every corner. It was so unlike the
rest of Kirkholm and the person who lived there. Nerissa
went to great pains to ensure she went unnoticed, her home
blending into the backdrop, plain and uninteresting. But this
was awash with unseasonal vibrancy and brightness. A patch
of summer dropped onto a quilt of autumn.

Layers of pinks and purples lined the walls, grading to
white as they approached the edge of flower borders. A
gravel path, in danger of being overwhelmed by the

burgeoning floral displays of blue and yellow blooms, weaved its way between the plants. No part of the garden was untouched by colour. Stems fought for space, stretching upwards to bathe in unexpected golden light, their heads swaying as a gentle breeze wafted through the flower beds.

Elspeth's mouth dropped open. She spun around, staring at the untamed beauty of the place, sensing the energy that reverberated through the air here.

'This is wonderful Nerissa! What a beautiful garden! How... the flowers? The weather?'

Nerissa laughed at Elspeth's ineloquence.

'There are some perks to being a Larimore Elspeth! This is where I love to be, where I feel most at home.'

Elspeth noted the sense of calm, of peace, that settled on Nerissa as she looked around her garden. A hint of a smile touched her lips and she looked genuinely happy, her red hair blowing gently around her face. It was as if she belonged in this place, surrounded by nature, at home in the feral majesty of the garden. Nerissa looked like she was part of it – the part that gave it meaning.

The opposite was true of Riordan. He stood stiffly in the entrance, a dim, grey slur on the vivid landscape. He seemed reluctant to step further in, almost afraid that his dull monochrome palette would become sullied by the colours that surrounded him. Elspeth watched as he cast narrowed eyes around the garden, no appreciation of the beauty evident on his face. There was, however, something in his expression, something Elspeth couldn't name but that quickly dulled her own wonder at the garden.

She felt eyes upon her and turned quickly away from her scrutiny of Riordan. With a smile fixed on her lips, she met Nerissa's gaze, whose serenity and calm from moments ago was now replaced with concern as she watched Elspeth from beneath a furrowed brow.

'What's wrong Elspeth?'

'Oh nothing,' she said with a feigned lightness. 'I'm just feeling a little overwhelmed by this place.'

Elspeth twirled around, looking at the garden again but not seeing. Her mind was still on Riordan, trying to discern what was going on behind the impassive expression. She couldn't help casting a furtive look towards her husband, a look that didn't go unnoticed as she came back to face Nerissa Larimore.

Neither woman spoke, their eyes locked, Nerissa's stare filled with questions. Elspeth's heart began to pound loudly in her chest, and she prayed Nerissa would not voice the thoughts she could almost hear parading through the perceptive woman's mind. Time seemed to slow, an understanding springing up in their silence.

Nerissa broke her stare allowing Elspeth to exhale.

'Right then, let's see what you can do,' Nerissa said, her tone practical but the look she gave Elspeth telling her there would be another conversation about Riordan Darroch in the future.

Nerissa moved to the centre of a lawned area where a large flowerbed brimmed with red and white petals towering over lush, green grass. Closing her eyes, she raised her arms out to both sides, welcoming something into her embrace. The air seemed to shiver around her, like she had entered a heat haze.

Elspeth watched intently as golden light formed in Nerissa's palms, stretching out towards the flowers until their colourful blooms were encased in a cage of shimmering energy. The movement in the stems as the breeze wafted gently through the garden stilled, and the floral display seemed trapped in a moment of time, immortalised in the amber glow. Slowly the colours faded, the red and green hues leeching out until only browns of desiccation and decay remained. The stems shrivelled, leaving empty husks, skeletal imprints of what had once been the vitality of life.

Nerissa opened her eyes and beckoned Elspeth to her side.

'Now you wake them up again.'

'I don't know how.'

'Just the same as you did with the plant in the kitchen on your last visit. Sense the life around you and draw on it. Fill the flowers back up with the energy you feel.'

Elspeth looked doubtful. This seemed a much bigger task than her previous, minor success. With a deep breath, she closed her eyes and imagined the flowers in her mind's eye. Nothing happened. She couldn't feel anything.

'I can't. There's nothing there,' she said petulantly, flicking her eyes open again, her brows drawn together, looking imploringly at her mentor.

'You give up too easily. Try again,' Nerissa said sternly.

Elspeth sighed heavily attempting to regain her focus although her confidence ebbed. She closed her eyes and imagined the flowers before her, saw them as they were before Nerissa had taken away their colour, visualised them as she wanted them to be. Her eyelids wrinkled as she closed them more tightly, her lips pursed together, her shoulders rising to hold in her breath.

The sounds of the garden began to fade away and silence surrounded her. She felt isolated, alone. Just her and the flowers. As she stood cocooned in her own concentration, she felt a tingling in her fingertips. Then a warmth spread up her arms, across her chest and face. She exhaled slowly, opening her eyes tentatively to let in the golden brightness, squinting until her pupils adjusted to the luminescence. She saw nothing but light enveloping her and extending to shroud the withered petals and leaves before her. Nothing else mattered. There was only the energy and the decaying flowers.

Elspeth felt in control now. Nothing from her surroundings disturbed her thoughts. She began to push energy into the flowers, watching as they filled like sponges taking in air after they had been squeezed. She seemed able to command the life force that was slowly being absorbed by the plants, turning the arid leaves green again, plump and lush, awakening them from their slumber.

Elspeth was transfixed as buds began to form and petals unfurled, reaching upwards towards the sun. Still, she pushed. The flowers grew taller, with more and more stems appearing through the damp earth, until there was no more room for new blooms to find space. In the distance, she heard a voice coming to her from beyond the light. She couldn't see the speaker but somehow, she could feel them, their words reaching her conscious mind some other way than by sound.

'The earth is dry. The flowers need water.'

It was Nerissa's voice. Elspeth didn't need telling what to do. She could feel moisture on her skin. She began to draw water droplets carried on the air into a mist that hovered above the newly grown flowers, forming a cloud that gradually darkened to an angry grey. Her mind condensed the water vapour until it could be no longer contained. Rain began to fall heavily, like a sudden summer shower laden with rumblings of thunder as the cloud rolled.

Elspeth watched as the flowers drooped a little, becoming leaden with water, droplets catching on their bright petals before running in rivulets to fall onto the earth below. The soil turned from brown to almost black as it became sodden, the air filled with heady scents as the smell of the garden mixed with damp earth.

'That will do.'

Again, the voice echoed inside her and she let go her hold on the captured energy. The rain stopped, the cloud dissipating with the fading golden light. All was still again. Blinking, she turned to look at Nerissa, whose broad smile greeted her. Elspeth looked back at the flowerbed to see the blooms waving full of vigour, dripping with water, the rest of the garden dry. Looking back at Nerissa, she broke into a grin that spread to become an excited laugh.

'I did it!' she said breathlessly. 'I really did it!'

Nerissa stepped forward and took Elspeth's hands in her own. She stared intently into her face, her smile fading. The scrutiny made Elspeth panic.

'What? What is it? Did I do something wrong?'

Nerissa's voice wavered, her brows drawing in to underline her worry.

'No, not at all,' she said quietly, emotion causing her voice to break, tears pooling at the corners of her cornflower blue eyes.

'Elspeth, you're amazing!'

Riordan's shrill voice pierced their reverie. Elspeth had almost forgotten he was there. Unnoticed, he had left the safety of the garden entrance and was striding purposively across to where the two women stood. Nerissa dropped Elspeth's hands and turned away as Riordan placed his hands on his wife's shoulders and pulled her into a perfunctory embrace. Elspeth did not return the gesture, her posture stiff as he clasped her firmly to him.

She found herself surprised to be this close to him and squirmed to get away. He held her too tightly and she couldn't extricate herself without it being an obvious rebuttal. She tried to relax into his hold. Over his shoulder, she could see Nerissa, still facing away from her but raising a hand to wipe away tears from her eyes.

After what felt like an age, Riordan released Elspeth, still professing her brilliance.

'That was so wonderful Elspeth! How did you do it? Can you do anything else?'

The words tumbled out of him ecstatically, his eyes dancing with fervency.

'I…I don't know,' Elspeth replied absently. She didn't want to talk to him now.

'Nerissa, are you alright?'

Elspeth pulled away from Riordan, walking over to where Nerissa stood.

'Nerissa?'

On hearing her name, she turned around, sniffing back unshed tears and composing herself. Elspeth felt Riordan behind her as he sidled over, and noted Nerissa's distrustful glance in his direction. Fixing her gaze back on Elspeth, her eyes still shone with tears languishing just below the surface.

'He's right. You are amazing. You're so much more powerful than I was before I inherited the gifts of my ancestors.'

'What do you mean – inherited the gifts? Elspeth already has some gifts from what I saw.'

Riordan couldn't keep the derisive note from his voice. Nerissa pointedly ignored him. An awkwardness sprang up, the tense silence permeated by Riordan's breathing as he fought to contain his irascible temper. To break the mood, Elspeth spoke.

'I don't know about being more powerful, but I do know I don't want your gifts if it means you have to die to give them.'

Riordan fidgeted, questions burning on his lips.

'There will come a time when you'll inherit my powers Elspeth. Neither of us can change that. My life will end, and I don't fear death. But before then, you must gain control of the gifts you already have,' Nerissa said. 'Then I know you'll be safe.'

She shot a stinging look at Riordan who balled his fists. Elspeth watched her husband fight some inner battle, eventually cementing a weak smile on his pale lips.

'I hope you don't think Elspeth is in any danger from me? I love my wife Miss Larimore and I assure you, I'll always protect her.'

There it was again. A statement of love. Elspeth felt an inexplicable shiver run down her spine. Nerissa did not answer. Her keen eyes stared coldly at Riordan but there was no suggestion of a verbal response forthcoming. The air felt suddenly heavy, hostile. Eager to put the conversation onto safer ground, Elspeth cleared her throat.

'Can I try something else?'

Nerissa somewhat reluctantly brought her attention back to Elspeth.

'I think you've done enough for today. Come back tomorrow and we'll begin your training in earnest.'

This seemed like a dismissal.

'Alright. I'll try to get back tomorrow afternoon,' Elspeth said, feeling disappointed but eager to get Riordan away from here. 'Thank you for today.'

Elspeth lent forwards to kiss Nerissa on the cheek, taking her hands and squeezing them in hope that the gesture communicated everything she wanted to say. Nerissa nodded, keeping her lips tightly closed as if afraid to let herself speak. Riordan also kept silent, giving Nerissa a cursory bow. He backed away, exiting the walled garden and turning towards the path back into the forest. He halted, waiting for Elspeth, too close for her to say anything more without being overheard.

'Until tomorrow then,' Elspeth said reluctantly, turning her back on Nerissa to follow Riordan.

They walked in silence for a few minutes, Elspeth lost in her own thoughts about what she had done, Riordan carefully watching his wife. As they approached the tree line, Riordan turned back to cast a look over his shoulder at Kirkholm Cottage. Elspeth found herself following his gaze and saw the door closing as Nerissa Larimore went back inside. No longer observed, Riordan lurched forwards and hugged Elspeth again. She was taken aback by his sudden show of affection and immediately tensed.

'Oh Elspeth,' he said stepping back but retaining his hold on the top of her arms. 'You were so amazing!'

'So you said before,' she said stiffly, looking into his face now alight with genuine pleasure.

'But it's true! I didn't think anything like that was possible. It's the most fantastic thing I've ever witnessed.'

Elspeth eyed him warily. She didn't trust the reasons for his obvious enthusiasm. Riordan sensed her guardedness, releasing his hold and stepping away. They continued towards the forest, Riordan holding his tongue until they were surrounded by the gnarled bark of the ancient pines.

'How did it feel? The power?'

Elspeth pondered the question.

'It's difficult to explain. I'm not sure I think of it as power. It's like I could sense the energy around me. I could direct it, put it where I wanted it to be.'

'That certainly gives you power over other living things.'

Elspeth didn't like this idea, not how Riordan was expressing it. Having power 'over' things implied superiority.

She didn't feel superior. She felt privileged to be able to see what others could not.

'I'm not sure I like the idea of having power *over* things,' she replied shakily.

'Why an earth not? Why wouldn't you want the power to manipulate other things? Think of what you could do...'

Something on Elspeth's face made his words tail off. Her mind raced as she tried to process what he had said. Or more the way he had said it. What could she do? What things was he thinking she could do that he found so exciting?

'What did Nerissa mean when she said you would inherit her gifts?'

His voice was gentle as he spoke, indifferent, as if the answer was unimportant. Yet he was bristling with barely contained exhilaration.

'When a Larimore dies, any gifts they possess pass on to another Larimore.'

'Any Larimore?' he asked, his head cocked as he looked at her, his eyes still burning with internal thrill.

'No, not any. Not all Larimore's have the potential to accept them. Nerissa told me it's usually one person in every generation.'

'And that's you then?'

'It seems like it. The potential manifests in the expression of some innate abilities. Nerissa currently holds the true Larimore gifts, but if she should die, they would probably pass to me. But only if she died, and I sincerely hope she doesn't,' Elspeth said firmly.

Riordan mused on this for a few minutes.

'If I understand then, the powers you displayed today are weak compared to those possessed by Nerissa?'

'Yes. Although Nerissa said I am already much stronger than she was before she inherited the gifts.'

'And when, I mean if, Nerissa dies, you will get the power she has as well?'

Elspeth fixed him with a stony stare.

'As I said, I hope I never do. I would much rather have Nerissa in my life.'

'Of course,' he said smiling. 'I'm just trying to understand.'

She stared earnestly at Riordan, feeling the need to underline that she didn't want Nerissa's gifts if it meant losing her. Riordan was nodding slowly but his eyes glazed over, something else going on behind his stare. A sense of uneasiness settled on Elspeth again.

'I wonder how much power Nerissa has? You seem very capable yourself Elspeth.'

'Oh, I don't know. I'm only just starting to understand it myself.'

Riordan whipped around, his eyes focussing again as he grasped her hands to pull her to face him.

'You must work hard to master these powers Elspeth. You must come here often to work with Nerissa... to gain control of your gifts. You need to reach your full potential my dear.'

Elspeth felt confused. Why was it so important to him? She looked into his pock-marked face, desperately trying to fathom what was going on in his mind. He seemed genuine in his desire for her to explore her gifts – the problem was, she just couldn't trust him. Having her become more powerful would make it difficult for him to control her as he had in the past. Maybe he really had changed? Or at least, was trying to.

'I want to study with Nerissa,' she said, still looking at him cagily.

'You must! I want you to become everything you can be!'

He beamed at her, the openness of his expression relaxing her a little. Tentatively, she returned his smile.

They walked through the forest in companionable silence, each lost in their own thoughts until the kirk came into view. Riordan stopped on the edge of the clearing.

'This place really is something else. It's the same as Cairndarroch in many ways. But it feels so very different.'

'Yes, there's something in the air that you can really sense, an energy. It's what fuels the gifts people here possess.'

'There are others with powers like the Larimores?'

'Not exactly. Nothing so extreme. But Nerissa told me there are other people with special abilities too. The Darrochs did when they lived here.'

He turned to face her.

'The Darrochs?'

Elspeth nodded.

'Nerissa said they could project their mind to observe other places. I don't think it was all Darrochs. I suppose it might work like the Larimore gifts in that it's passed down the generations, from one person to another on death.'

'My Mother? Do you think she has the gift now?'

'No...she can't have. All gifts fade with time away from Nethergar. I couldn't do anything until I returned here. My abilities awoke when I passed through the gateway.'

Riordan looked serious, his mind elsewhere.

'Riordan?' Elspeth ventured tentatively, interrupting his thoughts.

'Sorry. I was just thinking...wondering. I thought it might explain Morwenna's madness – you know, if she was seeing things she couldn't make sense of. But I guess not.'

He lowered his eyes and Elspeth reached out her hand

awkwardly and placed it on his arm. He responded to her comfort by smiling weakly and patting her hand.

'Right, well, I suppose we should get back.'

Elspeth nodded and together, they walked across to the kirk.

RIORDAN TOOK THE STAIRS TO THE EAST TOWER two at a time, bristling with fury. Elspeth had taken her leave as soon as they returned to Dalengour and he had immediately headed up to confront his mother. He burst through the door to Morwenna's rooms, breathing heavily both from haste and contained rage.

'Why didn't you tell me everything?' he spat through gritted teeth.

Morwenna looked up from her book, upturned eyes raking over her son. The malevolence in her stare stopped him in his tracks. She had been confined to the east tower now for over a fortnight and her character had not been softened by imprisonment. As far as she was concerned, Riordan was failing on every level. He should have secured access to Nethergar by now, and she should have control of the gateway. She should be free, and the insipid Larimore girl should be gone.

'What are you blithering about?' she said snarkily, standing and smoothing down her long black skirt.

She wasn't a tall woman, but her presence cowed Riordan, his anger instantly quelled.

'Why didn't you tell me how powerful Nerissa Larimore is? Or about the gifts being passed on from one Larimore generation to another? Or about the Darrochs having special abilities!'

His voice became higher as the words tumbled out and he

began pacing, trying to contain his agitation.

'How could I know? I haven't been to Nethergar have I?' Morwenna said pointedly, distain blazing in her eyes.

Riordan huffed and continued to walk the room, hands on hips, his black coat billowing in his wake.

'But you knew about the gift being passed on? You knew about the Darrochs?'

Morwenna pursed her lips to stem an outburst of fury and frustration. She must remember she was helpless while still locked in these rooms.

'My grandmother told me about the gifts from Nethergar and that they could be passed on from one family member to another on death. When you brought Elspeth here, I hoped she would have some ability, enough to enable her to reopen the gateway anyway. But I didn't know for sure until that day, when she came back from the kirk healed. I didn't know she would encounter another Larimore in Nethergar. This has been an interesting, but not unwelcome, surprise. Before this, my aim was to get through the gateway. Now however, the existence of another more gifted Larimore means there is much power to be gained – if we take the necessary steps.'

She deliberately emphasised every word during this monologue, her keen eyes tracking her son still stalking about the room. Riordan occasionally glanced at his mother as he changed direction but was unable to hold her gaze. A tic, visible in his left cheek, testified to the effort of leashing his anger. Morwenna too was bridling, containing resentment at being challenged, and at her prolonged imprisonment. But she knew she had to be smart. At present, Riordan had the upper hand. Elspeth was beginning to trust him.

'And the Darrochs? What about their abilities? Elspeth told me that in Nethergar, the Darrochs could see things, observe things without actually being present. Did you know that?'

Morwenna lowered her eyes, watching the lamplight catch the black beads adorning the hem of her skirt. She had told Riordan most of what she knew about Nethergar, but this she had kept to herself. Now she would have to tell him something.

'My father had the Darroch gift. However, he never knew it as such. He never used it. I suspect our abilities have faded over time as generations in Cairndarroch became more distant from our ancestors in Nethergar. Any vestiges of our gifts were easily ignored by my father.'

'And when he died? Did the gift pass to you?'

'If it did, I have never experienced it,' Morwenna lied easily.

She didn't want her son to know she had covertly observed him, could observe him sometimes. The gift wasn't strong in her... yet. She could only draw on it when she felt particularly calm, focused. And only for fleeting moments. But this would change once she got back to Nethergar. Then she would use it to her advantage.

Riordan seemed satisfied with her answer as he ceased pacing and sat down in one of the upholstered chairs. Morwenna also returned to her seat, their more relaxed postures discharging some hostility from the atmosphere.

'I think it's time Riordan,' Morwenna ventured calmly.

'Not yet Mother. I can hardly do what you want with Elspeth by my side. I need to be able to get to Nethergar alone, without her. For that to happen, she needs to trust me enough to give me a guide so I can access the gateway by myself.'

Small spots of colour burned on each of Morwenna's cheeks as she bit the inside of her lip. Her hands were clasped tightly in her lap, her spine stiff and straight as she sat forward in the chair. It wasn't Riordan's response that angered her. More that he was right.

'How long do you think it will take you to get to that?' she asked, keeping her voice light.

'Not sure. Elspeth is understandably guarded given your previous actions. Nerissa is also urging her to be cautious with me and I think Elspeth will heed her warnings. My wife seems heavily influenced by her opinions.'

The emphasis on his last sentence drawled, his irritation at Nerissa's distrust of him seeping through. Morwenna began twisting her fingers into her skirts, screwing up the delicate fabric.

'Riordan, I can't stay locked up here forever. You need to work harder to gain Elspeth's trust.'

Riordan stood up and moved over to place a kiss on his mother's cheek, preparing to take his leave, sensing frostiness creeping back into her words. He had no energy for another confrontation tonight.

'I will Mother. I promise.'

With this, he strode out of the room, eager to be away from Morwenna, but in no rush to hand her access to Nethergar. He turned the key, locking his mother away, smiling with satisfaction as he sauntered back to his rooms on the other side of the castle.

CHAPTER 13

A Good Deed

November 1921– Nethergar

Elspeth was physically exhausted. Her body felt weak, as if all her muscle fibres had turned to wool. Yet the thrill of the session with Nerissa still resonated in her. The path the energy had traced as it ran through her still tingled. There was a warmth where it had touched, a reminder in her now-wasted limbs.

She sat at the stark, wooden table in Nerissa's cottage, too lethargic to pick up the cup of steaming tea. A quiet smile played on her lips as she remembered the sensation of pushing trees skyward, letting them break in the wind she had created before repairing them again with new growth. It had been a good day. Better than yesterday.

'Drink your tea. The sugar will help restore your energy.'

Nerissa's voice interrupted her reminiscence. Elspeth reached obediently for the cup, her muscles protesting as she forced them to move. It wouldn't be long before she was restored to full strength. That was the power of Nethergar.

'I want us to do more today. You're ready to move on.'

'Oh Nerissa! I'm exhausted. Can't it wait until next time?' Elspeth pleaded with as much energy as she could muster.

'No. We have to do this today while he isn't here. I don't want him to see this.'

Today was one of the few times Elspeth had come to see Nerissa without Riordan. Her husband had accompanied her on all her frequent visits to Nethergar since she had first brought him here a fortnight ago. Today, business kept him away and Nerissa was determined to make the most of his absence. Despite Riordan doing his very best to assure her he cared for his wife, Nerissa was still wary of him. She didn't trust him and took every opportunity to tell Elspeth that she shouldn't either.

It was difficult though. Riordan really did seem different now. Elspeth had tried to keep her guard up with him. But she had found herself warming to her husband. He was very attentive and caring to both her and Robert. He had been as good as his word, keeping Morwenna away from them. They rarely even mentioned his mother except for Elspeth's infrequent enquiries into her health. Other than that, they talked about Elspeth, or Robert.

He listened patiently while she explained what she was learning with Nerissa and he seemed genuinely interested and even proud of her achievements. Together, they excitedly relived the experiences they shared in Nethergar and revelled in Robert's small developmental steps. Elspeth found herself feeling more comfortable with Riordan, even enjoying his company. She enjoyed sharing the growth in her abilities with him, and the parenting of their son. She might even say, she was happy.

The tea and powers of Nethergar were making her feel better.

'What are we going to do?'

'I think it's time you started to practice healing.'

'Healing? Healing people?'

'Yes. We'll start small.'

Elspeth found this idea quite alarming. It was one thing to make trees and flowers grow, but trying to heal people? This was something else.

'Do you really think I'm ready for that?'

'I do. You have a great deal of power Elspeth. Even now, without my gifts.'

Elspeth drank more tea, her eyes fixed on the porcelain cup.

'Nerissa, can I ask you something?'

'Anything.'

'It's about your gifts. You said they would pass to me on your death?'

'That's right?'

'But why me? I have two sisters and a brother. Surely, they could go to one of them?'

'Have any of your siblings ever displayed any abilities that suggest they have the potential to carry the gifts?'

'Kaliope definitely not, and Calder is so young. But Agatha? Maybe Agatha.'

Elspeth stared wistfully into her cup. She was suddenly ashamed because in admitting Agatha could have powers like hers, and could inherit the greater gifts from Nerissa, she felt disappointed. Nerissa watched her intently from across the table and as usual, Elspeth was sure she could see into her thoughts.

'It's unlikely Calder would inherit if there's still a female Larimore who has the potential. The gifts always favour women, and we know you already have some innate ability. It would also be unusual for there to be more than one person in every generation. Not unheard of, but unusual. I would expect the only ones with the potential now are you and probably, your son.'

Elspeth flicked her head up to look at Nerissa.

'Robert? I never even considered he could have gifts.'

Nerissa laughed.

'He is the son of a powerful Larimore woman and a Darroch. Both his parents are from Nethergar. I would find it very surprising if he didn't have some gifts of his own that would become apparent if he ventured through the gateway, just as they did for you.'

Elspeth shifted uncomfortably. This was information she was suddenly glad Riordan had not heard. The recent bond with his son was still new. She didn't want him to think of Robert as anything other than a normal toddler. And she certainly didn't want it getting back to Morwenna that he may be special.

'What makes you think Agatha has gifts?' Nerissa asked.

'She's very sensitive. She seems able to readily understand what people are thinking and feeling from the most subtle of behaviours. She seems able to see into my heart and mind with unnerving accuracy.'

'That sounds like a sister to me,' Nerissa said smiling warmly. 'It was the same for me and my sister. We knew each other so well we could communicate thoughts and feelings without uttering a word.'

'It's true, Aggie and I are very close. But I think it's more than that. Agatha sees things others don't in people's behaviour – not just family but friends and even strangers.'

'Agatha sounds like a wonderful person.'

'She is.'

Elspeth's eyes inexplicably filled with tears as she thought of her sister. She missed her so much. Although she visited Dalengour regularly, it wasn't the same as having her near all the time. She told Agatha as much as she could about Nerissa and Nethergar during her visits, but she was eager to bring her here, to see for herself.

Nerissa again seemed to know what was going though Elspeth's mind.

'You should bring her here. I'd love to meet her. Make sure she understands what coming here would mean for her won't you?'

The thought of bringing Agatha to Nethergar cheered Elspeth and she felt fortified. She nodded eagerly at Nerissa, wiping her eyes before draining the last of the tea.

'Right, healing. What do I have to do?' Elspeth said, rising from the table and placing her empty cup into the gleaming white butler sink.

Nerissa took a small silver letter opener from the pocket of her grey woollen dress. Deftly, she drew it along the palm of her hand leaving a deep welt that began to flow with bright red blood that pooled in the cup of her hand.

'Nerissa! Are you insane?' Elspeth cried, coming over and grabbing Nerissa's hand to examine the cut.

'Have you got something to stop the bleeding?'

Elspeth cast her eyes frantically around the kitchen for a tea towel or some other piece of linen that could staunch the blood now spilling over to drip onto the table.

'You can stop it. Focus your mind and stop the blood.'

'I can't! I don't know how.'

Elspeth's voice was panicky, shrill.

'You can. Calm down and focus your mind.'

Elspeth looked down into the firm, steely eyes staring out from Nerissa's pale face. What little colour she usually possessed was draining away as the blood continued to flow freely from her wound. There was now a large pool of red soaking into the woodgrain of the tabletop. Elspeth's heart was pounding as her hands began to tremble.

'You can do it Elspeth. Get a hold of yourself. Focus.'

Trying to block out the panic, Elspeth closed her eyes and visualised the wound on Nerissa's hand. She tried to focus on the blood, tried to slow it with her mind. Sweat beaded on her top lip, her teeth gritted in determination. Opening her eyes, she looked down to see red spilling just as quickly from Nerissa who was now ashen.

'Again!' she commanded weakly.

Elspeth tightened her hold on Nerissa's hand, urgency increasing her focus. She looked down at the blood noticing the flow pulsed with every beat of Nerissa's heart. As she watched, a feint glow of light stretched from Elspeth's fingertip to surround the laceration. Everything seemed to slow. The rhythmic surge of blood abated, and Elspeth could see the sharp tear in Nerissa's skin and blood vessels in her mind.

'Now heal it.'

Nerissa's voice was clear in her head although she had not spoken aloud. The golden glow intensified as Elspeth visualised the damaged tissues, imbuing them with energy to repair themselves. She kept pushing, accelerating the healing until no evidence of the cut remained.

As the energy faded, Nerissa withdrew her hand from Elspeth's grasp and held it aloft to examine her work. She stretched and wriggled her fingers, twisting the hand around.

'Look,' she said, forcing her palm towards Elspeth who

was fixated on the pool of blood remaining on the table, her stare glassy, her mind empty.

'Elspeth, look!'

Nerissa's insistence broke her trance, and she pried her eyes away from the blood to look at her outstretched palm. There was no sign of the wound. Nerissa's hand was completely repaired.

'You did it…thankfully,' Nerissa said with a wry smile.

Elspeth moved around the table and took her seat again, still dazed by what had happened. Nerissa left her in silence for a minute before reaching across the table to take her hands in her own.

'I knew you could do it. You just have to believe in yourself Elspeth.'

'What if I couldn't do it!' Elspeth shrieked, the vestiges of her panic giving way to a momentary flash of anger.

'I wouldn't have pushed you if I didn't believe you were ready. You healed me. You're a very powerful woman Elspeth.'

She felt Nerissa squeeze her hands and as she searched her face, Elspeth's anger immediately calmed.

'I did it…'

'Yes, you did.'

Now Elspeth couldn't contain the smile that spread across her face. Excitement reared in her stomach as she realised what she had been able to do.

'I healed you!' she said, her voice alight with the euphoria of her accomplishment. 'I really healed you!'

Nerissa laughed openly.

'Yes, you did.'

For a few moments, the two women enjoyed shared laughter before Nerissa's face became more serious.

'This is just the start Elspeth. You will need to practice

these skills to become proficient at healing though. Don't try to run before you can walk. It could be dangerous.'

Elspeth nodded, Nerissa's warning unable to dampen her spirits.

'Now, more tea I think. Then you should get back home.'

Elspeth raced back to Dalengour eager to tell Riordan what she had done with Nerissa. She burst through the door like an excited child, shouting her husband's name, hoping he had returned from the city.

'Gracious Elspeth. What is it?'

At the sound of her calls, Riordan emerged from the library, a stack of papers clutched in his hand. He still wore his long overcoat, the artificially broad shoulders and tailored waist accentuating his wiry frame. The blackness of the woollen cloth drained what little colour his angular face possessed, giving him a ghostly pallor in the dim light of the hallway.

'Oh Riordan,' Elspeth gushed, her excitement brimming over as she moved towards him. 'Nerissa showed me how to heal today. I healed a wound on her hand. It was such a wonderful feeling!'

Riordan grinned broadly at her, the smile not quite reaching his watery green eyes. He reached for Elspeth's hands, pulling her a little closer. Elspeth was still not used to his nearness but found she didn't mind it as much as she used to. Although she never instigated physical contact, she no longer recoiled at his touch. Riordan had never taken things too far and apart from the occasional embrace or kiss on her cheek, he had stayed away from her. She was grateful he had not pushed to reclaim his marital rights.

'You really are getting very powerful Elspeth.'

Elspeth flushed.

'Oh, not really,' she said coyly. 'But it was exhilarating.'

'Well, I think you're amazing. Let's go out for dinner to celebrate. I'll go and tell Mrs Pegg we won't want any supper, and you go and tidy yourself up.'

He smoothed an errant stray hair behind Elspeth's ear in an intimate gesture that flushed her face with colour.

'That would be lovely. I'll just go and look in on Robert. Then I'll change my dress. There's blood on this one!' she said looking down at the smears of red staining her cuffs.

THE INN IN THE VILLAGE WAS BUSY, BUT THE Darroch name secured them a secluded table by the fireplace. Elspeth was glad of the warming flames dancing in the grate, her favourite ocean blue gown offering little protection from the chill evening air. With her stomach full of ham and potatoes, her face pink with contentment, she relaxed back on the wooden chair. It had been a pleasant evening and Riordan had been good company. She had rambled on about Nerissa and Nethergar and he had patiently listened, contributing comments in the appropriate places with genuine interest.

A comfortable silence now settled between them, and Elspeth's eyes began to feel heavy.

'We should probably get you home before you fall asleep in that chair.'

The sound of Riordan's voice broke through her sleepiness. She sat upright nodding, stretching her spine to wake herself up.

'Wait here while I get our coats.'

Riordan left the table heading towards the coat pegs. Elspeth suddenly felt exhausted, the excitement of the day taking its toll. The thought of her warm bed at Dalengour had never been so appealing even though the clock had not yet struck eight. She sat for a few minutes, blinking back the tiredness, fighting the desire to relax back into the chair and shut her eyes. Riordan had been gone a while now, longer than it should take to retrieve coats and pay the bill.

Elspeth swivelled around on her chair and cast around for her husband. He was standing near the bar, coats in hand, talking to an agitated man waving his arms hysterically as Riordan tried to calm him. Elspeth shuffled around in her seat to get a better view. Riordan took the man by the elbow and guided him towards Elspeth.

The stranger's face was contorted, his eyes red from crying, tears shimmering on his craggy, weatherworn face. His clothes were those of a labouring man, simple and bearing the signs of toil in the fields. Elspeth guessed he must be a farmer. Married too, judging by the neatly darned patches on his well-worn shirt.

'Elspeth, this is Jim McNair. He's a farmer on the Dalengour Estate. He's been working the fields today with his young son, and there's been an accident.'

'Oh no!' Elspeth exclaimed, rising from her seat. 'What happened Mr McNair?'

The farmer stood with his head bowed, reluctant to meet Elspeth's gaze. He was still gasping for breath, trying to stem the flow of tears as he spoke.

'Davey...my son. He was so eager to come and help me. He's only eleven but he asks every day if he can come and work the fields with me.'

Jim wiped his nose on the edge of his sleeve and Elspeth caught the look of disgust that flitted across Riordan's pasty face.

'Go on Mr McNair,' Elspeth encouraged.

'Well, Daisy, my wife, she's not been too well of late. 'Bout to have another bairn you see. So, I thought it would help her out if I let the young un' come wi' me today. She'd be able to get some rest.'

His red eyes looked imploringly at Elspeth, hoping his explanation exonerated him from blame. He had no need of worry. Elspeth felt only sympathy for the man. She nodded encouragingly so he would continue.

'Anyway, he was interested in what we was doing for a while. But then, as bairns do, he got bored. Kept wandering off. I tried to keep me eye on him, but it's hard when the work still needs doing. He must have fallen just in front of the tractor. I didn't see him...'

His voice cracked and he fixed his eyes on his mud-covered boots, partly in shame and partly to hide the tears that were now dripping off the end of his heavily veined nose. He suddenly remembered that he was still wearing his cap and snatched it from his head, curling it up in his dirty fingers and stammering an apology to Elspeth.

'There's no need to apologise Mr McNair. Please go on. What happened to your son?'

'I couldn't stop it in. It went over him. I think I made it worse by trying to reverse it back...'

He bit his bottom lip, trying to stifle his cries. He couldn't go on. Elspeth looked towards Riordan, unsure of what he expected her to do or say.

'The boy is critically injured Elspeth. Mr McNair rushed to the village to find the doctor, but he isn't at home. His wife said he is out attending to a woman experiencing a difficult birth and may be some time.'

'My son doesn't have time Ma'am,' Jim stammered, finding his voice again. 'I think he might die...'

He looked pleadingly at Elspeth who shifted uncomfortably.

'Riordan – I – I don't know what you want me to do?'

She spoke quietly, trying to avoid seeing the immense sadness written across Jim McNair's face.

'I thought you might be able to... help him Elspeth?'

Her eyes widened as she stared disbelievingly at her husband.

'I can't!' she shouted, then quickly composed herself as she caught sight of Jim McNair dissolving into grief.

She took hold of Riordan's arm and steered him a few feet away from where the crying farmer stood. Leaning in to prevent patrons in the inn overhearing, she spoke tersely into her husband's ear.

'Why an earth did you bring him over? Did you tell him about me? Tell him I could help?'

'Calm down Elspeth. I just said that you might be able to help. I didn't give him any details or make him any promises.'

Elspeth exhaled forcibly, biting the inside of her lip in an attempt to control the urge to shout. Her anger was disarmed as she caught sight of Jim McNair collapsing to his knees, burying his face in his screwed-up cap in utter despair. Elspeth couldn't tear her eyes from the broken man, empathy for both his loss and his feelings of responsibility, weighing heavy on her.

'You could help him Elspeth.'

Riordan's voice was soft in her ear.

'I can't. Really, I can't. I've only healed a small cut and Nerissa warned me to take things slowly – not to do more than I'm capable of.'

The words came out, but Riordan sensed her resolve faltering.

'This is a special case and I'm sure Nerissa would understand. The boy will surely die if you do nothing. But if you tried... helped just a little bit, he may live long enough for the doctor to reach him.'

Elspeth's eyes were still fixed on Jim McNair who had sunk into torpor, his eyes vacant, staring into nothingness. His hands settled limply on his lap, the grubby cap laying discarded on the floor.

With a scathing look at her husband, Elspeth moved towards the kneeling man and placed her hand on his shoulder, bringing him out of his trance. He staggered apologetically to his feet, retrieving his cap, wiping his nose again on the back of his hand.

'Forgive me Ma'am. I'm sorry to have bothered you. I need to get back to me boy.'

Jim placed the hat back on his head and started to back away from Elspeth.

'Wait a moment Mr McNair.'

Elspeth could hardly believe she was saying this. But she couldn't walk away from this distraught man if there was any hope she could be of help.

'I might be able to help your son. I can't promise anything, but if you'll let me, I'll try.'

Some of the pain instantly left Jim's face as he stepped towards Elspeth.

'I'm very grateful Ma'am, grateful for anything you can do.'

'We'll take the carriage back to the Estate,' Riordan said, taking command of the situation.

As they rattled along towards Dalengour, Jim McNair looked as uncomfortable as any man could, attempting to stay as far away as possible from the Darrochs in the confined carriage. He avoided eye contact and Elspeth was glad of this, using the time to compose herself. What was she doing? She had no idea how to help this young boy. She might even make things worse! Her stomach churned, the wine she had so enjoyed now weakening her constitution. Riordan patted her knee, sensing her unease.

They pulled up outside a terraced line of workers' cottages on the edge of Dalengour land. The stone façade looked bleak, the peeling paintwork on the doors and windows giving the houses a dilapidated appearance. Jim McNair leapt out of the carriage before it reached a full stop and raced into the end house, shouting to his wife as he disappeared through the door.

'Are you ready?' Riordan asked her quietly, offering her his arm.

'Not really,' she replied. 'I don't know if there'll be anything I can do.'

'Just try your best.'

Elspeth was grateful for the feel of Riordan's hand as he helped her down from the carriage, entwining his fingers through hers reassuringly as they walked into the gloomy house. They entered a single room that seemed to act as parlour and kitchen. A heavily pregnant woman stood stiffly by the fireplace, her hands clasped under her swollen belly, her eyes bloodshot with the tell-tale signs of grief and worry.

'This is my wife, Daisy,' McNair said uneasily, throwing out his arm in the general direction of the woman.

Elspeth moved towards Daisy who dropped her eyes to the floor, afraid to breech some unspoken protocol by looking directly at Lady Darroch.

'It's lovely to meet you Mrs McNair,' Elspeth said, reaching out her arms and taking hold of the woman's clasped hands. 'I wish it was under better circumstances.'

Daisy raised her head to look at Elspeth, the candle on the

mantel reflecting in her watery eyes, her bottom lip beginning to tremble. The woman was unable to speak so she just nodded as Elspeth squeezed her hands.

Poverty seeped from every corner of the damp house. A paltry fire flickered in the grate, kept alight by a measly stack of logs and old newspapers, the flames ineffectual against the pervasive cold spreading through the drafty cottage. A small iron scuttle sitting beside the fire, contained only a few pieces of precious black coal, obviously rationed until more could be afforded. Elspeth shivered, drawing her coat more closely around her.

'Where is the boy?'

Riordan's voice came from behind her, and she turned away from Daisy to see Jim McNair indicate a small wooden bed she hadn't noticed in the corner of the room. Tenderly tucked into the charcoal-coloured blankets, his blonde head resting on a recently plumped, greyish-white pillow, was a small, skinny boy, dark circles surrounding his tightly closed eyes.

Elspeth turned towards her husband, his nod encouraging her towards the child. The only sign of life in the scrawny body was the slow rise and fall of his puny chest. The breaths came intermittently, a rasping noise accompanying each feeble exhale. There were very few breaths left in this boy.

Elspeth stood over the bed, feeling the eyes of everyone in the room boring expectantly into her back. She could hear her heart beating in her head and bile began to rise in the back of her throat. She didn't know where to start. She wanted to turn and flee, but then, the boy's eyes flickered open.

'Mamma,' he whispered, his voice thready as the word caught in his parched throat.

Daisy McNair came quickly to his side, falling on her

knees as she took her son's tiny hand in her own and maternally pushed sweaty tendrils of hair from his forehead.

'I'm here Davey, Momma's here.'

Fresh tears flowed down Daisy's face as she raised the boy's hand to her lips. Elspeth thought about Robert and her heart broke for the depth of this mother's worry. She placed her hand supportively on Daisy's shoulder, wishing she knew how to take away her pain.

'*But you can help,*' she told herself. Resolve flooded her and immediately, the nausea that had threatened to overwhelm her subsided and her head cleared.

'Davey, this nice lady is Lady Elspeth Darroch and she's here to try and help you.'

The boy didn't respond, his eyes closing again, his chest heaving. Daisy looked up at Elspeth, panic etched in the deep lines on her face. She still clung to her son, her face wet with tears.

'May I?' Elspeth asked, indicating the place where Daisy sat.

Wordlessly, the distraught woman stood and let Elspeth take her place beside the bed.

'I'm going to try and help you Davey. It might feel strange at first, but I promise, it will make you feel better.'

Elspeth had no idea whether the boy could hear her, but she felt the need to explain to him anyway. She gathered herself and tried to remember what she had done earlier in the day. Nerissa's warning not to run before she could walk rang in her ears. But she wouldn't let this family down. She would do her best to help.

Closing her eyes, she laid her hands on the small boy's chest, focusing on his irregular breathing, blocking out all other sounds in the room. At first, she could feel nothing except the weight of responsibility and the child's weakening pulse. She began to breathe deeply, slowly and as she did, the boy's breathing seemed to fall in time with her own. His lungs expanded with hers and his respiration strengthened.

Buoyed by Davey's response to her, she pushed out with her mind to strengthen the connection between them. She winced as she sensed pain in the boy's abdomen. Opening her eyes, she saw the familiar golden glow surrounding her hands. Slowly she moved her palms down the child's body. Blood. Somehow, she could see blood filling his body cavity, leaking from… somewhere. The view was obscured, her mind's eye swimming in a sea of red.

Trembling, she extended the energy radiating from her hands deeper into the boy, its light parting the blood and illuminating her way. Elspeth searched around, needing to visualise his injuries so she could focus the healing. There it was – a large laceration belching blood from the surface of the boy's liver.

Every muscle in Elspeth's body was aching with the effort of keeping the connection to Davey. Sweat gathered on her top lip and brow, the dampness accentuated by the cold air in the house. She wanted to let go. But that wasn't an option. If she stopped now, she wouldn't have the strength to try again, and the boy would die.

With renewed effort, she pushed the trail of light onwards until it surrounded the leaking wound. A golden mesh began to form over the hole, drawing together the edges until the haemorrhaging slowed, then stopped. Satisfied that the laceration was repaired, Elspeth slowly pulled back, taking time to ensure no more blood was leeching out from Davey's internal organs. All seemed well. She fought the desire to withdraw completely and carried on searching the boy's body for any other signs of injury. Other than bruising that would heal with time, there were none.

She let the energy retreat and with relief, she collapsed forwards bracing herself with both hands on the edge of Davey's bed.

Her breathing was laboured and hard, like she had been running for her life. Gasping for air, she stayed kneeling by the small wooden bed, her head bowed to control the dizziness that accompanied her intense feeling of exhaustion. After a few moments, she became conscious of the hard stone floor digging into her knees. She gathered herself and tried to stand. Her legs felt like jelly and she couldn't lift her own bodyweight.

Immediately, she felt someone hoist her to a standing position. Riordan was beside her, supporting her firmly around the waist. She took a few tentative steps as he moved her away from the bed and turned her to face the McNairs. Both parents were staring, wide-eyed, mouths slightly agape. Elspeth couldn't help smiling as she realised what this must have looked like to them. Some strange women producing light from her hands. She wondered how they would explain it to themselves. But then, if the boy was cured, they probably wouldn't dwell too much on how it had come about.

'I think your son will be fine now, with some rest,' Elspeth said croakily. 'I've stopped the bleeding, but he has lost a great deal of blood that will take time to replenish. He has a lot of bruising. But that should also heal with time.'

Her legs gave way, but Riordan caught her and pulled her more firmly into his side. The McNair's were speechless, continuing to stare in disbelief. A stirring from the bed roused them, Davey's weak voice calling for his mother. Daisy pushed past Elspeth to get to her son, followed closely by her husband. With no energy left to turn and witness their joy at seeing their son awake and stronger, Elspeth listened as Daisy reassured Davey he would be fine, the tears flooding down her cheeks now shed in joy.

'Please take me home,' Elspeth whispered to Riordan who escorted her towards the door and their waiting carriage.

As they reached the bracing evening air, Jim raced out to follow them.

'Thank you Lady Darroch! Thank you! Thank you!'

The lines on Jim McNair's face were filled with shiny tears of happiness as he bowed gratefully to Elspeth.

'You're very welcome Mr McNair. I'm glad I could help. But please keep this to yourself.'

'Yes Ma'am. I will.'

He kept his head bowed but Elspeth could see the bulging muscles in his cheeks, the smile of relief unassailable.

CHAPTER 14

Services Rendered

SETTLING HER ON THE SOFA IN THE LIBRARY AT Dalengour, Riordan tended Elspeth's every need when they returned from the village. He brought her brandy, some sandwiches she did not want, and a blanket that he tucked around her legs as she napped in front of the fire. After some food and a short rest, Elspeth had woken restored and buzzing with the thrill of what she had done.

She talked excitedly with her husband late into the night, reliving every moment as she explained the feeling of healing Davey McNair. Riordan had been an enthusiastic audience, eventually encouraging her to bed as the clock chimed one.

Elspeth had slept soundly and now laid in her four-poster bed watching ominous clouds rolling past the narrow window of her chambers. Even the gloom of the day couldn't dampen the excitement still reverberating through her body as she waited for the maid to come in and help her dress. She was growing impatient as she wanted to breakfast quickly and go back to Nethergar.

She was both eager and nervous about telling Nerissa what she had done. Elspeth wasn't sure how she would react. Would she be angry that she had pushed her abilities so far? Or would she be proud of what she had achieved? Elspeth rolled over and pulled the comforter sewn by her family tightly around her chin. She heard footsteps in the hallway hoping they signified the maid's approach, but they moved on past her door. Sighing heavily, she tried to close her eyes again. It must still be early.

She tossed and turned for half an hour, but sleep would not come. Every time she closed her eyes, the exhilaration of last night returned, filling her with a tingling excitement not conducive with rest. Throwing back the bedclothes, she got up and went to the washstand. Goosebumps pricked her skin as the cold air penetrated her thin nightgown. She washed quickly in the freezing water and brushed her hair into a tight chignon at the base of her neck. She had never been good with hair and this simple style was the best she could manage.

Her bare feet were now so cold they were painful as she padded across to the wardrobe. She pulled out a long-sleeved woollen dress in a heather colour. It was a more modern silhouette than she normally wore, with a straight shape finishing just below the knee, a dropped waist and high neck. It had been a gift from Riordan, bought on his last visit to the city. She hadn't worn it yet, feeling self-conscious in the shorter skirt. But it was the warmest dress she owned, and the weather definitely felt wintery today.

Selecting some undergarments, she took the dress over to the bed where the rugs lining the floor gave her toes some protection from the cold oak floor. She dressed quickly, shivering until the woollen dress warmed her skin. Pulling the tight neckline over her head disturbed her hair so she went over to the full-length mirror to fix it. Pushing her feet into some flat, black pumps, Elspeth stood back to look at her reflection. The dress suited her, the simple shape flattering on her angular body. Even motherhood had not managed to give Elspeth womanly curves, her body quickly returning to its boyish shape soon after Robert's birth.

Satisfied with her appearance, Elspeth left her chambers and made her way to the nursery. The castle was quiet apart from the occasional sound of one of the servants tending to their duties. They were not a large household with only the butler Gadsen, Mrs Pegg the cook, and two maids to tend their needs. Jenson Tanner had not been replaced after his departure.

Elspeth felt the familiar tightening in her stomach at the thought of Jenson. She missed him. So much had happened and despite her anger at the way he had spoken to her when he left, she still longed for him. The pricking of sadness behind her eyes encouraged her to put thoughts of Jenson from her mind. Pushing open the nursery door, the emotion she felt when thinking about the man she loved was quickly replaced by the overwhelming surge of love that always engulfed her when she looked into the crib at her sleeping son.

Seeing Robert safe and warm in his cot made her think of Daisy McNair. Nerissa might disapprove of her using her abilities to heal so soon, but she would never be sorry for preventing a mother from losing her son. Tenderly, she swept the reddish-blond curls back from Robert's soft face thinking she would need to speak with Miss Dennings about giving him a haircut.

Elspeth planted a gentle kiss on her son's cheek. He

didn't stir and so she left him to slumber on. She headed down the stairs to the dining room, grateful to see the fire had been lit. She stood in front of the hearth, rubbing her hands together to warm them by the flames. Gadsen's stealthy approach startled her. She jumped, wheeling around to face him at the sound of the silver platter being placed on the sideboard.

'Beg your pardon Ma'am. I didn't mean to disturb you.'

Elspeth had never warmed to Gadsen, the surly butler devoted to Morwenna Darroch. He had always treated Elspeth with courtesy, but still viewed her as an intruder at Dalengour. Even her mother-in-law's attempts to kill her and subsequent imprisonment hadn't dented Gadsen's reverence for Morwenna.

'It's fine Gadsen. I was just lost in thought.'

Gadsen stood stony faced, looking at her, waiting for some instruction.

'Am I early for breakfast? I didn't look at the clock?' Elspeth asked.

'It's a little before seven Ma'am. Mrs Peggs is sending up the breakfast now. Can I get you some tea?'

Gadsen indicated the steaming silver teapot on the sideboard he must have brought in unnoticed.

'That's fine Gadsen. I'll get my own tea.'

Gadsen raised his eyebrows, his lips pursed as he stared back at her.

'I don't think Lady Darroch would find it appropriate for you to serve yourself Ma'am,' he said disapprovingly.

Elspeth was used to his tone. He never missed an opportunity to point out when she failed to live up to Morwenna's high standards.

Elspeth stood up straight, her hands clasped and fixed her eyes resolutely on Gadsen.

'Well, Lady Darroch is not here.'

The butler opened his mouth as if to reply, but remembering his position, gave a reluctant bow. He turned and stalked out of the room, leaving Elspeth alone. She sighed, relaxing her poker-straight spine, irritated that she continually had to assert her position with Gadsen.

She retrieved a cup and saucer from the place settings on the table and served herself some tea, then sat at the dining table and stared out of the window. The rising sun was beginning to cast an orangey glow over the garden glistening with overnight rainfall. Elspeth watched as the trees swayed romantically in the breeze. The sparse leaves of the single ash tree fluttered to the ground, brown and shrivelled, leaving behind barren branches stark against the surrounding green firs.

'Good morning. You're up early Elspeth.'

Riordan entered the room, his tall, gangly frame draped in the usual black that drained any colour from his already ashen complexion.

'I couldn't sleep,' Elspeth replied excitedly.

Her husband took the seat opposite her, placing a newspaper on the table. Gadsen reappeared, carrying two more platters, domed silver lids hiding their contents. Placing them on the sideboard, he brought the teapot over to the table to serve Riordan, aiming a scathing look in Elspeth's direction as he did so.

'What can I get you Ma'am?'

Elspeth was too excited to eat, her stomach whirling with the anticipation of seeing Nerissa. Mrs Peggs' cooking hadn't improved from her very first visit to Dalengour, and the thought of it didn't stimulate her appetite.

'I'm not hungry thank you Gadsen.'

'You should eat something Elspeth.'

Riordan's tone was that of a grown up reprimanding a petulant child.

'Fine, I'll take some toast.'

The butler returned moments later with a plate of thick bread, slightly charred at the edges, and a small dish of butter. He set this down in front of Elspeth and served Riordan his usual porridge. They ate in silence, a legacy of Morwenna's mealtimes that Elspeth had been unable to change. With the plates cleared away and the servants gone, Riordan pushed his chair back a little, crossed his bony legs and disappeared behind the newspaper.

'You're fidgeting Elspeth.'

Riordan didn't raise his eyes from the headlines as he spoke.

'Sorry,' she said, sitting on her hands in an attempt to still them.

She looked at her husband and saw his lips were curled in a teasing smile. He folded his paper and gave her his undivided attention.

'I assume you're squirming is in eagerness to get to Nethergar?'

Elspeth smiled as she nodded, her eyes burning brightly.

'I want to talk to Nerissa about what happened yesterday.'

'Do I detect apprehension?'

'A little. I know it was the right thing to do – I couldn't have walked away from the McNair's without trying to help Davey. But I'm just not sure how Nerissa will see it. She warned me not to try and do too much too soon.'

Riordan lent forwards tenting his fingers together as he leaned his elbows on the table.

'Well, arguably, given your success in healing the boy, you didn't push yourself too far. What you did was well within your capabilities.'

Elspeth focused on his white, fanned fingers, thinking about what he had said. There was some truth in it. Riordan didn't speak again for a few minutes, leaving Elspeth to ponder his words.

'Elspeth, do you think perhaps Nerissa is trying to slow you down?'

She looked up at him, startled.

'What do you mean?'

He leaned back into his chair, crossing his legs again, his hands clasped over his pointed knee.

'She has commented on how powerful you are. More powerful than she was before she inherited the Larimore gifts. I wonder if perhaps... she is jealous of you, wants to slow your progress in case you become more powerful than her?'

Elspeth blinked disbelievingly at him. She knew there was no love lost between Riordan and Nerissa, but he couldn't mean this. Nerissa would never try and stop her developing her powers...would she?

'I can't believe that Riordan. Nerissa has always encouraged me. I would say she is even proud of my achievements. I don't think she would ever try and stop me reaching my full potential.'

'I hope you're right,' Riordan replied, reaching for the newspaper again. 'I think the hour is sufficiently late now for you to head to the kirk.'

'Are you coming with me?'

'Not today. I have some business in the village. You go. I know your visits with Nerissa are more relaxed when I'm not there.'

He was right, and for some reason, Elspeth was especially glad he wasn't going with her today.

'What business?'

She wasn't sure why she had asked. He never told her what his business was. Maybe just to deflect him in case he changed his mind about accompanying her.

'Nothing to concern you my dear. I'm going to drop in on Mother and then head into the village. I don't think I'll be back for lunch so if you are going to stay with Nerissa for the day, I'll let Mrs Peggs know not to prepare anything.'

Elspeth rose from the table, eager now to be on her way.

'That's probably for the best. Time always seems to run away with me when I'm in Nethergar.'

Riordan nodded and Elspeth raced out of the room. His eyes followed her and when she was out of sight, a toothless smile distorted his insipid lips. He listened intently until he heard Elspeth pull on her coat in the hall, waiting for the front door open and close. Shifting his gaze to the window, he watched his wife hurry across the lawn, her head tucked into her collar to protect against the chill as she disappeared into the tree line.

Standing, he smoothed down his jacket and went into the hall to retrieve his hat and a silver-headed cane he thought would add gravitas to his business today. He decided, uncharacteristically, to walk to the village. The day was bright if cold and he didn't want anyone to know where he was going. He couldn't risk one of the servants letting anything slip to Elspeth. Pulling up his collar and placing the black bowler on his head, he left Dalengour and headed towards Cairndarroch.

Half an hour later, he rapped the head of his cane on the shabby wooden door of the McNairs. He could hear a commotion inside and Daisy shouting to try and control unruly children. Moments later, Jim McNair threw open the door, his eyes wide as he saw Riordan standing there.

'Lord Darroch,' Jim stammered, lowering his head in a submissive bow.

The noise from inside the house stopped suddenly at the announcement of Riordan's presence.

'I wanted to check on the health of your son,' Riordan said calmly. 'May I come in?'

'Certainly sir.'

Jim stepped aside without raising his eyes from the floor and Riordan marched into the kitchen. Daisy stood stiffly, holding very tightly onto the shoulders of two boys to keep them from wriggling away. She looked tired, the strain of pregnancy and the vigil over her dying son telling on her face.

'Lord Darroch,' she murmured, bobbing her knees in some kind of mock curtsey.

Riordan took off his hat but kept hold of it.

'Forgive me for intruding on your day Mrs McNair, but Elspeth and I were eager to check Davey's recovery had continued.'

'Yes, yes sir. He's doing very well.'

She indicated towards the corner with a shaking hand. Davey McNair was propped up on greying pillows in the small, wooden-framed bed where he had been almost dead the evening before. He still looked weak, blueish circles around his sunken eyes. But his complexion had lost the deathly pallor and he was alert, his gaze fixed on their visitor.

Riordan stalked commandingly over to the boy's bedside, banging his cane on the barren wooden floor with every step. The child slipped further down into his bedclothes and drew the rough woollen blanket higher up towards his chin.

'How are you feeling Davey?'

The boy didn't speak. His father's voice came stern from behind Riordan.

'Answer Lord Darroch boy.'

Davey shot his father a frightened glance.

'I'm sorry Lord Darroch. He usually has a lot to say for himself.'

Riordan smiled at the boy in what he hoped was a reassuring way.

'No need to be shy Davey,' he said encouragingly, leaning forward so he wasn't towering so high above the bed.

'I feel better Mr...'

The child's voice tailed off with uncertainty over how to address Riordan, who didn't wait for him to continue. This had been sufficient pleasantries. He patted the boy's arm through his blankets and turned to face Jim McNair.

'I really am very glad Davey is doing better.'

'We can't thank you and your wife enough Lord Darroch.'

Jim's eyes glistened as he spoke of his gratitude. Riordan couldn't stand any more demonstrations of emotion, especially from a working man.

'Yes well... I'm glad Elspeth could help.'

There was an awkward silence as neither man spoke.

'Lord Darroch...'

Riordan spun around to face Daisy at the sound of his name. He had momentarily forgotten she was there. He worked hard to suppress a look of disgust at her fat, waddling form. Pregnancy did not suit any woman to his mind. Elspeth had been even more repulsive to him than usual when she carried his child, and he had been grateful she had avoided him as much as possible during her maternity.

'Yes?'

'I was wondering how Elspeth...'

She stopped as Riordan raised his eyebrows at the familiar address of his wife.

'I mean, how Lady Darroch did it? How did she heal my boy?'

Riordan sighed inwardly. He had suspected this might come up and he had no desire to try to explain anything to these ignorants.

'I don't rightly know. My wife has special sensitivities that allow her to feel things more deeply than you or I. She can see energy in all living things and is able to manipulate it, bend it to her will. This allowed her to force Davey's energy into healing his wounds more quickly than would usually happen.'

He turned back to Jim McNair who was listening avidly. He opened his mouth as if to ask another question, but Riordan cut him off.

'I'm afraid I can't tell you anymore than that. Now...'

Jim closed his mouth and shook his head at his wife who looked like she was going to press for more information on Elspeth's 'special abilities'.

'Mr McNair, we need to discuss the matter of payment.'

'Payment?' Jim said tentatively.

'For services rendered. My wife helped you out last night and now you must pay for her services.'

'But we haven't got anything!' came Daisy's cry as she moved towards Riordan and her husband.

'Calm yourself Mrs McNair. I am not an unreasonable man. I am sure we can come to some arrangement that will be suitable.'

The McNairs stood looking fearfully at Riordan, both too stunned to speak.

'Your farming on the Estate turns you a reasonable wage does it not Mr McNair?'

'I suppose it does sir. We manage.'

Daisy looked stony-faced at her husband and seemed about to argue before he clasped his hand around her wrist.

'And what, I wonder, would be a reasonable price for the life of your son?'

Riordan placed the tip of his cane on the floor and placed both hands over the silver handle, anchoring his narrowed eyes on Jim McNair's face. Neither he, nor his wife spoke.

'I think five pounds seems reasonable, don't you?'

'I haven't got five pounds Lord Darroch.'

'I didn't expect you had. I'll take what you have now and will return on the last Friday of each month to collect half a shilling until the debt is repaid,' Riordan said coldly.

'Please…please Lord Darroch,' begged Daisy. 'That will leave us barely enough to live on and with another bairn on the way, we won't manage.'

Riordan looked at the pleading woman through slitted eyes.

'Perhaps you should have thought about your poverty before you decided to add another parasite to your brood,' he spat.

Daisy drew herself up and for a moment, Riordan was impressed by her strength. She was staring back at him, hate flashing behind her steely expression. She wasn't going to break down in front of him. She moved over to a tin hidden behind the plates on the dresser and tipped two shillings and sixpence into her hand. Counting the pennies, she returned them and one silver coin to the tin. Her anger barely contained, Daisy pressed a shilling into Riordan's hand. He closed his fingers over her hand, trapping her near to him.

'Perhaps you could sell this child,' he said pointing at her swollen belly with the end of his cane, 'and settle the debt quicker.'

Daisy snatched her hand away, stepping back to where her

husband and children stood. Riordan smiled maliciously at the McNairs before brushing imaginary fluff from his hat and replacing it on his head. Jim looked at him in disbelief. Daisy glared at him, fire in her eyes.

'Until the end of the month then.'

Riordan rapped his cane on the floor, doffed his hat, then turned on his heel, leaving the house and feeling very pleased with himself indeed.

CHAPTER 15

The Raven's Flight

FEBRUARY 1922 - CAIRNDARROCH

'WHAT DO YOU THINK OF THIS ELSPETH?'

Kaliope was parading around the dressmaker's shop wearing a red cloche hat with an upturned brim and matching ribbon tied in a subtle bow at the side. She looked beautiful in it, her long dark hair secured in an elegant twist at the nape of her neck. But then, Kaliope looked beautiful in anything.

Elspeth turned to look at her younger sibling, earning her an angry stare from the spinster dressmaker, Temperance Bertram, who was trying to pin the hem of her new dress. Kaliope's hat matched the new maroon-coloured velour coat with bell-shaped sleeves and an ostentatious fur collar she had just collected from Bertrams. She couldn't keep from stroking the fur lovingly as she turned this way and that in front of the full-length mirror. Kaliope wore the coat over an elegant grey dress in the more fashionable straight design now favoured by society women, also just collected from the shop, along with underwear and a collection of six other dresses that would make up her new winter wardrobe.

Kaliope was never happier than when dressing up in pretty things and Elspeth smiled as she witnessed her sister's joy as she moved amongst the many fabrics and trimmings adorning the shelves of Bertrams.

'What do you think of this hat Riordan?'

Kaliope turned towards Elspeth's husband, seated on the chaise longue in the shop window. He had been perusing some business papers with occasional appreciative glances at Kaliope that hadn't gone unnoticed by Elspeth. Her sister was twirling around, her hands up at the brim of the hat, her head dipped so she looked at Riordan from under long dark eyelashes. He smiled a rare, genuine smile that sparkled in his pale green eyes as he placed the papers on the table in front of him.

'It looks very nice on you Kaliope. You should have Miss Bertram wrap it for you with the coat.'

Kaliope beamed. She had softened considerably towards Riordan recently, her fickleness allowing her good opinion to be easily swayed when she was being spoiled. This was their third visit to Bertrams dressmakers in as many months as Riordan had insisted that his wife and her family needed new clothes. Kaliope had been all too eager to accompany them on these shopping trips. Agatha on the other hand fervently refused all offers of clothes or any other gifts from Riordan Darroch. But today, she had relented under Elspeth's pleading and was now sulkily allowing a young assistant to fit her for a new dress.

'I think I will,' Kaliope said placing the hat on the counter and shrugging out of her new coat.

'Say thank you to Riordan,' Agatha shouted, her voice churlish as she reprimanded her twin's lack of gratitude.

'Thank you Riordan,' Kaliope said with exaggerated sincerity, bobbing her knees in a girlish gesture in front of Elspeth's husband.

Riordan smirked, then picked up his papers again keeping his eyes on Kaliope as she continued to browse around the shop.

Agatha fidgeted. The dressmaker's fussing was testing her patience. Elspeth looked over as Temperance, having finished shortening the hem on Elspeth's dress, draped cloths of different colours across Agatha's shoulders.

'Which colour do you prefer madame?' she asked haughtily.

Agatha looked pleadingly at Elspeth, shaking her head slightly.

'I don't know. They're all beautiful. But honestly, I really don't need a new dress.'

'Everyone always needs a new dress!' shouted Kaliope from across the room, amazed, as usual, by Agatha's lack of appreciation for all things pretty and expensive.

Elspeth intervened to make sure Kaliope and Agatha didn't embark on their usual bickering in front of Temperance Bertram.

'I think the blue is perfect with your eyes and hair Aggie.'

'But Elspeth, where on earth am I going to go in a dress like this?'

Agatha was holding out her arms that were now swathed in cornflower silk, Temperance having deftly removed the other colours when Elspeth mentioned blue.

'It'll be a beautiful dress to wear for dinner when we

entertain at Dalengour,' Elspeth said, walking over to Agatha and capturing her hands in both of her own.

Agatha stared at her, the furrow in her brow relaxing as she sensed Elspeth's desire for her to have something beautiful to wear. Until recently, there had never been money to splash out on new clothes, and growing up, their lives had been shaped by the frugal earnings of a clergyman – silk dresses were definitely well beyond the budget then.

'Blue it is,' Agatha said resignedly, but Elspeth was sure she had no intention of ever attending a fancy dinner at Dalengour in this, or any other dress.

'I really will need some new shoes to go with all these dresses,' Kaliope said matter-of-factly from the counter where the assistant was packaging her mound of new things. 'I don't have anything suitable to go with the green dress at all.'

As she spoke, she looked coyly at Riordan, her bottom lip pouting slightly.

'Kaliope! I'm sure you have enough shoes at home to find something that will do.'

Agatha sounded exasperated and rather embarrassed at Kaliope's obvious attempt to persuade Riordan to part with more money.

'But I really don't! I have nothing at all that will do justice to these beautiful fabrics…'

Kaliope was batting her eyelashes now and Agatha's cheeks coloured as she witnessed her twin's overt manipulation of Elspeth's husband. Riordan was easily won over when it came to Kaliope. He stacked his papers neatly on the table and slid them back into his leather briefcase.

'Well, we can't have that now, can we?' Riordan said with a broad smile that revealed his yellowing teeth.

Elspeth turned to look at her husband.

'Riordan, you really shouldn't spoil her anymore,' Elspeth said, creases forming on her brow.

But she knew she was fighting a losing battle as Kaliope rushed over and planted a kiss on Riordan's cheek. The familiar unease settled on her as Elspeth watched her husband's responses to Kaliope's affection and glancing across to Agatha, saw the same concern reflected in her sister's face.

Riordan stood and offered his arm to Kaliope who took it eagerly.

'I'll walk down to Sexton Shoes with Kaliope while you ladies finish up here. We'll meet you back here in say, half an hour? Then we can all go for lunch.'

Kaliope's eyes were alight with excitement at her successful manoeuvring. Agatha looked furious as her sister left the store on Riordan's arm. She turned exasperatedly to Elspeth obviously wanting to vent her anger but stifled by the continued presence of the dressmaker and her assistant.

When they were finally left alone, Agatha rounded on Elspeth.

'How could you let him give in to her so easily? She's spoiled enough and Riordan's attention... well it just makes her worse! And anyway, where is all this money coming from? Aren't you wondering how Riordan can afford all this?'

Agatha swept her hand across the many packages now piled high on the counter.

'Riordan has had a business investment pay off, that's all. He's quite shrewd when it comes to recognising fruitful opportunities.'

'That's what he tells you! But are you sure Ellie? It must be a very good investment to cover new wardrobes for all of us, especially with Kaliope's tastes and voracity for new clothes. Not to mention the cost of that!'

Agatha pointed to the new, black motorcar parked outside the shop that Riordan had purchased just last week.

'I'm telling you Ellie, something doesn't feel right about all this. And his attention to Kaliope – well doesn't it worry you, the way he behaves around her?'

Elspeth lowered her eyes, fixating on her toe that she trailed intermittently across the rug making the pile run against the grain, then lay flat again. She could feel Agatha's eyes boring into her face and was afraid to meet her gaze, knowing she could never conceal anything from her sister.

The truth was she was happier now that she had ever been since moving to Dalengour. Riordan had become her best friend. Although they had never restored the intimacy usually shared between husband and wife, she was spending a good part of every day in his company. He was attentive to her, even supportive and she had to admit that she was very much enjoying the prosperity that Riordan's business dealings brought them. Enjoying it so much, she hadn't bothered asking too many questions.

And Kaliope? She wasn't blind. She could see there was something more than affection for a sister-in-law in Riordan's actions, and that Kaliope was exploiting her husband's feelings. But she had chosen to push her concerns aside – refusing to dwell on things that might threaten her new-found contentment. Agatha made her feel guilty and she didn't like being unsettled again.

'I believe Riordan about the money Agatha. Where else could it be coming from anyway?'

'I don't know. It just seems… I don't know. I just have a feeling that there's something more going on.'

Elspeth usually trusted Agatha's feelings, but this time, she didn't want to.

'I'll talk to him about Kaliope though. You're right he shouldn't give in so easily to her.'

'Elspeth, that isn't what I meant and you know it!'

Elspeth was saved from having to respond by the return of Temperance Bertram.

'I've packaged the dress I shortened for you Lady Darroch, and the blue dress for Miss Larimore will be ready next week.'

'Thank you Miss Bertram,' Elspeth replied, taking the offered packages from the surly dressmaker. 'I trust my husband has settled the bill?'

'In full.'

Agatha shot Elspeth an angry stare as she snatched the remaining parcels from the counter and marched out of the shop. Elspeth smiled weakly at Temperance, muttered her thanks, then followed Agatha onto the street. The cold air of the February day stung against the heat of her cheeks. There was no sign of Riordan and Kaliope. As they were too laden down with bags to move very far, they waited on the pavement, Elspeth leaning against their shiny new car.

'How are your visits to Nerissa going?'

Elspeth was half glad of the change of subject – half glad because she hadn't been visiting Nethergar very often of late. Ever since the incident with Davey, Nerissa had been testy with her. She had been so angry with Elspeth at first that she had refused to help her develop her gifts any further. She had relented after much pleading, but now, spent a great deal of time criticising and berating Elspeth's efforts, always pointing out her weaknesses rather than her successes.

'They're going well.'

Elspeth lowered her face, not wanting Agatha to see her insincerity or the spots of colour that rose in her cheeks as they always did when she lied.

'I haven't been as much as I'd like. I've been so busy.'

'Busy with what?'

'You know, I've been helping people.'

Agatha stared at Elspeth, her expression unusually cold.

'You know Nerissa warned you about pushing your abilities too soon. Does she know that you're doing this 'helping'?'

Agatha's eyes flicked around the street to make sure they were not being overheard and Elspeth fidgeted uncomfortably. She hadn't mentioned any of it to Nerissa. She didn't want her reproaches to spoil the immense satisfaction of bringing someone back from the brink of death. Admittedly, not all the things she'd done had been that dramatic or worthy. Still, even the more conceited requests had value to the person who asked for them.

'Nerissa and I never speak of it. I'm not sure if she knows,' Elspeth said sharply.

'Oh Ellie! What are you doing? I can understand you wanting to help people like the McNairs, really I can. But some of the other things you've done…'

'I've saved a lot of people now from pain and suffering!'

'I'm sure you have, if having crow's feet constitutes pain and suffering!'

The two sisters glared at each other, both trying to contain their anger so as not to make a scene in the street.

'I may have done some things that are more… cosmetic in nature, but it doesn't mean those afflictions were any less distressing for the person concerned.'

Agatha smirked, shaking her head.

'Distressing! You're pandering to people's vanity Elspeth! What I don't understand is why?'

Elspeth was furious now, mostly because she didn't want to think about why she was doing these things.

Agatha was making her confront her recent behaviour and she had no desire for introspection today. The reality was, she was enjoying the reverence her abilities earned her in the village. It was intoxicating and she was revelling in the attention. She gave no thought to the morality of what she was doing.

'And how do these people find you anyway? You shouldn't be flaunting your abilities so openly in the village Elspeth.'

'I don't flaunt them! Riordan brings people to me when he hears they need – something. Others just seek me out themselves. Word travels in a small village like Cairndarroch.'

'Elspeth, open your eyes! Doesn't all this seem a bit odd to you? These people with problems just happening across your path? All this money suddenly appearing?'

'You're just jealous! Jealous of what I have. A nice home, a husband, money and special gifts that you don't!'

Elspeth regretted the words as soon as they were out of her mouth. There was no truth in any of them. Agatha had visited Nethergar and Nerissa confirmed she didn't have the Larimore gifts. But Agatha had been genuinely relieved. And as for coveting Elspeth's life and wealth, nothing could be further removed from Agatha's nature.

'Oh Aggie! I'm so sorry. I didn't mean that.'

Agatha stared at her, eyes glassy and lips clamped firmly together. They didn't have a chance to speak again as Riordan and Kaliope were walking towards them, weighed down with yet more packages.

'All finished?' Riordan asked Elspeth. She nodded curtly, too upset to speak.

Her husband opened the car door allowing her to settle in the back seat with all the packages. Agatha went around to the other side and climbed in next to her, staring out of the window to avoid looking at her. Kaliope took the front seat next to Riordan. They drove back to Kirkholm Cottage in silence.

'WELL, IT LOOKS LIKE JUST THE TWO OF US FOR lunch my dear,' said Riordan, patting Elspeth's hand as she took the front seat, now vacated by Kaliope.

Elspeth throat felt tight as she watched Agatha disappear, slamming the door behind her. They were all supposed to go for lunch together, but Agatha had said she felt unwell and wanted to remain at home. Kaliope had stayed with her, and uncharacteristically, had not pouted about missing the chance to dine out, sensing something was wrong.

'It seems so. I can't be too long though because I really must go and see Nerissa this afternoon.'

Agatha had made her feel guilty, even ashamed of her recent behaviour. Now she had an overwhelming urge to see Nerissa, to explain, to put things right.

They arrived at the inn and took their usual table near the window. Nods of greeting came from every corner as they entered, Elspeth returning them with a smile, Riordan stalking past, ignoring every gesture. She had never noticed before, but many of the stares that followed them were not from people glad to see them. In fact, many glared at them with open hostility. Elspeth frowned, shocked by what she saw, wondering why she had never noticed this before. Probably because she had never really looked. She had seen what she wanted to see. The row with Agatha had made her look at things differently.

Riordan ordered for them both and Elspeth listened to him belittling the service, the food, and the other patrons without really hearing him. She was lost in her own thoughts, running through the argument with Agatha in her head again and again. A pause in Riordan's speech caught her attention and she looked up to see him looking at her intently. He was evidently waiting for her contribution to the topic, to answer a question she hadn't heard.

'Why do you bring us here if everything is below your exacting standards?'

Her voice gave away her irritation. Riordan didn't answer.

'Something happened between you and Agatha today didn't it?

Elspeth really looked at him now for the first time since they had entered the inn. She was surprised by his astuteness. He didn't usually pick up on her mood that easily.

'We had a fight.'

'About what?'

'Mostly about you spoiling Kaliope.'

Elspeth didn't want to broach some of the other reasons with Riordan. He laughed.

'I spoil Kaliope because she is so willing to be spoiled! I would happily buy you and Agatha things but it's very difficult to get either of you to accept my generosity.'

Elspeth had to agree this was true. She relaxed a bit. It seemed a perfectly acceptable explanation. She was willing to accept it anyway. And the money? He couldn't be lying about the money. The Darrochs had always been wealthy and although cash flow was more limited when they first married, Riordan's business acumen had simply restored the family's prosperity to what it had always been.

Elspeth was still upset about her row with Agatha but did feel better about Riordan. By the time their food arrived, her mind was settled again. With the intention of visiting Nerissa that very afternoon to clear her conscience, she readily dismissed Agatha's words, assuming it had been annoyance over Riordan's behaviour towards Kaliope that had made her lash out. Eager to leave at the end of the meal so she could get to Nethergar, Elspeth encouraged Riordan not to linger once the plates were cleared. Always happy to oblige her these days, he paid the bill and collected their coats, foregoing the brandy he usually enjoyed when they ate out.

As Riordan helped her into her coat, a woman appeared at her side. She was well-dressed and looked out of place standing alone in the inn.

'Lady Darroch, please forgive my intrusion into your day. I went to Dalengour, and they told me you were here. It's very important that I speak with you.'

Elspeth looked at the middle-aged woman who spoke eloquently, the soft lilt of her Morningside accent giving away her class. Although she was immaculately turned out, the dark blue coat looked too big on her tiny frame, as if she had recently lost weight very quickly. Her face was pinched, her eyes puffy, implying recently shed tears.

'What can I do for you Mrs…?'

'My name is Jocelyn Tanner. I think you know my nephew, Jenson?'

Elspeth's face froze, her heart skipping a beat at the sound of Jenson's name. She felt Riordan stiffen at her side as he took a step closer and placed a possessive hand on the small of her back.

'Yes, yes I do know Jenson,' Elspeth replied, her voice trembling as she aimed for a nonchalant tone. 'But I haven't seen him for some time. I believe he moved down south.'

The woman nodded but offered no further information about Jenson. Instead, she moved straight to the point of her intrusion.

'I need your help Lady Darroch.'

'Help with what?' Elspeth enquired.

'My husband, he's very ill. We have had many doctors come to see him, but none have been able to help. They say he doesn't have long left.'

She swept her elegantly gloved hand swiftly below her eye to capture an errant tear.

'I'm very sorry to hear that Mrs Tanner. What's wrong with him?'

'He's in the final stages of consumption.'

Jocelyn lowered her eyes and Elspeth intuitively reached out and placed a comforting hand on her arm. She had seen the devastation this illness caused, had watched her mother nurse her father through his final days. She didn't wish that on anyone.

For a few moments, Elspeth didn't speak, allowing the woman time to regain her composure. With a toss of her head to shake away the sadness, Jocelyn met Elspeth's gaze, all business-like again.

'I understand you might be able to help my husband Lady Darroch.'

'Why do you think that?'

'There is talk in the village. I've heard about some of the things you've done and I'm here to ask…to beg you, to try and help my Jack.'

Elspeth didn't speak, her mind in turmoil. Agatha's words were still echoing in her head, and she had been determined to come clean with Nerissa today. She had resolved to listen to her mentor, to do as she instructed. To take things more slowly. But this woman… could she in all good conscience subject her to watching her husband die if she could help him?

'Mrs Tanner, I'm not sure what you have heard but I…'

Jocelyn interrupted, sensing her request was about to be refused.

'Lady Darroch, please. I can't live without my husband. Everyone said I was a fool to marry him. You see, he's a working man, and considered well below my class. But I didn't care. I gave up everything to be with him and I haven't regretted it for a single day. I just can't lose him now.'

Jocelyn took a step closer, laying a hand on Elspeth's arm. Her story struck so many cords. Losing her father, giving up Jenson, settling for a man she didn't love for the comfort and privilege his position would bring her. Elspeth struggled with her conflicting thoughts, her brows drawn in, her ego nipping at the resolve to abide by Nerissa's teaching.

'Elspeth, you could at least try and help Mrs Tanner couldn't you?'

It was the first time Riordan had spoken since Jocelyn appeared. His voice was quiet, but cajoling. Elspeth lowered her eyes to the floor, wanting time to think. But it seemed time was the one thing Jocelyn Tanner didn't have.

'Jenson told me a great deal about you Elspeth.'

The familiarity of using her name drew Elspeth's gaze back to the woman's face.

'He said you are a wonderful person, kind, considerate and very powerful. I need you to prove him right now and try. If not for me, then for him, so that he doesn't lose his uncle.'

These words hit home. Protecting Jenson from grief cleared her thoughts and she made up her mind to try. She didn't want Jocelyn Tanner to have to watch the man she loved wither away as her mother had. But she especially didn't want Jenson to experience the pain of loss if there was something she could do to prevent it.

'Mrs Tanner, I'll try to help you, but I can't make any promises.'

Jocelyn's face erupted into a smile and tears, temporarily stifled, flowed down her face.

'Oh thank you, thank you! Will you come now? Please, do come now.'

'I will. I need a moment to speak with my husband. How did you get here?' she asked.

'I have borrowed a car and chauffeur from my brother. They're just outside.'

'You should take your car and go home to check on your husband. Riordan will drive me to you as soon as we're done here.'

'You won't be long?' Jocelyn asked, panic in her tone.

'No, I'll be no more than fifteen minutes behind you.'

When Jocelyn didn't move, Elspeth added 'I promise' and the women hurried out of the inn.

'Riordan, I'm supposed to be visiting Nerissa today. She's expecting me and I don't feel I can let her down. I really need to speak to her too.'

'Do you think you'll be long at Mrs Tanner's?'

'I can't say. I have no idea how ill her husband is or even if I'll be able to help.'

'I'm sure you'll be able to do something for the man. Your powers haven't let you down so far, have they?'

Riordan smiled at her reassuringly.

'Do you want me to go and apologise to Nerissa for you? Tell her you'll be along tomorrow?' he asked offering his arm to escort her out of the inn.

'If only you could. But you can't get through the gateway without me.'

'Of course. I didn't think.'

Rain was beginning to fall as they came out onto the street. Heads bowed against the chill wind, they hurried across the road to where Riordan had parked the car. Quickly he opened the passenger door to let Elspeth in, then came around to the driver's side.

'Couldn't you do something so that I can get into Nethergar alone? I seem to remember Nerissa saying something when we first visited, something about a guide? If you gave me a guide, can't I go through without you?' he asked, brushing away the raindrops that had settled on his black woollen coat.

Elspeth looked at him. This wasn't something she had considered. If she gave Riordan a guide, he would be able to come and go through the gateway as he pleased.

'I understand if you don't want to. If you don't trust me...,' he said, eyes fixed down the street as he started the car.

'It's not that. I do trust you,' she said a little too quickly. 'I just hadn't thought about it. I forgot this was something Nerissa said I could do.'

Elspeth flushed, the colour collecting in patches on her cheeks giving away her untruth. Riordan was looking at the road now as he eased the car away from the kerb and towards the address Jocelyn Tanner had provided. They drove in silence for a while, Elspeth's mind reeling. She desperately wanted Nerissa to know she hadn't forgotten their meeting. Things were already uneasy between them and not turning up as planned would not help. She was also letting Nerissa down to do the very thing she had been warned against, the very thing Elspeth had decided to stop doing only an hour ago. The distress on Jocelyn Tanner's face flitted through her mind, and then the relief when Elspeth had said she would help. She couldn't let her down. She had to at least try.

'Riordan, I want you to go and tell Nerissa that I can't make today.'

'I'm happy to my dear. I just want to be of help. And the guide?'

Agatha's voice intruded into her thoughts - her distrust of

Riordan, her disappointment in Elspeth. She pushed it away. She loved Aggie, but she was wrong about this. Riordan could be trusted - she felt sure of it. And helping Jocelyn was important.

'I'll give you a guide so you can open the gateway.'

'If you're sure?'

She wasn't. She knew both Nerissa and Agatha would warn her against it. But she reconciled her conflicting thoughts with assurances that she was doing the right thing in trying to help the Tanners. And anyway, she could take away Riordan's access to Nethergar at any time.

Elspeth nodded as Riordan gave her a sideways glance.

They pulled up outside the Tanner's address. It was a well-kept house on the edge of the village that reminded Elspeth of Kirkholm Cottage. It had the same symmetrical façade of grey sandstone, with a central door and window to each side upstairs and down. Lights burned in every room, fending off the gloom that accompanied the rain. The garden was probably pretty in the summer months, but only ghostly bare branches and withered stems were evident now.

Elspeth turned to Riordan.

'Give me your hand.'

He obliged and she entwined her fingers in his. His skin felt dry, almost rough as he secured his grip. For a fleeting moment, she stalled, doubt clouding her mind again. But it was too late now. Jocelyn Tanner appeared at the door, her face pale in the greyness of the day, her brows furrowed as she peered through the downpour to see whether she was coming in.

Elspeth felt the pressure of responsibility at the sight of Jocelyn's expectation. She tried to shut it out, focussing on the feel of Riordan's hand. Closing her eyes, the familiar surge of energy built in her fingers. As it grew, she opened her eyes and saw a golden glow forming in the gaps between their hands. With her mind, she forced the light into a shimmering ribbon that weaved around their wrists, tying them together. The connection allowed her to pass part of herself to Riordan, a part that would be recognised by the gateway.

As the light faded, she released Riordan's hand. He stared at it, turning it around, as if looking for some visible difference.

'Is that it?' he asked.

'I think so. I've never done it before.'

She stifled a last moment of doubt and looked up towards Jocelyn fidgeting anxiously from foot to foot in the open doorway.

'I'd better go. Can you tell Nerissa that I'm very sorry about today, but please don't tell her why I'm not there. Just tell her I don't feel well.'

Riordan raised his eyebrow.

'I'll explain when I see her tomorrow,' Elspeth said in answer to his unspoken question.

'Fine, I'll make your excuses. I'll go to Nethergar and then come back for you in about an hour.'

He kissed her swiftly on the cheek and she got out of the car, drawing the collar of her coat as high possible to protect against the heavily falling rain.

Riordan watched her hurry up the path and vanish into the brightly lit house. A satisfied smile spread across his lips as he drove back to Dalengour.

WHEN HE RETURNED HOME, HE BRIEFLY considered going to see his mother to tell her of his success in securing a guide from Elspeth. But on reflection, he thought better of it. He was in no rush to hand control back to Morwenna. He had visited her less and less in the three months since he first went to Nethergar, unable to stand her petulant demands to be let out or that he force Elspeth to take her through the gateway.

Although he had always managed to convince her to be patient, waiting until Elspeth voluntarily provided him with the means to enter Nethergar, he was tired of being on the receiving end of Morwenna's anger and frustration. He was enjoying being free of his mother's moods.

Instead, he made his way to the kirk intent on delivering Elspeth's message to Nerissa as promised. Despite his arrogance at having manipulated Elspeth into giving him a guide, Riordan was apprehensive as he pushed open the wooden door and headed down to St Oda's window. It was dark inside the small church as he walked between the pews, the gloom of the day failing to provide any natural light even though it was still only mid-afternoon. The kirk seemed to sense him, the candles springing into life as he reached the altar stone, bathing the stained glass in a warm glow. He looked into the face of the blind Saint, his apprehension giving way to excitement.

Riordan reached out his hand to touch the window and immediately, the surface gave way to become a molten lake – the gateway to another world. Looking down, he saw mist gathering around his feet, twisting and undulating in waves that ebbed and flowed. He watched as the head of a bird seemed to form in the silvery vapour, rising up, wings erupting upwards as they were momentarily freed from the smoke, before sinking back beneath the surface.

Everything seemed to be moving in slow motion, his senses alert to every fluctuation in the environment around him. He could feel vibrations coming from the gateway, hear a gentle hum from the energy emanating from Nethergar. He had never felt so alive, so excited.

With a deep breath, he stepped through the window, emerging in the reflection of the kirk that was Nethergar. The mist was intensifying, the image of the bird becoming more opaque, solid. The feathers were clearly visible now, their silver silhouette deepening to a dense, glossy black. He watched as the black raven broke free, the diaphanous mist dissipating until only the bird remained. It soared down the aisle, coming to rest on the end pew, waiting for Riordan to follow.

He walked towards it. The bird held its position until he threw open the door. He was momentarily surprised by the brightness of the day, a marked contrast to the wintery damp and cold afternoon he had left in Cairndarroch. Here, the sun was high in the sky, bathing the clearing in unexpected light.

A sudden fluttering of wings startled him as the raven flew past his head and began to circle the kirk, cawing impatiently. It settled on a tree beside the path that led to Nerissa's home. A broad smile on his face, Riordan made his way through the trees, the raven flying from branch to branch, always staying ahead of him until they reached the edge of the forest. He looked down the path towards Kirkholm Cottage, plain and austere in comparison to the heather-covered hills surrounding it. The raven stretched its wings and took flight. Riordan watched as it soared overhead. He was here. He had done it.

CHAPTER 16

The Foolish Wife

ELSPETH HURRIED DOWN THE STREET, EAGER TO get back to Dalengour before lunch. Mr Tanner seemed to be doing better this morning and she was glad she had made time to call on Jocelyn. The woman's relief and gratitude had gone some way to alleviate the worrying thoughts that still plagued Elspeth's mind.

The argument with Agatha had affected her deeply. They had never exchanged cross words before, and she was shaken by her own behaviour towards her sister. She had lashed out angrily. And not because Agatha was wrong – but because she was right. She had been behaving rashly lately, carried along on a tide of conceited self-pride and preoccupation with the power she felt when changing the naturalness of things.

And Riordan? He had been very supportive of her trips to

Nethergar. Too supportive? Nagging worries still disturbed her. Had giving Riordan access to Nethergar been foolish? But she had no real reason to doubt him. He had collected her yesterday afternoon from the Tanners having delivered her message to Nerissa as requested. But still, she couldn't relax. She just couldn't bring herself to trust him completely.

She hurried along the pavement lost in her thoughts, head down as she resolved to discuss things with Nerissa that afternoon. It was time she came clean and told her the truth of what she had been doing these past few months. Nerissa would be angry, and rightly so. But she hoped her honesty would set their relationship straight.

Rounding the corner, not paying attention to where she was going, she ran headlong into a woman coming the other way, scattering the meagre contents of her shopping basket across the road.

'I'm so very sorry! I wasn't looking where I was going.'

Elspeth bent down as she spoke and began collecting the potatoes that were now rolling in the gutter. She placed them back into the basket along with a split bag of flour and a small package wrapped in butcher's paper. The box of eggs was irretrievably broken, the shells shattered and the yellow yolks oozing across the pavement.

'Are any of them saved?'

The woman's voice was panicked as she scooped up the smashed egg box to look for any salvageable contents.

'I don't think so.'

Elspeth met the woman's gaze for the first time and looked into the haggard face of Daisy McNair.

'Daisy, how are you? You had the baby!' Elspeth remarked noticing she was no longer with child. 'What did you have, a boy or girl?'

Daisy didn't respond. She looked at her with a cold expression, completely at odds with their last meeting.

'How's Davey doing?' Elspeth asked, wondering if her hostility was because something had happened to the boy she had helped.

'He's fine.'

Daisy didn't elaborate and began rearranging the contents of the shopping basket, obviously not wanting to engage in further conversation. Elspeth watched the woman check the box of eggs, feeling hurt and confused. Only one egg was intact. Daisy held it in her hand as if it were a precious gem. Her eyes glistened and Elspeth thought she was going to cry.

'Daisy, what is it? I'm really sorry about the eggs. I'll pay for the damage.'

Elspeth began to rifle through her handbag, searching for her purse that she knew contained a few shillings. She held one out to Daisy who stared at it. Still clutching the egg and never taking her eyes from the money, Daisy began to laugh, a maniacal laugh that confused Elspeth even more.

'You take everything we have from us each month and then stand here, offering me a shilling to pay for a measly box of eggs?' she wheezed, venom in every word.

Elspeth was lost. She had no idea what was going on. Lowering her hand, she pushed the shilling into her coat pocket.

'I'm sorry if I offended you. I was only trying to help.'

Daisy sneered. There was no mistaking the look she gave Elspeth. There was pure hatred in her eyes. Elspeth noticed now that the woman was extremely thin, dark circles around her eyes, her cheeks hollow, giving her pale skin a greyish appearance. She didn't look well at all.

'Daisy, I don't understand what's going on here. Have I

done something wrong? Is something wrong with the baby? Can I help you?'

'We can't afford any more of your help,' Daisy spat, small patches of colour appearing in her sunken cheeks, stark against her pallor.

'I'm sorry, I don't understand. What do you mean by 'afford my help'?'

Daisy drew her eyebrows together and she tilted her head, looking quizzically at Elspeth.

'You really don't know, do you?'

'Know what?'

'Your help with Davey came at a price. Don't get me wrong, I'm eternally grateful to still have my son, but we have been paying your husband half a shilling a month ever since. We have to pay until our debt of five pounds is repaid in full.'

The colour drained from Elspeth's face and the world suddenly stopped turning as everything fell into place. The sounds of the street faded away and all she could hear was her heart thudding against her chest.

'Are you alright Lady Darroch?'

Daisy's voice sounded distant, but the concerned tone penetrated Elspeth's consciousness.

'I...I...I'm fine,' Elspeth stammered. 'I'm sorry. I...I didn't know.'

She tipped all the coins from her purse still clutched in her hand. It totalled about four shillings that she pushed firmly into Daisy's hand.

'This should cover everything you've paid.'

Daisy stared at the coins.

'I can't take this Lady Darroch. I won't be in anyone's debt.'

'Consider your debt discharged. You owe us nothing. Please take the money and buy the food you need for your family.'

'This is too much,' Daisy murmured, thrusting her hand containing the silver back towards Elspeth.

'Please Daisy, take it.'

Elspeth curled Daisy's fingers around the money and was relived as the woman pushed the shillings deep into the pocket of her tattered coat.

'Thank you,' she said quietly. 'But what about your husband?'

'I will deal with Riordan,' Elspeth replied, repressed anger seeping into her words.

She took her leave of Daisy and hurried on down the street, fury fuelling her feet until she was almost running. Her mind was spinning. Riordan had been taking money from the people she helped and judging by the amount of spending he was doing, the five pounds from the McNairs was just the beginning. She suspected the pockets of the wealthier benefactors had been tapped more deeply. How could she have been so stupid!

Elspeth burst through the door of Dalengour twenty minutes later, the usual half hour walk shortened by her pace. Her lace-up boots and hem on her blue Devore coat were splatted with mud courtesy of yesterday's rains. She threw her leather gloves and bag onto the hall table, shouting for Riordan. No answer came. She began frantically searching each room, leaving muddy footprints in her wake.

'Is something wrong Lady Darroch?'

Gadsen appeared in the hall, the commotion bringing him up from the kitchen.

'Where is my husband?'

'I haven't seen him since breakfast,' he replied, his usual surliness exaggerated in response to her demanding tone.

'If you see him, tell him I need to speak with him urgently.'

Taking this as a dismissal, Gadsen nodded curtly and left Elspeth to her search. She looked in every downstairs room with no success and so headed up to the first floor. He wasn't in his chambers and there was no response to her shouts as she moved through each of the halls in turn. Maybe he wasn't here? He hadn't said he was going out. Frustrated, she started toward the staircase, intent on going downstairs to ask the servants if anyone had seen him leave.

As she made her way towards the main landing, she walked past the door that led to the east tower – to Morwenna's rooms. Riordan might be there. The door leading to the staircase was kept locked, but she knew there was a key in the drawer of the heavy mahogany dresser standing sentry beside it. Tentatively, she made her way over and tried the door. She was surprised to find it open, but not too alarmed. Perhaps Riordan was with his mother, or maybe Gadsen or the maid were tending to Morwenna's needs.

As she pulled the door wide, cold air caused her to shiver. There was no light on the staircase, with only a few narrow windows letting in the limited daylight to illuminate the way. The stone steps echoed with each footfall, giving Elspeth a sense of foreboding as she climbed higher, balancing herself against the barren stone walls as she went. For some reason, she felt nervous, shaky, unsure of what she would find at the top of the landing.

The stairs spiralled around as she climbed. She could see a door leading off a small landing. This went to the rooms occupied by Morwenna. The staircase continued to twist upwards beyond this, but she had never ventured to the top and had no desire to do so now. Riordan had told her it led to an old attic, once used for storage but now empty and locked as it was unsafe.

With a trembling hand, she reached out for the doorknob, swallowing hard as it turned easily. Opening the door a chink, she listened. Silence. She could hear no voices, no tell-tale signs that Riordan was visiting Mowenna or that one of the servants was fussing around the room. No sounds at all to say the room was occupied.

The hinges creaked in protest as she opened the door just enough to slip inside. It was dark, no lamps or fires lit to ward off the chill. In fact, the room looked as if had been vacated some time earlier. She turned on the light, but it did little to illuminate the space. Only the area immediately below it brightened, leaving all the corners of the room in shadows. She was standing in a parlour decorated in subtle pastel tones – very unlike any other room at Dalengour. Elspeth was certain this hadn't been designed by Morwenna Darroch given it lacked the crassness of the rest of the castle. She moved through the room, feeling as if she were disturbing the sanctuary of the previous occupant.

The bedroom led off the sitting room, the same delicate shades adorning the walls, lace bedding covering the neatly made bed. This room held some signs Morwenna had been here. Hairbrushes and cosmetics adorned the dresser, shoes were pushed carelessly under the bed, a nightgown thrown over the door of the large, imposing wardrobe. Elspeth looked inside to see a number of gowns, nearly all in Morwenna's favoured black. Water still filled the basin on the washstand, but it was cold, left over from the morning.

Bile began to rise in the back of Elspeth's throat and the

trembling in her hands spread through her entire body. Morwenna was not locked in these rooms and probably hadn't been for most of the day. Panicking, she fled back down the stairs and out into the hall of the main house. Robert. She needed to check on Robert.

As she burst through the nursery door, she bowled into Josephine Dennings, scattering the armful of folded laundry she was carrying across the floor.

'I'm sorry Miss Dennings. Robert, where is he?'

The nanny was picking up the clothes, a scowl on her pinched face.

'Lord Darroch came for him this morning. He said he was taking him for a walk with his grandmother.'

'With Morwenna! And you let him?'

Elspeth's heart raced, her voice high pitched, accusation in her tone.

Josephine Dennings drew herself up, her spine poker-straight.

'It's not my place to challenge Lord Darroch,' she replied waspishly. 'And why shouldn't Robert spend time with his father?'

Elspeth suppressed the desire to shout. The nanny didn't know about Morwenna threatening to harm Robert, about her attempts to kill Elspeth. She was sure she knew of Morwenna's 'illness' – servants gossiped. But as to the circumstances that led to her being confined in the east tower, anything she did know was likely conjecture rather than fact.

'What time did they go?' she asked, feigning a calm she didn't feel.

'A little after ten. He assured me he would have him back for his lunch so they should be here any moment now.'

Josephine glanced at the clock on the mantel that showed Robert had been 'out' for almost two hours. Elspeth nodded curtly to the nanny and walked out of the room as sedately as she could manage. Once clear of the nursery, she started to run again, her feet barely touching the stairs as she descended to the front hall.

She stopped dead in her tracks. Jenson Tanner was pacing back and forth by the front door.

'Jenson!'

He spun around to meet her stare and despite herself, her heart soared. He ran towards her and gathered her into his arms, crushing her tightly to him.

'Thank God!' he whispered into her hair, holding her longer than felt proper.

Remembering himself, he released her and stepped back. Elspeth saw tears glistening in his eyes, accentuating the golden flecks that swam amongst the greenness. Her panic was momentarily forgotten as she looked at him, love flooding her senses, disarming the anger she had nurtured towards him since he left her.

'What are you doing here?'

'I had to see you. I had to warn you.'

'Warn me? Warn me about what?'

'Oh Elspeth. There's so much you don't know. So much I should've told you.'

He looked down and a tear ran down his cheek.

'Tell me now,' she said, taking a step towards him again.

He didn't look up, ashamed to meet her gaze. He didn't speak.

'Jenson, I don't have time to play games,' she said shortly. 'A great deal has happened here since you left and right now, I have to go and find my husband and son.'

Jenson flinched as she mentioned her husband, but still

didn't look at her. Elspeth sighed heavily. She didn't have time to cajole information from him. If he wasn't going to tell her, then so be it. She turned away and headed towards the front door, intent on searching for her son.

'Wait! Please wait!'

Jenson grabbed her wrist, holding her firmly so she couldn't leave.

'What is it Jenson?' she asked angrily. 'I don't have time for this. Either tell me what's on your mind or don't. But I have to go!'

'Why do you need to look for Riordan and Robert so urgently?' Jenson asked, his eyebrows raised as he finally fixed his gaze on her face.

'Because…because they went out earlier this morning and I was expecting them back some time ago. I'm starting to get worried. That's all.'

'You're lying to me Elspeth. And not very well.'

'You can talk!' she spat, feeling heat rise in her face. 'You've been lying to me since I came to Dalengour!'

'Yes, I have,' he said sullenly, releasing her arm and taking a step back. 'But only because I had no choice.'

Silence hung heavily as Elspeth's anger faltered.

'What do you mean?' she asked more calmly now.

'Do you remember the young girl you saw in the carriage with me on the day I left?

Elspeth nodded.

'That was my younger sister, Gwen.'

Elspeth couldn't help the relief she felt. His sister. Not the daughter that had tormented her dreams.

'My parents died three years ago, and I became full-time carer for my sister.'

'Jenson, I'm so sorry. I didn't know about your parents. I didn't even enquire after them! I'm a terrible person!'

'No, you're not Elspeth. It was a long time ago and it isn't the reason I'm telling you this.'

She nodded slightly, encouraging him to continue.

'I was struggling for money and finding a job was difficult when I had to look after Gwen. Out of the blue, Morwenna Darroch offered me a job and said she would welcome my sister into her home as well. The arrangement was for Gwen to take up a post below stairs when she was old enough. Looking back, it was strange for someone I'd never met to provide me with a perfect solution to my problems. But I was desperate. I didn't want to think about it too hard, and so I took what was offered.'

He fell silent again. His eyes were pleading with her to understand as he searched her face.

'Then what happened?' she asked willing him to continue.

'We'd only been here a day when Gwen vanished from the servant's quarters. I came downstairs to look for her and Gadsen told me Morwenna wanted to see me. She told me if I ever wanted to see Gwen again, I had to do what she asked.'

'And what did she ask?'

'She knew that you and I were friends. She wanted me to encourage you to come to Dalengour, to marry Riordan.'

'But you didn't! You didn't encourage me. I thought you.. I thought you loved me,' Elspeth said coyly, lowering her eyes.

'I did. I mean I do. I do love you Elspeth. I always have.'

He took her hands in his, trying to communicate his affection for her. She tilted her head to look up at his, wanting to be happy that he loved her. But she still felt confused. He saw her the uncertainty in her face.

'When you came here, I played along at first. Morwenna wanted me to make you feel comfortable here. She thought my presence would make Dalengour seem more favourable to you, somewhere you could see yourself living. But she under-estimated how dreadful a place this is. My being here was never going to overcome how inhospitable Dalengour was going to feel for you after Kirkholm Cottage.'

Elspeth cast her eyes around the hall, remembering how oppressive she had thought it when she first visited. How happy she had felt to find Jenson here. His presence had reassured her. Morwenna was clever.

'When you agreed to marry Riordan, I couldn't do it anymore. I couldn't pretend that I was happy for you to become his wife. I was even angry at you for not seeing through what they were doing. You couldn't see how much I wanted you, couldn't sense that I was keeping something from you.'

'How could I? You seemed to do everything possible to avoid me once I moved here!'

'I know. I know it was unreasonable now. But I didn't know what to do. I was so worried about Gwen. I was afraid of what Morwenna would do to her if I stopped you marrying Riordan. So, I pushed my feelings away and went about my business. I asked continuously for Gwen's release, but Morwenna wouldn't do it. She told me she might still have need of me. So, I kept my mouth shut and waited for an opportunity to get Gwen back.'

Jenson paused, his head hung, his lips pressed tightly together. Elspeth's emotions were in turmoil. He loved her, but he had lied to her.

'You did get Gwen back. And then you left... left me.'

'Oh God Elspeth. How will you every forgive me?'

'Maybe if you tell me why you left it would be a start.'

Her tone was surly, her confusion giving rise to a sense of frustration with him.

'I tried to carry on as normal, even tried to be happy for

you when you became pregnant. I hoped I'd been wrong about Riordan and that he genuinely loved you. I convinced myself that you were alright, even content with your life here. Then, you vanished. The servants were told you were confined to your bed with complications from the birth, but I was afraid for you. So was Agatha. She came here every day asking to see you.'

Elspeth's stomach lurched as she remembered the argument with Agatha. She felt even worse about it now she knew her sister had been right all along.

'Eventually, they let Agatha sit with you two mornings a week. She still came every day to enquire about you, but on Mondays and Thursdays, Morwenna gave permission for her to spend an hour in your rooms. She would brush your hair, read to you. Anything to try and rouse you from your illness. But you never did. After every visit, she came to find me and told me how you were.'

'She never told me any of this! Nor did Riordan, or you!'

Elspeth was furious now. Angry at everyone else making decisions about what she should and shouldn't know. Jenson didn't respond to her outburst. Instead, he returned to his story.

'While you were ill, Morwenna called on my services again. She told me about the gateway to Nethergar.'

'You knew! You knew about the kirk? About me?'

'Not everything and I didn't believe most of it. She told me about the gateway and that you needed to be the person to open it. But Morwenna didn't know where it was. I think she'd been looking but couldn't find it. She needed you, but you were too ill to be of much help.'

'But it was Morwenna who was making me ill!'

'I know. She wanted to keep you weak so that when the time came, she could take what she needed – your blood to open the gateway. But first, she had to find it. So, I think she lessened the amount of poison she was giving you and you started to feel a bit better. Well enough to get up and go out for a walk.'

'And I found the kirk,' Elspeth said with a slow blink of understanding – Morwenna's manipulation of her had been complete.

'Yes. She wanted me to spend as much time as possible with you so that if you found the gateway, I would know and could tell her. If I did, she would let Gwen go.'

'So, you did as she asked and got your sister back,' Elspeth said, hurt in her blue eyes.

'No, no I didn't! I couldn't. I think Morwenna suspected how I felt about you and didn't trust me to do what she asked. I couldn't let her hurt you Elspeth. I just couldn't. When I saw you leaving the house, I followed you, intent on telling you the truth. I never thought you would find the gateway on your first day out of bed! Morwenna must have been watching you too because by the time I got to you, you were lying unconscious and bleeding in the kirk.'

'And when we came back from Nethergar, you told her I had opened the gateway?' she asked accusingly.

Jenson turned away from her and ruffled his tawny hair, leaving it sticking up untidily. He walked a few paces back and forth, gathering his thoughts before turning back to her.

'Please try to understand, she had my sister. I did tell her, but she already knew. She must have been watching in the kirk. I asked her to release Gwen again, but she wouldn't.'

Elspeth wanted to understand, but all she could feel was anger. Anger towards him for betraying her.

'Why didn't you tell me all this when we came back?'

'I was afraid of what she would do to Gwen, to you. I didn't know how far she would go to gain access to

Nethergar. So, I held my tongue and kept my distance, watching from afar but always making sure you were safe.'

'But you were supposed to meet me at the kirk the day you left!'

'Yes, I know.'

Jenson looked sheepish, his eyelashes shimmering with moisture. 'I couldn't stay away from you.

'I wanted you to know how I felt, I wanted you to know the truth about Morwenna,' he said grabbing her hands again, shaking them in his efforts to make her see.

'So why didn't you come?'

Elspeth's voice was higher now as her indignation swelled again at the memory of him leaving without explanation.

'Riordan cornered me as I was about to leave for the kirk. Elspeth, he knew. He knew about Nethergar, about what Morwenna had done to you, about Gwen, about everything.'

Jenson searched her face, looking for signs of shock or disbelief. There were none. Elspeth knew Riordan had been playing the part of dutiful, supportive husband these past months. Knew he had been manipulating her, getting her to trust him, using her as a puppet to get Morwenna what she wanted. The anger she felt now was only partly directed at Jenson. She was angry at herself for being so easily fooled.

'You left because Riordan knew?' she said waspishly, her face flushed with colour.

'No, I left because he told me that if I walked out of Dalengour then, and agreed never to see you again, he would finally let me take Gwen away. And so I did.'

His voice was quiet and trembling as he uttered these last words. He couldn't bear to look at Elspeth. She could feel his shame and disappointment in himself. Her annoyance softened as she looked at the top of his bowed head. They stood in silence for a few moments, both needing time for the implications of their spoken words to settle.

It was Elspeth who broke the silence, the need to find her son forcibly reasserting itself. She took a step towards Jenson and placed a hand under his chin to bring his face level with hers.

'You came back,' she said gently. Allowing her palm to come to rest on his cheek.

He covered her hand with his own.

'I have wanted to come back every day since I left. I love you so much. Can you ever forgive me?'

Her hand dropped. Truthfully, she didn't know if she could forgive him. She felt wounded by his deceit, by his lack of honesty, something Elspeth valued above all other.

'Jenson, I don't know how I feel having heard this. But I do know I don't have time to talk anymore about it now.'

His brows drew together, and she hastily summarised what had happened since he left. She told him about helping people in the village, about helping his aunt and uncle. About Riordan making the people she helped pay without her knowledge.

'I'm really worried Jenson. He might have gone to see Jocelyn to demand money. Perhaps you can go and explain to them? Make sure they don't give him anything?'

'Elspeth, I don't have an Aunt Jocelyn and I have no uncle on my father's side. The only relative I have is my mother's sister who is in London. I haven't seen her for years!'

The colour drained from Elspeth's face, Riordan's deception laid bare.

'He planned it all. Planned it so I would give him a guide...' she said wistfully.

Fury at her own stupidity flared up into tears of anger.

'How could I have been so stupid! Now he can get to Nethergar. What have I done!'

She looked pleadingly at Jenson, not expecting him to have an answer to her question.

'And Morwenna, Robert and Riordan are missing now?' he asked.

'Yes, I need to find them and quickly.'

Her voice was panicked, her hands shaking as Jenson took hold of them. She calmed a little at his touch. It was good to have him here despite her disappointment in his past actions. She knew his feelings for her were genuine even if she wasn't sure of her own anymore.

'Let me help you Elspeth. You stay here in case they come back. I'll go to look for them in the grounds and at the kirk.'

Elspeth's eyes glistened with the emotion of unshed tears. He looked tenderly into her face, tracing his finger down her cheek. As they looked at each other, understanding passed between them. Things would never be the same. They couldn't go back and start again. Too much had happened. They had missed their chance. Jenson stepped away. He would always love Elspeth Larimore, and she him.

'Elspeth, is there a reason Riordan would go through the gateway? Can he take Morwenna through?'

'No. I only gave the guide to him. Morwenna would need to be accompanied by me,' Elspeth said distractedly.

'Elspeth, what are you thinking? What do you think they're doing?'

She ran her hand across her forehead, trying to force the answer to the fore.

'I honestly don't know. But Riordan must have set me up for a reason. And with Morwenna free...'

'Let's not panic yet,' Jenson said, spontaneously pulling her into his arms.

She was grateful for his attempts at reassurance, but they failed miserably. She knew what Morwenna was capable of. Jenson released her, holding her at arm's length.

'Please be careful Elspeth – if he comes back. Be careful.'

'I can take care of myself,' she said, calm now, drawing on all the strength she possessed. The Darrochs would not win. They would not take everything she loved from her. She wouldn't let them.

CHAPTER 17

Murder Most Foul

FEBRUARY 1922– NETHERGAR

RIORDAN DARROCH COVERED THE GROUND EASILY, his long, bony legs striding out as he hurried through the forest towards Kirkholm Cottage. His raven guide was nothing more than a black blur silhouetted against the white clouds as it soared high above the trees just ahead of him. Excitement exuded from every pore as he moved, his skin prickling with the thrill of what he was about to do.

He had delayed the inevitable for as long as possible, but now he sensed Elspeth's suspicions, fuelled by that dowdy sister of hers. Agatha repulsed him. So unlike Kaliope who aroused every fibre of his being. Perhaps once Elspeth was gone, he could have her? With the power of Nethergar at their disposal, he could have anything he wanted. Only

Morwenna would stand in his way. And he was arrogant enough to think she could be handled.

Riordan had strung his mother along as far as he could manage. He had put up with her wrath every time he visited, never telling her about the people Elspeth was helping. Never telling her about the wealth he was steadily building. But now, his wife was acting strangely, more distant and he had to act before she took away his access to the gateway. If that happened, all the plans they had made, all the work he had done in playing the dutiful husband to his pathetic, unappealing wife, would have been in vain.

The caw of the raven brought his thoughts back to the present. He was approaching the edge of the forest. Soon, she would know he was here. The whirling in his stomach strengthened, his heart rate quickening. He paused for a moment, still concealed by the tree line, taking a few deep breaths to steady himself. He had to play this right. Nerissa Larimore was dangerous.

He took the small vial Morwenna had given him from his pocket and shook it so that the clear, odourless poison bubbled, confirming its presence within the glass. He smiled, then tucked it back from where it came. Next, he checked the knife was safely stored in the inside pocket of his jacket, the silver hilt cold to his touch. All was in place.

With a final slow breath, he stepped out into the open air and began to descend the path to Kirkholm Cottage. Nerissa saw him immediately. She was standing in the open doorway, waiting for Elspeth, arms folded obstinately, scowling in his direction.

'Nerissa, so lovely to see you,' he shouted as he came within hearing distance.

Nerissa didn't move. She continued to lean against the door frame, eyeing him suspiciously.

'Why are you here again? Where is Elspeth?'

'She sent me on ahead to tell you she's been delayed. She'll be along soon, but she didn't want you to think she wasn't coming.'

Nerissa humphed but unfolded her arms as she stood upright.

'You'd better come in then.'

She stood aside to admit Riordan into the kitchen. She was less than welcoming but he removed his hat and nodded to accept her invitation. He was inside and that was what he wanted.

Nerissa closed the door behind him and began to boil water to make tea as Riordan knew she would. Neither spoke while she busied herself, but he tracked her every move, running through the sequence of behaviour he had observed so closely every time he visited with Elspeth. He knew his opportunity would come any minute now. She would place the cups on the table, then turn back to the sink to wash the spoon before she came to join him. She had never deviated from this routine. Never.

On cue, Nerissa placed the tea in front of him, then turned her back. He slipped the small glass vial from his pocket and deftly emptied its contents into her cup. Small ripples appeared on the surface as it diffused through the dark brown liquid. To avoid raising suspicion, Riordan made to fidget, catching the table leg and causing both cups to slop some of their contents onto the table.

'I'm sorry,' he muttered apologetically as Nerissa brought a cloth over to mop up the spill.

As she did, she pulled her own tea over to where she would sit and pushed Riordan's closer to him. He smiled weakly in thanks and curled both hands around the cup. Nerissa threw the soiled cloth back into the sink and took her seat, fixing her keen blue eyes on him. Her lips were set in a thin line. He could sense her annoyance at Elspeth's failure to arrive along with him.

'Where is Elspeth then?' she asked tersely.

'She had to go and see Agatha. They had a bit of a falling out yesterday and it was playing on Elspeth's mind. She didn't think she'd be able to concentrate until it was resolved.'

Nerissa looked surprised, showing no sign of drinking her tea. Riordan took a long slurp of his own, hoping to encourage her to follow suit.

'Agatha and Elspeth get on so well. What could they disagree about?'

Nerissa looked interested and her tone was less accusatory now. She still didn't drink.

'It was about Kaliope actually,' Riordan responded, thinking on his feet.

He had rehearsed a reason why Elspeth was not with him but had expected any further conversation to be moot. But the damn woman wasn't drinking.

'It was silly really. They were in the dress shop and Kaliope wanted to get shoes to match her new dress. Elspeth agreed but Agatha was annoyed that we were spoiling her. They had cross words and Agatha refused to come to lunch with us.'

The bones of the truth were more convincing than an outright lie. Nerissa made him uncomfortable and concocting a complete fabrication under duress would have been too risky.

'That does seem silly and certainly not worth falling out over,' Nerissa said raising her eyebrows and glaring suspiciously at Riordan. 'But I know Elspeth has been worried about Kaliope for some reason. She never says anything, but I can sense it when we work together.'

Riordan shifted in his seat, red patches rising on his cheeks to disturb the grey pallor of his complexion as the image of Kaliope flitted into his mind. Quickly, he swallowed hard to calm his arousal and took another drink. This time, Nerissa joined him.

Immediately she swallowed the tea, she pulled the cup away, looking discerningly at the contents. She could sense something was wrong. She looked up at Riordan who smiled innocently.

'Is something a matter?' he asked, feigned concern in his voice.

He hoped one mouthful would be enough because she wasn't going to take anymore now.

'I…I…I don't know. The tea…'

Her voice trailed off as she started to sway on her seat. She was blinking hard as if trying to clear her foggy head, but he knew it wouldn't work. Nerissa's arms fell limply to her sides, all strength draining from them. The excitement erupted out of him in a perverted laugh. He threw his head back as he cackled while she drew on every ounce of her remaining strength to stay conscious.

Composing himself, he rose from his seat and walked around the table to stand behind her. He took the knife from his inside pocket and grabbed her chin, forcing her head back against him. He leaned in close, his hard, dry lips brushing her ear as he spoke.

'It seems your suspicions about me were correct Nerissa. It's just a shame you won't be able to tell my wife. Once you're gone, my way will be free to get rid of Elspeth. Then Nethergar and all the power you possess will be mine.'

Nerissa was helpless to struggle against him, the poison

coursing through her veins draining away all her physical and mental strength. As he straightened up, she managed to roll her eyes upwards so she could see his face. He stared back at her, the malicious smile twisting his thin lips, faltering. He saw no fear in Nerissa's eyes, only hatred. For a second, he was afraid. Afraid of what she would do to him if she could fight him off. No more time to enjoy the moment. He must do it now.

Riordan pulled Nerissa's head back firmly and placed the tip of the knife against her throat. Sadistic thrills rippled through him as he pushed the tip deep into her skin and pulled the blade swiftly across her neck. Blood exploded over the weapon in his hand, running down his fingers. It was warm and sensuous as it pulsed, leaving red splatters on the white cotton of his cuffs.

Nerissa's head fall onto her chest as he calmly took a white handkerchief from his pocket. He wiped the knife clean and put it back in his jacket, the stained cloth still wrapped around it. He picked up the cups and threw the undrunk contents down the sink, smiling as he washed his hands, the gurgling sounds of death emanating from his victim pleasing him. With one last look at Nerissa Larimore slumped in the chair, a bib of scarlet seeping down her grey woollen dress, he left the cottage, carefully closing the door behind him and whistling as he made his way jauntily back into the forest.

DARIAN MCGILLVARAY WATCHED FROM HIS HIDING place between the rocks as the ugly, skinny man left Kirkholm Cottage. Something was wrong and he could sense it. The small boy with amber eyes, a mud-stained face and bare feet, waited until Riordan Darroch was out of sight. Then he ran as fast as he could towards the house belonging to Nerissa Larimore. Usually, he was afraid of the red-haired woman with the surly manner. But today, he felt no fear. He had to go to her. She needed him.

Approaching the door, he knocked quietly and called out Nerissa's name. No answer. He reached out a small, grubby hand and twisted the handle. The door opened easily but with his eyes unaccustomed to the dim light beyond, he couldn't see far inside.

'Nerissa, are you here?' he called again, but there was no noise from within.

Tentatively, he pushed the door further open and stepped inside. He could make out the silhouette of Nerissa Larimore slumped on a chair at the kitchen table. Sleeping? No. This was an unnatural pose for sleeping. Darian ran over to where she sat, taking in the horror of the scene as the afternoon light filtered through the small kitchen window. Nerissa's head rested heavily on her chest surrounded by a collar of blood congealing in the tangled mass of her wild red hair. Her arms hung limply by her sides and her knees gaped open under her dull grey skirt as the power of muscle control ebbed away. Despite his young years, Darian's mind was clear. He knew what to do.

Gently, he pushed the blood-soaked ringlets back from her face and placed the palm of his small hand on her cold, ashy cheek. It wasn't too late. There was still a glimmer of life.

'I'm going to help you Nerissa,' he said determinedly.

She didn't respond as he pushed back her head, revealing the deep red slash across her neck, the blood thickening as it reached the air. Darian placed both hands on Nerissa's chest and closed his eyes tightly, his thick lashes fanning out onto his cheek. His face crumpled in concentration, and he began to breath deeply. Nerissa's body twitched as silver light surrounded the small boy's hands. The light intensified, became blinding as it engulfed the inert form of Nerissa Larimore.

For a few moments, they remained meshed together, Nerissa's chest beginning to heave with shallow but steady breaths as the blood loss slowed. Suddenly, her hand reached up and she grabbed Darian by the wrist, making him jump as he opened his eyes. He stared at the woman, now forcibly keeping him in his place. He wasn't afraid, his concentration still focused on keeping the light alive.

Nerissa opened her eyes, her deep blue irises locking with Darian's tawny gold stare. He could hear her now in his mind.

'Just a little more Darian.'

He nodded and closed his eyes again. The light brightened even more as Nerissa raised her hand to her throat. She traced the path of the knife with her fingers, her other hand still wrapped around Darian's wrists. As she moved across the open gash, it began to close until no trace of the mortal wound remained. Healed, she released the boy who staggered back as the light faded, panting heavily. He braced himself against the kitchen wall, bending with his hands on his knees to steady himself, while his lungs fought to pull in sufficient air.

Nerissa remained seated, watching the boy and waiting for her strength to return.

'Thank you Darian,' she whispered hoarsely, her throat dry and sore.

The boy was too exhausted to speak but nodded feebly.

'Come here, let me help you now,' she said, but his usual wariness of her seemed to have returned.

Darian looked at her from under hooded eyes but didn't move.

'Don't be afraid. You've given me so much today. I owe you my life. Now let me repay you a little for what you've done by making you feel better.'

Nerissa stretched out an arm encouragingly, not yet trusting her legs to carry her weight. The boy stood upright and walked tentatively towards her. She beckoned to him, and he quickened his step until he stood by her side. She reached out and took his hands. They felt warm and soft as she wrapped her cold fingers around them. Darian's gaze fixated on their clasped hands. His eyes widened as a tingling heat travelled from Nerissa, up his arms until it enveloped him, chasing the tiredness out from his small, weary body.

The boy smiled as she let him go, staring at his fingers before the last vestiges of Nerissa's energy left him.

'Do you feel better now?' she asked.

He nodded fervently, a huge grin splitting his handsome young face from ear to ear.

'Do you know what happened Darian? What you did?'

He frowned as if this was a stupid question.

'Of course I do. I used my gift,' he said proudly.

Nerissa laughed as he puffed up his puny chest and tilted his chin upwards in a knowing way.

'You did. But do you know what your gift is?'

Now, his ego faltered and he sank a little.

'Well, sort of. My father explained it to me.'

'And what did he say?'

'That I can make people well. If I concentrate really hard, I can make people who are ill better again.'

Nerissa nodded slowly, still smiling kindly at the boy.

'Have you ever done anything like this before Darian?'

'Not to people. But I did help a baby bird once that had fallen from a nest. I thought it was dead, but after I touched it, it woke up again, so I put it back in the tree. I tore my new shirt. Mother was furious.'

Darian sat down on one of the wooden kitchen chairs, more relaxed now they were talking. Once he had pushed himself back onto the hard seat, his feet no longer reached the floor. He swung his legs, kicking the back of his heels on the thick oak chair legs, watching Nerissa expectantly.

'Darian, you have a very special gift. You can pass some of your life force onto others who need it to get better. That's what you did for the bird. It's what you did for me. You gave me the strength to heal myself.'

Nerissa leaned forward suddenly, making Darian jump again. Her stare was so intense that he shifted uncomfortably, biting his bottom lip nervously.

'I'm very grateful for what you did for me Darian, but promise me, you'll be careful with your gift.'

The boy's eyebrows drew together, obviously unable to understand what she was saying. She sat back in the chair, not wanting to unnerve him any further.

'Whenever you help someone Darian, you give them a part of yourself. Here, in Nethergar, what you give away will replenish over time. But only if you don't give away too much. When you helped me, you gave away much more than you can safely lose, but I was able to help you get it back once I was well again. That might not always be possible. You must never give away that much again Darian, not until you are grown up and stronger.'

Darian blinked, his young mind trying to take in all that she had said.

'Promise Darian. Promise me you won't try to do something like this again?'

The boy nodded, never taking his eyes from Nerissa's face. She hoped he understood.

'Good. That's good,' she said, looking down at her stained clothes and shuddering at the memory of what had happened. 'Now, did you see what happened to me Darian?'

She hoped not. Hoped his innocent young mind had not been polluted by the murderous actions of Riordan Darroch. Relief flooded over her as he shook his head.

'What were you doing here then?'

'I saw that man, the skinny ugly one, come through the gateway without Elspeth. I followed him here. I don't like him. He's got a cruel face.'

'Yes, yes he has,' she nodded. 'And then what?'

'I hid in the rocks and watched you let him inside.'

'Why did you hide?'

'I don't know.'

Nerissa stared hard at the boy. He was very astute for one so young. He might not understand everything yet, but the McGillvaray gifts were strong in him. He'd sensed the danger much better than she had. But then, she had trusted Elspeth and had let that trust push away her fears about Riordan Darroch. She had been a fool.

'I saw him come back outside and I felt weird. That's when I came inside and helped you,' he continued, looking wary in case she was angry with him for entering her house uninvited.

'I'm very glad you were here Darian. Very glad,' Nerissa said, reaching over and patting his hand. 'Now, you should go home. Your mother will be worried about you.'

Darian hopped down from the chair and scuttled towards the door, glad to be leaving.

'Remember what I said Darian – about using your gift won't you?'

He paused and turned to look at her. He gave a quick nod of his head and then, was gone.

Once the boy had disappeared, Nerissa's fury reared like a spitting cobra ready to strike. She felt strong, fully repaired thanks to Darian McGillvaray and now, she needed to warn Elspeth.

Riordan's words echoed in her mind. He planned to kill her to control access to Nethergar. He wanted to take their gifts, use them to become powerful and rich. If he was successful, he would become far worse than the Darrochs of old. They had been tyrants, cruel and greedy, even without the Larimore power. With it, they would be unstoppable. Elspeth was in danger, her son too. She had to get to her, and quickly.

RIORDAN DARROCH WHISTLED CHEERILY AS HE crossed the entrance hall at Dalengour, intent on changing his blood-stained shirt before he searched for his wife. He glanced at his pocket watch. Morwenna should be at the kirk by now, with Robert. He had some time before she disposed of the child. As he placed a foot on the bottom step of the main staircase, he heard his name being called from the open door of the library. Elspeth.

Attempting a casual smile, he turned to face her, clasping his hands behind his back to conceal the blood spatters on his white cuffs.

'Yes dear?'

Elspeth's face was like thunder. Something was wrong. He needed to be careful.

'I need to talk to you. Now,' she demanded before turning to stalk haughtily back into the library.

He tried to tuck the stained shirt sleeves into his jacket and after a quick check that no further evidence of his misdeed was evident, followed her into the dimly lit room.

Even though it was only mid-afternoon, very little of the wintery daylight permeated the library due to the heavily draped small windows. He knew Elspeth usually hated this room, labelling it oppressive, but it would be a suitable setting for her demise. He laughed inwardly, fingering the second glass phial residing in his pocket.

'Whatever's the matter Elspeth?' he asked airily.

His wife stood stiffly by the unlit fireplace, her hands clasped in front of her, her chin tilted upwards on her tense neck. He noticed she was wearing a coat over her blue day dress, her boots spotted with mud from the rain-soaked pavements.

'I met Daisy McNair in the village today.'

His heckles rose, her tone warning him. He must tread cautiously.

'Oh yes,' he said casually. 'How is Davey doing now? Did she say?'

Riordan sauntered over to the sideboard and poured two glasses of whisky, surreptitiously slipping the contents of the glass bottle into Elspeth's before handing it to her.

'Here, drink this. It's freezing in here. We need to speak to Gadsen about getting the fires lit now the weather has taken a turn.'

He looked around as if expecting to see Gadsen lurking in the corner. Elspeth took the proffered glass but never shifted her eyes from his face. When he looked back at her, he could see hatred burning in her pale blue eyes. It thrilled him. He just needed to play along until she took a drink. Then he would finally be rid of her.

'You've been taking money from them. From everyone I have helped.'

Her words were cold, accusing.

'I have merely asked for recompense for your services,' he

replied reasonably. 'What you offer these people is very valuable Elspeth. It's only right they give something back.'

Elspeth slammed the drink down on the mantelpiece, splashing some of the amber liquid onto the stone hearth as her anger flared. Riordan looked at the untouched drink, fighting to conceal his frustration.

'You have no right!' she screamed. 'No right to take anything from these people. I help them because I can. Not for money!'

'I never ask them for more than they can afford,' he said indignantly. 'And you and your family have been enjoying the pleasures money can buy.'

Colour flamed in her cheeks as she opened her mouth to come back at him. But she changed her mind and closed it again. She couldn't deny she had enjoyed the money. An uncomfortable silence settled, and Elspeth absently picked up her glass again.

Riordan watched as she lifted the rim of the crystal tumbler to her lips, his breath held as he tried to silence the excited thud of his heart. She didn't drink. Elspeth stopped, the glass under her nose. Her brow furrowed as she pulled back to look at the liquid. Something was wrong. She could sense something was wrong. Slowly she lowered the whisky and looked pointedly at her husband. Now his heart was racing for a different reason. Panic rose from the pit of his stomach.

Elspeth's eyes burned into him. He could feel the fury in her stare, see understanding form in her mind. She enunciated every word, commanding him to answer her.

'Riordan, where are Morwenna and my son?'

CHAPTER 18

Mothers and Sons

MORWENNA PACED IMPATIENTLY AROUND THE altar stone trying to block out the infernal screaming of her grandson. She had been planning this day for months – waiting impatiently for it to come. She had plenty of time while locked up in Dalengour, the unsuspected puppet master guiding Riordan as he courted Elspeth, making her trust him so he could gain access to Nethergar without her. Finally, he had managed it and today was the day she would put her plan into action. She need wait no more. Today, she would take all the power from the Larimores. She would control Nethergar. She would have everything she ever wanted, everything she deserved.

She glanced at the pocket watch beside the screaming child. Morwenna couldn't help but smile at the thought of its previous owner. Her mirth was not due to fondness for her father's memory, but relish as she remembered the look on his face as he realised he was going to die at her hand. There were still fifteen minutes before she could do it.

She had to be sure Riordan had disposed of Elspeth. Then there was only Robert. He was the only one who could stand in her way. Without him, there would be nowhere for the Larimore power to go. Then their gifts and control of the gateway would be hers. Then she could go home, back to Nethergar. She would live forever exactly as she was now, frozen in time, restored whenever she passed through the gateway. She grinned, excitement bubbling over and temporarily lessening the irritating effect of her grandson's cries.

Morwenna looked at the watch again. Only one minute had passed. Time was deliberately slowing, determined to prolong her frustration. The child let go a particularly shrill scream, his distress building. She glanced at him, a sneer contorting her usually beautiful face. Morwenna felt no love for the boy. He may be the product of her son's loins, but today, he would die. Just ten more minutes…

Morwenna pulled her silver blade from within the child's blanket. Standing over the infant, she traced the tip of the knife across his face. The desire to push harder was strong. She wanted to hurt him. She increased the pressure just enough for small droplets of blood to appear on the soft, snowy-white cheek. The child screamed louder in pain. It thrilled her.

She continued to draw the blade across his skin, every now and again, pressing a little harder to draw another bead of red. Robert was bellowing with fear and hurt but she didn't hear him. She watched the knife leaving a trail of blood on his cheek, then down his scrawny neck, so easy to slit. Wanting to see what the child would look like with more blood oozing from his body, she drew the blade across her own palm and let blood splatter onto his naked chest, enjoying the aesthetic beauty of red on white. She hovered the knife tip just above his heart – just one quick movement and he would be quiet. She glanced at the watch again – still five minutes.

Completely lost in her thoughts, Morwenna didn't notice the stained-glass dissolve into shimmering silver. She looked up from the child to come face to face with the flaming red hair and barely-contained rage of Nerissa Larimore.

'WHERE ARE MORWENNA AND MY SON?'

Elspeth repeated her question when no response came. Riordan's face was even more ashen than usual as the little colour drained away under the weight of her stare. He seemed to be searching for an answer.

'I don't... I...'

Riordan started to turn towards the door and Elspeth thought he was going to run. But he seemed to recognise that would appear ridiculous and tried to casually change direction to move and perch on the edge of the desk instead. He clasped his hands together to conceal the shaking gripping him. But it was too late. Elspeth had seen his trembling, could sense his fear.

He cleared his throat, striving for an air of casualness.

'I expect Mother is in her rooms and Robert will be with the nanny.'

Elspeth smirked at the pathetic reply.

'You know that isn't true. Miss Dennings told me you collected Robert and took him out with your mother. I have checked the nursery and Morwenna's rooms and both are empty. Where are they?'

Riordan shifted uncomfortably.

'I assure you, I don't know. Mother did want to see Robert and as she is getting better, I didn't think it would hurt to let her. I supervised a visit in the gardens, then left Gadsen to escort Morwenna back to her rooms and our son to the nursery.'

Elspeth was shocked at the ease of his lie. It made her realise how readily he could adopt a plausible falsehood. She felt stupid for having been so easily fooled in the past.

'I see. And you don't know where they are now?'

'No, no I don't. I had no idea Morwenna had got out of her rooms.'

He started looking around the library as if expecting to see Morwenna just standing there.

Elspeth struggled to remain calm. Losing her temper now wouldn't help. Her heart raced in her chest, its dull thud echoing in her ears. She wanted to fly at him, hit him, demand he tell her where her son was. She wound her fingers tightly together, using the pressure to control her rising panic.

'Riordan, I know you're lying. You've been lying about everything. I've taken away your guide to Nethergar and once I've found my son, I am leaving with him. Now tell me, where is he?'

The fear suddenly dissolved from Riordan's body, his self-assured arrogance returning. His cold eyes narrowed as he fixed them on hers. Casually draining the rest of his drink, he placed the empty glass down on the desk. It made a loud clunk in the silence.

'You're too late Elspeth. Nerissa is dead and soon you and your brat of a son will follow her. Then we'll have everything. Your gifts will belong to the Darrochs and we will have control of Nethergar.'

The venom in his tone disarmed her. She staggered

backwards her legs unable to hold her weight. She felt the hard stone wall behind and was grateful for its support as she fought to arrest the wave of sorrow and loss threatening to overwhelm her. She needed to keep focused if she was to save herself and her son. There would be time to grieve for Nerissa later.

Elspeth took a deep breath and tried to right herself. Her head swam as air filled her lungs, her legs still shaking as she pulled herself up to full height. Blinking back the tears obscuring her vision, she tried to step forwards, needing to leave this place and search for her son. She took a few tentative steps, Riordan watching her every move, visibly enjoying her distress.

Determined to get away from his scrutiny to compose herself, she quickened her pace. Almost at the door, she was suddenly winded as her body slammed against the wall. Riordan held her arms behind her back, his weight pushing her against the cold stone. His rancid breath felt warm on her ear as he lent harder against her. It was difficult to breathe, her rising panic making her chest heave, trying to draw in enough air.

'Not so fast my dear. We have some unfinished business.'

Roughly Riordan turned her to face him, still holding her wrists tightly and using his body to subdue her. She felt his manhood stiffen against her stomach, her enfeeblement arousing him. He began rubbing his crotch against her, breathing excitedly into her face. Elspeth closed her eyes and tried to turn away from him, but he grabbed her chin forcibly and turned her head to face him.

His jagged nails cut into her flesh as she tried to resist. With one arm wrenched free, she pushed with all her strength against his chest, but couldn't move him. He pushed harder against her, laughing callously. Elspeth stilled. There was no point struggling. Memories of those first nights as Riordan's wife invaded her mind. The more she fought against him, the more zealous his abuse would become.

'That's better,' he spat, letting his hand slip from her face down to her neck.

She felt the pressure of his body ease as he released her other wrist. In a sudden movement, his hands closed around her throat. Elspeth looked up imploringly into his face as his grip tightened. She saw excitement there, his beady eyes wide and burning with relish.

She felt lightheaded as her oxygen depleted. She was scared, helpless. She was going to die. He was going to kill her.

'YOU CAN'T BE HERE! YOU'RE DEAD! HE ASSURED ME you were dead!'

Morwenna's screams verged on the hysterical as she stood, her green eyes fixed on the woman who had just stepped through the window.

'It seems he was mistaken,' Nerissa said calmly.

Morwenna's mind lurched chaotically as she tried to understand how this Larimore witch could be standing before her.

'You can't be here. You can't. He killed you!'

'As you can see, he did not. If it makes you feel better, he did try. When he left, I was almost dead. Almost...'

This didn't make sense. She should have died. How was it she hadn't died? Anger flooded Morwenna and she began pacing back and forth in front of the altar stone, blood pulsing from her cut hand dripping in her wake. That idiot! He should have waited. Waited until he was sure she was dead.

Fury boiled inside her. All her planning, all her waiting, all her sacrifice would be for nothing if any one of the Larimores with the gifts remained alive. Riordan was a fool! An inept fool!

Tears stung the back of Morwenna's eyes, panic welling up inside her. What was she going to do now? How could she turn this to her advantage? She began to mumble, rehearsing every scenario in her confused mind. Nothing made sense. She needed to get rid of Nerissa, but she must be careful. Riordan said she was powerful. She needed to get rid of her and hope her fool of a son had at least succeeded in killing his wife! Then there would just be the child…

Her pacing became more frantic, beads of sweat gathering on her brow. She had almost forgotten Nerissa was watching her until the calm, patronising voice penetrated her addled thoughts.

'Morwenna, the child is innocent. He may be a Larimore, but Darroch blood runs through his veins as well. Does that mean anything to you? Are you so corrupted by the need for power you would spill your own grandson's blood?'

Grandson! As if she could have feelings for a grandson shared with a Larimore! If her thick-headed son had managed to control himself, there would be no grandson. He was a mistake that needed to be removed. There would be plenty of time for grandchildren with a more worthy maternal bloodline. She would make sure that Riordan's next wife was suitable to mix blood with the Darrochs.

Morwenna stopped beside Robert, still squirming and whimpering, red welts swelling on his cheek and neck. As she placed a hand on each side of the infant, a scathing laugh escaped her lips at the stupidity of Nerissa Larimore. How pathetic to try and evoke her emotions for this screaming wretch.

'Do you really think I care about this mongrel?'

Her tone was sibilant as she scoffed at the child.

'He should never have been born! If my son had not been such an arrogant idiot, he wouldn't have been!'

Morwenna's nostrils flared, her lips downturned as she looked at the flailing child. Nerissa took a step forward and Morwenna glimpsed her fear. She could use the child! Although she had no sentimental feelings for the boy, Nerissa obviously did. She had come here to save Elspeth's son.

'Not so fast. One step nearer and the brat will die.'

Morwenna raised the knife above the boy's chest, irritated by the way it shook in her hand. Her mind reeled, continuing to search for an idea, for a plan to get what she wanted – Nerissa dead. Nothing would come. Her heart raced and she felt cold, shivery, her eyes shifting around frantically but not seeing anything. Her breathing felt laboured as she gasped to stem the dizziness welling up in her. She needed to get a hold of herself if she was going to get out of this.

She blinked hard, trying to focus her attention. The child was quiet now, his eyes fixed on the glinting blade hovering above him. Nerissa stood stiffly a short distance away, watching. If she drove the blade through the boy's chest, she was sure Nerissa would act. She would take the child to Nethergar where he could be healed. If she played this right, maybe she could force her to take her through the gateway as well. At least then, she would be in Nethergar. She could plan the rest when her gifts grew stronger.

Making up her mind, she drew back the knife, then thrust it downwards towards the boy's chest. Something was happening. Light flooded the kirk. It seemed to be coming from Nerissa, extending around her and the child. It felt warm, stifling. She tried to move but couldn't. Morwenna was trapped, held firmly by an unseen force within the golden halo.

Morwenna's anger and frustration bubbled over. She let out a wretched scream and pushed down harder on the blade. It wouldn't move. It was as if the air around her had become solid. Temper flashed in her green eyes as she looked at Nerissa from under cowled lids. She wanted to shout, scream, vent her fury at being thwarted so close to her goal. But the air around her was dense, crushing her lungs. It's thickness dulling any sound she made, her screams deflected back towards her as low meaningless rumbles.

The blade pulled out of her hands, moving slowly as if it had a will of its own. As it broke free of the light prison holding her, it flew across the kirk, skidding noisily along the stone floor. Defeated, Morwenna stopped struggling. As she stilled, the air around her relaxed a little, allowing her to breathe more easily.

Nerissa walked steadily over to the child and drew him into her arms. Morwenna watched as the Larimore woman ran her hand tenderly down the boy's face, covering the wounds she had inflicted with a trail of gold iridescence that quickly faded to reveal freshly healed skin. With the child safely cradled against her, Nerissa met Morwenna's venomous gaze. She didn't speak but shook her head, closing her eyelids to momentarily hide the golden glow invading her usually blue eyes. With one last pitying look at Morwenna, Nerissa turned away, comforting the child in her arms as she walked away.

Morwenna's eyes leaked tears of frustration as she began to struggle again against her unseen bindings. She wouldn't be beaten, not by this woman who had the audacity to pity her! Fury fortified her strength, but it was still insignificant against the power holding her.

A sound from the back of the kirk caught Morwenna's attention. A man was moving down the aisle towards them. She recognised him. Jenson Tanner came to a halt at the end of the pews, his hazel eyes flicking from her to Nerissa.

'Get the knife!' Morwenna screamed, but Jenson didn't move.

'Get the knife you imbecile!'

Her anger roared as he turned away and fixed his gaze on Nerissa Larimore.

Why had she let Riordan take away her leverage over this idiot! And just because he was jealous! If she still had his little sister, Jenson would do as she said. Her mind raced.

'I swear, if you don't do as I say, you won't live to see another day!'

Jenson flinched. Nerissa took a step towards him, speaking calmly, extending the precious bundle towards him. Morwenna's scream reverberated around the kirk.

'Pay her no heed. She's in no position to make threats. Take the boy back to his mother. I'll deal with Morwenna. I promise she won't be able to hurt you.'

Morwenna was momentarily stunned into silence as Jenson tenderly took Elspeth's son. He turned to leave the kirk, walking slowly so as not to alarm the child coddled in his arms. Rage erupted from Morwenna, her screeched, rambling threats echoing around the cold stone walls.

CHAPTER 19

Two Become One

'ELSPETH! ELSPETH!'

Her name. Someone was calling her name. She could hear it echoing in her head as Riordan's hands tightened around her throat. She had no air, everything was fuzzy. She just wanted to close her eyes – let everything fade to nothing.

'Elspeth! Elspeth! Focus. Listen to me!'

The voice in her head dragged her back. Nerissa. It was Nerissa!

'Elspeth, I'm at the kirk on the Cairndarroch side. I have Morwenna.'

Nerissa was talking to her. Nerissa was alive! Elspeth opened her eyes to look at her husband's contorted face, his eyes glowing with excitement as he wrung her neck. She wouldn't let him win. Nerissa was alive.

The voice came again.

'Jenson has your son. He's bringing him to you. Elspeth,

you must close the gateway. I'm going to transfer some of my power to you – to give you the strength to close it. I will deal with Morwenna. Close the gate Elspeth and don't ever open it again. Then you'll be safe. Robert will be safe.'

Elspeth tried to focus on Nerissa's voice through the haze of unconsciousness threatening to overwhelm her. She understood. She knew what she must do. She struggled against Riordan, trying to throw him off but his vice-like grip tightened again.

'Hurry Nerissa.'

She cast the thought in her mind, hoping it would reach Nerissa. Then she felt it. The familiar warmth as she became connected to her Larimore ancestor. She could feel Nerissa all around her. The energy began to build inside her, more energy than she had ever felt before. Her hands moved up to grasp Riordan's wrists. This time, she pulled them away from her throat with ease. He staggered backwards, eyes wide in astonishment, quickly replaced by panic as he stared at Elspeth, now standing tall, the strength within her palpable.

As the breath returned to her lungs, she inhaled deeply, empowered by the gifts of Nerissa Larimore. She looked down to see sparks of gold bristling around her palms, light tracing the outline of the veins in her hands and arms. The power was intoxicating.

Her head was spinning with memories that weren't hers. Nerissa's memories. She saw her as a small, red-headed child running through the forests of Nethergar, holding the hand of a younger girl who shared her bright blue eyes but with strawberry-blond hair – like Elspeth's own. This must be Nerissa's sister. She saw two children connected by golden threads as they forced red and yellow flowers to grow up from the earth, causing a dense ring of riotous colour to form around them as they played.

Then, she felt fear. Fear as the two adult Larimore sisters ran for their lives from a group of men pursuing them. Men with the slim build and green feline eyes of the Darrochs. She watched as they dragged Nerissa and her sister into the town square, the youngest man plunging a sword into the belly of one of the women, gutting her from abdomen to chest.

Tears formed in Elspeth eyes as the visions from Nerissa's past played out in her mind. Then she saw the present. Nerissa holding her son, healing his wounded cheek before passing him to Jenson Tanner. Then finally, Morwenna, held captive in a cage of golden light.

The scrapping of furniture on the wooden floor dragged her from Nerissa's mind and back to her own present. Riordan had caught the table leg in his haste to run from the room. Elspeth threw out her hand in his direction and he was immediately held in an invisible grasp. He struggled for a moment, not knowing what held him. Elspeth walked around until she was facing him, her whole body tingling with vitality.

'Elspeth, please. Please. I didn't want to hurt you but my Mother...you know how much influence she has on me...'

Riordan's begging appalled her. Even now, just moments after he had his hands around her throat, he was trying to weasel out of blame. Bile rose in her gullet as she looked at this pathetic man. More hatred than she thought possible rose like acid burning her skin. She wanted him dead. But she wouldn't be the one to kill him. She wouldn't let him make her a murderer. Not today. But he didn't know that and now, he was afraid. Afraid of her.

'You disgust me Riordan. After everything, you're still trying to rationalise your actions. You tried to murder Nerissa and now, me. You've stood by while Morwenna planned to kill our son. You don't deserve to live!'

'Please Elspeth. Please..'

He attempted to move towards her, but she held him fast in the grip of her power. Tears were streaming down his pallid cheeks. Not tears of sorrow or remorse. Tears of panic and fear. She relished his terror. He deserved to feel it. She stared hard at the revolting person before her and felt a rush of shame. She had allowed him to use her, to fool her. She had even defended him, claimed a fondness for him.

Elspeth released him and he fell weakly to his knees, staring up at her, his nose running, his thin pale lips coated in saliva. Repugnance swelled in her stomach not only for Riordan, but for herself. She had let this happen and now she must make it right.

Riordan snivelled, wiping snot on the sleeve of his coat. He was a broken shell of the man she knew, his rounded shoulders heaving through renewed sobs.

'Get up!'

He looked up at her, then doddered unsteadily to his feet.

'I'm not going to hurt you Riordan.'

A smile faltered on his face as he tried to look appealing.

'I'm not going to hurt you today,' she corrected.

The smile faded.

'But if you come near me or anyone I love again, I will kill you. Don't ever doubt that.'

Riordan bowed his head and looked at his scuff-marked shoes.

'My Mother?' he stammered.

'I don't know what's happened to her. Nerissa has her trapped at the kirk and I believe she intends on taking her back to Nethergar.'

Riordan's head jolted back up.

'Before you let the idea of Nethergar seed another plan in

your evil mind, you should know I'm going to close the gateway – permanently.'

'Can you do that?' He sounded more like his old self, a sneering undertone doubting her ability.

'Nerissa transferred some of her powers to me, so I am strong enough now.'

Her husband's eyes widened. Elspeth could sense his emotions. The fear that had gripped him, quickly ebbed, giving way to the excitement of opportunity. He couldn't help himself. He was already planning how he could use her gifts to his advantage.

'Don't waste your time.'

'What?'

He looked at her, confusion on his face.

'Don't waste your time planning how my gifts could be of value to you.'

The little colour that had returned to his face drained away.

'I don't know what you mean…'

'Yes, you do. I can see what you're planning, and I assure you, I'll never be used again, by you or anyone else. I'm leaving you Riordan. I'm taking Robert and going back to Kirkholm Cottage once the gateway is closed.'

'Oh, please don't go Elspeth. Now, with Mother gone, I'm sure we can make things work. I…I love you Elspeth. You're my wife.'

Elspeth laughed.

'Riordan, you don't know how to love, and you certainly have never loved me.'

He lashed out, made to grab her, but she saw it coming. The energy still pulsing through her body pushed outwards, shards of golden light shrouding Riordan's body, holding him in a glimmering prison. He breathed heavily, struggling to reach her, his face twisted in rage. She was reminded of the image she had seen in Nerissa's memory of Morwenna in the same position. The irony was amusing, and she smiled enraging Riordan more. She enjoyed the vision of him looking ridiculous as he strained frantically against unseen restraints. But now she must focus, she must close the gateway.

NERISSA HOPED HER MESSAGE GOT THROUGH, hoped Elspeth had heard her, felt her transfer the power. She would know soon enough because if it had worked, the gateway would close. Nerissa glanced over at Morwenna, still captive in shackles of light. The woman was screaming empty threats at the retreating Jenson, intermingled with insane ramblings of how she planned to escape. Now was the time. She must pull her through to Nethergar and hope Elspeth worked quickly.

Nerissa approached Morwenna and grasped her hand, pulling her towards the window, a lasso of light winding around their wrists to bind them together. Morwenna did not struggle but followed her obediently towards the gateway, her eyes wide with excitement. Nerissa trailed her fingers across the molten, shimmering surface of the window, causing ripples to echo through the liquid glass until they broke against the frame. She turned to cast a last look at the kirk in Cairndarroch. She would never see it, or Elspeth again.

She watched for a moment as Jenson reached the door, cradling Elspeth's son tightly in his arms. Robert was safe. Comforted by this knowledge, she stepped through the gateway emerging in Nethergar, the subservient Morwenna Darroch still lashed to her. It was dark inside the church, with only the silver reflection from the gateway providing any light. The chill of the night made her shiver, the sadness of what had happened tonight threatening to drown her. She'd lost the only family she had left. She was alone again. There was no time for maudlin now.

Nerissa pulled herself together and looked intently at her prisoner. Morwenna's green eyes reflected the silver light from the gateway as she stared around the kirk. Her face wore an excited grin as she looked back at the window, then towards the door leading outside. She threw back her head and let go a raucous, triumphant laugh that bounced around the deserted space.

'I'm here! I'm finally here!'

Her words were barely understandable between the high-pitched cackling, but Nerissa understood. All Morwenna's life, she had dreamed of getting through the gateway and now, she had made it. Not the way she had hoped, but still, she was here.

'You are here and here you'll stay.'

Morwenna's laughter stopped abruptly as her eyes flitted to Nerissa.

'What do you mean?'

'Elspeth is going to seal the gateway - permanently. You'll be trapped here in Nethergar. You can never go back, so the benefits you imagine will be yours by coming through the gateway will never be realised. You'll stay here in Nethergar Morwenna, and I'll be watching you.'

Morwenna's smile tarnished as her sly eyes shifted furtively this way and that, the cogs of her mind turning frantically. Nerissa sensed her turmoil, the disorganisation of many thoughts running rampant through her consciousness. Elation at being here, excitement at being fixed in this moment, the potential to stay forever youthful. But for that, she needed continued access to the gateway. She needed to be able to pass through to Cairndarroch and back again. If what Nerissa said was true, she would be stuck here, growing old in a different place.

Nerissa saw the beginning of a plan forming in Morwenna's mind but realised it too late. She was caught off balance as her captive lurched towards the gateway. The binds tying them together pulled taught as Morwenna stepped through the shimmering surface of the window. Nerissa leaned back, intensifying her hold, trying to keep her in Nethergar. The gateway began to flicker as the ground rumbled beneath her feet. Elspeth! Elspeth was closing the gateway!

Nerissa pulled harder against the forces trying to transport Morwenna back to Cairndarroch, bracing her feet against the window frame and putting her full weight behind the struggle. The tremors rising up from the earth grew more violent, the gateway growling as it prepared to close. The tips of Morwenna's fingers were just visible now as they broke the surface of the window as Nerissa heaved her back. The noise became deafening as the gateway pushed against Elspeth's attempts to close it while someone was passing through.

The whole kirk seemed to be shaking as somewhere on the other side of the gateway, Elspeth fought to seal it. Nerissa tried to reach out her mind to her, but knew it was futile. Elspeth would not hear her from this side. She felt Morwenna's wrist slipping away again. She was losing her grip. Focusing her mind, she fortified the bindings holding them together. She felt Morwenna struggle against the tightening of the restraints, but Nerissa held fast. She was beginning to tire. Her powers were depleted after the transfer

to Elspeth. She didn't know how much longer she could
hold on.

As the ground shook, the surface of the window became
turbulent, silvery ripples becoming waves that smashed
against the stone. Nerissa's hand dipped below the surface as
Morwenna continued to pull against her. The sensation of
being straddled across two worlds was unpleasant, as each
place attempted to tear the two women apart. But she
wouldn't let go. She couldn't let Morwenna get back to
Elspeth's world.

Nerissa's heart thumped wildly in her chest, now
drenched in sweat. The light of the gate was beginning to
fade, the vibrations coming from beneath reverberating
around the stone walls of the kirk. It was closing. With a last
show of strength, Nerissa hauled Morwenna back towards
Nethergar. Then suddenly all was still. The rumbling ceased.
The light gone. Silence.

Only a stained-glass window depicting Saint Oda stood in
place of the gateway. The moonlight cast a silvery light from
behind, outlining the crumpled shadow of a woman lying on
the floor of the kirk. Slowly, she began to stand, straightening
her soiled woollen dress and smoothing her dishevelled wild
red hair.

Unsteady on her feet, the woman walked over to the
window and ran her hand slowly over the solid surface.
Nothing happened. The corners of her lips turned up in a
rueful smile, then grabbing the sides of her head, she let out
a scream of frustration. Wringing her fingers through her
hair, she staggered back, wails of anger exploding from her
slender frame. She collapsed to the floor, leaning against the
altar stone, her cries echoing around the barren kirk.

Then, just as suddenly as they started, the cries stopped.
The woman rose from the floor, as serene now as she had

been manic moments before. She walked quietly down the aisle, threw open the door, and stepped out into the cold night. She watched as her breath turned into puffs of silvery mist with each exhale. Shivering as the frosty air enveloped her, she cast her eyes skyward to look at the full moon hanging brightly in the sky. Beams of moonlight reflected in her eyes, momentarily highlighting a green ring surrounding the cornflower blue iris.

She blinked hard as she tried to focus, rubbing her eyes in an attempt to rid them of the shadows staining her retinas from looking at the moon. With her vision becoming more accustomed to the darkness, she stepped out into the forest clearing, hugging her arms around her body to ward off the chill.

The woman walked purposefully towards the tree line, then winced. She staggered against the gnarled trunk of a tree standing guard by the path winding through the forest. Her hands clutched the sides of her head and she screwed up her face in pain. She was unable to move as the throbbing rampaged through her brain. As it subsided, she slumped panting, trying to catch her breath. After a minute, she wiped her hand across her face, using her sleeve to mop up the tears leaking from her eyes. Eyes that were no longer blue. Eyes that were cat-like and vivid green.

CHAPTER 20

The Woman in the Tower

April 1946– Cairndarroch

Josephine Dennings closed the door leading to the east tower at Dalengour, trying not to make a sound. It was early and no-one else was awake. She wanted to keep it that way. She had been nanny to the Darroch children for over twenty-five years. First Robert, and now Lord Darroch's four children from his second marriage. Today, she would leave this place. The children were grown and had no further need of her. It was time. She needed to get away. She needed to leave this place now she knew...

She leaned back against the door, her heart beating noisily in her chest from a combination of nervousness and exertion. She had done it. She had helped. Now she could leave here with a clear conscience. Heaving herself upright, she began to walk slowly back to her room beside the long-abandoned nursery, a dull ache from her bare, arthritic feet accompanying every step.

Back in the sanctity of her parlour, she breathed more easily. She felt safer here. She looked around and was surprised by the swell of emotion that overtook her. Tears prickled in her dark eyes, the realisation of what she had done, of what *they* had done, rattling her usually unshakeable countenance.

'Pull yourself together Josephine! It's not your fault. You didn't know!'

She wiped the sleeve of her demure, floor-length nightgown across her eyes and smoothed her tightly plaited, greying hair. She pulled the knitted shawl more closely around her shoulders, the inevitable cold of Dalengour penetrating the flimsy fabric of her garment.

Josephine looked around for slippers to protect her sore feet from the hard wooden floor. She hadn't worn them on her excursion to the east tower for fear the soles would clack on the barren floors, accentuating her footfall. She regretted it now. The stone stairs she climbed to reach the woman in the tower had been freezing, the achy joints in her toes protesting at their exposure to the cold.

With her feet more comfortably ensconced in the tatty, quilted lilac slippers, a Christmas gift from the children a few years back, she hobbled through the parlour into the adjoining bedroom. Her chambers were simply furnished compared to the rest of Dalengour, but they were comfortable, and she had been happy here. Until she had found her.

Josephine busied herself, folding the clothes strewn across the ruffled comforter of her unmade single bed, placing them neatly into a battered leather suitcase. Soon she would be out of here. Her meagre belongings would not take long to pack. She reached for the photograph on her nightstand. The sepia tones depicted three children, two boys and a girl. She was seated in the middle of them, a baby dressed in a frilled robe sleeping peacefully on her knee. A young woman stood behind, her hands placed tenderly on the boys shoulders. These people had been her family.

She trailed her fingers tenderly over the images in the worn gilt frame, tears prickling her eyes again. Lady Leona Darroch had married Riordan a year after Elspeth left. She had been glad to see the back of Elspeth Larimore having long despised her. But her son, Robert, she had loved as if he were her own. He had been a beautiful child, calm and giving. She missed him.

Josephine was set to leave Dalengour after Elspeth took him away but had been convinced to stay by Lord Darroch who had seemed certain Elspeth would return. She hadn't, but soon Leona was the resident Lady of the house. A sweet girl and fertile too! Six pregnancies. Although two girls did not survive their birthing.

The tears threatened again as she thought of Leona Darroch. She had been exceptionally fond of her, taking on a motherly role in the girl's life, nursing her through pregnancy, supporting her through stillbirths and looking after her surviving children before and after her death. Leona had been a frail creature who suffered frequent bouts of depression and ill health. When she succumbed to illness, Josephine had been devastated but not suspicious. Now, if what she had learned was true, Leona's death was the fault of her husband. Josephine shivered, then tucked the precious picture between the folds of her best dress already packed in the suitcase.

She didn't hear him come in, so lost in her memories of

happier times. She didn't know how long he'd been standing there, observing her, his shoulder leaning casually against the door frame. It wasn't until she finished her packing and turned to check for belongings in the parlour that she came face to face with Riordan Darroch.

RIORDAN HAD WATCHED THE AGED, CRIPPLED FORM of Josephine Dennings dodder around the room for five minutes before she realised he was there. Today, she would leave Dalengour for good. Just not the way she expected to. He couldn't risk her telling anyone what she knew.

He felt unusually sombre. The thought of killing this woman who had shared his house for over a quarter of a century, did not give him the usual thrill. Riordan liked Josephine Dennings. She had always been a good influence on his children and had dealt well with his insipid wife when she was still alive. He was glad of that as it meant he had hardly seen Leona Darroch during his ten-year marriage, leaving him free to devote his time to the woman he truly loved. It was a shame Josephine had found out. If she had just kept her nose out, he would have let her leave today to enjoy her well-earned retirement.

Riordan sighed. His long, noisy exhale had caught her attention and now she stood staring at him, a wooden hairbrush clutched in her hand, her saggy backside silhouetted by the rising sun in the window filtering through the sheer material of her nightgown.

'Lord Darroch!'

Her eyes were wide at the shock of seeing him there. She shifted uncomfortably and drew the well-worn shawl more tightly around her low-slung bosom.

'Do you need something?'

Her voice shook slightly as she asked him the question, but this was the only sign of nervousness. She stood her ground, her wary eyes planted on him. Riordan was impressed. Even his unexpected presence in her rooms when she was undressed, unprepared, had not disarmed the formidable nanny. She glared at him – the same look he had seen directed to his misbehaving offspring. He smiled. He really did like Josephine Dennings.

Riordan sauntered into the room, rolling up the sleeves of his hastily thrown on shirt. He had grabbed the clothes he had been wearing at dinner last night, not wanting to waste time once he saw her leaving the tower.

'Forgive the intrusion Miss Dennings. I see you are readying to leave?'

'Yes Lord Darroch. I have booked a taxicab to collect me and take me to the station for the ten 'o' clock train to Leeds.'

'You're going to your sister's then?'

'That's the plan, for now.'

Riordan began to circle around the nanny as they talked. Still, she didn't flinch, her eyes cannily tracking his every move. He liked this part. The dance before the inevitable. He made a mental note to cancel the cab. He didn't want to dally too long. He needed to get this done before the rest of the household awoke.

'Why were you in the east tower earlier this morning Josephine?

Josephine blinked but held his gaze. She was good – good at controlling outward signs of her emotions. She didn't answer, taking her time to form a suitable excuse to placate him.

'I was taking my last look around Dalengour. I'm going to miss this place. I wanted some time to myself before everyone stirred.'

'That's nice. I'm glad you have fond memories of us. But why were you in the east tower? In all your time at Dalengour, you've never set foot in that section of the house before. I know this because my personal rooms are in the east tower. I always keep the door to the tower locked and I have never had need of a nanny there.'

Josephine shifted from one slipper-clad foot to the other. Her fidgeting told him he was unnerving her. He smiled.

'I'm sorry Lord Darroch. My curiosity got the better of me and I tried the door. It was locked as you say.'

She suppressed her nervousness again and stared directly at him, the steadiness of her gaze trying to convey the truthfulness of her words. But he was not fooled. He had seen her exiting the tower and returning the key to its hiding place in the dresser drawer. It was a perk of his mother's disappearance. Morwenna had not been seen for twenty-four years and the night she had vanished, he inherited an unexpected gift – the Darroch gift that allowed him to see, to watch people without them knowing.

This morning he had been laid in his bed, his love the first thing on his mind when he woke. He had let his mind roam the halls of Dalengour, heading towards the east tower where he would be able to look upon her while she slept. But he had not seen her. Instead, he watched as Josephine Dennings descended the stairs leading from the east tower, locking the door behind her before making her way back here, to her rooms. She knew. She must have seen her. And now, he couldn't allow her to leave.

'I see,' he said, raising an eyebrow and continuing to pace around the nanny, a predator toying with its prey. 'The problem is Josephine, I know you're lying to me. You see, I saw you come down the stairs from the tower and lock the door behind you.'

Riordan's pale eyes met the nanny's steely gaze as he traced his mouth with a bony finger in mock consideration.

'Now I'm curious what made you go up those stairs Josephine?'

Riordan seemed to weigh every word, punctuating each with a short pause to add sufficient gravitas.

Panic flitted across her usually composed face. She was cornered and she knew it.

'You're an animal,' she spat. 'How could you imprison that girl? Inflict yourself on her by force? I always knew you were a cruel man. But I never thought you capable of this!'

She didn't sense danger. If she had, she wouldn't have risked irking him. Riordan's anger swelled. She had no right to make judgements on his relationship with the woman in the tower. He loved her. Loved her as he had never loved anyone before. Loved her more than he ever thought himself capable of. She was everything to him.

'You don't know anything Miss Dennings!' he said venomously, trying to control the desire to wrap his hands around her throat.

'I know that you've been keeping her here against her will for fifteen years! That you rape her almost daily! That she wants to die!'

These last words stalled him, alarm bells ringing.

'What do you mean? She wants to die?'

'That girl would rather die than spend one more day living with you.'

Josephine Dennings' spine stiffened, hatred for Riordan emanating from every pore, a self-satisfied smile playing at the corners of her thin lips. He was surprised by the vehemence of her tone. She had always been stoic, emotionless in their dealings. But now, he could feel her animosity, even disgust as she glared at him, a triumphant look on her face. He cocked his head to one side, trying to decipher why she exuded a sense of winning. Panic started to whirl in the pit of his stomach.

'What did you do Josephine?'

Now she broke into a broad grin, her hard eyes relishing his discomfort.

'You won't be able to hurt her anymore.'

Anger roared to the surface. Unable to contain his fury, he lurched forwards, gripping her flabby neck in his bony hands. He drove her backwards with the force of his movement until she was pinned against the barren stone wall, her arms flailing around her as she tried to grab at anything to steady herself. Her back hit the cold surface and she grabbed at his wrists, trying to pull them from her throat, struggling for breath. He held on tighter, enjoying the blue tinge of her skin, watching the air drain from her lungs.

Riordan's eyes bulged with excitement as Josephine Dennings issued her last gurgling breaths. The woman slumped against his grip but still he held on, needing to be sure she was really dead. As he let go, she slid down the wall, falling in a contorted heap, her eyes staring but seeing no more. The exertion of the murder caused his breath to come thick and fast. He staggered backwards, wiping sweat from his top lip.

He would have liked to savour the moment, but something in her last words had frightened him. He needed to get to the east tower. He would come back and deal with the corpse of Josephine Dennings later.

Hastily, Riordan threw the comforter from the bed over the crumpled heap that had once been the long-serving nanny to his children, and left the room. The halls were still deserted, silent except for the sound of his feet as he ran, and the pounding of his heart. Reaching the landing of the east wing, he reached into the top drawer of the sideboard beside the door to the tower, feeling for the key that lived in a secret compartment set into the bottom.

Swiftly, he turned the lock and took the steep stone steps two at a time. He passed the door on the first landing that led to the rooms where his mother had once been held captive, continuing up, his legs shaking with the effort of his haste. Throwing open the door nestled on the very top landing, he burst into the dimly lit room, holding a stitch in his side, his breath heaving in an out of his puny chest.

Squinting, he tried to focus on the imposing iron cage that occupied the greatest part of this dour, cold room. The outline of a small metal bedframe came into view, the threadbare, unwashed blankets pulled tightly around the form of a woman laid on her side, facing into the grey, damp wall. Riordan let out a sigh of relief. He had thought Josephine might have set her free.

He began to creep towards her, not wanting to disturb her slumber. He enjoyed her most when she was sleeping, her face peaceful and calm rather than full of fear and loathing. Although he really didn't mind that either. She was his.

Riordan's foot fell on something that crunched loudly as he stepped on it. The noise reverberated around the dank stone walls, but the sleeping woman did not stir. He lifted his foot carefully, trying to see what he had stepped on. Glass. He dusted the shards from the sole of his shoe, looking around to see where it had come from. A small empty bottle lay on the floor to his left, the stopper now crushed on the bottom of his shoe. It was the last of the phials of poison his mother had given him years ago.

His eyes flicked to the shelf where it had stood for over twenty years, the dust marking the empty space where it had once lived. Slowly, realisation seeped into his mind, and he ran the last few yards to the cage door. Fumbling, he withdrew a small key from his pocket and tried to steady his trembling as he placed it into the lock. The mechanism turned with an echoing clunk, but still the woman did not move.

He moved slowly to where she lay, his heart like a battering ram. With a sweaty palm, he reached over and touched the woman's shoulder. Nothing. With uncharacteristic tenderness, he pulled her shoulder towards him to move her onto her back. Her arm flopped lifelessly away from her body, her glassy eyes unseeing as they stared at the ceiling. Vomit stained the front of her tattered dress, spreading into her long dark hair and across the blood-stained pillow. Riordan let out a racking scream. Kaliope Larimore was dead.

CHAPTER 21

The Girl with the Green Eyes

'ELSPETH! ELSPETH! WAKE UP!'

Elspeth rubbed her eyes, trying to focus on Agatha who had flown into her bedroom and was now frantically trying to rouse her.

'What is it Aggie? What's the matter?' she asked, bleary-eyed, her head still foggy from deep sleep.

'It's Kaliope. Something's happened to Kaliope. I felt it.'

Agatha's cornflour blue eyes were full of tears, her brows drawn together, a pained expression on her tired-looking face. Elspeth dragged herself wearily to a sitting position, trying to comprehend what her sister was saying.

'What do you mean?'

'I felt something. Kaliope…'

Agatha broke down into heaving sobs, collapsing forward into Elspeth's arms. Wrapping her in an embrace, Elspeth tried to console her sister, stroking her untidy hair and pulling her tightly to her breast. She had no idea what was wrong. Kaliope had disappeared over fifteen years ago. They hadn't heard from her since she left Kirkholm Cottage six months after their mother's funeral. Kaliope had taken the loss of Charlotte Larimore badly, sinking into depression that would not relent. It had been Elspeth's idea to send her to London for a while, to spend time with her mother's brother and his daughters, hoping that a change of scenery and society would do her good. It was on route to London that she vanished.

The police had looked for her, somewhat half-heartedly in Elspeth's view. When they discovered Kaliope had been in a state of depression, they lost interest in the search, convinced she had either run away from her dysfunctional family, or taken her own life. Elspeth had never given up looking for her, never given up hope. But deep down, she knew Kaliope was gone forever. Deep down, she suspected Riordan Darroch, but had never been able to prove anything.

Agatha calmed and sat up, her tear-stained face blotchy and gaunt. Elspeth brushed her hand tenderly down her cheek.

'Now, tell me. What did you feel?'

I...I don't know exactly,' Agatha stammered, wiping her runny nose on the sleeve of her nightgown. 'I saw Kaliope. She was crying. It was dark, cold and she looked ill. I couldn't see where she was. There was no light. But she was afraid, so very afraid.'

Tears began to spill from the blue eyes again.

'It was just a dream Aggie,' Elspeth said soothingly, but Agatha stood abruptly from the bed, her face resolute, glowering at her sister.

'No! No! It wasn't a dream. I could feel her. I could feel how scared she was.'

'It's alright Aggie. Come, sit back down and tell me what else.'

Agatha continued to stare at Elspeth for a moment, then sank back down on the end of the bed and began picking at the embroidery flowers adorning the quilt.

'I couldn't see her properly Ellie, but she felt so close. She seemed sick. She was moving very slowly. Then suddenly, she wasn't moving at all.'

Agatha's watery eyes pleaded silently with Elspeth. Pleaded for an explanation. She always trusted her sister to be able to answer her questions, to make everything alright. But this time, she couldn't. Elspeth's heart ached. She had watched Agatha slip away piece by piece since her twin's disappearance. Her mind had begun to wander, losing her grip on reality at times. There had been days when she had forgotten their mother was dead, that her sister was lost. Elspeth had struggled as she watched Agatha grieve for them all over again each time she explained.

'Agatha, you remember that Kaliope has been missing for a long time?'

'Of course I do,' she replied, a note of irritation in her tone.

'Good. Then you know that it was probably just a dream? You were very close to Kaliope. It's not surprising she would come to you in your sleep.'

Agatha's brow furrowed as she processed Elspeth's words. Uncertainty crinkled up her face as she tried to reconcile what she had believed to be true with the possibility that Elspeth was right.

'But it was so real,' she said shakily.

'Dreams can feel real. Especially ones about people we love.'

She pushed a few strands of wayward red hair from

Agatha's damp cheek and tried to give off an air of assurance.
She wished she could be sure Agatha's feelings were just a
response to a dream. But it was possible that she was sensing
something. She had always been remarkably perceptive, able
to read people's behaviour, understand the emotion driving
their actions much better than she. And she did have an
extraordinary connection with Kaliope. Maybe she was in
trouble...

Agatha saw the frown on Elspeth's face and cocked her
head as if waiting for an explanation of her thoughts. She
shook them off quickly, reprimanding herself for allowing
hope in. She had long ago accepted Kaliope was probably
dead and would never return to them.

Throwing off the bedclothes, she planted her bare feet on
the rug and stood up, pulling Agatha to her feet.

'I want so much for Kaliope to come back to us Aggie. But
we looked everywhere and for so many years. I think we have
to accept she's gone.'

Agatha stared blankly at Elspeth, then forced a smile.

'I try Elspeth. I do. But I can't shake the feeling that she's
still here – somewhere close. I know it's unlikely and I know
everyone thinks she's dead. But I don't! I still hope we'll find
her, that she'll come back.'

Elspeth looked surprised. She had never mentioned the
possibility that Kaliope might be dead to her sister. She was
already so fragile. Tears threatened to spill from Agatha's
eyes again.

'I really hope you're right Aggie,' Elspeth said, wrapping
an arm around her and pulling her close to plant a kiss on
her lined cheek. 'Now, why don't you get dressed and we can
get started on baking the bread for the party.'

Baking was one of the few things that calmed Agatha and
Elspeth was keen to take her sister's mind from the

distressing dreams about her twin. With a brief nod and hint of a smile, Agatha nodded and headed back to her room.

Elspeth sank back down onto the bed as she heard her sister close the door, then let out a deep sigh, allowing her own tears to leak slowly from her pale eyes. Tears for Agatha, for Kaliope. She let herself wallow in sorrow for a few minutes, listening to the soft creaking of the house as Agatha moved around her bedroom getting ready for the day. The sound of her sister descending the stairs into the kitchen pulled her from her sad thoughts.

She reached into her bedside cabinet and pulled out a handkerchief with her initials and a small daisy carefully sewn onto the corner by her mother's hand. She wiped her eyes forcibly, reprimanding herself for a moment of weakness. What time was it? The sun was visible in her window, peeping over the crest of the hill. It must be getting late.

Elspeth rose and sat down at her dresser. She looked at the small clock that resided there. It was almost nine. She had slept in. Fussily, she smoothed her hair and wiped the last signs of sleep from the corners of her eyes. She looked pale. Leaning forward so she was closer to the mirror, she examined her reflection carefully. She was not a vain woman and usually paid no heed to how she looked. But today, the crow's feet marking her otherwise still youthful skin caught her eye. Today, she turned fifty-two years of age.

She stared at the reflection looking back at her. Where had the time gone? Twenty-four years since she had walked out of Dalengour and closed the gateway to Nethergar. She let the image of Nerissa Larimore float through her mind. What had happened to her? She missed her. Missed her straight-forward nature, her ability to get to the crux of the matter with just a few well-chosen words. She missed

Nethergar, the way it made her feel, the advantages it offered. If she went back now, the crow's feet nestling in the corners of her eyes would be banished.

But she couldn't go back. She still had the power to open the gateway, the gifts Nethergar had awakened. still strong in her. But she had sworn never to use them again. Her cheeks reddened at the familiar shame of remembering how arrogant she had been, how materialistic she had nearly become with Riordan pulling her strings. And Morwenna. She was trapped in Nethergar, and Elspeth was determined it would stay that way. She didn't want anything else to pose a threat to her family.

She dressed quickly, choosing a lilac day dress with a high neck and long sleeves to protect against the chill of the day. Although spring was threatening, the Scottish hills still bore a smattering of snow, and the grasses wore a mantle of frosty dew. She pulled back her hair into a severe chignon at the nape of her neck and surveyed her work in the full-length mirror before heading down to the kitchen. Agatha was bustling around pulling flour and milk from the pantry to join the plethora of bowls and spoons already on the table.

'There's tea...somewhere,' she said, her good mood showing no signs of her earlier distress as she moved things around on the table looking for the cup buried amongst the chaos.

Elspeth smiled, taking a small cup from Agatha that contained lukewarm tea, a dark skin beginning to form on top.

'Thank you. Do you have everything you need?' she asked indicating the packed table.

'I think so. We're getting low on sugar. I might run down to the store.'

Agatha didn't look up as she spoke, too focused on the

baking ingredients strewn around the kitchen. It was one thing Elspeth was grateful for. Agatha was easily distracted. Her mind and her mood lurched from complete sadness to happy contentment in an instant. Baking always shifted her to the happy side.

Elspeth watched her sister as she pulled on her coat, getting ready to leave the house for the village.

'Is there anything I can do while you're gone?'

Elspeth knew the answer to this. Agatha hated it when she 'interfered' as she called it.

'No, no. It's fine. I won't be long anyway.'

Elspeth smiled the first genuine smile of the day, the predictability of the response reassuring. Agatha was right to keep her from the kitchen chores. She was a terrible cook. With a basket swinging on her arm, Agatha opened the kitchen door, letting in the cold morning air and making Elspeth shiver and wrap her arms around herself.

'There's a note on the table,' Agatha called absently over her shoulder. 'It's from Robert.'

She shut the door and left Elspeth alone to move cookbooks and bowls, looking for the note from her son. She found the envelope underneath the flour bag. Blowing away the dust of white powder that had settled on the paper, she unfolded it and read the quickly scribbled note. He must have left it before he went to work that morning.

Robert had grown into a wonderful young man, with very little trace of his father's looks or character. The only tell-tale sign that Darroch blood ran in his veins was the green of his eyes. But thankfully, the size and shape were distinctly Larimore rather than the narrow slits his father possessed.

Elspeth felt a stab of guilt when she thought about Riordan. She had never told Robert he was his father, instead concocting a lie about a good and kind man who had been tragically killed in an accident when Robert was three. Her son had never questioned this, and Riordan had never shown any interest in his first-born son, becoming too involved with his second family. For this she was grateful. She had divorced Riordan shortly after leaving Dalengour, reverting back to the name Larimore and trying to forget she was ever a Darroch. On the odd times she had seen Riordan in Cairndarroch, he had purposefully ignored her. He was as eager as she to wipe their marriage from memory.

The note wished Elspeth a happy birthday and said he would be home in plenty of time for the party. She smiled tenderly, admonishing his dreadful handwriting, and absorbing the genuine love and best wishes expressed in the written words. Her thoughts were disturbed by the sound of the doorbell. It must be the mail. No-one ever used the main door on the front of the house except the postman. Everyone used the back door that led straight into the welcoming kitchen, but the mail man resolutely walked past the back door to go around the front and ring the bell.

Elspeth walked down the short hall to open the door to the post man who handed her a hand-written envelope. She recognised the writing at once. Jenson. Clutching the letter, she sauntered back into the kitchen and settled down on the window seat to read her correspondence. She hadn't seen Jenson in years, but he always remembered her birthday. She read quickly as he filled her in on his news and congratulated her on making it through another year. By the time she reached the end, she was laughing. He had always been able to make her laugh.

Once she finished, she let the letter fall into her lap and stared wistfully out towards the rocky path leading into the forest. But she didn't see it. She was lost in thoughts of Jenson Tanner. She had loved him so, loved him still, but their time had long past. She had been so angry with him when they had left Dalengour. He had betrayed her, not trusted her with the truth and she hadn't been able to forgive him then. Elspeth had said she needed time. Now, so much time had passed, they had missed their chance.

When she had first left Riordan Darroch, she had been so focussed on Robert, on repressing the shame of her actions as his wife and shame at her stupidity, there had been no room for love. Jenson had his sister Gwen to think about and so had taken a position in the city, working for his cousin, a wealthy self-made banker. It was a good job and Gwen had settled into service in Bellendon Hall, their home. Not wanting to uproot her again, and with Elspeth seemingly too focused on her own family to have time for him, he had never returned to Cairndarroch. But they kept in touch, and she still missed him.

The sound of the small brightly painted gate swinging open dragged her from her meanderings down memory lane. Calder Larimore was coming down the garden path. He had been only ten years old when their mother had passed away and Elspeth had been both sister and parent to him for most of his life. At almost twenty-six years of age, he had grown tall and muscular due to his work in the fields, his natural freckles augmented by long days outdoors, his strawberry-blond hair hanging too long across his cornflower blue eyes. He was so much like their father.

Elspeth smiled as she saw him. He was clutching a small, badly wrapped package in one hand and waved with the other when he saw her. She stood up waving back and was heading to open the door when something caught her eye – someone else. Calder wasn't alone. A petite, dark-haired girl, bundled up in an emerald-green hat and woollen coat was trailing behind him. Suddenly remembering his company, Calder turned around and took the girl's hand, helping her navigate the uneven gravelled path, a broad smile on his face as he chatted to her. Elspeth couldn't hear what they were saying, but from the look on her face, it was well-received.

Elspeth moved to open the door. Her brother had never brought a girl home before. This must be someone important for him to have thought to introduce her to Elspeth. She smiled, hoping he had met someone special. It was about time.

She flung open the door and Calder rushed at her, gathering her into a tight embrace. The girl hung back, not wanting to intrude on their greeting.

'Happy Birthday Ellie!' he said, releasing her and thrusting the brown paper package hastily into her hands.

Calder seemed nervous. He stepped back, wiping his hands anxiously down the front of his best brown trousers.

'Ellie, there's someone I want you to meet.'

He stepped aside so the girl who had been waiting patiently was visible in the doorway. Elspeth cocked her head so she could see around Calder. The young woman bowed her head as she waited to be introduced, clutching gloves in her hands that Elspeth noted were reddening with the cold.

'Come, let's get inside and you can make your introductions in the warm.'

She went back into the kitchen and Calder held the door open in a gentlemanly way for his companion. She followed Elspeth into the kitchen and slid off her hat, smoothing her long dark curls that hung free and wild down her back. She was undoing the buttons on her coat as Calder came to her side.

The young women raised her eyes to Elspeth's face as she felt Calder's presence beside her. Green cat-like eyes that sent a chill down Elspeth's spine.

'Ellie, this is my friend, Freya Darroch. Freya, this is my big sister, Elspeth Larimore.'

For a moment, the two women's eyes locked. Elspeth felt the colour drain from her cheeks. Freya's brows drew together with the strain of trying to comprehend the look on Elspeth's face. The girl shifted her gaze to Calder, looking for reassurance in the uncomfortable silence.

'Ellie?'

Calder's voice brought her back to the moment.

'It's very nice to meet you Freya,' she said, her voice, despite her best efforts, holding no sincerity.

This was unmistakably Riordan Darroch's daughter. She looked at the young girl who was now smiling warmly at her. Elspeth tried to smile back, the skin of her lips feeling tight as they twisted into a feigned smile. She gazed at her brother, hoping her attempts at a welcome were convincing, but Calder wasn't looking at her. He was completely transfixed by Freya Darroch.

Elspeth scoured her brother's handsome face, alive with the first flush of young love. Blinking slowly, she sighed deeply as her heart plummeted into the pit of her stomach.

THE END

The story continues in *Cunygar* - out December 2021

The Nethergar series continues in the second book, **CUNYGAR**, out in ebook and paperback in December 2021.

Elspeth Larimore lies awake, frail and alone in the emptiness of Kirkholm Cottage. The consequences of decisions made during her abnormally long-life weigh heavy. Everyone she loved is gone. If only she could reopen the gateway, she would have time to make things right.

Tobias Darroch lies awake in the squalor of his London lodgings, roused from sleep by agonising pain in his infected leg. Hatred festers in his puny chest as he plots revenge on those that took away his chance at immortality.

Jacob McGillvaray lies awake on the mossy forest floor, looking up at stars so clear in the autumnal highland sky. He made a mistake coming back here. Now he's lost everything. Only one thing remains – to kill the man who murdered her.

'Cunygar' is the second novel in the Nethergar series by C.L Holland. The books follow the story of three families whose lives become entwined when a gateway is discovered linking the small Highland village of Cairndarroch to the world of Nethergar. Cunygar is home to the McGillvarays, distant, elusive and new to the village. Elspeth Larimore protects their secrets but now, decisions she made to protect her family decades ago threaten to ruin many innocent lives, unless she tells the truth.

Turn to the next page to read a preview now.

CUNYGAR

BY CLARE L. HOLLAND

Prologue

The Letter

The Gateway – May 1997

Animal silhouettes reared up from the silvery haze loitering at her feet, their diaphanous forms cavorting through the smoky swirls as she paced agitatedly back and forth. The minutes ticked by, her movements becoming more deliberate, every turn fracturing the ghostly shadows that resolutely reformed in her wake. Tired of walking, she leaned against the wall of the gatehouse, pushing hard on the blank expanse of granite, hoping it would miraculously give way.

'Come on!' she spat, her voice gravelly, the words escaping through clenched teeth.

Frustrated, she pushed back forcefully, turning away from the still, unmoving wall. With a deep sigh, she propped her hands on her narrow waist and walked back towards the surrounding forest.

'I see you're as petulant as ever Freya.'

She spun around to look at the owner of the condescending tone. Elspeth Larimore was framed in an open doorway, her piercing eyes fixed on her sister-in-law.

'Nice to see you Elspeth. It's been a long time, and I see time hasn't treated you well.'

Folding her arms stubbornly across her chest, Freya waited for a reaction, but none came. Instead, Elspeth smiled politely, standing aside to let her enter the gatehouse.

Freya started around the barren room whose only occupants these past fifty years had been hairy-legged spiders, diligently adorning every nook and cranny with gossamer webs to capture unsuspecting prey. She wrinkled her nose at the fetid smell of stale air carried on the breeze from the open door, her emerald-green eyes taking in the layers of dust settled on every surface. The piles of ash in the grate whipped up as Elspeth closed the door behind her, blocking out the comforting golden glow temporarily casting life into this neglected room.

Freya shivered in the darkness, sensing the power harnessed in this liminal place, standing on the threshold between two worlds. Pools of dim light began to illuminate the gloom as Elspeth ignited the candle-filled lamps adorning the bare stone walls with a wave of her hand. Dust burned in the flames, causing the light to flicker and dance, adding a smoky aroma to the musty air. As the glimmering brightness settled, Elspeth turned to face her, an icy expression set on her heavily lined face. Determined not to show weakness, Freya drew herself up to full height and met the challenge of the older woman's stare.

Elspeth remained stoic, continuing to look at her from

beneath hooded eyes that had once reflected fondness for Freya, but were now cold and flinty. She was a tall woman, her height emphasised as she stood looking every inch the dowager, hands clasped tightly together, spine as straight as a lamppost. Elspeth's woollen shawl hung loosely around her stiffly held shoulders, the soft lavender hue complimenting her tightly drawn back hair, pale auburn in her youth, but now, almost completely silver grey. This was not the kindly woman Freya remembered. There was a hardness in her countenance borne from the pain of loss. However, the aura of power surrounding her had not dimmed.

The silence weighed heavy, mutual hatred settling like an impenetrable barrier between them. Freya succumbed to the pressure of Elspeth's glare first, breaking their stand-off and sauntering aimlessly around the unwelcoming room.

'Given your obvious displeasure in my being here, I wonder why you sent for me?' Freya asked, attempting indifference.

Elspeth's expression tightened, the vein at her temple pulsing as she fought to maintain her composure.

'I need you to deliver this letter to Cassie.'

Elspeth held out a sealed, ivory envelope, puckered by the tightness of her grip. Freya didn't take it, folding her arms defiantly like an obstinate child.

'Why can't you give it to her yourself?' Freya asked impudently.

'Because I made a promise – to Agatha.'

A smile played around the corners of Freya's mouth as she saw Elspeth's fleeting discomfort at the mention of her younger sister.

'What does it say?'

'That doesn't concern you. Will you take it?'

Freya's brow creased as she fought an internal battle

between her hatred of Elspeth Larimore and an intense desire to get back through the gateway.

'Why does it have to be me?'

'Because the letter is written as if it comes from you.'

'If it's supposed to be from me, I have a right to know what it says!' Freya snapped, her sense of self-righteous injustice sounding truculent.

Elspeth sighed, relaxing the arm back to her side.

'The letter explains things – explains why she must leave him.'

A derisive laugh escaped Freya's lips as she sensed the balance of power tipping in her favour.

'You need me to deliver a letter to my granddaughter laying the blame for your mistakes at my door? You must be mad!'

'You owe me this Freya,' Elspeth said, punctuating every word with the hatred burning in her steely blue eyes.

Colour rose in Freya's cheeks as the shame of what she had done all those years ago forced its way uninvited into her mind. The intrusion was fleeting, and she quickly regained her audacity, determined not to let this woman take the moral high ground even though it rightfully belonged to her.

'That still doesn't explain why it has to be me! Why do I have to deliver the letter?' Freya asked, disappointed to hear her own voice falter.

'Because I need Cassie to believe it,' Elspeth replied, her calm demeanour slipping. 'I need her to act on it. Your appearance will force questions into her mind. She won't be able to deny you. You're so like her mother…'

Elspeth tailed off, her eyes looking suddenly watery. Freya sensed a moment of weakness and pounced.

'Yes, but unlike my daughter, I'm not dead!' Freya snarled.

The fury erupting inside Elspeth was palpable, her

emotions stirring the power so readily awakened, even after all these years of dormancy. Freya's eyes widened as she fixated on the halo of gold surrounding the older woman's clasped palms. She had gone too far. Despite her bravado, Freya was afraid of Elspeth Larimore. She pointed accusingly at the envelope still held in Elspeth's hand, a note of panic in her voice.

'You can't blame me for the contents of that letter.'

Elspeth's power surged within her. Freya watched as she took a deep breath, blinking slowly, pulling the energy bristling across her skin back inside as she fought to keep control. With the light around her hands fading, Elspeth settled her gaze back on Freya, and smirking, shook her head pityingly.

'But I do blame you Freya.'

Elspeth proffered the envelope again, her eyes blazing, etched in gold as the power slumbering beneath her cold exterior roused.

Freya snatched the letter from Elspeth's outstretched hand who did not relinquish her hold. The two women stood glaring at each other, connected by the envelope at risk of tearing as both held their ground. It was Elspeth who gave way, the amber lights in her eyes waning, an air of tranquillity restored.

'I've opened the gateway for one hour and no more. If you're not back by then, your guide will return, with or without you, and you'll be trapped in Cairndarroch.'

This was not something Freya wished to contemplate. With a heavy sigh, she pushed past Elspeth, heading towards the door on the opposite side of the gatehouse.

'One hour Freya.'

She glanced back over her shoulder at Elspeth Larimore, then with a curt nod of her head, threw open the door. The transient spring sunshine forced its way into the forsaken room and Freya squinted to protect her eyes from the sudden onslaught of light. The forest surrounding the Cunygar Estate stretched ahead of her as far as the eye could see, but now, everything was different.

Sunlight fought against the thick, grey clouds overhead, failing to take the chill dampness from the air. She could feel droplets of moisture landing on her skin as she stood there on the threshold, the greenness of the surrounding trees subdued compared to the vibrancy of Nethergar.

Silver mist gathered around her feet, summoned from some unseen place. As it churned around her legs, the translucent form of a large bird rose and fell, trying to escape the haze before being repeatedly pulled back. Freya's legs felt heavy, her muscles quivering feebly resisting her attempts to move forward. The fully formed ghost of a buzzard burst from the fog as she took a purposeful step into Cairndarroch for the first time in over fifty years.

Emerging from the gatehouse, Freya shivered, the scowl on her face portraying her displeasure at being here. Her foul mood could not detract from the otherworldly glow that surrounded her, making her seem out of place in this forest muted by leaden light. Her long, dark hair fell in waves around her lightly freckled, olive skin, that thanks to the powers of Nethergar, denied her seventy years of life. Only the crinkling of crows' feet around her feline eyes gave any indication of age.

The wine-coloured silk dress accentuated her slender figure, fitting snuggly at the waist and hips, before relaxing to a flared, feminine skirt. The delicate fabric was decorated with silver flowers that shimmered as she moved, giving the appearance of growing upwards, straining towards a non-existent sun.

She wrapped her arms tightly around her body as she walked, trying to subdue the goosebumps standing proudly from her skin that testified to the fact she had not dressed for the Scottish spring. Freya scanned the clearing with her brilliant green eyes before heading towards the ancient trees, their gnarled trunks seeming impenetrable as they stretched upwards to the overcast sky. The morning dew was still fresh on the mossy floor, the moisture seeping through her inappropriate shoes, making her feet feel cold and wet. She hated this world.

Her now corporeal buzzard guide circled above her, coming so close, her hair caught in the breeze it created. As if to remind her not to dawdle, it soared upward just ahead before coming around and flying over her again.

'I know, I know' she muttered impatiently.

She wanted a moment to calm herself after her altercation at the gatehouse, but time was not on her side. The buzzard let out a plaintive call from somewhere above as if to remind her they must return to Nethergar before the hour was up. Heeding the warning, Freya quickened her step, stumbling over tree roots undulating through the earth in her haste to reach more open ground.

After a few minutes of scrabbling through thick ferns that formed a tangled carpet between the trees, the dense vegetation gave way to clearer sky, allowing the weak sun to cast dancing polka dots on the forest floor. Grateful for easier passage, Freya raced ahead, breathing heavily from exertion as she emerged into a sylvan glade.

Cassandra Fenmore, walking the grounds as she did every morning, stared wide-eyed, startled by her abrupt appearance at the edge of the clearing. Freya's tawny skin and abundant, waist-length mahogany hair, contrasted sharply with her granddaughter's copper-red elfish style that framed her pale face. Here, the differences ended, their shared ancestry obvious in every other characteristic.

Recovering from the shock of Freya's sudden arrival, an easy smile spread across Cassie's face, filling her vivid emerald eyes with genuine openness.

'Hi, I'm Cassie Fenmore. Can I help you?'

Freya considered the self-confident woman before her, and for a moment, felt uneasy in her task. She shifted her weight from foot to foot, musing over what to say, trying to push the unwelcome feelings of concern away.

Cassie's brow furrowed, the silence going on too long. Mentally chastising herself, Freya threw off the uncharacteristic sensations of guilt, reasoning she had no part to play in this other than being the messenger. Despite what Elspeth had said, this was not her fault. Yet still, she couldn't help feeling mildly sorry for Cassie. She was about to blow her world apart after all.

'My name is Freya Darroch and I'm your grandmother,' she said assertively.

Cassie stared incredulously, and Freya, always a fan of the melodramatic, smiled at the internal sense of gratification.

'I'm sorry – I – that's not possible,' Cassie stammered, her convivial expression replaced by confusion. 'My grandmother's dead.'

Freya thrust the envelope, now looking dog-eared and stained, into Cassie's hand.

'Read this,' she said without preamble. 'It will explain.'

Cassie's name was scrawled across the front in ornate letters reflecting a different era in penmanship. The young woman, a bewildered expression on her face, stared down at the letter, then began to unfold the heavy, ivory pages. Freya was again troubled by an intrusive sense of remorse. She needed to get out of this place. She must return to Nethergar where this unpleasantness could not touch her.

'Goodbye then' Freya said abruptly, the suddenness and inadequacy of her words rousing her granddaughter from her reading.

Cassie stared at her with eyes so like her own except for amber flecks that perforated their greenness. Uncomfortable and at a loss for what else to say, Freya turned away and scurried back towards the gatehouse. She could sense Cassie's gaze following her, dubiety transmitted wordlessly across the glade.

Freya did not slow until she was hidden by the dense trees. Breathing heavily, she leaned against the peeling bark, surprised by her own empathy for her granddaughter. She peered around the tree to look back at Cassie, watching as she read down the page, the trembling in her hands increasing until she reached the end.

Suddenly aware of an errant tear running down her face, Freya wiped the back of her hand across her cheek. Cassie sat motionless, clutching the letter in her lap, her expressionless face concealing the workings of her mind. Abruptly, she folded the letter, jamming it back in the envelope and stuffing it into the pocket of her jeans before striding purposefully out of the clearing. Freya continued to stare after her until she disappeared from view, and against her nature, couldn't help but wonder if Cassie would be alright.

The call of the buzzard overhead brought her back to her senses. She had done her job, now it was time to get what she wanted. She made her way back through the forest more steadily now, using the time to distance herself from Cassie and the unwelcome feelings the meeting had awakened.

As the gatehouse came back into view, the last vestiges of concern were quickly replaced by excitement. Freya was relieved to find no sign of Elspeth Larimore inside. The candles still burned in the wall lamps, their illumination augmented by diluted sunlight now finding its way through dusty windows on each side of the door. Her guide flew in, settling on the ground close to her feet.

Freya was unsure of what to do. She had only passed through the gateway once before and then, she had been close to death. She stood for a few moments, her eyes scouring the walls, looking for some hint of an exit that would take her back to Nethergar. There was nothing – only the open doorway back to Cairndarroch that she definitely did not want to go through.

The floor beneath her feet shuddered, the sound of the door slamming startling her. The buzzard at her feet faded into a smoky reflection of itself as the tremors intensified. It was a few moments after the room had stilled that she realised a second door had appeared on the opposite side of the gatehouse. Sun was streaming in through the sparkling windows on either side of this new door, bathing the room in warmth, banishing the gloom.

A smile formed on her lips, her stomach somersaulting with exhilaration. She was back. Freya ran to the door and turned the handle. Heat radiated through her fingers as she touched it, the skin on her hand tightening, becoming youthful and clear. She threw open the door and took a step back into Nethergar, her euphoria bubbling into laughter that erupted, free and spirited to shatter the peace of the forest. She spun around, arms outstretched, her face raised towards the glorious sun.

Freya Darroch left the gatehouse in Nethergar, a young woman of twenty-seven. The possibilities of youth stretched before her and this time, she would get everything she wanted.

AFTERWORD

Thank you so much for reading Dalengour. I hope you enjoyed it.

I would really appreciate it if you could spare a few minutes to leave a review either through Amazon, or if you prefer, via the 'contact me' form on my website (www. nethergarpublishing.com).

I look forward to hearing from you through Amazon, the website, or through my social media pages.

Happy reading!
    Clare L.Holland

ABOUT CLARE L. HOLLAND

For more information about the author and to read extended free samples of **Cunygar**, visit www.nethergarpublishing.com

Follow the author on Facebook, Instagram and Twitter for all news about forthcoming releases from Clare L. Holland.

Twitter: @ClareLHollandNP
   Facebook: ClareLHollandNethergarPublishing
   Instagram: clarelhollandnp

Printed in Great Britain
by Amazon